NOV 0 4 2017

D1485835

MURDER IN JULY

*A Selection of Recent Titles from Barbara Hambly
from Severn House*

The Benjamin January Series

DEAD AND BURIED
THE SHIRT ON HIS BACK
RAN AWAY
GOOD MAN FRIDAY
CRIMSON ANGEL
DRINKING GOURD
MURDER IN JULY

The James Asher Vampire Novels

BLOOD MAIDENS
THE MAGISTRATES OF HELL
THE KINDRED OF DARKNESS
DARKNESS ON HIS BONES

MURDER IN JULY

A Benjamin January Novel

Barbara Hambly

This first world edition published 2017
in Great Britain and the USA by
SEVERN HOUSE PUBLISHERS LTD of
19 Cedar Road, Sutton, Surrey, England, SM2 5DA.
Trade paperback edition first published
in Great Britain and the USA 2018 by
SEVERN HOUSE PUBLISHERS LTD

British Library Cataloguing in Publication Data
A CIP catalogue record for this title is available from the British Library.

ISBN-13: 978-0-7278-8740-5 (cased)
ISBN-13: 978-1-84751-855-2 (trade paper)
ISBN-13: 978-1-78010-915-2 (e-book)

All Severn House titles are printed on acid-free paper.

Severn House Publishers support the Forest Stewardship Council™ [FSC™],
the leading international forest certification organisation.
All our titles that are printed on FSC certified paper carry the FSC logo.

Typeset by Palimpsest Book Production Ltd.,
Falkirk, Stirlingshire, Scotland.
Printed and bound in Great Britain by
TJ International, Padstow, Cornwall.

For Dad

ONE

1839

The offer was good.

In the sweltering nadir of a summer season wherein everyone with any money in New Orleans had left town for the lakefront or the North – and even the barkeeps of the saloons were paying musicians in booze rather than coin – Benjamin January was sorely tempted by the words: 'a hundred dollars, in addition to recompense for whatever expenses you may incur'.

He had, however, no desire to be hanged for treason.

And he suspected that 'a personal service requiring both intelligence and the utmost discretion' from Sir John Oldmixton of the British Consulate might very well involve that.

'I thought you said Sir John Oldmixton helped you find Dominique, when she and her daughter had been kidnapped by slave stealers when you were in Washington?[1] Benjamin's wife Rose straightened up – carefully – from mixing the tub of plaster, the latest in the unending cycle of small repairs required to keep the crooked old Spanish house on Rue Esplanade looking its best. On the roof above the low attic dormitory, January could hear his niece and nephew moving cautiously about, digging out the sprouts of resurrection fern which would grow anywhere in New Orleans the moment the owner of the property turned his or her back.

In two and a half months, the first students in two years would arrive at the boarding school which had been the dream and occupation of Rose's lifetime. And the place had better, January reflected, look like somewhere a well-off man would feel comfortable sending his daughter, albeit the daughter of a mistress of color.

[1] See *Good Man Friday*

He stepped quickly to Rose's side and gave her a hand up. She was a strong woman, for all her thin gawkiness, and she had borne one child already in safety. But Little Secundus (as they called the prospective newcomer) was due, literally, any day, and over twenty years' experience as a surgeon had shown January a hideous spectrum of ways in which childbirth could go wrong.

Another reason, he reflected wryly, not to get himself hanged as a traitor if he could help it.

'Sir John Oldmixton,' he said, 'looks like the most respectable man in the world. He's efficient, self-effacing, well-dressed, with impeccable manners, tactful, charming, and can carry on a conversation about anything. Towards the end of our stay in Washington City I began to realize that that was his job at the British Ministry. To be the person that nobody would suspect of running a spy-ring that employed everyone from professional slave stealers to the wife of the assistant to the Secretary of the Navy. I don't know what he's doing in New Orleans, but my guess is that he's up to no good.'

Had it been winter instead of summer, January would have walked the length of the attic and put Oldmixton's note into the little brick fireplace. Or perhaps, had it been 1836 – before the bank crash that had closed the doors of a third of the businesses in the twenty-six states – instead of 1839. But he put the note in his pocket, before beginning to plaster the weak or flaked spots in the walls of the dormitory – in the muggy humidity of the Louisiana summer it would take weeks to dry – and resolved to think no more about it.

The fact was, that a hundred dollars would come in extraordinarily useful.

The house – bought with windfall cash shortly before the cascade of bank closures had swallowed up every penny January and Rose had saved – was an old one. It had stood for three-quarters of a century some five or six streets back from the river on the wide thoroughfare that led from the wharves to Bayou St John. For a long time it, and the neighborhood that stretched behind it along Rue Burgundy and Rue des Ramparts, had been well-kept, if slightly shabby; streets of pastel stucco cottages owned by *plaçées*, the free ladies of color who had achieved a 'place' as the mistress of a well-off white gentleman. The arrangement was a common one in the French Caribbean, where law forbade the union of black and white. Men frequently maintained these shadow-marriages for years in a world where real marriages – white marriages – were often entered into from considerations of family, property, and position in society.

Both January's mother, and Rose's, had been *plaçeés*. Rose's white father had paid for her education, even as the white protector of January's mother had paid for his, despite the fact that January's father had been some other man's cane-hand. But times were changing. The French society that regarded it as only right that a man should care for his own children, though they be by a woman of mixed race, was rapidly being replaced by American planters who thought nothing of selling off the children they begot on slavewomen – none of this *plaçeé* nonsense for them! And the financial ruin that had for two years now gripped New Orleans – along with the rest of the United States – had demolished the annuities of many of the ladies of the Rue des Ramparts, forcing the sale of the cottages given to them by protectors a decade or two before.

The men who bought these cottages, seeking to turn a speedy profit in the harder times, had found it easy to put in two or three girls and a madame, to take what advantage could be taken of the river trade, since nobody in the history of mankind ever lost money running a whorehouse. And prospective investors in such property could be assured that complaints from the neighbors – mostly free men and women of color annoyed and revolted by the deterioration of their neighborhood – would be disregarded by the white city council.

Many city council members owned these shabby little bordellos themselves.

Thus January, with the district behind his school growing coarser and poorer than it had been, thought it behooved him to invest what little money he and Rose had in setting apart their ramshackle house as distinctly as possible from those along Rue des Ramparts. The wide esplanade onto which the house faced still had its rustic charm, and the inhabitants of its larger houses still had influence. In these harder times every toehold of advantage had to be made the most of.

So January turned to – nervously watching Rose from the

corner of his eye – and plastered, swept, painted and whitewashed for all he was worth . . .

And didn't throw Sir John Oldmixton's note into the fire, an omission he later regretted.

A few days later – Wednesday, the third of July – January took advantage of the relative cool that followed a particularly long, afternoon rainstorm to paint the front shutters the bright, clear blue that his aunties back on Bellefleur Plantation in his childhood had described as 'haint blue': proof against evil spirits of any ilk. Education at the St Louis Academy for Young Gentlemen of Color – and subsequent training in the sciences of healing, both in New Orleans as a youth and later at the great hospital of the Hôtel Dieu in Paris – had largely erased his early belief in the platt-eye devil and the efficacy of graveyard dust, but he still liked the color. Good pigment was costly, but, he guessed, worth it. Once the outside was spruced up, the six rooms of the main floor could be done (eight, if one counted the tiny 'cabinets' that served as pantry and stairway to the attic) in the cheerful yellows and oranges that the Creoles – French, Spanish, and African alike – adored. He already guessed that this would make some of the furniture look shabby . . .

But first things first. Assisted by his niece and nephew, who had lived under his roof since the hard times had set in (his sister Olympe's husband, the upholsterer Paul Corbier, hadn't worked at his trade in two years), and by his friend the fiddler Hannibal Sefton, January laid tarpaulins over the boards of the high gallery, and had just gotten Gabriel and Zizi-Marie started when a neat, open carriage drawn by matched grays drew to a halt before the house, and Sir John Oldmixton stepped out.

There was no mistaking the sturdy form, broad-shouldered and barrel-chested in tailored linen that rendered him deceptively ordinary. He looked just as he had two years ago, when January had met him in the national capital: smooth black hair, smooth pink face, twinkling blue-green eyes. These brightened as he looked up at the high gallery – like many of the oldest Spanish houses of New Orleans, built to ride out Mississippi floods that had at one time regularly submerged the streets five and six feet deep. 'My dear M'sieu Janvier!' His French was perfect and his smile one of genuine pleasure as January descended the steps and took his extended hand. 'So this is your castle? Your description didn't do it justice.'

'Mine, and my wife's.' On the gallery, amid the ladders and draped canvas, January made introductions. If Sir John thought it uncommon for a scrawny white gentleman in shirtsleeves to be helping a family of color paint their shutters – Hannibal was probably the only white man south of the Mason-Dixon Line who would have done so – he didn't by the slightest blink betray it, and Hannibal's bow of greeting wouldn't have been out of place at the Court of St James. 'You'll take coffee, won't you, sir?' asked January. 'Zizi-Marie, my niece – Sir John Oldmixton. Sir John, my nephew Gabriel Corbier, Mr Hannibal Sefton . . . Zizi, if you'd do the honors . . . You must excuse Madame Janvier today, Sir John. I fear she's indisposed.' Women in Europe weren't immured during pregnancy as they were more and more coming to be in 'good society' in America, but even the very French society of the French Town in New Orleans drew the line at the concluding weeks of a woman's term. (Not, reflected January, that the very Americans who frowned upon a woman venturing forth from the moment she suspected herself with child, weren't perfectly ready to work a slave woman until she gave birth in the fields . . .)

'I'm afraid you find us very much at sixes and sevens . . .'

'I abase myself.' Oldmixton inclined his head. 'Yet I feared that, having had no reply to my note, my communication with you had perhaps gone astray . . .'

'No, sir.' January ushered him through his study – the room traditionally allotted as the bedroom of the master of the house, in the accepted French Creole fashion – and into the parlor, while Zizi-Marie went in through Rose's bedroom at the other end of the house and then through to the pantry where the coffee was. 'I received it.'

'Ah.' Oldmixton met January's eyes, still with his slight, elfin smile. 'It is a personal favor,' he added after a moment. 'It has nothing whatsoever to do with my capacity as a representative of Her Majesty.'

'I would never dream of thinking such a thing, sir.'

The Englishman's smile widened, and he laid his hat, stick,

and gloves on the side table, and took the chair January offered him. 'The fact is that a friend of mine has met with an . . . unfortunate accident. His body was found Sunday morning in the turning basin at the end of the canal from the lake. A dangerous neighborhood, I am informed. Certainly an insalubrious one, and I did notice that poor Harry wasn't attired to be inconspicuous in such surroundings. He was usually quite careful about dressing to blend in with his company.'

January nodded. As a free man of color in a city dominated more and more by Americans, to whom all black men were slaves or potential slaves, he had early learned the value of camouflage.

A white man, of course, would do the same thing only to avoid being mugged and robbed by the local plug-uglies.

'I have reason to believe he was carrying personal papers,' Sir John continued. 'Papers important only to myself and to members of my family, but it is of the highest importance that I find them, and find them quickly.'

'So the interest is in the papers?' January settled in the chair opposite the swept, cold hearth. 'Not primarily in poor Henry's murderers?'

'Naturally, I would like to see the fiends brought to justice—' He didn't bother to put much indignation in his voice, nor did the twinkle leave his eye. But it was more of a glint than a twinkle, like the blade of a stiletto, small enough to hide in a sleeve, but long enough to penetrate the heart.

'Or at least learn who they were?'

'Oh, that, at the least. When last we met in Washington City, m'sieu, you impressed me as a man who can gather information from a wide variety of sources not available to me as a foreigner, and a white man. In London one may disguise oneself as a servant, since servants see and hear what polite society veils from its own members. In New Orleans this is not the case. And you impressed me, if I may say so, as a man capable of extrapolating from fragments of information, where and how to search for the next fragment – something, again, which a man not familiar with the patterns of New Orleans society would be unable to do. This is not a quality one encounters in the official police force, whose concern is primarily – and rightly – with the vast majority of crime, which hinges upon simple violence and opportunistic greed. The broad, outer circles of Dante's Hell.'

'You flatter me.' January turned and smiled thanks as Zizi-Marie – seventeen and uncharacteristically scatterbrained these days in the throes of first love with a harness-maker's apprentice – brought in a japan-ware tray with the coffee things and a little plate of pralines.

'If I intended to flatter you, my dear m'sieu,' purred Oldmixton, 'I would be much more fulsome. I speak only the truth. I need a man of your capabilities. Can I count on your help?'

January dunked an edge of praline into his coffee, and savored the combination of chicory-bitter and molasses-sweet. His nephew Gabriel had made the pralines, as he did all the cooking for the household. Rose, though she could tell you why *vicia fava* had to be soaked in soda overnight and what the followers of Pythagoras had thought about them, could barely boil beans and rice. The parlor walls around them were already blotched with plaster repair-patches and it was here that the painting would start, and his estimate for paint for the whole house, inside and out, was almost equal to the little hoard of coin tucked behind the bricks of the parlor chimney. Three students were scheduled to arrive on the fifteenth of October, when the wet heat of summer finally began to ease and the danger of hurricanes abated. He had three piano students starting around then as well. Until that time, beans and rice was going to figure prominently in the lives of everyone in the household.

Quietly, he said, 'I'm afraid you're going to have to excuse me, sir.'

The Englishman's eyebrows went up.

'You're offering too much,' January explained. 'That tells me that there's something about these "personal papers" that you're not telling me. If you're that worried that the New Orleans police might recover the papers, instead of a private party, I'm wondering why. It's not that I don't trust you, or Her Majesty or Lord Melbourne or any of those other nice folks. But there's just . . . something about the situation that doesn't listen right to me, as my old aunties used to say. And I can't really say what it is.'

Oldmixton laughed, and threw up one hand. 'There! Serves

me right for offering what you're worth. I suppose I couldn't
interest you for twenty-five dollars . . . I didn't think so.' His
smile vanished, and his tourmaline eyes turned hard. 'There's
something about the situation that troubles me as well,' he went
on. 'Brooke's body had begun to stiffen when he was taken out
of the water – Brooke was his name, Henry Brooke. So he'd
been dead for some hours when he was thrown in. And, as I said,
he was dressed in morning-wear. He and I were to meet Saturday
evening, an appointment he never kept. He'd never have visited
the neighborhood around the turning basin in bottle-green superfine and a silk vest, let alone a top hat – which was retrieved
this morning from a local mudlark. And I suspect that were he
shot in that neighborhood, it would have been with something
more formidable than a muff pistol.'

'A muff pistol?'

Oldmixton must have heard the sudden sharpness of January's
voice, because he looked at him curiously. But when January
said nothing more, he explained, 'The way the ball deformed, it
looked like it came from one of those old screw-barrel kinds . . .
Do you know them?'

'Yes,' said January softly. 'Yes, I know them.'

'Does it mean anything to you?'

'Nothing,' said January, 'now.'

TWO

Nine years.

It felt like another lifetime.

In the sweltering heat, with the whole house smelling of plaster, January lay awake in the darkness and listened to the grumble of thunder, far off across the lake. Rose lay beside him, brown curls – silky, like a white woman's – scattered on the pillow, her belly a smooth white mountain in the thin stripes of moonlight through the jalousies. The faintly musky perfume of her flesh was comfort, a joy to him in the darkness most nights.

But there was no comfort for him anywhere tonight.

A screw-barrel muff pistol.

He could almost feel the weight of it on his palm, as real to him as the remembered smell of the French countryside that had drifted on the chill dawn breeze, and how it had yielded to the reek of Paris when the breeze failed. As real as the recollection of the clammy gloom of the Saint-Lazare Prison. As real as new-risen light on the guillotine's blade, against gray autumn sky.

What had happened to that pistol?

He had never learned.

1830

Another lifetime.

Summer was the slack season for musicians, whether in New Orleans or Paris. The summer of 1830 had been worse than most. In the dry heat the wealthy left Paris early. Aristocratic families who'd returned to France in the wake of the Bourbon King when the Allied armies had put him back on his dead brother's throne. New-rich aristocrats as well, promoted to noble estate by Napoleon in his fourteen-year reign, or businessmen who'd grown fat on twenty-five years of war. When Benjamin January had arrived in France in 1817 it had been with the goal of studying to become a surgeon, a career he'd pursued even after he realized that few whites, even in the homeland of The Declaration of the Rights of Man, were going to let a huge black man come anywhere near them with a scalpel in his hand. Only with his marriage to the beautiful Berber dressmaker Ayasha had he turned to music – the other great passion of his life – to earn his living. Though like every other musician in Paris he counted his pennies with great care in the summers, in the winter season of Christmas and Carnival he earned far more than he had as a junior surgeon at the Hôtel Dieu.

But in that summer of 1830, three years of bankruptcies in high places, of runs on banks, of workshops closed for lack of credit, had left thousands of the working people of Paris in the street. When the Chamber of Deputies had refused to pass yet another law tightening censorship of the press, King Charles had dissolved that representative body, then delayed the election of a new chamber for over two months. In the back rooms of cafés and the garrets of newspaper offices, groups of students, journalists and workingmen had read and argued and labored over schemes to canvass support, with one ear cocked for the White Terror, the king's secret police. Even the splendor of the French army, as it had gathered to invade Algiers back in May, hadn't impressed the people of Paris. When the new king had ridden out from beneath the triumphal arch of the Tuileries gate to review his departing troops, they had greeted him with stony silence.

Most of those troops were still in Africa when, on the twenty-sixth of July, the conservative newspapers had published the king's proclamation, dissolving the Chamber of Deputies yet again (since the delayed elections had gone overwhelmingly to those who opposed him). The same ordinance suspended freedom of the press, and announced that businessmen and the owners of factories no longer had the right to participate in elections or to run for office. The government of France, said the king (from the comfort of his summer palace at St-Cloud), would henceforth be by royal ordinance alone.

That had been a Monday.

Both January and Ayasha went down to the offices of *The National* – the foremost of the newspapers that had been ordered to close for not agreeing with the king – late in the afternoon to cheer and support the journalists who met there to sign a protest. Crowds of printers surrounded the offices, men who'd been put out of work by the ordinance, by the prohibitively high tariffs set on other printed matter, and by the king's new laws of censorship. It was the same at every newspaper in the city. January had expected to find hundreds gathered in the Rue St-Marc, despite the blistering heat of the afternoon.

Instead, they found thousands.

'The workingmen of Paris have had their fill of the Bourbons!' cried a young artist named Aristide Carnot – a member of the political (and illegal) reading group that January belonged to, the Société Brutus. 'We had a Republic once! We will stand no more, of the king's idiot friends making rules for their own profit . . .'

'They are trying to turn back the clock!' yelled someone else, closer to the looming soot-stained wall of the building where the crowd was almost impassable. 'To put us under the scarlet heel of the aristos again!'

'Well, actually, it's on account of the Bourse.' Daniel Ben-Gideon, another friend from the Société Brutus, shouldered gently through the press, in his coat of antique lilac brocade looking like a monstrous peony in a basket of turnips. The black silk of its collar set off a pale, plump oval face upon which sweat made long tracks in his rouge. 'The businessmen and bankers—' he nodded down the street towards the Parthenon-like bulk of the Paris stock exchange – 'declared this morning that since they're permitted no participation in government, they shall henceforth loan nobody any money nor sell stock nor finance anybody's endeavors, with the result that most banks and half the businesses in Paris are closed. Hence—' he gestured at the shouting crowd – 'we find a great many more workingmen of all stripes on the streets this afternoon with not much to do. And no surety that there'll be anything for them to do for some time to come. *Not* the best time to have one's army in Africa.'

In his frogged and nip-waisted coat, his luxuriantly-dressed brown curls wilting in the heat, and exuding the delicate scent of patchouli, Daniel had all the appearance of one whose intellectual horizons were confined to the season's newest dictates in the cut of waistcoats. In fact, though such great questions did comprise much of the man's usual conversation, January had always found him – as the son of one of Paris's wealthiest bankers – to be a shrewd observer of both politics and humanity.

'Imbeciles!' Ayasha clinched her arm around January's waist. Her face, like dark ivory against the white of her linen bonnet, sparkled with a kind of fierce exasperation. She never could abide stupidity.

'*Precisely* my opinion, madame.' Daniel's latest sweetheart, the devastatingly handsome and (as far as January had ever been able to tell) comprehensively wooden-headed heir of the Comte de Belvoire, dabbed at his sleeve with a spotless linen handkerchief. Something – probably a thrown dog-turd – had left a little smear of brown on the immaculate cream-colored wool of his coat, and this seemed to preoccupy the young man to the exclusion of any larger issues of political catastrophe or personal danger. 'Why should businessmen want to poke their noses into affairs of state anyway? And in the *summer*, of all the absurd times, when everyone is out of town?' He cast a reproachful glance at Daniel. 'Or *should* be out of town . . .'

'My dearest Philippe.' Daniel put a genial arm around his friend's shoulders. 'I vow to you, we shall make our way to more agreeable climes just as soon as I've ascertained what's actually going to come of all this. God knows the only entertainment in town, if one can call it that, is the French opera—'

Philippe de la Marche shuddered elaborately.

'—unless of course one regards rioting as a form of sport.' And Ben-Gideon nodded toward Carnot, now haranguing a group of shouting men about the king's friends.

Quietly, January asked, 'Do you think this is all a form of sport, then?' His eyes met Daniel's, nearly on the level with his own: Daniel was within an inch of January's six-foot, three-inch height, and the Vicomte de la Marche – who had gone back to dabbing worriedly at his coatsleeve – was not much shorter.

'Dearest Benjamin, do you think that for one man – or woman – out of three here, that it isn't?' Daniel raised his manicured brows. 'Do you think that there's really any chance of France returning to a republic, just because the people of Paris break some windows and loot some shops? I suspect that all of this—' he waved toward Carnot, and beyond him to the open windows of the *National* – 'has a good deal more to do with the fact that a man can only aspire to membership in the cream of society by election to the Chamber of Deputies, than any real desire to abolish that society.'

'And the rights of the people?' asked January, with the quiet anger of a man who has grown up having no rights. 'Are we to pretend those don't exist?'

Ayasha added something extremely rude in her native Arabic.

'I do assure you, my Mauritanian gazelle, the king's party would like nothing more than to exclude jumped-up businessmen like my father and his cronies from all voice in the government. They can see very well that it's the factory owners who'll be ruling England openly inside of five years. Who do you think owns the *National*? Certainly not the working people.'

'If the Lafitte brothers—' January named the owners of the largest banking firm in France, who financed the embattled newspaper – 'hope to increase their power – or their place in society – by scaring the king, they'd better watch out what they're doing. These people are angry. Not just at the king, but at kings. A lot of them served with Bonaparte's armies, and armed force doesn't impress them. The businessmen may have a bigger storm on their hands than the one they whistled for.'

Shouting redoubled at the edge of the crowd. 'Precisely the reason,' said Philippe, taking Daniel by the arm, 'that we should get ourselves out of town until things— Now see here!' he cried, genuinely roused, as a spoiled peach struck him juicily in the back. 'This is impossible! I only got this coat from my tailor yesterday, and already it's ruined! Honestly, Daniel, there's nothing you can do in this town about all this—'

Someone yelled that royal troops were coming to shut down the newspapers, and the crowd began to scatter into the surrounding streets. Carnot sprang down from the box where he'd been standing and caught January's arm. 'We're not going to let them get away with this!' he cried.

And Maurice Pleyard, another of the Société, called to them in passing, 'Are you with us, Benjamin? We have guns – and we *will* be free!'

Twilight was approaching. January guessed that the royal troops weren't going to try anything with night drawing on. At the end of the Rue St-Marc he saw the city's frock-coated lamp-lighters come around the corner and hesitate, with their keys and staffs, flints and jars of oil. Someone flung a paving-stone at them; someone else hurled a half a brick at the lamp that hung over the street nearest the *National*'s offices, shattering it and showering those below with broken glass.

A sensible precaution, January reflected, as the lamplighters fled and people began smashing the wall-boxes that guarded the ends of the chains which held up the lamps above the streets. If the king's troops were on the way – 'Such of them as aren't in Algeria,' scoffed Pleyard, as he dove back into the crowd – it made sense to destroy any lights that might have helped them, once darkness gathered in the narrow Paris streets.

As January and Ayasha walked home in the long northern twilight, he heard more glass break along the darkening streets. Windows, it sounded like. Knots of men gathered outside cafés along their route, and by the lamplight from within those windows January saw men he knew from the Société, or from other groups like it, gesticulating and shouting. Cries of 'Down with the Bourbons!' and 'Long live the Charter!' cracked from street corner orators – as if the Bourbon king hadn't already twisted the charter of the peoples' liberties to support his own intentions on a number of occasions.

'I hope Anne has the sense to stay out of this,' remarked Ayasha, as January led the way toward the river.

Anne was Daniel Ben-Gideon's wife.

'Or at least that she'll take someone with her,' returned January, 'if she doesn't.'

'Who's her lover, these days?'

'That Irish fencing master of her brother's, the last I heard.' Though Daniel had little practical use for a wife, it still vexed January that the girl his friend's family had forced him to marry the previous year betrayed him so publicly. They kept separate establishments – the funds that old Moses Ben-Gideon had settled on Anne de la Roche-St-Ouen's ancient but impover-ished family made that easily possible – and Daniel spoke of the flamboyant seventeen-year-old with avuncular fondness. Now January wondered whether it was concern for Anne, as well as the urge to gather information about the slow-boiling rage in the city, which had drawn his friend to the offices of the *National*.

They crossed the bridge to the Ile de la Cité, and Ayasha flattened against the wall of a line of ancient houses along the Rue de la Juiverie, as a group of rough-clothed men streamed past them in the direction of the Palais de Justice. 'Is he a revolutionary, too, this fencing master?'

'I don't know about his politics.' January glanced before them and behind. The Rue de la Juiverie, like most of those on the Ile de la Cité, was barely a dozen feet wide and hemmed on both sides by high old houses of timber or brick. 'Though I can't imagine the Comte de la Roche-St-Ouen hiring a genuine troublemaker to school his boy.'

'I can't imagine a genuine troublemaker admitting what he is to someone like the comte,' returned Ayasha with a shrug. 'I wouldn't.'

'They'd know *you* for a genuine troublemaker, my nightingale,' said January, wrapping one powerful arm around her waist, 'no matter what you said you were.'

'*Majnun.*'

Few street lamps hung above these narrow ways at the best of times, and of these, all save one had been broken. The survivor's feeble rays glinted on the shattered glass underfoot. A dim slot of yellow glow ahead marked the Petit Pont and the river, and between, in the absolute blackness, January could hear men's voices still shouting, 'Down with the Bourbons!'

His friends – the artist Carnot, and Maurice Pleyard from the Société Brutus, and his fellow musician Jeannot Charbonnière – along with any number of his fellow medical students during his years at the Hôtel Dieu – were enthusiastic participants in the riots that periodically swept Paris. They'd cheerfully rain roof-tiles or cobblestones on royal troops, or help to erect barricades across the narrow streets. Raised on a sugar plantation and witness, before the age of seven, to the killings of two men he knew for being 'uppity', January had a healthy respect for armed authority and his senses prickled at the tension palpable in the sweltering night.

'In any case, Daniel's the only one she'll ever listen to,' he added. 'And not always, to him.'

Which was curious, given what he knew of Anne Ben-Gideon's ardent nature. Having been forced into the marriage for the financial and social benefit of their respective families, Daniel had spent his wedding night chastely playing backgammon with his bride before going out to breakfast with the *eromenos* who had preceded Philippe. Daniel had a mistress as well, hired several years previously for the purpose of convincing his parents that his tastes in the bedroom were orthodox. January wondered if he'd kept her on after the wedding, for good measure.

January encountered Anne Ben-Gideon early the next morning at the Palais Royale, that great emporium of the fashionable and clearing house of news. The Société Brutus met in the basement of one of its cafés, whose proprietor concealed guns for them in the rafters of the building's garret. At a guess some of its members, at least, would be there.

Leaving the tall house near the river where he and Ayasha had rooms, January hoped guns wouldn't be needed. By the light of day, last night's apprehensions seemed exaggerated. Though the streets still teemed with unemployed, angry workingmen – clustering in cafés and around the offices of newspapers (which seemed to be operating as usual despite the king's ordinance) – there were also the usual number of women coming and going from the market. Small shops were open, knife-grinders plied their trade. Barbers shaved customers on the street corners, and in the Rue de la Monnaie every imaginable variety of *camelot* was engaged in hawking everything from rabbit pelts to lemon juice.

Yet the tension remained. As he walked, January found himself remembering the king's notorious stubbornness, and he listened all the way for the crack of gunfire, and the unmistakable, elemental noise of a mob.

The Palais Royale, when he reached it, was jammed with men and women, four or five times as many as yesterday. Students had joined the working people. More seemed to be arriving all the time, and many of them, he observed grimly, were openly armed. Even at this early hour, orators were shouting in the cafés.

'They're saying the king's going to send troops into the city,' reported Anne, emerging from one of the excited knots of working-folk gathered in the pilastered shopping arcade. A broad-shouldered, extremely handsome young man stood protectively at her elbow, presumably her brother's erstwhile fencing master. He wore the out-at-elbows coat and the over-emphatic waistcoat of a student, and now and then turned his head – January observed – to catch a glimpse of his own reflection in the nearest shop window, and to straighten his cravat or the curl of honey-golden hair that fell over his forehead.

'There's going to be a demonstration in the Place du Carousel at noon,' the girl went on. 'Not that the king's at the palace, but you can bet that swine Polignac' – she named the first minister – 'is there. We stoned his carriage yesterday.' She grinned like a schoolboy at the recollection. 'There'll be twenty thousand of us at least.'

Anne Ben-Gideon was dressed like a woman of the people, her skirt of striped drugget kilted up to show pink lace stockings, the sort worn by shopgirls when out with their sweethearts. Her shift was patched and the leather bodice that sheathed her slim form stained and supple with wear – January guessed she'd bought the outfit at a slop-shop. But her shoes were incongruously expensive, the sort that English countrywomen wore to go shooting in with their husbands. She sported a tricolor sash, the colors of the revolution, and a pistol was stuffed into it, a small silver weapon of the sort called a muff pistol, with a screw-on barrel. 'He'll be a fool if he doesn't listen.'

'And you'll be a fool,' returned January, 'if you think there won't be trouble.'

'Of course there'll be trouble!' Her grin sparkled as she looked up at him, brown eyes –bright and lively as a squirrel's – fairly dancing at the thought. 'Nobody has *ever* accused His Majesty of not being a fool!'

The daughter of aristocrats who had fled France in 1789, January guessed that Anne Ben-Gideon looked forward to a battle with the royal troops far more eagerly than she'd looked forward to any of the balls, operas, and court levées she'd been forced to attend since her 'presentation' to polite society. She pulled the pistol from her sash and brandished it, competently. 'But we'll make him listen . . .'

'With that?' January took it from her hand, weighed it in his own. It was small, but the barrel was large, designed for defense against highwaymen or footpads. The chased silver barrel was designed to be screwed into the breech after the lead pistol-ball had been seated; a silly nuisance, January had always thought of such weapons, but it did mean that it could be carried inconspicuously, if you didn't have to use it in a hurry.

'With these.' From the back of her belt she drew two other weapons, heavy horse-pistols, capable of knocking a man down. 'And this.' Replacing them, she reached back to her decorative lover and took from him a handsome Wilkinson hunting-rifle. 'And don't think I don't know how to use them.'

That, at least, January believed. Anne de la Roche-St-Ouen, despite everything her despairing parents could do, had managed, as a child, to learn to shoot, to hunt, to ride astride *à l'Amazone* and to fence, as if fitting herself for the role of the intrepid heroine of any of a thousand novels she had read; according to Daniel, she was getting her current lover to teach her to box. January didn't know whether to feel exasperation or pity when his friend spoke of her. She had studied chemistry and astronomy by turns, and had tried to get the artist Carnot to teach her to dissect corpses, in her quest for arcane and flamboyant areas of knowledge wherewith – January suspected – to shock parents and a brother whom she held in good-natured contempt.

Had she been a boy, he knew, the Comte and Comtesse de la Roche-St-Ouen would have welcomed her taste for adventure and hard-riding, for cigars and swordplay, with proud delight. Nobody January knew would have striven to squeeze a son's over-brimming energy into the narrow tracks of fashion, sketching, and embroidery. No parent on earth would have considered it laudable to train a male child to sit, straight-backed and gracious, for hours at a time doing *absolutely nothing*, for the sake of social discipline and proper court manners. At the age of fourteen Anne had discovered newspapers and politics, and her parents had been even more horrified by that than they'd been when they'd discovered that she'd been bribing the old gardener at the convent of Notre-Dame-de-Syon to teach her to handle a gun.

'Any other demonstrations?' he asked now.

'Vendome,' she said, 'and L'Elephant,' meaning the Place de la Bastille, where Napoleon had intended to erect an eighty-foot-tall bronze elephant to memorialize one of his battles. The Emperor of the French had only gotten so far as to raise a full-size plaster model, which, sixteen years later, still stood, filthy, crumbling, and rat-ridden in a tangle of weeds on the site of the ancient fortress. She took the silver muff pistol back from him, and shoved it once more into her sash. 'And a march along the boulevards . . .'

Since the stylish boulevards were also the site of a number of gun-shops – not to mention establishments that sold silks, jewels, and other lootable commodities – January suspected that it was there that troops would be sent.

She glanced at the handsome fencing master for further information, but he was adjusting his cravat in the reflection of a nearby window. 'Gerry?'

The dimple in his chin deepened with his dazzling smile. 'That'll be enough to have 'em on the run, *acushla*.'

Maurice Pleyard, the Norman divinity student who had formed the Société Brutus, emerged then from the Café de la Chatte Blanche with the news that the Société would meet at noon and join the demonstration in front of the Tuileries Palace. At shortly before that hour, Ayasha closed up her shop – none of the girls who worked for her had come in that day in any case – and went with January to the Palais to meet the others. But they found the gates to the immense courtyard of shops and cafés closed, the doors of the adjoining theater locked, and shutters over the windows of the palace of the Duc d'Orleans who owned (and collected rents on) the entire complex.

Guards in the blue-and-scarlet of the king's troops were stationed among the archways that fronted the small square. Gangs of children skirmished around the soldiers, pelting them with stones. A young man – no child – in the shirtsleeves and patched breeches of a laborer ran out to join one of these bands, with a torn-up cobblestone the size of a man's two fists. The whores who customarily populated the central garden of the Palais stood around at a safe distance and jeered.

January took Ayasha's hand, and retreated into the Rue des Bons Enfants.

By late afternoon – that grilling Tuesday seemed endless – troops had begun to concentrate in the Place du Carrousel before the palace, in the Place du Vendome and along the boulevards.

More were said to be moving into the city, 'Proving that His Majesty would rather shoot his subjects than listen to them,' proclaimed Pleyard, when the Société Brutus finally gathered in the twilight at a café on the Quai du Louvre.

Most of the shopkeepers of the city had boarded up their establishments by this time, and the strollers and carriages which had earlier promenaded in the mellow warmth of the early evening had vanished, like birds seeking shelter at the growl of thunder. 'It's the Allies who put the kings back onto us,' cried Carnot, shaking back his tangle of dark hair from his blazing eyes. 'And foreigners – our enemies! – are the ones who seek to keep them there! They know that the republic cannot be stopped—'

January didn't think it was quite the moment to bring up the fact that the Republic had been succeeded, in fairly quick succession, by a corrupt directory and then by a military dictator who had had himself crowned emperor. At thirty-five, he was older than most of the members of the Société, and remembered, as a young man, both hearing from witnesses, and reading in the New Orleans newspapers, accounts of Napoleon's ruinous ambitions. At least the republic had tried to right the accumulated wrongs of centuries. Thanks to state education, it might now have a better chance to do so again.

Thus when the fighting started – crowds raining the troops with broken roof-tiles, bricks, and the torn-up cobbles of the streets, the soldiers firing back, first into the air and then into their attackers – January and Ayasha joined their friends in building barricades across the mouths of the Rue des Capuchines and the Rue St-Denis, to hem the royal troops into the Boulevard. Against the evening sky the tricolor of the republic could be seen flying from the towers of Notre Dame and from the spire of the Hôtel de Ville, and through the night – which they spent in Pleyard's garret near the barricade – even after the crackle of rifle-fire died down January heard dimly the great bells of the cathedral sounding an alarm, answered by those of half the churches in the city.

What was later called the July Days had begun.

Troops moved through the city on Wednesday. Twice they attacked the St-Denis barricade, a six-foot redoubt built clear across the street, over five-feet thick: carts, furniture, packing-crates filled with dirt; doors and shutters torn from houses, empty barrels and baskets, the timbers of a dismantled shed. The interstices of all these were packed with the granite squares of cobblestones torn from the roadbed, and further filled in with the black, heavy Paris dirt. Guns had come out of hiding, or had been distributed (voluntarily or otherwise) by the owners of the gun-shops along the Rue de Rivoli. Other barricades – some large, most barely breastworks of cobblestones and chairs – were going up all over the city.

'I actually suspect you're better armed than the royal troops,' said Daniel, when he slipped through the back door of the house that faced onto the Rue de Rivoli, where the defenders of the barricade had taken refuge. 'They've only got eleven rounds apiece, you know, and General Marmot's made virtually no provision for them to get food or drink.' The back room of the building's tight-shuttered ground-floor shop had been converted into a sort of guard-post for the men firing from the upper windows or manning the defensive wall itself. Local women and children brought in buckets of water and what food they could spare through most of the night and into the morning. Even his old master on Bellefleur, January reflected, had taken care that his field hands had water in heat like this.

Daniel himself looked bathed, barbered, rouged, rested, perfumed and free of powder-stains. His coat today was a marvel of changeable green silk with golden buttons – January wondered that one side or the other hadn't picked him off like a gigantic bird as he'd made his way through the tortuous streets behind the barricades.

'You haven't seen Philippe, have you, darling?' he asked, and January and the others – Ayasha, Carnot, a handful of printers and stevedores from the market district – all shook their heads.

'I thought Philippe wanted nothing to do with politics,' said Ayasha, loading guns with the mechanical speed of a Yankee factory line.

'He doesn't, poor lamb.' Daniel adjusted his beautifully-tied cravat in the glass of a shuttered window. 'Not any more than I do, really. He and I were leaving town this morning – I've rented us an absolute *bijou* of a house outside of Vouvray, as far as possible from that frightful family of his – but he didn't come to my house this morning as we had agreed. I went to his apartment – not that awful mausoleum of his family's on the Ile St-Louis, but a most charming *pied-à-terre* I rented for him on the Rue St-Honoré . . . Here, let me help you with that, my beautiful one . . .' He picked up one of the rifles from the table and, with surprising adeptness, measured powder from one of the several canisters and proceeded to charge the weapon. The war ministry had been broken into early that morning, so there was no shortage of guns or powder.

'He wasn't there, and his man tells me he went to my house yesterday afternoon, and didn't return. Freytag – my man, you know – had told me Philippe was there whilst I was at that demonstration at the Elephant – *fearfully* ill-organized, and I won't even speak of the so-called logic of the speeches . . . but that he'd left before I got back. I must say I'm a bit concerned about him. The dear boy is as beautiful as an angel but has *no* sense whatsoever . . .'

Someone shouted down the stairway from above, 'They're coming!'

'Either get out of here, *tapette*,' put in a thickset man whose ragged shirt was stained rusty with tanning liquor, 'or come out with us.' He snatched up an army musket and shoved it at the dandy. Daniel backed away in surprised alarm.

'What about Anne?' January caught up his own rifle and headed for the stair.

'Good Lord, I expect she's with Gerry,' said Daniel. 'O'Dwyer . . . Her fencing master, you know . . . He'll take good care of her. Anyway she's a thousand times smarter than poor Philippe – although I'm afraid the same could be said of my dog!' And he darted out into the Rue St-Denis.

General Marmot's troops drove the rebels back from the barricade shortly after that, and January, with the others, retreated in good order through the houses along the Rue St-Denis to the next barricade, while those remaining in the upper stories of the buildings along the street continued to hurl paving-stones, roof-tiles, and broken furniture on the heads of the advancing soldiers. The tortuous streets of Paris seemed built for the 'little war' – the *guerilla* – tactics pioneered by the Spanish against Napoleon's troops twenty years before. The men crouched behind the barricades simply broke and ran when the troops finally came storming over, and disappeared through a hundred doors opened for them. When barricades were taken, the royal troops frequently found the walls rebuilt behind them, trapping them in the open between one barricade and the next. In the baking-hot day their water-carriers were shot, their messengers – with pleas for more ammunition – intercepted.

All over Paris, fashionable perfumers or tailors or bootmakers took down the fleur-de-lys signs which had marked them as 'Perfumer (or tailor or bootmaker) To The King'.

By the time the shadows began to lengthen, the royal troops were pulling back to the Palace of the Tuileries and the long, rambling courts of the Louvre.

January and Ayasha slept that night on the floor of a family of plasterers on the Rue du Temple. Four bare walls, a curtained bed for their host (and his wife and five children) and an assortment of rags and dishes stacked on goods-boxes. Pleyard and four other students shared the floor with them, their guns lying ready beneath their hands. Ayasha's hair had smelled of gunpowder, January recalled. Now and then, lying awake in the heat, he'd heard the furtive scratching of rats in the corners of the room.

1839

Like tonight. January remembered it vividly, nine years later, lying in the dense heat of a New Orleans summer in his own house, his wife – not Ayasha – by his side. Suffocating darkness, and lying awake, listening . . .

Nine years ago it had been the tolling of the *bourdon* of Notre Dame.

Tonight it was thunder, across the lake in a place where – at that other time, in that other place – he had held in his heart the iron determination never to lie again.

Louisiana. The land where he had been born a slave.

In Paris at least he could fight for the hope of justice for the poor, and freedom from the tyranny of kings.

It is true, he thought, *that you can't step twice into the same river . . .*

1830

It was barely light when he'd gone downstairs, seven flights, rifle in hand, to piss in the courtyard and see if anybody in the building had water left, or if any of the city's thousands of water-carriers were afoot yet. The streets were still, the smell of gun-smoke everywhere. The hoarse croaking of ravens sounded very loud. When he turned the corner and made his way towards the last of the barricades they'd abandoned – on the Rue St-Croix – the birds flew up in their hundreds, from the dead men lying there.

He walked through the twilight streets – as he was to walk, over and over again for years, in dreams – a clear gray world inhabited by stray dogs, by rats, by scavenger-birds. For several blocks the streets would appear perfectly usual for this time of the morning, save that they were utterly deserted, and strewn with broken bricks and shattered roof-tiles. Then he'd come on a barricade, or the remains of one – or sometimes two, one that had been stormed by the troops, and then re-erected behind them, trapping them in crossfire. The blood had darkened on the ground, blending with the infamous Paris mud. But the smell of it, and of the waste the dead men had voided, was everywhere.

In the Rue St-Martin, near the church of St-Nicholas-des-Champs, a huge barricade had been erected. January paused to admire it: an omnibus had been commandeered, the horses unhitched, the passengers debarked, and the whole vehicle turned over on its roof as the core of the makeshift fortification. Around this cobbles and earth, barrels and furniture and planks, had been reared nearly ten-feet high, and the men of the district had made their stand against the royal troops who'd been attempting to clear a way around the fighting in the nearby Rue St-Denis. The dead lay where they'd fallen, though January guessed General Marmot would have bearers out later in the day to collect them.

They were already beginning to stink.

He glanced warily down the street – the mud blood-soaked and denuded, from edge to edge, of paving-stones – and would have passed by, but for a glimpse of incongruous color on the barricade.

Among the dark-blue uniforms of the troops, the rough browns and grays of the students, printers, clerks, butchers who'd considered their freedom worth dying for, there was a single, gaudy splash of lilac, like a peony in a basket of turnips.

January crossed to the barricade, scrambled up the steep slope littered with the dead.

Even smeared with black Paris mud, the brocade coat was unmistakable.

Terrible grief closed his throat. Daniel had been an observer of the world, not a participant in its violence. *How will I tell Anne? If I can locate her?*

He turned the body over.

But the dead man wasn't Daniel Ben-Gideon. The angelic features, the Cupid-bow lips beneath their soft brown mustache, the gem-blue eyes staring blankly up at the paling sky, belonged to Philippe de Gourgue, Vicomte de la Marche. Heir to the Comte de Belvoire.

And the hole in the lilac coat, the green silk waistcoat beneath, hadn't been made by a trooper's musket.

January saw this at once. He had fought on the cotton-bale barricades at the Battle of New Orleans as well as in the streets of Paris. He knew what musket wounds looked like.

This wound was bloody but neat, the silk of the coat burned by powder, and the wound small.

A small pistol, fired at close range.

A muff pistol, almost certainly.

THREE

1839

A s a member of the Board of Directors of the Faubourg
Tremé Free Colored Militia and Burial Society, it was
part of January's responsibility to march in the Fourth
of July parade along Rue Royale – in the First Municipality of
the now-tripartite city of New Orleans – and thence up St Charles
Avenue through the Second Municipality, to Tivoli Circle. Though
celebrating the Birth of Freedom in a nation which not merely
tolerated, but actively defended, human slavery struck January
as incongruous when he was in a good mood and blasphemous
in his angrier moments, he was careful to lobby every year for
the society's continued place in the proceedings. He, and a number
of other members, had fought under Jackson at the Battle of New
Orleans, and he considered it vital to remind the Americans of
this fact. To remind the white Americans as a whole that it was,
in fact, legal, under certain circumstances, for men of color to
possess or carry guns. (What the police would have said about
the two rifles, two pistols, and the smoothbore musket hidden
in the rafters of his house was another matter.)

Dressed in his red and blue uniform – and pardonably proud
that, at forty-four, it still fit him as it had when he was in his
twenties – he led the militia band, playing bright proud marches
with the other members in step behind them. He was nevertheless conscious that once they crossed Canal Street into the
American municipality, the cheering of the crowds that lined
the parade route significantly lessened as their group marched
past. White men didn't like to see black ones – even the fairest-
skinned quadroons and octoroons – in uniform, much less armed.
They didn't like to see the smart military formation, the sharp
discipline and soldierly turnouts, that gave the lie to the conten-
tion that those of African descent were lazy, shuffling cowards.
Before dark, he guessed, there'd be planters and cotton-brokers

clustered on the porches of the big houses farther up the Avenue declaring that such displays were a 'bad influence' on 'good niggers who know their place'.

After the parade they all stood in well-mannered silence while the local (white, American) politicians made speeches about democracy and the Birth of Freedom under red-white-and-blue awnings erected in the circle. Then the various militia companies dispersed into the crowd and the society made their way back to Congo Square.

It was at Congo Square that the issue of Henry Brooke's murder re-entered January's life.

Congo Square, known also as Circus Square or Circus Place, opened off of Rue des Ramparts next to the turning basin of the Carondelet Canal: not, as Sir John Oldmixton had observed, the most salubrious district in the city. For as long as January could remember, on Sunday afternoons there had been a market there, for slaves to bring garden produce or handicrafts to sell. At the markets someone had always brought along a drum. They had danced – ancient rhythms, African rhythms, that men and women had brought from home or had learned from their parents in this new land of slavery. When January had first known the place it had lain just outside the city's wall – if the crumbling palisade could be honored by that term – a few hundred yards upriver from the lake-ward gate. When he'd returned from Paris, seven years ago now, it had been to find the old rampart torn down, small houses built up in the new streets back from the new Rue des Ramparts over what had once been the municipal cow pastures. The Sunday slaves-market square was now surrounded by an iron fence and the turning basin hemmed about by a grimy collection of saloons, boarding houses, warehouses and bordellos constructed of flatboat planks and tent-canvas.

And the slave dances were still being held.

Congo Square was one of the few places where the colored population of New Orleans could gather – probably, January guessed, because the iron fence made the whites feel safe. Thus when celebrations for the Birth of Freedom were discussed by various of the free colored benevolent societies of the city, it had been arranged to hold them in the square. There was an unspoken understanding that they'd be 'American' – by which January guessed the City Fathers meant 'no drumming'. But tables had been set up under the plane trees around the square's edge, and the ladies – both *plaçeés* and artisans' wives – had brought of their best: 'dirty' rice, gumbo, hoppin' john, sweet potato pies. Society funds had been expended on barrels of beer and cauldrons of boiled shrimp and crawfish. Pits had been dug that morning, to roast a couple of pigs, donated by the better-off *libré* businessmen or the white relatives of several of the *plaçeés*. Though the picnic was officially the province of the free people of color – the *librés* – and only those from 'downtown' in the French district, January met and greeted men and women he knew were slaves, and welcomed the uptown blacks.

'Hmph,' said his mother, elegant as a dowager queen in butter-yellow voile. 'You should be more careful who you let in, Benjamin. They're barely more than slaves and they certainly have manners straight from the cane-patch.'

January knew better than to remind the Widow Levesque that she'd cut cane herself, up til the age of twenty-five, and merely said, 'It does no harm to get to know the uptown folks, Maman. Some day we may need to work together.'

'God forefend. They're completely without the slightest notion of how things are done.'

Meaning, January knew, the delicate systems of favors and families by which the Creole French and their Creole African cousins did business.

Turning, he caught sight (*Thank you, God!*) of his sister Dominique, his wife Rose, and their children (*My child! My son!* The sight of Baby John still filled him with ridiculously cataclysmic delight). 'Minou!' he called. 'Rose!' and his mother sniffed.

'Don't you think Rose is a little far along to be appearing in public?' she asked, ignoring the fact that she herself had carried cane-stalks to the grinding-mill only hours before giving birth to January's sister Olympe.

Rose's friends gathered around her, chattering and laughing – a Fourth-of-July picnic being a far different thing from a formal party, much less a gathering of white folks. Among the artisans and small shopkeepers of the *libré* community far too many women were obliged to tend to business in an advanced state of pregnancy to turn up their noses at a mother-to-be attending a picnic. This matter-of-fact attitude about the so-called facts of life, January suspected, might have had something to do with the attraction many 'well-bred' white men felt toward the free colored demi-monde: the relief at being able to drop polite pretense. (To say nothing of a different attitude about what could be done between the sheets.)

While his mother went to embrace Dominique – the only one of her children for whom she actually cared – and to kiss four-year-old Charmian, he strode to Rose's side and kissed her hands.

'How do you feel?' he asked in an undervoice, and her friend Cora laughed up at him.

'Ben, Rose is pregnant, she hasn't got a broken leg!'

'I'm told there's going to be ice cream,' smiled Rose, watching Baby John – eighteen months old – toddle purposefully off to investigate the resurrection-fern growing along the iron fence. 'I have no intention of giving birth until after I've had some.' The afternoon was growing hot but breeze still wafted from the river; Rose faced it, eyes shut behind the thick ovals of her spectacles.

Someone had set up a makeshift awning over some goods boxes, and a pack of January's fellow-musicians were playing, those who hadn't been employed to perform at a dozen white militia picnics elsewhere in town. January took Rose's arm, collected Baby John from beside the fence, and led them in search of beer and lemonade. He himself had had offers to play for the Urban Guards (Second Municipality) and New Orleans Fensibles (First Municipality), and while he admitted that they needed the money, it was good beyond measure just to be here with his wife and his son.

He later reflected that he should have taken the paying jobs . . . not that it would have done him any good in the long run.

'Benjamin!'

His other sister, Olympe – Olympia Snakebones, the voodoos called her – came through the clumps of revelers to where January and Rose had found seats on some goods boxes beneath the trees. She was tall like their mother but thin, and like January himself, African-black, a complexion not admired among the free colored. The five points of her headcloth that marked her as a voodooienne flicked and wavered in the river breeze. A girl followed her, skinny and coltish, her face vaguely familiar. January thought he'd seen her along Rue Burgundy, when he'd walked through those neighborhoods that had grown dirtier and more crowded. The child of one of the whores, maybe, or at her age perhaps a whore herself.

Certainly her eyes, when she looked up at him as Olympe stopped before him, were the eyes of a child too old for her years. A child who no longer trusts anyone or anything. He'd seen the same look in the eyes of children on the slave blocks.

'This is Manon Filoux,' Olympe introduced them, laying a long, bony hand on the child's shoulder. 'Manon, this is my brother Ben. He's going to help get your mother out of jail.'

The huge eyes – turquoise-gray, a color often seen among the fairer-skinned *librés* – returned to his face, not believing a word of it. Manon said nothing. It was far from the first time that someone in the *libré* community at the back of the French Town had come to January to solve a puzzle.

'And what,' asked January gently, 'did your maman do, Manon?'

'She killed Mr Brooke.' The girl's voice was startlingly deep for a child's, and vicious satisfaction roughened her tone. 'And I'm glad she did it. I wished I could have done it myself.'

'Brooke?'

'An Englishman,' said Olympe. 'Henry Brooke. They pulled him out of the turning basin Sunday morning.'

'The girl's mistaken.' Olympe bore an old blanket over her arm, and she spread this on the ground beside the goods boxes where January and Rose sat. January got to his feet to give her and Manon his seat.

'I hope the police believe so.'

His sister sniffed. 'The police want to arrest someone,' she said. 'They don't care who.'

He couldn't argue with her there. 'Does . . . What's your maman's name, Manon? Does she own a muff pistol? And had she reason to kill M'sieu Brooke?'

'She's called Jacquette. She killed him because he deserved it,' returned the girl, but Olympe's eyes narrowed at the question.

'How did you know it was done with a muff pistol?'

January shook his head. 'I take it she knew the man?'

'The pistol was stolen from her a week ago.'

January raised his eyebrows.

'Don't look at me in that tone of voice,' added Olympe, which was exactly what their mother – with whom Olympe had not willingly spoken since 1812 – used to say to them. 'Jacquette is on the verge of losing her house. Without what *he* gave her, her children would be in the street. And she knew that in three weeks he would be gone.'

'Did she, now?'

Zizi-Marie wove her way to them through the crowd, balancing gourd bowls of red beans in her hands. Her harness-maker's apprentice – Ti-Gall L'Esperance – lumbered behind her, bearing a half-dozen roasted corn-ears wrapped in newspaper. Olympe's two middle children, Chou-Chou and Ti-Paul, trotted at his heels. 'Papa says, Zéphine needs to be fed,' Zizi reported. Zéphine was the family baby.

'Tell your papa I'll be along in a minute.' Olympe's whole thin, sharp face altered when she spoke to her daughter, anger dissolved by love. 'Take Manon along with you, *chère*.' She took the gourds, handed them to Rose and January. There were girls in the *libré* community – mostly the daughters of the *plaçeés* whose white fathers were paying for their upbringing – who avoided girls like Manon. January guessed Manon's mother was of the type who called herself a *plaçeé* rather than a prostitute, but was in fact somewhere between the two categories. She owned a house, where she lived with a white lover, not for years or decades after the older French Caribbean custom, but in the fashion that had become more and more common in the past few years, for a few months or as little as a few weeks. The long-time *plaçeés* felt their own standing – and that of their daughters – threatened by this new pattern, and usually didn't hesitate to express their scorn.

But Zizi-Marie had grown up seeing everyone in the world of black New Orleans pass through her mother's parlor: slave or free, dark or fair, *marchande* or *plaçeé*, wealthy or desperate. Olympe dealt in secrets, and through those secrets saw clearly into the dark waters of their souls. January had stood sponsor to his niece at her first communion, and knew – from living with

her since the time of the bank crash – how deep was her faith
in Christ's teachings. Yet the voodoo's all-accepting understanding showed now in the way Zizi-Marie took the younger
girl's hand.

In the trees around the square the metallic drumming of the
cicadas quickened its rhythm with the slow approach of
the afternoon's rainstorm, and far off over the lake the coming
thunder growled.

'I take it Jacquette was living with this Brooke?'

'Since he came to town, the middle of June.' Olympe's voice
was neutral, her shrug a sneer. 'He's one of those, says it's cheaper
than a hotel. She has the house her grandma left her on Rue
Toulouse.' Her nod down Basin Street – which dead-ended into
Congo Square opposite where they sat – indicated the snaggle
of low cottages just across the way, which had seen better days.
'That, and just about nothing else.'

January nodded. Over the past year or two he'd seen the Blue
Ribbon Balls, where the wealthy of the French community came
to dance with their *plaçeés*, become more mixed affairs. European
and American travelers were more prominent at the balls, drawn
to the gambling rooms on the ground floor of the Salle d'Orleans
where they were held, and as French wealth had declined a
number of women of the free colored demi-monde were willing
to settle for what they could get. In turn, the more traditional
plaçeés withdrew a little, drawing a line which divided the
demi-monde itself.

Jacquette Filoux (as Olympe gave the woman's full name),
though the daughter and granddaughter of *plaçeés*, was one of
those on the wrong side of that line.

'What was Brooke doing in New Orleans?'

'What do any of them do?' Olympe shrugged again. 'He said
he represented a group of Englishmen looking to invest, either in
steamships or cotton-presses or land—'

'It's a foolish time of year,' commented January, 'to come to
New Orleans for business.'

The voodooienne's eyes narrowed sharply at that.

'Everybody with any money is at the lake, or has gone north.
Even most of the slave dealers have left town.'

Olympe turned the matter over in her mind. 'Smuggling, do

you think? For all Britain's acts and treaties, men are bringing in more slaves than ever, through Cuba and Cartagena.'

'I have no idea.' He tried to sound as if he hadn't been approached by an unofficial representative of Queen Victoria on the subject of 'family papers' that needed locating. But Olympe, who had spent decades making deductions from secrets, still watched him, with her huge dark eyes so like their mother's, as if she could smell Sir John Oldmixton's Parma violet lingering on his clothing.

Or maybe she really does have a familiar spirit who tells her things.

He wouldn't put it past her.

'Sounds like you and I, brother, need to have a look at Jacquette's house. The City Guards took his clothes and things, but a man leaves his marks. And those marks will point to his killer.' All around the square, men and women were finishing up their picnic, complimenting one another on the excellence of each others' biscuits or callas, shaking out picnic-cloths and glancing at the sky. They'd all be back after it rained, in the evening when darkness mitigated the heat. There'd be drumming and dancing then, under the inevitable watchful eye of the First Municipality City Guards. But even the most hardline slave-holders would hardly forbid Fourth of July celebrations.

'You have friends in the City Guard,' Olympe went on. 'Sounds like you might have heard from one of them already . . .?'

'I haven't said I'll look into this.'

Her eyebrows disappeared under the red-and-gold line of the tignon that wrapped her hair.

'The woman's daughter sounds pretty sure Jacquette shot her "friend"—'

'That's her anger talkin'.'

'That doesn't mean it isn't right. If his body turned up in the basin – which is handily across the street from her house, as you say – the gun could be down there, too, swallowed up in the mud. Any of her neighbors hear a shot on Saturday night?'

'In this neighborhood? There's seven saloons around the basin itself and a dozen more you could hit with a rock from the water.' Scorn smouldered in her voice. 'You got to tell what shots you talkin' about by what time you heard 'em – "Was that the ten o'clock shootin' or the one at eleven-fifteen?" And you haven't yet said how you know what he was shot with.'

'I don't remember. Somebody said a man had been found . . . and it sounds to me like whoever killed him, gave him what was coming to him. Even a frightened woman – or a good one, or a careful one – will turn on a man if she gets angry enough, or sufficiently scared.'

'I don't give a chicken's dream about this Englishman.' Olympe folded her arms. 'I agree with you, brother, he probably did get what he was asking for. But Jacquette didn't do it. And whoever did it walked off and left her holding the bag.' Her gaze remained steady on him, as if she saw in his eyes the chill autumn dawn in the Place de la Nation. The silver glint of the guillotine's blade.

'She'll hang for it,' Olympe said.

Whatever the evidence, January knew that nobody was going to bother to defend a young woman of color for killing a white man who was sleeping with her. Particularly if her daughter had gone about the neighborhood crying that he'd deserved to be shot by the woman he had used.

Damn it.

Damn it.

There was more to the killing than met the eye. That much he knew.

And also that he'd be very, very sorry for the next words out of his mouth.

'Let me get Rose home,' he said. 'I'll meet you there.'

FOUR

Of course Rose insisted on coming as well.

'If Jacquette – she wouldn't be Lucette Filoux's granddaughter, would she? – did the murder, she's safely locked up and no threat to me.' She wrapped her hand firmly around her husband's arm, and walked close, partly for better balance on her iron shoe pattens and partly to share the shelter of his black silk umbrella. 'And if someone else did it I can't imagine they'd still be hanging around in the house.'

'Lucette Filoux . . .?' January vaguely remembered the name. His mother, who knew every *plaçeé* in the French Town, had mentioned her, though he couldn't recall the context. He did remember his mother's tone, though, as she spoke of the woman to her cronies over coffee. Patronizing, and full of contempt.

'Lucette Filoux was *plaçeé* to a shipowner named Jean Filoux, in Port-au-Prince.' Olympe named the town that had once been the administrative center of the French sugar colony of St-Domingue. She and the girl Manon were waiting for January and Rose in the dining room – or what had once been the dining room – of the shabby stucco cottage on Rue Toulouse, at the very back of the old French Town in the narrow block between Rue des Ramparts and Basin Street. By this time it was, as January's mother often put it, 'raining pickaninnies', and water poured off the edge of the little dwelling's abat-vent in gray curtains.

It was raining indoors as well. Through the door at the back of the dining room that let into a tiny 'cabinet' in the rear of the house, January saw buckets on the floor to catch the drips. The cottage, like a scaled-down version of his own house, consisted of two rooms and two 'cabinets', plus the half-story of attic above: fewer rooms than the house on Rue Esplanade, but laid out in the same fashion. Across the drenched yard behind it, visible through shutters wide open to the exquisite wet coolness of the air, a dilapidated kitchen boasted a little *garçonnière* on its upper floor.

From the gallery of the *garçonnière*, two little boys watched the house. Presumably Manon and her brothers were relegated to the upper floor of the kitchen building, as January himself had been in the larger cottage that his mother's white protector had given to her. The dining room was furnished with factory-wrought American chairs and sideboard, fairly new and extremely cheap. Any decent furniture had clearly been sold years ago.

'When the slaves rose up in '91 Lucette managed to get on one of the boats to New Orleans, with her four-year-old daughter Galianne.' Olympe crossed to the sideboard, where coffee things stood ready, as January helped Rose to one of those gimcrack chairs. 'Jean Filoux was away at the time. From all I can tell he never even inquired for Lucette or their daughter. Lucette found another protector in New Orleans – a wine merchant named Madrazo, I think his son still has a shop on Rue Bienville. He bought her this house.'

She poured out coffee into cups; Manon brought it to them on a japanned tray. The girl had clearly been 'talked to' on the subject of speculating about the murder, but she seemed still to vibrate with resentment, like a piano string's soft drone lingering on after a note.

'Galianne started going to the Quadroon Balls as soon as she was old enough and eventually became *plaçeé* to Gilbert LaBranche.' Olympe's grasp of the biographies of everyone in the French Town was as comprehensive as their mother's. It thoroughly entertained January that his sister was so like their mother, whom she despised and by whom was despised in her turn. 'She died of the fever when Jacquette was two. Madrazo was dead by that time and Lucette took Jacquette in; when LaBranche died his wife and her family managed to get hold of not only the cottage LaBranche had bought for Galienne, but the annuity he had settled on Galienne and their child. Lucette took Jacquette to the Quadroon Balls when she was fourteen and got her placed with a man named Revel, a banker. That lasted about five years.' Her dark glance touched Manon, who looked aside. 'She still comes to the balls.'

And probably keeps to the groups in the lobby or the gambling room, with the younger women, and the poorer ones, thought January. The women of the generation who didn't have long-term protectors, who made short-term liaisons with men passing through town: in effect, a single-resident boarding house with sex thrown in. Walking up Rue Toulouse, he had noted two cottages on the block, including the one next door to that of Jacquette Filoux, that were clearly bordellos – not the fancy parlor houses like that of the Countess Mazzini uptown, but simply establishments where four or five women lived and received their customers in cottages that had once belonged to *plaçeés*.

He sipped the coffee. A woman who presented herself as a *plaçeé* would never serve even a *pro tempore* lover coffee with this much chicory in it. At a guess, Olympe had brought it, as she'd brought the pralines on the German china plate. 'So tell me about Henry Brooke.'

Manon perched on the end of the daybed beside Olympe, opened her mouth, and Olympe raised a finger for her silence.

'He's an Englishman – or he was – and came into town in the middle of last month, on the *Hannah Crowder* from London. Where he went and what he did with himself in the daytimes I haven't had time to find out. I'll start asking around tomorrow.'

'Manon?'

'He'd rent a buggy and a horse sometimes.' The girl spoke with a kind of gruff hesitancy, as if she feared being shushed again. 'He said he was driving out to look at plantations, or out to Milneburgh. He'd be dressed up, you know, in a nice coat and a silk waistcoat and all that. He had some mighty pretty things, and he talked like a gentleman. You got to,' she added wisely, 'if you're gonna get anybody to lend you money, or buy something from you. That's what M'am Boudreaux says, that runs the house next door. When he'd go out on foot he dressed cheap, a calico shirt and big boots like the Kaintucks wear.'

'Did he, now?' January remembered Oldmixton's description of Brooke's instinct for protective coloration. 'You happen to see which way he went, either time?'

'I'd only see him when he came out to use the *couillon*.' She nodded toward the outhouse, against the tall brick wall that bounded the rear yard. 'Maman told us – Tiennot and Jean-Luc and me—' she glanced in the direction of the yard behind the house, and the *garçonnière* where the two little boys watched – 'to stay out of his way. I think he wore them cheap things to walk over to the basin and drink at the barrooms there, so he wouldn't look like a mark. When he'd come back late, drunk, he'd be dressed that way. It's how he was dressed the time he came up to my room,' she added, turning her face aside.

January said nothing, but only regarded her in silence.

'I hope you brained him with the chamber pot and threw him off the gallery,' Rose said calmly.

The flicker of Manon's grin told January before the girl spoke that the rape hadn't been consummated. Told him, too, that Manon understood that Rose wasn't going to ask, *What did you do to lead him on?*

'I should have. If he'd broke his neck then nobody'd be saying . . .' She shook her head. 'I bit him, and then screamed and screamed, and Maman came running out of the house. He told Maman I'd asked him to come up to my room. She didn't believe him . . . but she didn't make him leave, either.' The girl's face tightened. In her turquoise eyes was the understanding of why her mother hadn't defended her more, mixed with anger at the betrayal. 'After that he was meaner to me and the boys than before. But that time he was dressed like that, and I smelled the liquor on him.'

'That the only time he tried?'

Her voice strengthening in the face of January's tone – adult to adult – she replied, 'Yes, sir. But he did poke Lili Estevez next door. She's a friend of mine. I couldn't really tell Maman because Maman doesn't want me talking to Lili or any of M'am Boudreaux's girls.'

I'll bet she doesn't. The line between a *plaçeé*, who theoretically chose which men she gave access to her body, and a whore who could be raped with near-impunity, was all-important but razor-thin. A girl of eleven who strayed – or was dragged – across it would lose the greater part of her choices in life thereafter.

'And he'd hit me sometimes,' added Manon. 'Or hit the boys. He broke Tiennot's wrist. Or he'd yell at me, like if he'd ask me something and I'd say "Yes, sir," or "No, sir," and he'd yell, "What the hell you mean by that, girl?" Once Maman got on him about it and he slapped her 'cross the mouth.'

'Well,' said January, 'I can see why the police think she shot him. Tell me about Saturday night.'

'He wasn't here Saturday night!' Manon turned on her seat, caught his hands in her anxiety. 'Swear to Jesus he wasn't! Maman made dinner and supper for him both, and I didn't see her come out to get either one from the kitchen. He'd never tell her if he was going to be in or not,' she added. 'But he'd get mad if he got home and dinner wasn't waiting for him, or supper if he came in late. Or if she was out when he got here. When I came downstairs Sunday morning, there was dinner and supper both, still on the trays where she'd left them, with covers on them, on the kitchen table: chicken and rice for dinner, and cold ham and tomatoes for dinner. We ate them up, Sunday dinner and supper. Saturday night from the gallery we could see candles burning here in the house until three in the morning.'

'But you don't know for certain your maman was here?'

'Don't be silly, Benjamin,' said Rose. 'No woman would go off and leave candles burning in an empty house. Do you happen to know if the candles burned themselves out, or were blown out?'

'Burned themselves out,' returned the girl promptly. 'I cleaned out the holders Sunday and there was nothing left in them but a puddle and the wick. And anyway, Maman said as how he hadn't come in. Then later that day our uncle Juju, Maman's brother, came in and said as how Michie Brooke had been found in the basin shot dead. Juju said, he and Maman better go through the house and round up any money Michie Brooke might have left, in case he owed money someplace in town.'

The grin returned for a moment to the girl's strong-featured face. 'He said, "You search downstairs while I go through the attic," and Maman said, "No, how about you and me search together." You can't trust Uncle Juju with twenty-five cents. Maman stuck to him like a leech and together they found about twenty dollars in his suitcase and something Maman said was a bank credit-paper for fifty more. She kept that twenty dollars and the credit-paper on her, in case Uncle Juju sort of came back when she was out, and they were still on her when the policeman came this morning, and arrested Maman for killin' Michie Brooke, and took away all his papers and things.'

She looked aside then, her eyes filling. Rose moved over to the daybed where the girl sat, and she and Olympe both encircled Manon's shoulders in brief hugs.

January asked, 'Do you really think your maman did it?'

'Of course she didn't—' cut in Olympe, and it was January's turn to motion his sister silent.

'I don't know,' Manon whispered. 'She was mad enough to. I wanted her to. It would serve him right, he treated her so mean. But we really needed the money he gave her and she was just waiting for him to leave. It's the first time Maman ever said to me she wanted one of her gentlemen to leave.'

He glanced across at Olympe. 'What do the guards say?'

'That Brooke came home at one in the mornin'. Bridgie Danou, that lives across the street, says she saw him unlockin' the door, lettin' himself in as she was comin' home – she's a maid at the Verandah Hotel. She says she was waked up by shots at around two. Other neighbors say the same.'

'You hear shots, Manon?'

The girl nodded. 'I thought they were at M'am Boudreaux's,' she said, as if not entirely convinced of it herself. 'Or at M'am Tonnerre's, or down over at Vidi Vigaud's that runs a crap game most nights in her parlor—'

'You can't pass a night in this neighborhood without hearin' shots,' reiterated Olympe impatiently, and January, who lived only blocks away, knew she was right. It was one of the things he knew he'd have to talk his way around, to the parents of Rose's young scholars.

'And you can bet your Sunday shoes,' his sister went on, 'that Effie Boudreaux and all her girls will swear nothing of the kind went on under their chaste roof.'

And the owner of the place – a wealthy gentleman on the municipal council – would, January knew, back them up.

His glance returned to Manon. 'Does your maman own a pistol?'

'I told you it was stolen.'

January wanted to ask Olympe how she knew this, but guessed that she'd have an answer ready.

'Like as not by that good-for-nothing brother of hers.'

From what he'd heard of Jules-Jérôme Filoux – whose name was not unknown to the members of the Faubourg Tremé Free Colored Militia and Burial Society – this also sounded not unlikely.

'She had a little one,' said Manon, with a worried glance at Olympe. 'I only saw it once, more than a year ago. She kept it hid, on account of the boys. Lili told me—' Manon's voice grew hesitant again, like one who has been forbidden to discuss the subject (or maybe just forbidden to talk to Lili) – 'if there's trouble over in M'am Boudreaux's house, M'sieu Alvarez sorts it out: if one of the men causes trouble with a girl, or tries to rob her, or something. But Lili said, Maman not working in a house, she needed a pistol. Monday afternoon, when I was doing the chores, I went and looked in the place where Maman hid it, and it was gone.'

'Why don't you show me where that was?'

There was a false back on one of the drawers of the bedroom armoire. One would have to pull the drawer all the way out, to get at the little compartment there. A few grains of powder dusted the bottom of the compartment, and the smell of gun-oil lingered.

Trailed by the ladies, January went on to search the rest of the cottage, while the afternoon's rainstorm gradually wore itself out overhead and blew on up the river toward Baton Rouge. Shortly after the last drops rattled on the abat-vent, January heard music start up again in Congo Square.

The City Guards had already cleared out the armoire in the bedroom and the small desk in the dining room which, Manon said, Henry Brooke had appropriated for his own use. All the furnishings – bed, armoire, desk, chairs, the dishes in the dining-room cupboard, the curtains and the toilette articles on Jacquette Filoux's bureau – were new and cheap, while the few older objects which remained, stored in the attic or relegated to the *cabinets* at the back of the house, were of infinitely better quality, though worn and scuffed. False economy, his mother would have sneered, but January understood that when one needs something that doesn't scream *poverty*, it isn't always possible to purchase good quality. Observing how the fabric of Jacquette's dresses had been carefully picked apart and re-cut to more recent fashions was like reading a bank book.

January located two other hidey-holes in the attic and one in the *cabinet* that housed the attic stair. One of these held five dollars in silver, an ivory miniature of a beautiful, dusky-complected woman in the extravagantly-wrought tignon characteristic of the

Caribbean, and the deed to the house. Another held receipts and notes pertaining to two loans from the Bank of Louisiana, one against the house, the other against a slave woman named Nanny (foreclosed, January assumed, since there didn't seem to be any servant on the property and Jacquette had made dinner and supper for her lover herself). There was also a bank book from the First Commercial Bank, one of those which had closed its doors in the spring of 1837 and had never re-opened. The third held only a few receipts, and, jammed into a corner where the bricks of the house-wall had been removed behind the attic stair, a pistol-ball about the size of a pea.

A tiny gun, thought January, turning the ball in his fingers. Easily palmed, but any salt-river roarer who pulled a weapon that size in a Basin Street saloon would be laughed out of the place with his tail between his legs and a nickname on the river that he'd never live down.

'Have you got anyone to stay with?' he asked Manon, as they descended the attic steps, and he saw a flicker of panic cross the girl's eyes.

As well it might, he reflected, given the neighborhood and the proximity of such entrepreneurs as Madame Boudreaux and M'sieu Alvarez next door. The parish orphanage, January was well aware, didn't have any more money than anyone else did in these times, and it wasn't a place he'd have wanted any child of his own to stay.

'They can stay with me.' Olympe gathered up her skirts, to follow them down the narrow stair.

'I'll speak to the board of the society,' said January, 'about getting you a little money to help with their keep. Can the house be locked up?' The entire contents, if carried off and sold second-hand, probably wouldn't have realized twenty dollars, but they were all Jacquette Filoux owned. 'Obviously it can,' he added immediately, 'if Bridgie Danou saw M'sieu Brooke letting himself in with a key—'

'There's bolts on the back doors,' provided Manon. 'Good key-locks on the front.' Like most of the older Creole cottages, Jacquette's had long French doors to provide both entry and light. Dining room and bedroom each had two sets of 'doors' on the street side, glazed and equipped with simple latches but defended with stout pairs of shutters, whose louvered jalousies would admit a striped light even when the shutters were closed. One French door of the dining room, and one of the bedroom, were equipped with bolts on the inside, the second set in each chamber fastened with nearly new brass Chubb locks. Each chamber also had one set of French doors that looked into the rear yard – fastened with an interior bolt rather than a lock. The little *cabinets* that extended into the yard had American-style sash windows, latched at the top of the sash in the usual way. They looked like they'd been forced more than once, but not recently.

'Did your maman have the back shutters closed Saturday night?'

Manon nodded. 'You can see the stripes of light through them. Tiennot and Jean-Luc and me, that's how we'd know sometimes when Michie Brooke came in at night. We'd see Maman's candle go out.' She spoke matter-of-factly, her chin up, and January remembered well creeping out onto the gallery of his own *garçon-nière*, all those nights of his childhood, and seeing those threads of light in the windows of his mother's cottage on Rue Dumaine. In his own case, the memories were merely nostalgic: knowing that Michie Janvier was in residence – or, later, after the sugar broker had married, that he was paying a call on his lovely *plaçeé*. Sometimes he'd see the candlelight from Olympe's room – the cottage had four rooms plus the *cabinets*, not two – and would wonder if his sister was getting ready to sneak out with the voodoos.

Nothing, he thought, to what these children would think, and wonder, when they saw candlelight in their mother's room.

His own worst days of slavery and fear had ended when he was seven. Looking at the defiant calm of this girl's face, he felt an ache of pity for her. To live dependent on such men as Brooke – on their mother's precarious shifts to hold such men, to extract from them the money to keep her children sheltered and fed – was bad enough. To lose even that tiny hold on sustenance . . .

'These look like markers,' commented Rose, who had remained in the bedroom to search through the bureau drawers. She held up a slim sheaf of torn-out notebook pages, jotted with the names of men and sums of money. 'No notebook, but that was probably in his pocket when he was dropped into the basin—'

'I wonder,' said January.

'I'm sure Lieutenant Shaw will let you see everything—'

'I haven't said,' put in January quietly, 'that I'm going to take this up.'

Rose and Manon looked at him, startled and protesting as Olympe had been.

'There's something else going on here,' he said. 'Something that's probably dangerous. Until I know how dangerous—'

'It's mostly dangerous—' Rose's voice was that of gently reminding him of something he may have forgotten – 'to Jacquette Filoux.' She spoke softly, but behind her spectacles her hazel-green eyes challenged him to say, *That isn't my business* . . .

He knew it was.

He had never encountered any of these people – Henry Brooke, eleven-year-old Manon, Jacquette Filoux – before in his life . . .

But he knew he couldn't walk away.

In a city ruled by whites and for whites, they had no one else.

'This is his.' Olympe came in from the dining room, turning a card-case over in her hand. 'I can't think how the police would have missed it – and I can't think how Uncle Juju would have missed it.' She held it out. 'But it's got his cards in it.'

When January didn't touch it – when he only stood staring at it – she glanced at him and raised her brows. 'You *are* going to look into this, brother, aren't you?'

January felt exactly as if he'd been descending a staircase in the dark, which had ended, abruptly, before it was supposed to. Jolted, and slightly disoriented.

There couldn't be another case like that . . .

Well, he told himself, *there probably could* . . .

Expensive, and French, slightly curved to fit the shape of a man's waistcoat pocket. Its lid was outlined by a simple double line of enamel, green and dark red. The lines met in one corner in an intricate Grecian knot.

He took it, and opened it, though he already knew what he'd see there.

He read the inscription, '*Cras amet qui nunquam amavit; quique amavit, cras amet.* May he love tomorrow who has never loved before; may he who has loved, love tomorrow as well.'

It was signed, *Daniel.*

FIVE

'Who did it belong to?' asked Rose, as she and January made their way back toward Congo Square. The rocks were burning, as the inhabitants of New Orleans said. The renewed heat of late afternoon turned the rainwater that lay on the brick banquettes to steam, and the whole city smoked in an eerie veil of white. Men, women, children were making their way back to the square, for the music and the dancing. Crowdie Passebon and Mohammed Le Pas, January's fellow-directors of the FTFCMBS, waved to him as they rolled a barrel of what would become tafia punch through the iron gate. 'From the sound of it, M'sieu Brooke doesn't seem the type to be getting love gifts from people named Daniel. Certainly not with inscriptions from *The Vigil of Venus*.'

Under the plane trees that surrounded the square, men were settling down on boxes and stools, their drums between their knees: the goblet-shaped *djembe*, the little hand drum and the big *bamboula*, old names from places half-forgotten, rhythms passed down from fathers and uncles who had brought them from Africa or Sainte Domingue. The morning's musicians, the professionals, had mostly gone to play for white peoples' parties that would extend into the muggy night. The slaves – who were not legally allowed to possess drums – lingered inconspicuously in the background, waiting until the crowds got thicker before they would begin to play. Cicadas whirred in the trees. In the gutters, and along the canals, frogs croaked in many-voiced chorus; guardians, the ancient Greeks had said, of the road to the Underworld.

January touched the smooth, small rectangle of worn gold in his pocket.

Smelled again the stink of blood and powder-smoke that had hung over the barricade in another July, when he had been able, at least, to fight for the cause of freedom.

'It belonged to a man named Philippe de la Marche,' he said.

* * *

There had been, of course, a hideous uproar when Daniel had purchased the case for Philippe, at the most expensive shop in the Palais Royale. The de Gourgue family – Comtes de Belvoire, Vicomtes de la Marche, barons and chevaliers of God knew how many lesser titles going back eight hundred years – might possibly (Daniel had said) have accepted Philippe's infatuation with a duc or a marquis, or even an Italian prince if he'd had sufficient quarterings to his coat of arms, but a banker's son? *Oh, the horror*!

Anne had only laughed.

Now in the parlor's dim lamplight, after curfew had closed down the dancing in Congo Square, January turned the slim case over in his fingers, remembering that shop in the Palais Royale, and the sonnets that Daniel had written to his friend's beauty.

They'd been awful. Daniel was no poet. The most one could say was that he penned fresh effusions for each new love, and didn't re-use those relics of former passions.

Philippe, Vicomte de la Marche, for his part, though neither intellectual nor intelligent, had nevertheless shared Daniel's huge curiosity about the world that lay outside the bounds of his own upbringing and the expectations that his family had of him. Tall, broad-shouldered, heroically beautiful and raised in the most ancient traditions of the French aristocracy to look with scorn on the lower classes, he had instead sought to learn about the way they lived.

And he had loved Daniel, who was everything that his family wasn't.

The air that stirred through the shut jalousies on the French windows bore on it the swift click-click of carriages and fiacres passing, and the distant shouting of drunkards outside the whore-houses of Rue des Ramparts.

Twice January heard the snap of gunshots, from the direction of the basin.

Somewhere, someone was still playing a drum.

Philippe de la Marche.

1830

He'd started to lift the young man from the barricade, meaning to carry him to some inconspicuous doorway or courtyard, then hasten to the city's central marketplace to rent a barrow, for who knew when the police would start sending men to cart away the bodies? His first thought was only that Daniel would be distraught. *At least let him be spared the additional horror of going down to the Morgue to fetch him . . .*

But the body came up all of a piece, like a plank. Grotesquely, the arms swung down free from the shoulders, though the elbows remained flexed at an angle of about forty degrees. A second look at the young man's eyes confirmed what January had been too shocked – and too grieved for his friend – to note in that first instant. The corneas were cloudy, the eyeballs flattened back into the sockets.

It was hot last night . . .

But he couldn't recall ever encountering heat that brought on rigor so complete, so swiftly.

He edged over on the barricade, to where a man in the uniform of the Guarde Royale lay, the top of his head blown to pieces by musket-fire. January picked up the man's arm, and let it drop, limp as boned fish. Then he felt the muscles of the soldier's jaw and neck. They'd just begun to stiffen. The guard lay as Philippe had been, face-down against the clayey snarl of chair-legs and cobbles, and his face had turned livid purple with the slow drain of blood to the bottommost tissues.

Under streaks of dust and mud, Philippe's face was pale as wax.

The backs of his ears, the back of his neck, were dark, like the poor guard's face.

January lifted the young man carefully. Six feet three and massively strong, he still found the vicomte's height and magnificent stature – complicated by rigor mortis – nearly impossible to maneuver. His training in the handling of cadavers at the Hôtel Dieu held good, however, and he bore him, awkwardly, to the tightly boarded-up doorways of a Benedictine monastery a few streets away. It was barely seven o'clock by the chimes of St-Nicholas-des-Champs. The monks had decamped on Tuesday, when the trouble had begun in earnest. The monastery – St-Honoré – backed onto the far older ruins of the demolished medieval fortress of the Temple, whose debris had, since its demolition twenty years previously, still not entirely been cleared.

January left Philippe's body in a deep-set doorway, found a couple of planks and an old shutter lying in the middle of the Rue du Temple where someone had dragged them toward a barricade, and arranged them over the body. It was a twenty-minute walk through the silent streets to the Halles. He encountered en route two other people carrying corpses: neither, he noted, displayed advanced signs of rigor. As he'd suspected, a handful of country-men from Gonesse and Batignolles had opened up shop in the great central market: milk, mushrooms, cherries, newlaid eggs. *Even revolutionists have to eat.*

Though he hated to do it, January left his rifle with a farmer whom he knew named Villayer in trade for the man's barrow and a sheet of canvas. He fetched Philippe's body, and trundled it through the re-awakening streets of Paris, first to the home of Broussard the plasterer where everyone was trying to talk Ayasha out of sallying forth to look for him, and then – with Ayasha's assistance – three miles back across the river to the gem-like eighteenth-century hôtel purchased by old Moses Ben-Gideon in an ecstasy of misplaced parental hopes when his son Daniel had married Anne.

'And we have to get the barrow back to Père Villayer by six,' said January, as the Ben-Gideon porter unlocked the stout gates that guarded the hôtel's central court. 'Or sooner, if the shooting starts again and he decides to leave town. My gun's worth twenty times the cost of this barrow . . .'

Ayasha gave her opinion – fortunately in Arabic – as to what Mâitre Villayer could do with himself if he grew impatient for his barrow. 'My nightingale, as a medical man I have to inform you that what you describe is physically impossible.'

She gave him a grin, poked him with her elbow, and said, 'And you can do it, too, *Malik*, twice,' as the porter opened the door. He was a stout man with an expression of dread and January thought it was just as well that the canvas hid the barrow's occupant.

In fact, though it was full daylight now, the streets remained quiet, particularly here south of the river. North of the river, towards the center of the city, they had passed gang after gang of Parisians – men, women, children – building or re-building barricades. Later January heard that over four thousand of these had been erected in the city. In the more stylish thoroughfares, trees had been cut down to re-enforce the defenses, and on their way to the river with the laden barrow he and Ayasha had passed dozens of lanes completely stripped of their cobblestones. In one place they'd also passed two companies of the Fifth Infantry, surrounded by cheering revolutionaries, on their way to the home of the banker Lafitte, to offer their services to the revolt. Someone had shouted from a window on the Rue de la Juiverie that the Louvre had been taken.

Waiting for Daniel in the courtyard, January felt strange, almost as if dreaming. He grieved for Daniel's grief, yet triumph electrified him. *We did it! We actually overthrew the Bourbons!* A part of him felt as if he'd helped storm the Bastille, the first time the power of kings had been broken. And in spite of all that, deep within him quivered a cold seed of dread, born, he supposed, from a childhood spent in slavery. That sense that the 'Man', as the folks in the quarters had called the whites, would always win in the end.

The butler who opened the door was pale and shaky to begin with and blanched further at the sight of the covered barrow, so that January stepped forward quickly to steady him, fearing that the man would actually faint. There were tears in the servant's eyes as he whispered, 'It isn't . . . Madame?'

'Madame?' Through January's mind flashed the recollection of Anne Ben-Gideon, ablaze with triumph in her borrowed cast-offs, brandishing her silver pistol. 'No,' he stammered quickly. 'No, I'm very much afraid it's M'sieu Ben-Gideon's friend, the Vicomte de la Marche.'

'Oh, dear God.' The butler looked aside. Then his training took over, and he straightened. 'I shall tell him at once, m'sieu. Was he . . .? Should you . . .?'

'If there's a storeroom, or a scullery, with a table—'

'Yes,' said the man quickly. 'Yes, of course. Laurent!' he called out, and a young footman appeared behind him, neatly liveried in blue but also haggard with sleeplessness. 'Please take Monsieur and Madame to the scullery and help them in whatever way they require. It's M'sieu le Vicomte,' he added, with a nod at the barrow.

Laurent opened his lips as if about to ask what the hell M'sieu le Vicomte was doing out on the barricade – a question which had exercised January's mind as well, all the way here – but the footman mastered himself and only said, 'This way, m'sieu.'

The storms of revolution shake the earth like thunder, reflected January, *but a well-trained servant's* amour propre *looks upon Armageddon unmoved.*

They spread canvas from the stable over the scullery table, and January stationed Laurent at the door to keep the other servants of the house (including an incandescently indignant cook) out of the big stone room.

Philippe de la Marche had been dead, January calculated, for some eighteen to twenty-four hours. Immediately after his death, he had lain on his back for six hours at least, with his hands folded over his middle. The dark bruising of *livor mortis* on the back of his head was unmistakable, under the light-brown curls. Someone had wiped away the blood that had trickled thickly from his mouth, but it had soaked into his shirt collar and the black silk collar of Daniel's gorgeous coat. 'Whoever did that was probably the one who broke the rigor on his shoulders,' he opined, as Ayasha helped him turn the body over gently onto its back. 'You see how his arms flop free, though the elbows and wrists are still stiff as wood. Whoever put him on the barricade broke them loose because nobody would be lying on the barricade in this position.'

'How were they when you found him?' She was already checking the dead man's pockets, her nose wrinkled against the stink of the mud that smeared the delicate silk.

'Flung above his head, as if he'd fallen forward.' January demonstrated. 'It's how many of the others lay. Anything?'

'Nothing. I mean, not *anything* – not even one of Daniel's handkerchiefs. Faugh,' she added, pulling out a kerchief of her own to wipe her fingers. 'This smells like he was dragged through the sewers!'

'He may have been.' Gently January unbuttoned the young man's fancy waistcoat, and pulled up his shirt, which stuck to the wound with crusted blood. 'Someone has to have got him onto the barricade somehow, from where he was actually killed. Look, there's a spot of wax on his coat. It's fresh, Daniel would never tolerate such a thing. Someone broke the rigor on his shoulders, in order to make it look like he'd been caught up in the melee.' As had been his first impression, the wound simply wasn't big enough to have been made with a musket. Muskets – and a few rifles, like his own – were the usual weapon of the rioters, and of the Guarde Royale, whose armories the mob had looted. There was only the single wound on the body, in the left thorax from behind. 'Most of the men around him had been raked by other shots after they fell.'

'The shooting ended – what? Around nine?'

'On the St-Denis barricade, anyway.' January frowned. 'But there were people re-building the barricades, or moving about the streets, or looting shops, far into the night. He must have been put there in the early hours of the morning. How far do those sewers stretch?'

Ayasha shook her head. 'Anne would know,' she said. 'Or Pleyard. I gather revolutionists who're being chased by the police dodge through them all the time.'

'I suppose it would work,' said January. 'Once you came out, though, everybody would know where you'd been. Not somewhere I'd like to try carrying a completely stiffened corpse.' Carrying poor Philippe a dozen yards through the street had been difficult enough. He pushed the shirt further up, and turned the body again – at the Hôtel Dieu his great strength had made him the man always elected by the others to manipulate the cadavers – seeking an exit wound. 'He may have been laid out with his hands folded like that, simply because his killer had to find someone to help him move the body.'

'Daniel's cook will fillet you,' warned Ayasha, as January looked around for something to use as a bullet-probe, 'if you take one of his knives. What's this?' She picked a fragment of straw from the fragile silk of Philippe's coatsleeve.

Then from the doorway, Daniel whispered, 'Oh, dear God . . .'

January stepped back, and his friend crossed the scullery in two strides and flung himself on Philippe's body, his arms around the broad shoulders as if he could somehow warm him back to life.

'Oh, dear God. Oh, Philippe.'

Ayasha retreated to January's side, glanced up at him sidelong, the coal-dark eyes of a desert witch under a working-woman's

linen coif. 'But who would want to kill him in the first place?'
she breathed.

January shook his head. For the first time since finding the
body, he had time to think of something other than the immediate
issues of what to do with it and what could be learned from it,
and his thoughts now raced to put together what he had found.

He whispered, no more loudly than she, 'He was wearing
Daniel's coat. Remember Daniel said yesterday he'd been here
Tuesday and then gone away again. If he'd run into another gang
of children on his way here and been pelted with garbage, he'd
have borrowed it to go outside . . .'

'You think someone mistook him for Daniel?'

'I think someone could have.' He turned back, even in his
grief for his friend noticing how Daniel's hair, long and curly
and a rich brown, mingled with Philippe's golden-bronze curls.
'They were nearly of a height, and the collar of that coat would
make anyone look broad in the shoulder.'

'But who—?'

Daniel let out a sobbing cry, with the full force of his lungs,
like Achilles' cry at the death of his friend, then sank to his
knees. A slender young man in the livery of a valet slipped past
Laurent in the doorway, and helped his master to his feet. At a
nod from January, Ayasha joined him in leading Daniel, weeping,
from the scullery.

January picked up Daniel's coat, turned it over in his hands.
It stank of the sewers, the silk still damp in long smudges on
arms or sides, randomly, where the carried body had brushed the
foul bricks. Dots of beeswax marked one sleeve. Flecks of packing
straw still clung to the collar and cuffs. When he returned to the
body and checked the young man's lips and eyes, fingertips and
earlobes, his observation was confirmed: the body had been
protected from both rats and the flies that were even now, he
knew, transforming the corpse-strewn barricades into crawling
nightmares of mortality. In this week's savage heat, the body
would have been almost unrecognizable within hours.

And but for the chance of his having emerged early – but for
the chance of his knowing Daniel's incongruously brilliant coat
– what was clearly murder would have vanished into the greater
toll of the dead, and the victim's body into a common grave.

With one of the cook's filleting knives, and a slender lark-spit skewer, January began to probe for the bullet.

Daniel's valet, Freytag, returned a few minutes later, with the request that when M'sieu le Vicomte's body was cleaned and decent, would M'sieu Janvier be so good as to have Laurent, and whatever other servants were required, carry it across to the house? A room was being prepared for him. 'For surely, m'sieu,' said the valet, 'there will be no one at the Prefecture of Police today, to whom this can be reported. All they will do is recommend that M'sieu le Vicomte be taken to the public morgue. Shall I send word to M'sieu le Comte de Belvoire?'

'Thank you.' January had reflected at the time only upon the comte's grief for the death of his heir, though later he regretted the agreement. But in truth, when he looked back on it, there was nothing else really that he could do. The pistol-ball lay on a Limoges-ware saucer, distorted where it had lodged against Philippe's shoulder blade after tearing through both heart and lung. Examining it, January had already observed how characteristically the soft lead had deformed, from being loaded first, before the barrel of the weapon was screwed on.

When Anne returned to the hôtel two days later, the first thing January observed of her, was that her little screw-barrel muff pistol was gone.

Those two days, of grilling July heat and nerve-racking confusion, blurred together in January's later recollections. Sitting in the light of his single candle, in this other July, this other world, with the cicadas' droning rattle outside in the darkness, he had difficulty piecing together which events had taken place on what days, and what had been said to whom, and when.

He remembered someone – Emil, the older of the two footmen – coming in to Daniel's room to whisper that the tricolor flag now flew over the royal palace of the Tuileries. Even in the midst of his concerns for his friend, and his sorrow for that handsome young man whom he had barely known, January had felt elated.

The Bourbons were defeated. Humankind – the voices of

rationality, education, tolerance, and the rights of all mankind
– had finally had their say.

*We will no longer suffer ourselves to be ruled by men whose
only qualification for their post was the offchance of birth. We
will no longer have to watch them give away to their friends – or
keep for themselves – that which our hands bled to produce. We
will no longer see their friends take away from us, for their own
convenience, those things which are ours by right: our lives, our
property, our liberty.*

The Louvre had also been taken. Freytag had told him that,
when the last twilight was fading in the windows and the house
was filled with shadow. The people of Paris, the young valet had
said, had joined together to keep the rioters from laying a finger
on the royal art collection there. It was the property, they said,
of the people, not the king. Those who sacked the palace of the
Archbishop of Paris and hurled all his books, vestments, and
furniture into the river, had threatened to drown any thieves or
looters who attempted to fish the valuables out.

Sometime – it must have been Thursday night – the servants of
the Comte de Belvoire arrived with a coach, to take the body
of their master's son away. January and Ayasha had remained in
the house, for Daniel was devastated with grief. 'Who would
harm him?' he kept asking, raising a face pasty and haggard with
weeping from the pillow of his bed. 'He hated politics. He didn't
care who ran the government.' Creased and rumpled on the pillow
beside him was a coat of pearl-gray superfine, which, Freytag
had whispered to January, had lain across the end of Daniel's
bed when he'd come home Tuesday.

As January had suspected, street urchins had thrown offal at
Philippe on his way to Daniel's that day: 'He must have taken
M'sieu Ben-Gideon's lilac brocade when he left the house
Tuesday afternoon.'

'Do you have any idea why he left?' January asked quietly.

The slender little man shook his head. 'He said he would wait
for M'sieu Ben-Gideon. Indeed, I had no notion he had left the
house until M'sieu Ben-Gideon came home and looked about for
him.'

On the bed, Musette, Daniel's fairy-like Italian greyhound,
pawed anxiously at her master's shoulder, and licked his ear.

'No one saw him leave, but then, he was a very quiet man in his ways, M'sieu le Vicomte, and quite willing to sit without a sound in the library, reading one of M'sieu Ben-Gideon's books.'

Freytag set down the candles he bore, and went to pick up the tray of food he'd brought earlier, which lay on the bedside table, untouched. He bent to speak to his master and January didn't hear Daniel's reply. Freytag only murmured, 'Very good, m'sieu,' and took from the tray a bottle and glass. Daniel's hand groped for the tumbler, and January smelled the unmistakable swoony musti-ness of laudanum. Freytag took it back, empty, his face a non-committal mask, and closed the diaphanous, linen bed-curtains.

'Was there anyone who *would* have harmed M'sieu le Vicomte?' January asked on another occasion, a sweltering afternoon, the windows of Daniel's bedroom thrown wide to the garden and a clanging of church bells all over the city on the air. 'Or,' he added, 'was there any who would have harmed M'sieu Ben-Gideon himself? For it is clear to me that M'sieu le Vicomte was killed sometime Tuesday night, and his body sneaked onto the barricade early Thursday morning.'

Freytag sighed, and glanced across at the blur of summer gauze that curtained his unconscious master from view. 'It is . . .' he began, and then stopped himself, as if debating on how much to say, gently tugging on the ears of the dog Musette whom he held cradled in his arm. 'You must understand,' he went on after a time, 'that the circle of M'sieu Ben-Gideon's friends . . . The way they lived their lives . . . It is hard to explain. I don't really understand it myself.' His lips pursed. January recalled that the valet was Bavarian, and of a strict Protestant sect.

'Many of the young men of his circle, though they dress and live in the first style of elegance, are practically indigent. They live, as one would say, as parasites on their wealthy friends. In consequence of this, there is a great deal of jealousy, should a gentleman like my master transfer his . . . his *affections* . . . to someone else.'

January raised his eyebrows, recalling the gold card-case, the 'charming pied-a-terre' and a dozen other costly love-gifts Daniel had bestowed upon his beloved. Beyond the dreary tolling of the bells there was no sound, no gunfire at least. 'And who was M'sieu Ben-Gideon's dear friend,' he asked, 'before he became

dear friends with M'sieu le Vicomte? Someone of a nature sufficiently jealous to do harm to a rival? Or to m'sieu himself?'

'His name is Apollon Michaud.' Freytag's tone was a world
of professional restraint. 'The son of a good family, I understand,
who was at one time in the Guarde Royale. A young man of
volatile temperament, yes. At one time he threatened violence
against M'sieu le Vicomte, when they encountered one another
at a ball shortly after m'sieu began – ah – "keeping company"
with M'sieu le Vicomte. I know not whether the threat was
serious.' The valet's upper lip seemed to lengthen and thin.
'M'sieu le Vicomte himself was a notable shot, and, I am told,
a nimble and powerful swordsman. Considering the amount of
money m'sieu spent on this Michaud, he may well have considered himself aggrieved. And then of course, the Comte de Belvoire
himself, M'sieu le Vicomte's father, might well have wished my
master harm. There is also his younger son, M'sieu le Vicomte's
brother Celestin . . .'

He stopped himself, and shook his head again. Setting Musette
on the floor, he whistled softly to her, and she followed him from
the room.

'The flics are going to have their work cut out for them,'
remarked Ayasha later, when January spoke to her of these pos-
sibilities, 'if they decide to go after de Belvoire or his number
two son for trying to murder either Daniel or Philippe.' She spoke
in a whisper, with a glance toward the dim shape lying behind
the gauze curtains, his lover's coat still clutched in his arms, in
a stupor of laudanum and grief. Musette was back on the bed,
curled on the pillow, a worried little ball of bones.

It was night, January recalled, though he couldn't remember
whether it was the Thursday or the Friday. He remembered only
that it was very late, and still gluily hot, and that the city outside
was silent. Even the great *bourdon* of Notre Dame had stilled.

'That is, if they investigate at all,' his wife went on with a
shrug. 'Belvoire's one of the old crowd that's been with King
Charles since he was having picnics on the lawn at Versailles
with Marie Antoinette. His wife's a Noailles . . .' She named
one of the wealthiest, most ancient noble families in France.
'Catch either of *them* admitting that they snuffed the heir to the
title, either by accident or on purpose. Or that Number Two might

have done the deed himself. What will you bet me they push off the blame on this poor *branleur* Michaud?'

'Who might actually have done it,' January reminded her softly.

Ayasha only sniffed. Her opinion of the aristocracy was not high.

And what chance, January had wondered – on that hot Paris night when everything had been simple – would the unknown M'sieu Michaud stand against a man of wealth and nobility who either believed Michaud to be guilty of the murder, or who simply wanted everyone else to believe it? Though the servants had been bringing in a steady stream of rumor and information – that the king had backed down from his resolve to rule the country in the old style, by royal ordinance alone; that a republic was going to be proclaimed ('It is plain,' had remarked Freytag dourly, 'that they don't recall what happened to their *last* republic.'); that the king had called for Austrian troops; that the minister Polignac had resigned – it was clear by this time to January at least that the old nobility would keep their hold on the government of France. How would they not? It was they who had the money. It was they who had the land.

Maybe you *couldn't* fight The Man.

It was into these families that the bankers, the factory owners, the new-rich proprietors of railroads and canals and mines, sought to marry their sons and daughters, desperate for the cachet of nobility and the social connections that it brought.

And though the king's stubborn determination to hand the country back to the Pope might be thwarted, it was unlikely that the son of a Jew, be that Jew ever so wealthy a banker, would get a hearing when he demanded that his lover's true killer be brought to justice.

Nobody would want to hear it. Much better that a simple solution be found, sordid though it might be. A disgusting love-spat, but easily dismissed, particularly if there was another heir to the title of Comte de Belvoire.

And perhaps – January glanced back toward the bed, where his friend tossed in his sleep and muttered Philippe's name – a killer who had sought Daniel's death, not Philippe's, was still out there. Waiting, with his little gun that would slip so easily into a pocket or a muff.

On Saturday, the last day of July, Anne returned. Daniel was up for the first time, moving about the paneled and sun-drenched rooms like a man dazed, fumblingly trying to collect the threads of his life once more. Once, when Musette stood up in his lap to lick his chin, he even smiled.

Ayasha had returned to their rooms on Rue de l'Aube, and had re-opened her workshop, though between the hot summer season and the paralysis of the king's government nobody was buying dresses. January remained at Daniel's, sleeping on a pallet that Freytag had made up for him in the dressing room; the neighborhood children brought January notes from his wife. All was quiet, she said. There hadn't been a riot anywhere for twenty-four hours. January watched Daniel's face when the butler carried in tea late in the afternoon, trying to gauge whether he should bid his friend farewell and return tomorrow, or remain another night.

The milk, he could not help noticing, was fresh. 'It is, m'sieu,' affirmed the butler, when January remarked on it.

'A sure sign,' murmured Daniel, pouring a little into a saucer for the dog, 'that the trouble is over, if the farmers are bringing their milk to market.'

'Not only that, m'sieu.' The butler bobbed a bow, and January could see that the man was as pleased as he was himself, to see his master rouse himself to speak of the commonplaces of the living. 'It was not only in the markets, but Mademoiselle Constitution – the woman who sells it in this quarter, m'sieu – was back this morning peddling it in the street.'

'Mademoiselle *Constitution*?'

The servant allowed himself a grin. 'I understand that her mother was a sans-culotte of the republic, m'sieu.'

'Good Lord. I should think—'

A sound – a closing door – on the floor below made Daniel jump as if at a gunshot, spilling the milk, and January reflected on how deeply grief and stress had pierced him. His plump face had a fallen-in look, and his soft flesh seemed to have collapsed down onto his bones. This was the first time since Thursday that he was dressed and shaved, but his eyes were still red with weeping. Without rouge he seemed pasty and old.

Yesterday – Friday – he had talked incessantly of Philippe,

blaming himself for not having been home on Tuesday afternoon; asking again and again if word had come from the Comte de Belvoire regarding a funeral.

'But of course they won't tell me,' he would say, instants later. 'They regard me as Moloch, the Anti-Christ, the corrupter of their precious boy – as if he hadn't been struggling for years against what they wanted him to be. What they demanded that he be, a . . . a family stud-horse, a good administrator of their property, a presentable dummy . . .' And then he would cram his fist into his mouth again, trembling all over, and whisper, 'Philippe . . .'

And fifteen minutes later would return to the subject of his friend again.

Now he looked up as footsteps clicked on the parquet of the stair, his face ghastly. But Musette dashed to the door, whiptail lashing frantically, and a moment later the door opened and Anne stood framed in it. Her chestnut hair was uncovered and unwashed, the striped skirt and leather bodice she had worn Tuesday outside the Palais Royale stained with gunpowder and Paris mud. She strode to him with outstretched hands. 'Oh, Daniel, they just now told me—'

He clasped her to him, his face pressed to her breast and his grasp so tight January thought he would snap her in two. She bent over his head, folded the heavy shoulders in her arms, as if he had been a brother, or a child. January took his teacup, and quietly left the drawing room.

But not before he had noted that the silver pistol was gone from her side.

SIX

He attached little importance to that fact at the time.

Walking back along the Rue de l'Université in the twilight on Saturday, the last day of July, he found scant evidence of the week's rioting until he was almost opposite the Ile de la Cité. Even those barricades that he passed had been cleared of bodies, and the local workingmen and students who still manned them were mostly smoking and talking in the nearby shops and doorways. The barricades had also, January observed, been cleared of any weapons dropped in the course of the fray. The only muskets he saw were obviously broken. The smell of powder and blood had dispersed days ago.

Handbills plastered the city trumpeting the defeat of King Charles, and praising to the skies the virtues of the king's cousin, the Duc d'Orléans. It crossed January's mind even then to wonder who'd paid for printing – much less distributing – those. 'That dear good friend of bankers and factory owners and men of wealth!' sneered Maurice Pleyard, who was waiting for January – with half a dozen friends, Ayasha, several loaves of bread and a couple of bottles of wine – at January's rooms when he reached them. 'Lafitte the banker had them printed up, of course! Every shopkeeper and café owner in the Palais Royale is saying how Orléans should be made king – those of them that want to keep their leases there! And idiots all over the city are starting to say, "H'mn, well, the republic actually didn't work out too well . . . Maybe we *should* have another king!" Imbeciles!'

'Well, they have a point,' argued Dumare, a very young law student who had only joined the Société Brutus the previous winter. 'What glory did the republic ever bring to France?'

'The glory of opening the doors to an age of righteousness, you—' began Carnot furiously.

'Yes, of course, but how those idiots can even think about a slick *enfonceur* like Orléans when the son of Napoleon himself dwells just across the border in—'

'Napoleon was a tyrant!' shouted Pleyard. 'Napoleon deserted his own armies – *twice*! – when he thought his power might be in danger. Napoleon was responsible for the deaths of over half a million of our countrymen—'

January sprang in at this point to avert a fistfight over the respective merits of republic and empire, and informed all parties concerned that he would throw any and all combatants out the window.

'Deputations went back and forth all day yesterday between Lafitte's house and the Palais Royale,' said Ayasha, disengaging a couple of candles from the bundle Pleyard had brought and puffing gently on the banked embers of the little cooking range to light them. 'Not that any of the gambling dens in the Palais closed – I think even the naughty theaters stayed open.' Outside the air was still infused with light, but blue shadow filled the narrow streets of the Left Bank, and from every rooftop, swallows dipped and darted in quest of flies.

'The king's still out at St-Cloud,' added Chatoine, a skinny little street urchin whose brother Poucet, at the age of twelve, had been one of the youngest members of the Société – and one of the youngest to die on the barricades. 'He's supposed to be assembling troops, but me, I don't believe it.' She divided the bread and cheese Pleyard had given her with the other members of her little gang, dirty, shock-headed infants who ran errands for Ayasha in return for food. 'The man's got no *couilles*.'

'The prince imperial—' insisted Dumare.

'The prince imperial is a boy of nineteen!' yelled Carnot. 'A boy who's been brought up in Austria, for God's sake – in the very palace of our country's foe! This is our chance, the chance France has waited for since 1795! The chance to have a *real* republic, for workingmen to have a voice in their own government, to make the laws that will benefit themselves and not take ordinances handed down by the whores that surround the throne!'

But January heard the note in his voice – a kind of frantic urgency – that told him that somewhere, the tide had turned. That there would be no republic.

The following morning Pleyard came again to January's rooms, meeting him on the stair as he descended to go once more to

Daniel's, and gave him the news that King Charles had offered the Duc d'Orléans a position as Lieutenant General of France.

'Whatever the hell that means,' grumbled Ayasha, pouring out coffee for the three of them when January led the student back upstairs to share a spartan breakfast with them.

'He turned the offer down.' Pleyard slumped into a chair, ran a tired hand through his fair, thinning hair. He had formed the Société Brutus six years ago, January recalled, when the feckless King Charles had succeeded his obese and wily brother on the throne of France. Had dedicated his time and energy to running reading groups, making plans, speaking to workingmen and as a result hiding from the secret police. 'Orléans has already formed a cabinet, appointed ministers, taken over the government, in effect. His men are dismantling the barricades, re-paving the streets, just as if someone had given him the authority to do so . . . And so they have. The banker Lafitte. The Rothschilds. The landlords of Paris who want to protect their property and the owners of railroads and factories who want laws made to keep the workingmen's heads down. Whores,' he whispered, staring out the open window into the hot, morning brightness, and his voice broke with grief. 'Whores.'

That afternoon, January and Ayasha went (with pretty much everyone else in Paris) to watch the parades in the Tuileries and the Champs-Elyseés. There were still no carriages in the streets, on account of the remaining barricades, but the prostitutes, January saw, had reappeared in force. 'You can tell the fighting's really done,' Ayasha remarked.

Tricolor flags – the colors of the republic – flew from every window and building. But it was as if a dark lens of apprehension covered the sun, and over the shouts of the populace and the marching feet of the companies of National Guard and neighborhood troops, January found himself listening for gunfire in the distance.

None came.

All day Sunday, the first of August, Paris waited with held breath. The following day – Monday, the second of August, 1830 – King Charles X of France abdicated, bypassing his son Louis, the Duc d'Angoulême, and leaving his throne to his nine-year-old grandson the Duc de Bordeaux. The Duc d'Orléans, a chubby and undistinguished (and phenomenally wealthy) cousin of the king's, was already firmly ensconced in authority, and ignored the claims of the new king – who had taken the name Henri V. On the third, Orléans dispatched troops to escort the deposed King Charles and all members of his family to Cherbourg, to take a ship for England.

A week later, on the ninth, the Chamber of Deputies proclaimed Louis-Philippe, Duc d'Orléans, 'King of the French'. The revolution was over. Again.

January himself barely felt either the exultation of triumph: 'We have defeated the House of Bourbon forever!' proclaimed his fellow musician Jeannot Charbonnière in ecstasy – or the disgust of defeat: 'We didn't bleed on the barricades to get ourselves another fat king!' yelled Pleyard, when he read the news. This was because on the previous day, the eighth of August, news reached him that Anne Ben-Gideon had been arrested for the murder of Philippe de la Marche.

1839

Vachel Corcet, attorney at law, had an office on Rue Bourbon, in the courtyard of what had once been a townhouse but was now being rented out as offices and flats. The elderly little lawyer greeted January with pleasure – they had worked together frequently over the business of the FTFCMBS – and agreed at once to go with him to the Cabildo, 'Though in all honesty I have to advise you, when Madame Filoux's case comes before the court, hire a white lawyer as a senior colleague to plead. I never know from one week to the next,' he added, in a voice that he strove to make annoyed rather than deeply discouraged, 'when the gods that sit up in Baton Rouge might decide to forbid *gens du couleur librés* to appear before the bar, and never mind that we've been doing so – and I've *personally* been doing so! – for longer than most of them have lived in this state . . .'

His soft little mouth pursed tight under its wisp of moustache. 'And in any case,' he added, with a resigned quirk of his brows, 'it seems to go over better with juries.' Meaning, January knew, that since the juries were all white they tended to believe white attorneys. 'Though as a *placeé*, as I'm sure I have no need to tell you, Madame Filoux is going to need a very strong case.'

'And we'd better hope the actual murderer isn't white.' January sighed, and picked up his hat as Corcet rose from behind his desk.

'Now, there's no need to prove that any specific person actually committed the crime.' The attorney donned his own hat – a new and stylish silk tophat, like January's own an investment in avoiding the appearance of shabbiness – and slid into his frock coat, though the morning outside was already stifling. 'Just that *she* could not have done so.'

January had taken the precaution of speaking to Corcet – and having the little lawyer accompany him to the Cabildo – in case Lieutenant Abishag Shaw of the City Guards was out, but in the event he was lucky. The tall, stringy Kentuckian stood beside his desk in the corner of the stone-floored watch room, clearly just returned from his morning mosey of inspection along the levee, and was going over his notes on the experience with three men of the guard. The Fourth of July being as much a day of celebration among the flatboat men, filibusters, and steamboat crews as it was among the planters and businessmen of the American community, Shaw sported a cut on one cheek and a bandage wrapped around his left wrist. In his yellow calico shirtsleeves, his greasy dust-brown hair straggling to his shoulders, he had the look of someone who was in the Cabildo on his way to the cells himself, rather than of a minion of justice.

'Maestro,' he greeted January, when the three policemen left and January and Corcet approached the desk. 'Figured I'd see you this mornin'. You here about that li'l gal they pulled in for shootin' the Englishman? Mr Corcet . . .' He extended his hand to the lawyer. 'Always a pleasure.'

Corcet shook hands and nodded, though he looked, January thought, slightly pained. Like most natives of the French Town, he found Shaw's pronunciation of the language an abomination.

'We'd like to speak with Madame Filoux, if we may,' said January. 'And, if you have a few minutes, we'd deeply appreciate hearing the police side of the story. If possible, might we see Mr Brooke's effects?'

'Got 'em right acrost here.' Shaw led them through the rear doors of the watch room and through the courtyard – its high walls still guarding what little coolness the night had brought. 'Such of 'em as we found at Ma'm Filoux's, though I will say there was a couple of things that shoulda been there as wasn't. You have a look at the place?'

'Yesterday afternoon.'

'You find any Bank of England stock sustificates?'

'Stock certificates?'

Something Mama said was a bank credit-paper . . .

'She had a fifty-dollar stock certificate from the Bank of England in the pocket of her dress when she's arrested.' Shaw opened the door to what had once been the only prison in Orleans Parish, at the rear of the Cabildo courtyard. Though the male prisoners had been moved to the new prison a block away, and the town whipping-post removed from the courtyard, the stink of decades of filth and human waste seemed ground into its bricks. 'She claimed it was hers, but it was fresh – hadn't been folded up but the once, an' there was no scuffin' or smudgin' on the back of it. An' she couldn't give any good account of where she'd got it from. An' it so happens this Brooke jasper used Bank of England stock to back up land he purchased, out on Bayou St John an' Bayou des Avocats—'

'*Land?*'

He had assumed Olympe's tales of 'a group of Englishmen looking to invest' had simply been the usual verbal smokescreen that men put up, to explain their presence in a place where they had no business being.

'Brooke actually *purchased* land?' He wondered if Oldmixton had known about this, and if so, why he'd kept that particular card concealed in his hand.

'Bought the old Chitimacha Plantation.' The policeman ambled ahead of him into what had once been the prison's tiny infirmary and opened its single, barred window. Watching January – January was well aware – out of the corner of his cold rain-gray eye. 'Also about an arpent of land on Bayou St John that you could get rich off of the minute somebody figures out a way to make money raisin' mosquitoes. Both places worthless – myself, I wondered if'n he had some plan goin' to bilk investors back in England, sellin' 'em "plantations" that don't exist. He was negotiatin' with the Labarre brothers, an' with Angelica Aury, 'bout small parcels they own along Bayou Metairie. Same story: nuthin' there but palmetto an' gators. You didn't happen to find the deeds to any of them places whilst you was goin' through the house, did you?'

January said, 'No,' with such patent bafflement in his voice that Shaw half-turned from the stack of boxes in the corner, to consider the expression on his face.

'Had he anything in his pockets?' asked Corcet, who had remained back in the doorway as if unwilling to get closer to the smell of the room.

'Nary a huckleberry.' Shaw spit a stream of tobacco juice at a cockroach that stomped grumpily from among the other boxes by the wall – such containers formed a sort of inner wainscot about four-feet high along one side of the room, reeking already of mould. Blobs and stains of tobacco spit dotted the boxes, the wall, and the floor: Lieutenant Shaw was far from the only man in the guards who chewed. The lieutenant carried the box to the room's central table and set it down with a thump. Another roach emerged and fled.

'Them's his duds.'

The attorney looked appalled at the thought that he'd have to touch anything that had been stored here, but advanced, gingerly, nonetheless to look over January's shoulder.

Shaw drew down a lamp on its chain over the table, kindling it with a lucifer-match, for the room's tiny window let in only a few spoonfuls of light from the courtyard. The lamp helped only a little, its chimney not having been cleaned, January estimated, since Thomas Jefferson purchased Louisiana from the French. 'Rest of his wardrobe's here.' He crossed back to the wall of boxes for another crate.

'Would it be possible also to see the body?'

'Lord, no! We planted the poor bastard same day we pulled him outen the basin. Heat like this, he's already startin' to go off. Wisht I'd known,' he added, 'that you's gonna take an interest in the case, Maestro. I would purely have liked to hear your opinion of that corpse.'

January paused in the act of leafing through the letters which had evidently been found in the dining-room desk, tucked into the front cover of an octavo copy of *The Lustful Turk*. All were recent, from assorted tradesmen in New Orleans and property owners in the surrounding countryside. Two were, indeed, from Alcinde Allard – former owner of the abandoned Chitimacha Plantation – and Angelica Aury, who owned land along Bayou Metairie in which, to judge by her brief description, Brooke had been interested. 'Tell me,' he said.

'Well, for starters—' Shaw ticked off points of observation on his long, bony fingers – 'he sure weren't dressed to go drinkin' down on Basin Street. An' he hadn't been drinkin', on Basin Street nor noplace else, 'cause when I cut open his gut there was no smell of alcohol. An' I asked around some, among the sweepers an' the whores an' the small-time gamblers that don't care one way or t'other. They knew Brooke, all right – he'd sometimes drink at the Four Kings – but nobody'd seen him that night till they pulled him outen the basin.

'Two.' He held up another finger. 'His neck an' jaw was stiffened up already, like they get after six-seven hours. Brooke's head was tucked for'ard—' he demonstrated, tucking his gargoyle chin down onto his breast – 'like as if he'd laid someplace too short for him. He was a tall man,' he added. 'Six foot I'd make him. Then too, he'd laid on his back long enough for the blood to settle, an' stayed put long enough for it to *stay* settled when he was dumped in the drink. That's what? Five hours?'

'Five or six. Who found the body?'

'Railspike Adams.' Shaw named one of the most notorious prostitutes of the back of town. 'Says she saw him floatin' in the basin when the Blackleg Saloon closed down, which was right around sun-up: six a.m, accordin' to the almanac. How much earlier he's there, we don't know. No lights thereabouts save what comes through the barroom windows. This neighbor of M'am Filoux says she seen a man she figured was Brooke lettin' hisself into M'am Filoux's house with a key, round about one thirty, by which time accordin' to my reckonin' Brooke, wherever he was, was long dead an' turnin' cold. An' the shot they heard was somethin' after two. But Cap'n Tremouille—' he nodded back towards the main Cabildo across the court – 'says on a hot night corpses stiffen up quick. Which is true, but not that quick. An' he says likewise M'am Filoux don't give just anybody keys to her house, which is also true, so I hear from her neighbors.'

'And no key was found on the body?'

Shaw spit at another roach. 'Not as Railspike says.'

'Railspike find anything else in his pockets?' Any girl who worked around the basin, January knew, wouldn't have reported a floating cadaver without hauling it to shore first and helping herself to whatever pickings she could find. He was a little surprised the woman had reported a corpse at all.

'She says not. An' generally they just keeps money an' rings an' such, not keys. Nor, as you'll see—' he nodded at the assortment of pens, ink bottles, cuff-buttons, hairbrushes, and stickpins in the box on the table – 'was there a house key anyplace in the house but the one M'am Filoux herself had on her ring, which don't mean she didn't drop Brooke's in the basin, Tremouille says. An' he could be right.'

'Rigor *can* start within a few hours, on a hot night,' agreed January slowly. 'But I've never heard of hypostasis fixing itself in a body in under four hours. And I still haven't heard anything that explains how Jacquette Filoux got Henry Brooke's body from Rue Toulouse to the basin.'

Brooke was six-feet tall. Almost as tall as Philippe de la Marche had been, all those years ago – the question had been asked about Anne Ben-Gideon almost at once. An accomplice, the police had said, and had begun a search for her handsome fencing master.

'There was a handcart she kept in her yard sometimes, for a friend of hers – Cuff Bazaire, his name is. He works on the wharf, couple days a week, an' lives over on Girod Street an' has noplace to keep it.'

'Anybody find any blood in this handcart?'

'Hard to tell. It'd been used two-three times 'tween Saturday night an' Thursday when we arrested her. Hell, that thing's so filthy there's probably six kinds of blood soaked into them planks, an' God knows what else besides. The cart was in her yard that night. Tremouille thinks that's why the corpse's head was tucked up like that. She put him someplace til the ruckus that goes on ever' night sort of calmed down.'

'Her brother have a key?'

'Not no more, he don't. The neighbors all say as how M'am Filoux turned Brother Juju out six months ago an' got a new lock on the door. I guess Brother Juju waxed mighty eloquent on the subject of the relative thickness of blood an' water. Even the evenin' of the killin' he was still complainin' of it, accordin' to Short-Change Jimmy at the Proud Cock on Franklin Street.'

'What time did he leave the Cock?' By Hannibal's accounts of having played there, January knew the Proud Cock was a gambling parlor and house of prostitution which boasted the cheapest drinks in New Orleans: watered rum (said Hannibal) mixed with camphor and opium-sweepings.

'Sometime 'fore three. Nobody can say rightly how much before. An' he ain't been seen since, barrin' the visit he paid to M'am Filoux Sunday, which ain't much of a surprise given what he owes all over town. But all Tremouille sees is how the neighbors all say how M'am Filoux said to more'n one of 'em how she hated Brooke. A week ago he give her a black eye, an' it was no secret in that neighborhood as how she had a purse-gun. Woman who runs the place next door said as how Brooke had tried to rape M'am Filoux's little gal.' He spit again, missing the sandbox beside the door by feet.

'Tremouille don't hold much by medical evidence.'

'Regrettably,' spoke up Vachel Corcet in his soft, prim voice, 'neither do juries in this state, when they have what appears to them to be a clear motive—'

'An' specially,' added Shaw, 'if so be the culprit's a black woman, accused of shootin' a white man.' From the box on the table he drew a little screw of paper, from which he took a pistol-ball roughly the size of a chickpea, and held it out on his callused palm. January needed only a glance to note the characteristic deformation of a screw-barrel muff pistol. 'That's what they're gonna pay attention to.'

January set the book aside, and fished from his pocket the pistol-ball he'd found in the hidey-hole in Jacquette Filoux's back cabinet. 'She have more than one gun?'

'Where'd you find that?' Shaw set his own bullet down, took the smaller one from January's fingers. 'No gun with it, I suppose . . .?'

January shook his head.

'Well, consarn.' The Kaintuck scratched his long nose. 'We didn't find no gun of any description on the premises. Given that neighborhood, wouldn't surprise me none if she had more'n one.

An' that's what the gentlemen of the jury gonna say, if'n we got no better evidence – 'specially if we don't got neither one of them guns in hand. M'am Filoux claims she never had no gun—'

'Who's Gerry O'Dwyer?' The attorney Corcet had picked up the battered copy of *The Lustful Turk* from the table, and was gingerly thumbing its pages.

January swung around, shocked at the name. Shaw began to remark, 'Some friend of Brooke's with the same taste in—' and then broke off, seeing the look on January's face. 'Somebody of your acquaintance?'

January took the book, stared at the inscription scrawled on the flyleaf.

Scribbled but readable, it said: Gerry O'Dwyer.

'He was,' he said. 'Once.'

SEVEN

Gerry O'Dwyer.

For a moment he was entering that narrow cell in the Saint-Lazare prison, with Daniel, with Anne's dandified younger brother Armand, with old M'sieu Sarrien, the lawyer hired by the Vicomte de la Roche-St-Ouen for his daughter.

1830

'The police are saying Gerry helped me carry Philippe's body to the barricade after I shot him.' Anne Ben-Gideon sprang to her feet and crossed the room in two strides to catch January by the hands. 'Has he come to you? Has anyone in the Société seen him? It's ridiculous, it's nonsense—'

'They know about Gerry, then?'

The young woman waved impatiently. '*Everybody* knows about Gerry. I've never believed in hiding what I felt—'

'One could wish, madame,' intoned M'sieu Sarrien disapprovingly, as the turnkey closed the door behind them, 'that you had been a little more circumspect—'

'As Papa is circumspect about his mistresses?' Anne flared. 'As my uncle Louis is circumspect about what goes on in that social club he frequents? As—' She stopped the flood of her angry words with a glance at Daniel, who had his own reason to be circumspect.

And her brother Armand, sixteen years old and nearly in tears of anxiety, cried, 'All the *juge d'instruction* is going to say is that of course a woman who takes lovers would do murder!'

'Where is Gerry?' asked Daniel reasonably.

Anne turned her face away, her body trembling as if under the lash of a whip. She whispered, 'Dead.'

1839

'I never asked.' The way Jacquette Filoux looked aside at
January's question, like a woman expecting at the best a tirade
of shouts, at the worst a blow, brought that meeting in the Paris
prison back to him in all its detail, and for a moment it seemed
to him that he was, in fact, stepping into the same river that had
nearly drowned him nine years before. Dimness, window bars,
the stale taste of despair. 'How stupid does that make me?'

Jacquette's face – dark ivory features that barely whispered
of African descent – was dusted with a galaxy of freckles which
most of the quadroon and octoroon ladies of Rue des Ramparts
would have scorned as ugly. Tinier than her sturdy daughter,
she wasn't beautiful by classical standards – by white standards.
But there was an elfin prettiness to her thin features and large
gray eyes that made the classical standards seem lifeless. She
was a woman, January felt at once, who would have been something other than what she was, had she had the slightest chance
to do so.

'Everything I've heard about Henry Brooke,' returned January,
'tells me you did the smartest thing you could. He'd probably
have lied to you anyway.'

Brought down to the watch room from the women's cell, she'd
sat drawn into herself, in the chair beside Shaw's desk, intimi-
dated by the three men gathered around her in the grilling
forenoon heat. Now she glanced up at January with eyes that
really saw him, and a little wry twist pulled one corner of her
mouth. 'That he would, sir. He lied fast as a dog can trot. I didn't
know that when I met him.'

'Which of us does?'

She returned his tiny, rueful smile with one of her own, in the
moment before she glanced around her, at Corcet and at Shaw.
Beyond them, the watch room had quieted, except for a fat,
sloppy journalist from the *True American* arguing with the desk
sergeant in bad French. The doors to the Place des Armes stood
open in the vain hope of something resembling a river breeze,
but all that came in were flies and the pong of horse droppings
in the Place. January noted that Jacquette Filoux had taken
the trouble to wash her face in what water was available in the

women's cell, and to re-wrap her tignon, the head cloth once required by law of women of color in Louisiana. That law itself no longer existed officially, but it would take a brave *librée* indeed to risk an unofficial beating by offended whites for being 'uppity', or the possibility of arrest on some other charge by a guard who thought that women of color needed to be 'kept in their place'.

'Henry—' she began, and then stopped, as if trying to gather a description of him that wouldn't get her into worse trouble for criticizing a white man. She glanced at Shaw again, and then toward the desk sergeant. 'It wouldn't surprise me to hear Michie Brooke wasn't his real name. Most men, they'll relax sometimes, they'll tell you things, over breakfast, or when you're having a smoke out on the gallery. Little things, things they remember, like, "You ever been to Havana? Well, they have these ladies there who sell mangos in the streets . . ." Or, "My daddy used to tell me when we'd go walk on the riverbank in Philadelphia . . ." That kind of thing. Things that lead into stories. Michie Brooke wasn't like that.'

'You think he might have kept silent because he feared enemies in town?' Corcet leaned forward a little, notebook in hand.

'That wouldn't surprise me, either.' Her French was the sort taught by the nuns at the Ursuline convent; educated and grammatical, better than that of many white ladies January had heard. 'It was like with the stories: most men will let it slip out how they make their living, when they brag about the money they've got. Henry didn't. He'd go out, and come back smelling of liquor, and I saw gambling markers in his pockets and in the desk. Of course I never asked him – what man likes to be asked where he's been or what he's been up to? The markers weren't enormous – I think the most I ever saw was for eighty dollars – but I don't know what else he owed. And he had a temper. He'd get furious, if he thought that anyone was asking where he'd been, or what he'd been doing.'

January wondered if she'd found that out in connection with the fading bruise under her left eye.

Shaw, perched on a corner of his desk, asked in his execrable French, 'An' you got no idea who that mighta been that M'am Danou seen lettin' himself into your place Saturday night?'

'I told Michie Tremouille,' she said pleadingly, 'I heard

nothing. I saw no one. I swear it! I dozed off in my chair in my room, waiting for Michie Brooke – I'd prepared supper for him, he liked me to wait up for him and sometimes he'd come back later than that. Only he had a key to the house – I take good care . . .' She hesitated, suddenly painfully self-conscious at the admission that she might have to take good care to keep track of which men had keys to her house.

She still clung, thought January, to the polite fiction that she was a real *plaçeé* instead of merely 'cheaper than a hotel'.

She finished with, 'If he'd come into my room I would have waked.'

'Would you have waked if he'd let himself into the dining room instead of your chamber?' inquired January. 'I noticed yesterday that the lock on the shutters to that door was freshly scratched around the keyhole, as if someone had unlocked it in the dark. It's a new lock-plate – six months, isn't it? – and the scratches showed clearly. And it would be dark, under the abat-vent, if he was at the dining-room door and not your chamber where candles burned. Could your brother have stolen a key?'

Jacquette's mouth tightened, hard and suddenly, at the mention of her brother. 'If he had a chance, yes.'

'Do you know your brother's address?' inquired Corcet, pencil again at the ready, and the young woman shook her head.

'I know he had a room with Lallie Gardinier on Girod Street,' she said. 'But when I asked him about it Sunday he said he couldn't stand her drinking and stealing everything he owned – meaning she'd asked him for rent money and he'd left, I assume. He asked me for money Sunday, when I wouldn't let him go through the house. I gave him what I could spare.'

'Could he have sneaked in Saturday night?' asked January. 'Sneaked in through the dining-room door and poked around looking for what he could steal?'

Again her lips compressed. 'If he saw a body floating in the basin – he often gambles at the Proud Cock on Franklin Street – he would certainly have pulled it ashore long enough to go through his pockets. And then of course he'd know that Michie Brooke wouldn't be at my house. He could have taken his key . . . I did waken,' she added, 'some time late in the night. I took the candle and went into the dining room, thinking Michie Brooke might have returned. But I saw no one . . .'

'One candle,' drawled Shaw, 'throws damn poor light. Your brother's lucky you didn't shoot him.'

Fear sprang immediately into her eyes. 'I have no gun—'

'Accordin' to M'am Boudreaux you do. An' the maestro here found a pistol-ball on the premises—'

'I had no such thing!' she cried, trying to sound innocent and puzzled and not succeeding in the least. 'I . . . Madame Boudreaux just hates me because I try to keep my girl away from the trash that hangs around her house. Ask anyone on the street! Please,' she said. 'Please . . .'

Shaw said nothing.

'M'sieu, it's true I hated Henry Brooke. But I would never, ever have harmed him! Maybe if I thought he was going to remain with me for any length of time I'd have asked him to leave. But he said he was going on the twenty-first. I told myself I could hold out til then.'

'He say why he was leavin'? Or where he was headed?'

She shook her head. 'I don't know if you'd understand how it is, sir,' she went on after a time. 'Living with such a man. But I have to keep the house. I have to keep Manon and the boys in school. The nuns teach fine sewing, good manners, the proper way of speaking that the white ladies, the rich ladies, look for in a maid. Or that the shopkeepers look for when they hire a girl . . . or when they look for a wife for their sons. I don't want Manon to live as I do. I don't want my sons to be what my brother is, cheating at cards and living off women. You can't do that, washing clothes, or selling pralines on the levee. For men it's different,' she finished in a whisper.

'It is.' Shaw spit again in the general direction of the sandbox near his desk. January had seen Shaw kill a man at fifty yards with a rifle by starlight, but with tobacco he couldn't hit the side of a barn.

'What did he look like?' asked January. 'Henry Brooke?'

'Like an angel,' replied Jacquette promptly. 'A Greek god. Short little straight nose, wavy hair, golden like honey. Just a hint – the tiniest thread – of silver, but a man in his full prime. Thirty-five? Thirty-six?'

Her eyes narrowed, calling his features back to mind. 'There was a little cleft in his chin.' She touched her own chin, as many people do when describing such a feature. 'Blue eyes – dark-blue, like a new bandanna, and eyelashes that curled. Handsome . . .' A flicker of pain crossed her face, or shame, at having once taken him into her bed. 'He was always sort of catching his own reflection in things – windows, or the looking glass in the parlor. Always touching his neck-cloth or fussing with his collar, or pushing a curl of his hair straight.'

January whispered, 'Ah.'

1830

'I looked for him,' murmured Anne Ben-Gideon, returning to the cell's single chair. 'When the rioting finished, I went back to his rooms on the Rue L'Asnier, thinking he would come there. I waited, all day Thursday. Friday I went to the morgue—'

She shook her head. The Vicomte de la Roche-St-Ouen might have provided the family lawyer – a white-haired, vague-eyed man who had served the family for sixty-three of his eighty-plus years – but it was Armand who was responsible for the fact that Anne's cell had a curtained bed, a small rag rug on the floor, a little dressing table, a lamp, and a prie-dieu. The going rate for such amenities – according to Maurice Pleyard, who had reason to know – was two hundred francs. January wasn't sure whether Armand had borrowed this money himself at some shocking rate of interest, or whether he'd gone to their parents with hysterical visions of the daughter of the family being tossed into a prison dormitory with the floozies for whom Saint-Lazare was primarily intended. In either case the youth had met them at the prison gates with a bulky packet of linens, clothing, and toilet articles, which he now stood clutching in his arms.

'He wasn't there.' Anne looked up, her voice a little stronger. 'Most of the bodies, they simply dragged off the barricades and buried where they could. Or put them in mass graves in the Cemetery of the Innocents, or the Champ de Mars . . .'

'But you were with him,' said old M'sieu Sarrien, 'on the night of Tuesday the twenty-seventh?'

'Of course.'

'Did others see you?'

'Of course! Armand . . .' she added impatiently, as her brother spread out on the narrow bed a frock of sage-green foulard cut high to the throat, a schoolgirl's dress almost and certainly something January had never seen Daniel's wife wear. With it, the young man had brought a small gold cross on a golden chain, which he held out to her. 'Where did you get that thing, for Heaven's sake?'

'You can't let them think you don't love God, Anne!' Armand pleaded, nearly in tears. 'It doesn't matter what you really feel! But they have to see that you're innocent!'

'Quite right,' agreed M'sieu Sarrien, 'quite right. Now . . . What did you say this young man's name was, Hèléne?'

'I'm Anne,' Anne reminded him, her voice gentle. 'Hèléne is Mother.'

'Ah, yes! Quite right, Anne.'

1839

The stink, and the heat, of the New Orleans morning brought that cell in Saint-Lazare back to January as he stepped out of the Cabildo, spoke his automatic goodbyes to Vachel Corcet, turned his steps back toward Rue Esplanade. The last freshness of the morning remained only in the alleyways beside the cathedral, where the shadows clung, and in the open doors of the church itself. January knew if he didn't hasten his steps back home and begin mixing paint, he'd be working into the insufferable heat of the day.

Yet as he crossed in front of the cathedral's shallow steps he turned sharply, and made his way inside. The sanctuary was empty. A small galaxy of candles burned before the image of the Blessed Virgin, the protector of women, and to these he added four more, dropping a coin he couldn't really afford into the slit metal box and whispering their names as he worked the stumpy cylinders of white wax onto their spikes.

Seeing their faces, as if they stood before him in the gloom. His beautiful Rose, approaching the ordeal of childbirth for a second time, with the full knowledge of how many women did not survive that experience. (*Holy Virgin, Mother of God, uphold*

her in your hand.) Jacquette Filoux in the dark sweating cavern
of the women's cell, for a murder that January's instincts told
him had more to do with Sir John Oldmixton's deadly games.
(*Holy Virgin, Mother of God, lead her safe from that darkness*.)
Ayasha . . .

After seven years, he could still not even pronounce more than
her name.

Anne Ben-Gideon.

He retreated to a bench, one of the several arranged to face
the Virgin's little side altar, and sat for a time, looking up into
the calm face of the Mother of God.

Anne Ben-Gideon.

1830

'We stood together on the barricade at the Place des Trois-Maries,'
Anne had said that hot morning in Saint-Lazare. 'You needn't
look like that, Armand, I wasn't the only woman in Paris, fighting
for our freedom from oppression! The king's soldiers attacked
twice, in the morning and again just as it was growing dark.
After we threw them back from the barricade the second time
we waited, to see if there'd be a night attack. Some of the local
women brought food, and we all shared it, sitting there behind
the barricade. Finally the man in command – people called him
Grand-Jean – told us we had best get some sleep. He'd keep half
his force on the barricade through the night, he said, and the rest
of us should come back just before dawn. I went to Gerry's
rooms with him—'

Armand flinched and waved his hands, as if he could not bear
his sister's open admission that she'd spent a night with a lover,
and M'sieu Sarrien muttered, 'Tut-tut!'

Anne met their eyes defiantly and continued, 'And I was there
the rest of the night.'

'What time did you get there?' Speaking to her, January
recalled poor Philippe's board-stiff muscles, mentally calculated
arguments to the *officiers de la sûreté* . . . Surely the new king
(they had heard the news of the duc's confirmation in that office
on their way to the prison) wouldn't summarily get rid of experi-
enced men of the Paris police, just because they'd been put into

office by the ousted King Charles? The men in the prison courtyard had worn the blue-and-white uniforms of the old National
Guard, and the dark-clothed nuns who looked after the prisoners
seemed not to have been touched by the events of the past weeks.

Anne grimaced at the question, as if she couldn't see its
relevance, but said, 'It must have been one or one thirty. I wasn't
looking at my watch,' she added, with a touch of sarcasm.

'Not much time for rest—' old M'sieu Sarrien laboriously
noted something on his old-fashioned set of ivory pocket-tablets
– 'if you were to return before the sun rose.'

'Gerry let me sleep.' The hardness of defiance – the fearless
brightness that gleamed in her like a sword-blade – softened at
the recollection of her lover's consideration. 'I don't think I
stirred until noon.'

'And I take it,' went on the lawyer, 'that you then returned
to the Place des Trois-Maries and your – er – toils of the previous
day?'

The disapproval in his voice made her lift her chin angrily.
'I did. Well,' she added, 'I didn't go back to the Place des
Trois-Maries, because Gerry's landlady Madame Gruen woke
me up running in and saying the guards were attacking the
barricade on Rue de Rohan and they needed every hand. I pulled
on my clothes and followed her. That was the worst of the
fighting,' she added. 'I think that was the only time – that day
– that I feared we'd be driven back.' Her lips tightened. 'And
after all that, after all the men – and women too! – who died,
to have that pussy-footing lickspittle Orléans . . . "King of the
French" indeed! I—'

Sarrien held up an arthritic hand. 'We can debate the fitness
of His Royal Highness to rule this kingdom upon another occasion, madame. But Mr O'Dwyer – if he can be found – can
testify to your whereabouts from when? The morning of Tuesday
the twenty-seventh until . . . when? When did you finally part
from him?'

Her butterfly-wing brows pulled close over her sunburned nose.
'He was gone when I woke,' she said. 'I think he must have
waked before me, and gone out to find breakfast, and gotten
swept up, as I was, by those running to one of the barricades
when we were attacked again that morning. I was among those

guarding the barricade on the Rue de Rohan. I slept that night in a courtyard near there, with some of the other women. After things quieted down I went back to his rooms and asked Madame Gruen if he'd been in, and he hadn't.'

She shook her head, her brown eyes filling again. 'I think he must be dead. I've asked everyone I can think of—'

'So you have not seen his body?'

Young Armand opened his mouth to snap something – *probably*, reflected January, *Who cares*? – and then closed it as the truth seemed to come to him. He stammered instead, 'He must be found . . .'

'Very inconvenient.' Old M'sieu Sarrien tut-tutted again, and looked through his shaky notes. 'Most awkward, of course. But we'll come up with something. Let this be a lesson to you, though,' he added, frowning at her as if trying to bring her face into focus. 'I'm sure you're facing a very severe sentence – a year in a convent at the very least, though we can almost certainly have it commuted to be spent at Notre Dame de Syon. Your aunt is still Mother Superior there, isn't she?' He glanced for confirmation to Armand. 'Your family name should still count for something, with King Charles—'

'Charles isn't the king anymore, m'sieu.'

'Oh!' He made an impatient little gesture. 'Of course . . . That's right. All that rioting . . . Though how anyone could possibly accept the cadet line when the real king still lives . . .'

January's eyes met Daniel's, and he felt as if a shadow passed across his heart.

1839

'And was Michie O'Dwyer in fact dead?' Rose paused, needle in hand. Much as she hated sewing, January had ruled (as firmly as anyone ever could pass a rule upon Rose) that she would not assist in the repair of the parlor plaster but would instead occupy herself with a mild task fitted to her condition, such as repairing all the sheets and pillowslips that the school would need for its (*three-so-far!*) scholars. She had thrown a pillowslip at his head, but had agreed that she had lately felt so drained and heavy – and her back ached so much – that she would even accept the burden of mending, if it allowed her to sit down. Gabriel, Zizi-Marie (resplendent in one of Gabriel's old shirts and a tattered pair of his trousers), and young Ti-Gall (gazing upon his beloved, so attired, in smitten adoration) all waited with trowels and 'hawks' for January to finish mixing the tub – over which task he'd related the events of the morning.

'Up until this morning,' said January, 'I thought that he was. I didn't know him, but gave him credit for having died for the revolution – and it was a revolution,' he added quietly. 'In its way, a continuation of the revolution that had started in 1789. And he may indeed have died. The book, and Philippe de la Marche's card-case, could have been taken by Brooke, who may have been one of the fighters at that time or even one of the French king's soldiers – they weren't all Frenchmen, you know. Or Brooke's path may have crossed that of the original looter years afterwards.'

'What about the gun?' asked Rose.

'And what was he doing here?' demanded Gabriel, enraptured, as if the whole were a tale by Scott or Dumas.

'And why did you need to find him back then anyway?' added Zizi-Marie. 'I mean, hundreds of people must have seen Lady Anne in the fighting, besides this worthless Irishman.' Her eyes – brown and velvety like Olympe's – sparkled with delight at the thought of taking potshots at enemy soldiers from behind a wall of dirt and broken furniture. 'Couldn't you go around and find other people who could say, she'd been where everybody could see her, when this poor *couillon* was killed?'

'I doubt any of those with her on the barricade knew her name,' said January. 'She didn't give her right one to whoever might have asked, you know; she told me that. Believe me, in between everything else I did over those next few weeks, I tried to find someone who remembered her clearly enough to swear to it in court. But once Louis-Philippe set up his own police, nobody was willing to admit where they'd been. And there are few things harder than to prove a negative, especially to a jury. The safe thing to do – her family's lawyer, and the lawyer Daniel hired to help him, and all of us agreed – would be to find out who'd really killed Philippe de la Marche . . . if it was Philippe they'd meant to kill. Or to find some way around the fact that he'd been her husband's lover, and had been shot with her gun.'

He scooped plaster from the tub with his trowel and dropped it – three thick wads of snowy mud – onto the 'hawks' of the three young people. The tarpaulins that covered the parlor floor were strewn with plaster dust and little chunks chipped and scraped away from those places where damp and time had loosened areas like moulted scales. The shutters, usually closed over the French doors in a mostly-futile attempt to block the heat at this time of day, stood open to Rue Esplanade, and the noon sun streamed pitilessly in, emphasizing every ripple and bump in the parlor walls. 'I want those walls smooth as a fresh-ironed sheet,' he said, 'when I get back,' and they grinned and nodded, delighted to be undertaking so important a task on their own.

He went into his study, sponged off in the tepid water on the washstand, and dressed again in the corduroy trousers, good boots, linen shirt and jacket that marked him – as surely as if he'd worn his freedom papers pinned to his lapel – as a free householder of the French Town rather than as somebody's slave loafing off for the afternoon. Thus attired, he kissed Rose, and set forth to cast the wide nets of gossip, and see what he could find.

EIGHT

The French Town had changed in the seven years since Benjamin January had returned to it from seventeen years in Paris.

Changes for the better, some of them. The commercial streets closer to the river were paved now, and the three-foot gutters that had separated the thoroughfare from the brick banquettes – crossed at the corners by planks for the benefit of pedestrians – were mostly covered over and transformed into proper sewers, though in the back of town the old-style gutters still reeked to heaven and provided lodging for innumerable crawfish and frogs. In several streets the old-style lanterns on their chains had been replaced by the bright glare of gaslamps, and on Rue Royale and Rue Bourbon, modern banks and hotels shouldered the old Spanish town houses. The new parish prison had relieved the overcrowding of the Cabildo's cells. Some shops had new windows, wide sheets of glass instead of small latticeworks of panes that January recalled from his childhood.

Few of these modern amenities, however, had reached Rue Gallatin, the insalubrious stretch of mud between the market and the levee given over to cheap rooming-houses and even cheaper saloons. Lallie Gardinier's house combined the two establishments, offering near-toxic forty-rod for five cents a glass and accommodations abovestairs for those who came ashore and those who preyed upon them either by games of chance or more violent expedients. The landlady herself was fat, only a few inches shorter than January's impressive height, and muscled like a stevedore. When he saw her – as he did every morning at early Mass – January was invariably reminded of an overweight black lioness in a pink tignon.

'Michie Janvier!' She paused in the task of sweeping her back steps and held out her hands to him. They knew one another slightly from the social gatherings of the FTFCMBS, which she seldom attended but to which she was a regular financial contributor, and he guessed that he was known to her by reputation. Her brother Cochon was a friend and a fellow musician, and he suspected that she'd heard a good deal about him through Olympe. This was confirmed when she said, 'I hear you're lookin' into poor Jacquette Filoux's trouble,' and any question about Jacquette's brother was postponed for the moment while he related what arrangements were being made for the care of Jacquette's children.

When the topic of Uncle Juju was broached, however, the tavern keeper had little good to report of her former tenant. 'A gilt-edged weasel,' she pronounced, her dark eyes narrowing. 'He sweet-talked Polline an' Doucette, that works the levee, into breakin' off with Suggie Labeaue – that was their man – an' workin' for him instead, 'til Suggie came 'round an' took 'em back. They was ready to go by that time. Juju never gave those girls a penny of what they made for him, an' I will say for Suggie, he's clock-stoppin' ugly an' he don't smell so good but he don't skimp his girls. Juju's pretty as a girl himself an' comes across like the sweetest man in the world 'til it comes time for him to lay out so much as a silver dime.'

She jerked her chin towards the stair that led up the side of the building to, presumably, the rented rooms above the saloon. 'When I told him in April I needed his rent if I'm gonna make the note on this house he was all, "Oh, I'll get the money for you by the tenth, I got money comin' in" – humph! You know where that money was comin' in from? Playin' poker at the Proud Cock! An' when he got cleaned out there, which any idiot could tell you he was gonna, that walks into any joint owned by that skunk Jared Ganch, he went an' got the money out of that poor sister of his. In May it was the same story, only on top of owin' money to Jared Ganch an' every other gambler in town, he goes an' borrows more from Ganch himself, which if you ask me is like cuttin' your own throat. He never paid me in June, but it was always "Oh, please, m'am, I got money comin' in, just give me til Tuesday"' She shook her head.

'I locked up the room on the twenty-eighth – I wasn't gonna have him go clean out his things some night an' leave me stuck – an' he didn't have the stones to come in that night nor the Saturday, nor any night since. You can go up an' have a look at

it if you want, but there's nuthin' there worth sellin'. It's all at
the pawnshops – Bisson's, Houssaye's, an' Oviedo's over on
Canal Street – an' I've asked all three of 'em to let me know if
Filoux ever walks in. Marie-Louise Houssaye say Ganch – the
snake that runs the Proud Cock an' the Flesh an' Blood over on
Girod Street, an' two whorehouses out in Faubourg Pontchartrain
besides *an'* smuggles in slaves from Cuba – was into her place
yesterday an' asked him the same thing. So if Ganch's lookin'
for him, I'm guessin' Juju's lyin' pretty low.'

'Any idea where he'd go to do that?'

Lallie Gardinier shook her head again, and reached out to
catch a skinny boy of six who came rocketing out the back door
of the saloon. 'Whoa, there, Ritchie! I been out here twenty
minutes and I ain't seen you go near that woodpile.' She shoved
the child in the direction of the woodpile, where he began to
gather up kindling. To January, she explained, 'My sister's boy.
Juju . . . I got no idea where he's at, but my guess is, he's sweet-
talked some other woman into puttin' him up.'

She fished in the pocket of her apron and brought forth a
bunch of keys, each with a scrap of colored ribbon tied through
it. She sorted a green one from the others, handed it to him. 'You
can go have a look at his things, but Jacob Greenfeld the Jew
tailor come by Tuesday an' took back the coats Juju hadn't paid
him for, an' Wednesday Dirksen from over the Second
Municipality, an' Risteau that has a shop on Rue Bourbon, came
by an' took back his boots an' three of his waistcoats, so there
ain't much up there but empty liquor bottles now. Sure as fleas
on a dog, nuthin' that'd tell me where he might be hidin'.'

And so, January found, it proved. The room formerly occupied
by Juju Filoux was small, furnished plainly but comfortably, and
contained little beyond a few shirts and three very stylish hats
whose seller, January was almost certain, would be by within
the week to collect them. As Madame Gardinier had said, a dozen
empty liquor bottles were lined up along one wall, and a formidable pile of gambling markers heaped the neatly-made bed,
presumably emptied from Uncle Juju's coat pockets by the
defrauded Mr Greenfeld. These, plus a few crumpled and well-
used handkerchiefs and a plethora of pawn tickets, were the only
personal items remaining.

And yet, reflected January, there was no mention that Uncle Juju had left town. He'd tried – unsuccessfully – to search his sister's house for her lover's money. At a guess, he was waiting for his chance to do so again.

January thanked Madame Gardinier ('Now, you give my regards to your sister, Michie Janvier, hear?') and turned his steps to the Verandah Hotel on St Charles Avenue, in the so-called Second Municipality of New Orleans – the American district.

Even in the French Town – now the First Municipality – January was more conscious than he had been, upon his return in 1832, of the presence of Americans. In 1803, when his mother had become St-Denis Janvier's *plaçeé*, she had told the seven-year-old Benjamin not to go beyond the old city wall, and above all not to cross the common pastureland that separated the French district from that of 'the American animals', for they would have no compunctions about kidnapping a black child and selling him back into the slavery from which he had so recently come. When he'd returned from Paris the wall had been gone and what was left of the common pastureland had become the 'neutral ground' along Canal Street, but the warning remained. It was more true than ever, that Americans tended to see all free blacks as potential money on the hoof, if they could be but separated from their freedom papers and from the members of the white French community who knew them and could attest to their legal status. And despite the feverish summer heat, there were more Americans on the streets of the French Town itself: sailors from the wharves, carters, draymen. Clerks from the steamboat companies and those big new hotels. The clamor and chatter of English, threading through the softer music of French as he made his way along Rue Bourbon, seemed to him more insistent, and he noticed how many of the cafés along that street had changed their names to make themselves more attractive to an Anglophone clientele.

He had never felt safe crossing Canal Street. Now he didn't feel safe in the French Town either, and when he left it, as he did now, he found himself mentally measuring the distance between himself and any white man he passed, and calculating his chances of escape.

Several of the new, elegant American hotels graced St Charles Avenue a short distance upriver from the French Town; it was said that the Verandah, with its splendid balcony and marble statues, was the most home-like, a statement which made January reflect that whoever said that must have had an extraordinary home. He entered, as was considered proper for a man of his ancestry, through the rear yard, and sought out the concierge Louis Naquet – reflecting again upon the general usefulness of the FTFCMBS in acquiring a nodding acquaintance with pretty much everybody in town.

He located Naquet in the pantry, through which waiters carried food from the kitchen into the spectacularly painted dining room. Elegant in livery, the concierge stood with three or four waiters and table captains beside the padded doors, looking through the small glazed windows into the dining room itself. Even from there January could hear the soft clamor of lunchtime customers, the voice of one man – a thickset American businessman with a rufous beard, he saw when he joined them in looking through the windows – raised in carping complaint. 'Damn it, boy, when I say I want chicken I mean I want something that's *hot*, not that's been sitting on a counter somewhere while those lazy niggers take their sweet time fetching it out.' His tablemates – all with dishes already before them – nodded and growled agreement as a harassed-looking waiter set a plate of chicken and cream sauce on the table.

'And don't think this is the end of it, boy,' the man snapped at the waiter. 'I expect this to be taken off my bill, for all the trouble you've caused me.'

Naquet, at whose elbow January stood, shook his head, and January said softly, 'M'sieu Naquet, if I—'

Naquet held up his hand: *Wait.*

All eyes were on the window, with a sort of breathless anticipation.

Then Naquet grinned. 'Well,' he said, with great satisfaction, 'he ate it.'

The waiters dissolved into silent guffaws, slapping one another on the back in congratulation – for what, January could only speculate with a shudder. The concierge turned from the little windows with a shake of his head, said, 'Janvier,' in greeting, and grasped his hand. 'It plumb amazes me,' he added, with a glance back toward the dining room as he led January toward his own little office near the pantry, 'that so many of those white men ain't yet figured it out, that you don't cause trouble for them that handles your food. What can I do for you, m'sieu?'

Naquet recalled Henry Brooke – it was his job to remember everybody who stayed at the Verandah, sometimes over years between visits – but had little to say of him. He'd arrived with a single heavy trunk – something January already knew from Shaw – and a valise. He tipped adequately, was gone most of each day, didn't bring prostitutes up to his room, and had departed after two days. 'The morning after he'd gone to one of the Blue Ribbon Balls, I understand. I assume he met someone there with whom he reached an understanding.'

'He did,' said January quietly. 'She was arrested yesterday morning for his murder. I'm certain she didn't do it and I'm certain she's going to hang for it – she can't prove where she was at the time – and I'm looking to see who he knew in town. Did he meet anyone here?'

It was a bow drawn at a venture, and January wasn't surprised when Naquet shook his head. If the man Brooke was working for Oldmixton, he'd be taking pains to cover his tracks. 'You have any samples of his handwriting?' he asked, and the concierge took him to the manager's office and fetched the hotel's register, and one of the folders of dining-room records. January wasn't sure – he was no expert in handwriting – but he thought the slightly cramped 'r's in 'Brooke' and 'Henry' were identical to those in 'Gerry'.

Did it prove anything? He didn't know.

And if Gerry O'Dwyer had fled from Paris in 1830 – if he'd been completely unaware that his lover faced the guillotine for lack of evidence as to her whereabouts on that hot Tuesday night – it wasn't beyond the bounds of reason that he would come to New Orleans one day.

Or even that he'd be working with, or for, the British.

Why property? he wondered, as he made his way back to the French Town, glancing over his shoulder all the way. *And why* worthless *property?*

There was a man named Ti-Jon, whose master usually rented him to one or another of the stevedore gangs that worked the steamboat wharves: Ti-Jon was the hub and facilitator of a network of slaves that covered the riverfront and half the city. Since his master – who owned a steamboat, a cotton press, four goods wagons and a hotel – was one of those who let his slaves find their own lodgings and food and demanded only a weekly cut of their wages, Ti-Jon was the man other slaves went to in quest of side work to earn extra money, or bargains of one kind or another for clothing or food.

Knowing, as he did, that it was the slaves of the white folks who knew everything in any town, January inquired along the wharves for him, and was directed to the blacksmith shop of Mohammed LePas on Rue St-Pierre. Ti-Jon was there, with four of his master's draft horses being shod. He and the blacksmith greeted January, and asked after Rose's health, and the rumor that it was January who was inquiring into the matter of Jacquette Filoux's arrest.

'That would be me,' sighed January, and explained the principle problem: that almost nothing was known of Henry Brooke, except that he was mixed up in some reputedly strange and illegal doings someplace. 'The City Guards want to hang somebody for the murder, and right now there's no alternative candidate. We don't know who else in town *would* want to murder the bastard. How many enemies can you make when you've only been in town two weeks?'

'Depends on who you play cards with,' remarked Mohammed LePas wisely. He was a wiry old man, with old and faded 'country marks' scarred into his face. He'd been the apprentice blacksmith on Bellefleur Plantation when January was a child, and had known him almost literally from birth: his freedom papers were one of the finest examples in town of Hannibal Sefton's talents as a forger.

'On the subject of playing cards,' said January, 'I'm pretty sure when his body was dumped in the basin it was dragged out and robbed by Juju Filoux. So whatever he had on him that would tell us what he was up to and who he was involved with, is probably in Juju's pockets right now. Either of you know where he might be found?'

'You lookin' for Juju,' said Ti-Jon, 'you standin' in the back of a long line. What I hear, that boy owes money to every crap game in town – and to half the girls in town that he's sweet-talked into lendin'. I don't know what that boy's got,' he added, with a shake of his head, 'but I would surely make my fortune if I was to bottle and sell it.'

'You heard if he's left town?'

The slave considered the matter, while LePas went back to his bellows and his hammer; at length he said, 'You know, I think if he had, he'd have taken some girl with him, and I haven't heard any of their men cryin' *thief*. So I may be wrong, but I'm thinking he's still around someplace.'

'Would you keep your ear to the ground?' asked January. 'About Juju, and about Brooke – and anything you might hear about the old Chitimacha Plantation, which Brooke apparently bought—'

'*That* place?'

'Good Lord, my uncle Dom worked on that place,' exclaimed LePas – meaning, January knew, not the blacksmith's literal uncle, but one of the older men who had been part of the Bellefleur workforce at some point in the man's childhood. 'He said that bayou would change course damn near every time it rained. They got a steamboat stranded just about on the front porch of the house one winter . . .'

'I'll ask around,' promised Ti-Jon. 'Mr W—' this was the man who owned him, Jean-Francois Wachespaag – 'has me drivin' for him, now work's so slow on the docks; which beats Jesus out of workin' Jem Mayhew's brickyard, which is what he had me doin' last week. He'll have me waitin' tables next. Somebody should have heard something.'

Olympe, whom January found in the shaded loggia outside her kitchen on Rue Iberville, scrubbing out her jelly-making kettle, had heard nothing of the errant Juju's whereabouts either. 'And that Brooke, he come and go quiet.' Though like Jacquette Filoux she'd been sent to the convent of the Ursulines for an education, her French was still the coarse patois of the cane patch, a gesture of defiance against the *plaçeé* mother who, like Jacquette's, had tried to make her into a *plaçeé* in her turn.

In the afternoon heat the yard behind her cottage was still cooler than the streets, and in the shadows of what had been her husband's workshop – back when customers had had work for him – Tiennot and Jean-Luc Filoux picked through baskets of berries with Olympe's seven-year-old son Ti-Paul, removing rubbish and leaves.

'He was up to something.' January shed his coat, and carried the big terracotta pitcher to the cistern to refill it for his sister. 'Four days ago a man offered me a hundred dollars to find Brooke's killer, and get back some papers he might or might not have had on him – which for certain weren't in his pockets when they pulled him out of the basin. So something tells me it wasn't just buying up worthless plantations and selling them to ignorant Englishmen.'

His sister set down the porcelain jelly-pot she was drying on the table before the kitchen, and her velvet-brown eyes narrowed. 'Buying *plantations?*'

He related to her what Shaw had told him, adding, 'Uncle Juju might have made off with the deeds when he let himself into Jacquette's house Saturday night. He was gambling at the Cock that night, and I think he found Brooke's body and took the key. I notice Bridgie Danou said she didn't see the man's face, which means he was letting himself into the dining-room door rather than the bedroom where there was a candle. If he found the deeds – and the stock certificates, or whatever else Brooke had in the desk – he might well be afraid to sell them now, for fear of being traced. That might be why he went back Sunday. For cash money.'

'For sure he couldn't sell somethin' like a deed or stocks on his own,' agreed Olympe slowly. 'He'd have to go through one of the big bosses, like Ganch or Shotwell at the Blackleg. Dobo at Lorette's livery tells me he drove Brooke out to Alcinde Allard's plantation, and out to the Labarre place. Other times, he said, he'd rent a buggy an' drive himself.'

'So Saturday afternoon,' said January thoughtfully, 'he got dressed up and either walked down a few streets to Rue Bourbon or Rue Royale—'

'To see who?' Olympe glanced over her shoulder at him as she entered the kitchen, came back out with a cone of sugar and a scraper. 'The Merieults are at the lake.' She named one of the most socially prominent of the Creole French. 'Chesneau and his family left for Mandeville last week, the Almonesters and the de la Rondes are in Spanish Fort for the summer. Near every family that's got a town house you can reach by foot from Rue Toulouse. Yet he was dressed up fine to go callin'.'

'So he took a fiacre someplace.' January bore the kettle into her tiny kitchen, which throbbed with the heat of the hearth, and hung it on the gallows-iron in the big fireplace. 'So far as I can tell, he was shot early in the evening, with daylight still in the sky.'

'Can happen, down by the basin.'

'Somebody would have seen it, that early. There's enough coming and going, someone would at least have seen the body. If you could ask among the drivers who were out that night – quietly,' he added. 'If Brooke was up to something that was worth a hundred dollars to somebody, I'd rather not have my name bandied around as looking for him.'

'I'll do that.' She took a poker, and tidied the heap of searing coals beneath the kettle, turning with a smile as the boys brought in the cleaned berries – trying to pretend their mouths and fingers weren't stained purple. 'That's very good, gentlemen. Now you put these little pots in a row there, and fetch me the big ladle . . . I'll burn a green candle for you,' she added, turning back to January, her dark eyes somber. 'And I'll ask M'am L'Araignee, if she has anything to tell me of this. Don't laugh, brother.' She nodded toward the house, where the altar of her gods occupied its niche in the parlor, and the spirit she called M'am L'Araignee dwelt in a black-painted bottle among a litter of silver pins and split peppers, graveyard earth and mouse bones. 'M'am, she tell me last night, it's the gold they want.'

'What gold? I thought it was stock certificates . . .'

Olympe shook her head. 'She showed me in the ink bowl. Bags of coin, boxes of rubies, Our Lord with his body all made of pearl crucified on a cross of gold. "It's the gold they after", madame said.' The stifling heat of the afternoon seemed to darken with the shadowing of her eyes. 'The gold smelled like honeysuckle, she said. The diamonds like sandalwood. Diamond combs . . .' Her brow creased in thought. 'Diamond combs. The moon and three stars.'

And seeing how his eyes changed, she asked, 'You know what those mean, brother?'

'No. But I've seen them.'

And from the house, the treble voice of nine-year-old Chou-Chou called out 'Mama! Mama, M'am Maurepas here!'

'I must go.' Olympe laid a hand on January's, her eyes still intent on his. For two years Olympe's trade in gris-gris, in hoodoo, in magic candles and fortunes read by the patterns of beans dropped on her carven tray, had put food on her family's table. Maybe darker things as well. Big, good-natured Paul Corbier, a skilled upholsterer, had for two of those years rolled cigars in one of the cramped little factories along Tchoupitoulas Street, to keep Chou-Chou and Ti-Paul in school while those who'd been wealthier before the bank crash made do with shabby chairs. When the Mesdames Maurepas of the world came calling, it behooved Olympe not to keep them waiting.

'You go careful, brother.' With unaccustomed concern she laid a hand upon his shoulder, and tiptoed to kiss his cheek. Then she strode back to the house, straight as a sword blade in her faded red dress.

'Gold is what anyone would be after, obviously,' said January to Hannibal Sefton later, as the afternoon's rainstorm pounded like an avalanche of stair rods on the tiled roof of the marketplace arcade.

'Boxes of rubies and solid gold crucifixes somehow don't sound like Sir John Oldmixton's style,' remarked the fiddler, and added, 'Beautiful damsel, "dusky like the night, but night with all her stars" . . .' as the old coffee vendor La Violette brought him a couple of pralines on a square of newspaper despite the fact that he had not a penny to his name.

She bridled and said, 'Go 'long with you, with all your pretty talk! These was dropped on the ground, I figured you might as well have 'em—' Patently untrue, January knew, as he'd been facing her for the past fifteen minutes, and Hannibal took her hand and kissed it.

'If they fell at your feet, gracious madame, they would be all the sweeter for having been crossed by your shadow,' and she walked back chuckling to her coffee stand.

The fiddler continued thoughtfully, 'But certainly not something you'd find in the same cache with good, marketable Bank of England stock certificates. Though I quite agree with you about gold being at the bottom of it. *Non quid mortalia pectora cogis, auri sacra fames!*' He pressed his hand to his side and coughed as if the life were being wrung out of him.

January watched him uneasily, but in fact his friend sounded better than he had earlier in the summer, when the two of them had returned from a somewhat rough-and-tumble stint playing for a minstrel show up-river[2]. For years Hannibal had controlled his periodic pulmonary crises by liberal use of opiates, with predictable results, and his stubborn adherence to abstinence from the drug – it was nearly two years since his last binge – had results just as inevitable. He must, he had said, be back at the Eagle of Victory after dinner to play for the evening trade: he looked rather like the ghost of an undertaker's mute who had been run over repeatedly by a hearse.

'This is easier at any rate,' said January after a time, 'than it was trying to find Gerry O'Dwyer in Paris nine years ago.'

'If it is the same man,' agreed Hannibal, 'he was probably more lively then than now.'

At the next table an American who looked like a steamboat pilot slammed a newspaper impatiently down, demanded of the man with him why the hell didn't the United States government just send troops down to New Grenada and take the whole place and be done with all these damn uprisings and revolutions? 'What the hell do them bean eaters know about revolution anyways?'

What indeed? January reflected, remembering the barricade on the Rue St-Denis.

'There's good land down there, cotton land, just for the askin'! An' what do them Spanish do but fight amongst themselves an' screw up the trade! I lost a whole shipload of Yoruba – two hundred prime niggers straight from Africa, the ones that survived the voyage – just disappeared in Cartagena in the street-fightin'! An' for what?'

'Hell, with fifty guys I could take that place myself, while they's all fightin' each other . . .'

'Serve them Pope worshipers right, too, for what they done in Texas—'

[2] See *Drinking Gourd*

'One of the first things Louis-Philippe did when he became king,' January went on thoughtfully, 'was to abolish the royal police and replace them with his own infantry and cavalry, mostly to keep "public order", as they called it – but presumably also to keep control of the old Napoleonnistes who wanted the emperor's son back on the throne, and those of us who'd *thought* we were fighting for a republic, the more fools we.'

He had himself barely escaped arrest, he recalled, one night when he'd hauled Carnot out of an altercation with the *guarde municipale* at the Scarlet Monk in the Rue St-Denis. That was the occasion on which he'd discovered that Anne had been perfectly right about the sewers being a useful escape route. He'd had to burn his clothes afterwards, to Ayasha's loudly-expressed disgust, but he'd seen the chalk marks on the curved brick vaulting of the walls, and guessed he could have traveled for miles in that fashion, unseen.

Gerry O'Dwyer could easily have gotten out of Paris that way . . .

And anyone could just as easily have transported Philippe de la Marche's corpse.

'I wonder that anyone was sufficiently organized to arrest your friend Madame Ben-Gideon in the first place,' remarked Hannibal, and sipped at the tin cup in which La Violette served all of her customers. 'Much less bring her to trial.'

'Louis-Philippe d'Orléans is a man who never lets the principles of liberty interfere with good order,' returned January, a little drily. The recollection of the smell of sewage and of his friend's blood faded – not quite completely – from his hands. 'Immediately after the revolt he dismissed the old king's prefect, but he kept on most of the Sûreté – two-thirds of them were former criminals themselves – and *sergeants de la ville*. The man he put in charge was a minor nobleman who practically fell over himself when a member of the Noailles family came in demanding that the atheistic trollop who murdered her precious son be arrested.'

'Ah,' said Hannibal, who had himself had acquaintance with the powerful Noiailles. 'Not good.'

'No.' January turned his head, looking out into the sheets of rain that half-hid the Place des Armes, and across to the fiacre drivers clustered beneath the green pride-of-India trees. Above the levee, the black stalks of the steamboat chimneys poured black smoke into the soot-gray clouds.

The Americans at the next table had departed, and a woman in an elaborately-dressed silk tignon walked past. 'It is all very well to love,' she said to the young girl beside her, 'but to raise your children in poverty, colored in a white world where the whites own all things and can do as they please, does them no kindness. We can be sure of nothing . . .'

'No,' repeated January softly. 'It was not good.'

'We all took refuge in Ramboulliet,' said Hannibal after a time of gazing into the battered tin cup. January recalled again that though their paths had never crossed, his friend had also been in Paris in the days of the Restoration. A well-born wastrel in a 'merry band' of wastrels, he had gathered, from things Hannibal had spoken of in the past, when he'd been more than usually drunk: latter-day goliards who had abandoned the families who asked of them what they were not able to give, to pursue the fairy-gold of pleasure, wine, and song.

The fiddler had his own memories, of nine years ago.

'It was ghastly hot in Paris that summer. Achille Tremaine – his father had made an indecent amount of money selling shoddy boots to Napoleon's soldiers – had a chateau that had used to belong to some relative of the Duc de Soissons. Very stylish, even without most of its furnishings, which of course Achille's father had sold off . . . Achille called me out, I remember, for flirting with his mistress. As the challenged party I stipulated blowpipes of cognac at twenty paces, and after the first ten attempts nobody had any very clear recollection of the duel. But it was assumed honor had been satisfied.'

He was silent for a time, long insectile fingers tracing the rim of the cup. Behind them in the arcade the voices of the last of the *marchandes* echoed, packing up lettuces and tomatoes they had been unable to vend, and calling good-natured curses down on the weather.

'In effect,' continued Hannibal softly, 'we left Paris at the end of June under one king, and made our way back there sometime in December to find another solidly in residence. I fear my memories of the Three Glorious Days concern only the scent of cut hay and the reflection of the moon in the chateau's lake, and music played in the night.' His brows pinched together. 'Not very creditable, I'm afraid. I left Paris, soon after that.'

You can't step twice into the same river, reflected January again, studying the thin profile half-turned from him, the deep, exhausted lines around the fiddler's dark eyes.

And was it worse, January wondered, to have the remembrance of cut hay, stolen kisses, and moonlight, than the burnt back-taste of anger that still filled him, when he remembered crouching in the scorching heat behind the barricade, killing men he had never met because he thought he was finally going to be able to live in a republic of which he could be proud? Worse than the revulsion he had felt clambering up that same barricade the following day and seeing the corpses of the men who had died – for what?

We can be sure of nothing . . .

Died – left their families bereft and in poverty – so that Louis-Philippe d'Orléans and his rich friends could rule France in the place of his arrogant cousin Charles and *his* rich friends?

Quietly, January replied, 'It doesn't matter. Not at this distance. You know Juju Filoux? I'm looking for him, and I'm looking for Henry Brooke, whose other name might just possibly be Gerry O'Dwyer. Any information would be welcome. I understand he spent time in the saloons around the basin – probably in the Swamp as well. God knows what he was actually up to – on behalf of Oldmixton and Company on the one hand, or possibly playing them false.'

'The ears of King Midas,' promised the fiddler, raising his left hand in avowal and crossing his heart with his right, 'shall be as the blunt organs of adders, compared to mine.'

'Thank you, Your Majesty.' January bowed gravely. 'I've asked among the uptown musicians, and among the voodoos, and among the slaves along the wharves and in the French Town. Anyone, I hope, who won't get word of my quest back to Sir John and his minions over at the British Consul. I don't precisely suspect him of having had a hand in Brooke's demise, but if Brooke worked for him, and happened to decide to use consulate funds to purchase worthless real estate – for what purpose I am too simple of soul to imagine! – I'd rather keep my distance until I have a better idea of what's really going on.'

'*Timeo Danaos,*' agreed Hannibal. 'You cannot trust the

sassenach, least of all when they're offering you money. Will you be riding out to have a look at these desirable properties on Bayou des Avocats and in such other charming places?'

'I was just going to ask you,' said January, 'if you would be free to accompany me tomorrow?' He had learned long ago that a black man accompanying a white one outside the narrow confines of the French Town was usually safe from kidnappers – the assumption being that the black man was the white man's slave and that probably someone would go looking for him if he vanished. 'In payment for which, would you care to repair to my house for dinner before you have to return to the fields of your honorable labor?'

'It is well known in the Swamp—' Hannibal lifted his hands – 'that I may be had for any purpose whatsoever for the price of a plate of beans. *Claudito iam rivos, pueri,*' he added, with a glance past the arcade, where the downpour had thinned to a glittering drizzle. '*Sat prata biberunt.* I think we have just time for that.'

NINE

Diamond combs.

The perfume of sandalwood.

For a long while after Rose had gone to bed, and Olympe's children had retreated upstairs to the long room that so soon would become the dormitory for the school's students once again, January sat at his piano, his fingers tracing out the tunes he recalled from that summer of 1830. The overture from *La Dame Blanche*. 'I Know a Bank Where the Wild Thyme Blows'. 'Highland Mary'. All the popular dances he'd practiced, knowing they would be in demand when the best and the beautiful of France returned to Paris – like Hannibal and the 'merry band' of his companions – with the fading of the leaves.

Diamond combs. The moon and three stars.

Why, he wondered, had the vision sent by his sister's private god been of *her*?

1830

January had located Daniel's former 'friend' Apollon Michaud without difficulty, at a high-class gambling-hell on the Rue de Rivoli. Though the new king was said to be moving his residence from the Palais Royale to the Tuileries, and the Opera and many of the gambling houses (and up-scale bordellos) of the Palais Royale remained open ('Lest His Majesty should lose some rents,' grumbled Pleyard), a number of gamblers had moved their custom elsewhere for the time being – 'At least until things calm down,' said Jeannot Charbonnière.

Daniel had also provided the name of Michaud's newest 'friend' ('A man whose family makes boot blacking! After all his comments about Jew parveneux . . .'), and had offered to go the rounds of the gambling parlors and identify the suspects. ('Not that I think Apollon would actually *do* such a frightful thing. He was greedy and vain – Anne positively detested him, and was forever warning me against him – and spiteful as a child. But *murder . . .*')

January, whose youth in New Orleans and six years at the night clinic of the Hôtel Dieu had taught him what men do when wounded both in pride and in pocketbook, went instead with Jeannot Charbonnière and old Lucien Imbolt the violinist, who between them knew pretty much everyone in Paris's demi-monde and were less likely to be recognized by their quarry. Daniel's pomaded curls, kohl-lined eyes and coats of antique brocade – puce or lavender or parakeet-green – weren't likely to be missed or forgotten.

At six feet three, January was aware that he wasn't exactly inconspicuous either – there were numerous other Africans in Paris, but only a few were making their living as musicians. But at least his friendship with Daniel wasn't known to half the gamblers and Cyprians present at Chez L'Alouette that evening. Charbonnière pointed out Michaud, broad-shouldered and soldierly in a blue superfine coat of rather pronounced cut and trousers strapped tight beneath his insteps; Imbolt quietly identified the over-pomaded dumpling of a man who leaned over the roulette table at his side as Jacques Troue, proprietor of the aforesaid string of blacking factories. Inquiries among the musicians – playing discreetly behind screens at the far end of the room – established that Troue had abandoned Paris weeks before the rioting, with Michaud in tow, and hadn't returned until all was quiet and Louis-Philippe was safe on the throne. One of the waiters added that he'd heard they'd gone to Dieppe.

From there it was a simple matter to wait outside Chez L'Alouette until three in the sultry August morning, and follow the Troue carriage (four horses and one of the most ostentatious coats of arms January had ever seen) when it conveyed the young man (and his infatuated *erastes*) to Michaud's apartment on the Place de Vendome. On the following evening – summer being the time of leisure (and short commons) for musicians – January made his way to Les Quatres Chiminees in the Rue des Capuchines. It wasn't the nearest tavern to the apartment, but it was the cleanest, and the haunt of every valet and hostler in the district. Michaud's valet had been newly hired – only a week after the start of Michaud's association with M'sieu Troue – and was far from enthusiastic about his employer.

'Now, my granddad was the Marquis de Trebeche's coachman,' the valet groused over the pint of ale January bought for him (at Daniel's expense). 'Yeah, he'd treat you like you was a dog, but those old aristos, before the revolution, some of 'em treated their dogs damn well. Trebeche was one of 'em. Granddad'd have to wait for the family in the square outside some Versailles town house in the rain til near dawn, but he'd always tip an extra couple of sols for our trouble, or make sure that stuck-up daughter of his didn't call for her carriage 'til she was damn well ready to walk out the door. Pig-headed and head over ears in debt, the lot of 'em, but they had a sense of *noblesse oblige*. Not like the trash you've got now, callin' 'emselves noble – T'cha! Marryin' factory-owners' daughters, an' bankers' sons, an' hirin' the children of real nobles to teach 'em manners that they feel deep in their spoilt hearts that they don't have to learn since Dad's got money . . .'

It was a simple matter and a few francs – and the sympathetic ear that January had early learned worked almost as well – to ascertain that Michaud had been nowhere near Paris on the night Philippe de la Marche had died.

'Which clears some of the underbrush,' he remarked on the following afternoon, when he joined Charbonnière and Lucien at Carnot's tiny attic studio. 'Troue – and Michaud – and Madame Troue – were all at Dieppe from mid-July until just last week, though madame wasn't aware that her husband was renting rooms in the Rue de l'Epée for the "Paris friend" they coincidentally met every evening at the Petite Theatre.'

'Nor that her husband had purchased that "Paris friend's" new coat, new hat, and new boots for him either, I'll wager.' Carnot, blacked eye fading and the bruises on his jaw and lip diffusing to an unsightly yellowish-green, delicately blended cast shadow with background darkness on the face of Medea, staring wildly around a pillar at her husband Jason and his frail blonde princess.

'A pity, in its way,' the artist continued. 'Not only would I not mind seeing Apollon Michaud go to the guillotine – the man can't hold his wine and lies like a serpent – but nobody would much care if he were taken for the crime. He doesn't have family – at least, not family who'd work to have him cleared. Something tells me old Moses Ben-Gideon isn't going to have a conveniently disgruntled valet to question, and if the de Belvoire family themselves – *père* or *fils* – were behind it . . .'

'The de Belvoires?' Lucien dropped the string he'd been dangling for Thaïs the cat, and sat up in the attic's single, dilapidated bergère chair. 'Dear boy, what are you saying? Philippe was madame's curly-haired lamb. By all I've heard, she's the one who's pushing so hard to have poor Anne executed for the crime.'

'And was this Comte de Belvoire so enthusiastic about his curly-haired lamb of an heir dallying with men?' Ayasha, sitting in the dormer stitching buttons on Carnot's good visit-the-clients shirt (Carnot's girlfriend being apparently ignorant of which end of the needle the thread went through), raised her brows. 'Or is his perfectly robust little brother – who according to de la Marche's prospective mother-in-law, the Marquise de Taillefer, lost thousands of francs in the gaming rooms of every party they took him to last winter – happy to see the family fortune turned over to one who'll never get an heir in his turn?'

Charbonnière protested, 'You can't go so far as to say—'

'And in any case—' January set aside the sheaf of sketches he'd been perusing – 'according to the *Gazette de France*, the Comte de Belvoire and his family were at Etamps during the rioting. At the Comte's chateau at Noisette-le-Comte, to be exact, where they'd been since—'

'But they weren't.' Lucien detached Thaïs from his shin, and gathered her compact fluffiness into his lap. 'I saw Celestin – the younger son – at Au Mandragore on the twenty-sixth, the night before the rioting started. Old Moulard who owns the place practically begged me to play there this summer,' he added, as if he expected one or both of his fellow musicians to cry out in horror at the mention of this low-grade den. 'Even Orpheus played in Hell.'

Charbonnière grinned. 'You could catch the pox just breathing the air in there.'

'I have better ways, dear boy,' retorted Lucien grandly, 'of catching the pox, should I desire to do such a thing.'

'You're sure about seeing him?' January leaned forward, from the corner of the table where he perched. 'Because I checked in the *Gazette*, and it says the whole family was at Noisette-le-Comte—'

Ayasha set Carnot's shirt aside and dug from the untidy pile of broadsheets, magazines, and newspapers in the goods boxes along the wall a slightly yellowed issue of the court periodical in question. Like many artists in Paris, Carnot kept track of the great families of the court: one needed to know where one's clientele could be found. January took it from her hand, and read aloud: '

Friday, 23 July, 1830. The Comte de Belvoire remains at Noisette-le-Comte, summer residence of the family. Enjoying the country air with him are Madame la Comtesse de Belvoire-Clianrouge, his younger son Monsieur Celestin de Gourgue, the Marquis and Marquise de Taillefer, Monsieur le Vicomte de Brancas – 'that's Taillefer's oldest son' – and Mademoiselle de Chouvigny. One daily expects an announcement of considerable interest.

'Mademoiselle is Taillefer's daughter,' Ayasha put in. 'I was originally inclined to feel sorry for the girl, given the degree of resemblance she bears to a stoat, until the third or fourth tantrum she threw while I was fitting a court dress for her last fall.'

'Celestin de Gourgue – though I suppose we must call him de la Marche now – is mentioned as being at Etamps again on the twenty-sixth,' said January, scanning the column of print. 'He may have sneaked into town to go gambling, if he's as enthusiastic about it as you say—'

'According to Madame de Taillefer, the family hired some frightful old clergyman to follow the boy about and keep him out of trouble. At twenty-three you'd think they'd recognize him as an adult.'

January queried Lucien with an eyebrow.

'No sign of a pedagogue, frightful or otherwise. Myself, I'd hardly say the boy was the fiendish gambler his mama seems to fear. To my recollection he was only in Au Mandragore for half an hour.'

'I wonder his throat wasn't cut as he walked out the door,' Charbonnière commented, and Lucien shook his head.

'The proprietor pays two hundred francs a month to Cut-Throat l'Allemande to make sure the customers aren't robbed coming out. A great many of the Good and the Beautiful come in of an evening – to play a few hands, or watch part of the show – before going on elsewhere. Particularly in the summer when there's nothing on but the Comedie Francaise and everyone is out of town.'

'And you're sure it was de Gourgue?'

'Reasonably so,' said the old violinist. 'Like a plump version of the Beautiful Philippe, but six inches shorter and with a half-grown Van Dyke and spots. And one could scarcely mistake that heinous black-and-yellow waistcoat he wears—'

'Ah!' said January, recollections from the previous winter's engagements dropping into place. 'That's the fellow.' He barely remembered the face of the wearer – glimpsed across the lawn at a Venetian breakfast at which he'd played – but the gaudy embroidery of ebony and daffodil (and Charbonnière's *sotto voce* comments thereupon) were unforgettable.

For a time he watched Carnot catch a delicate rim-light on Medea's curls, on the knuckles of the hand she clenched at her breast. Thinking of Anne in Saint-Lazare, and of the difficulties of proving a negative.

At length he crossed to the dormer where Ayasha had resumed her seat, and laid a hand on her shoulder. 'My nightingale, I suspect that a journey to Etamps is in order.'

January's fingers stilled on the keys of his piano, and he sat for a long time looking into the darkness past the candle's single flame.

Remembering.

The smell of linseed oil, the voices of friends. The warmth of Ayasha's shoulder through the faded print cotton of her dress – that blue-and-black frock that two years later he was to pack in a trunk with all her other clothing and throw into the Seine in the wake of her death.

Pain constricted his heart, then opened it like a red-and-black flower.

Gone. Not just Ayasha, but that time, those days, the taste of Carnot's cheap wine and the way the sunlight came through his studio windows. *That time is gone.*

And all the days with her, with them, that I would have had.

The rattle of hooves in the Rue Esplanade outside had nearly stilled. The only sound, from far off to the north across Lake Pontchartrain, was the dull grumble of thunder. Closer to, the whine of a mosquito which had escaped Rose's vigilance as she'd closed up the house at sunset.

They visited Anne at Saint-Lazare the evening before they left.

The evening had been hot, like this one, and Anne, restless as a caged panther. 'An officer came and questioned me.' Her glance passed from January's face to Ayasha's, half contemp-tuous, half-scared. 'He asked me about Daniel, about Daniel's "little friends", as he called them. I said of course I knew he had lovers, everyone in Paris knows it. Some of them I like, some I don't, but I certainly didn't think shooting any one of them was going to stop him from running after every pretty boy he sees. I liked Philippe, the few times I met him, and he was never anything but polite to me. This man carried on as if I spent my nights in tears of mortified pride and my days in plotting revenge, like a character in one of those awful novels Mother's always reading!'

While she was speaking she paced the length of the room three times – three of her long strides, the sea-green silk of her skirts billowing gently. 'Bad enough I should get an hour's worth of such nonsense from Armand, every time he's in here! And Mother.'

A pile of fabric was heaped on the end of the bed, fashionable pale-pink silk, and with it a huge square sewing box of tortoise-shell and ebony. January guessed that some member of her family had brought her embroidery to occupy her time. Since the nuns would have taken away even the small scissors that such a kit would have included, there probably wasn't much she could have done with it anyway. The inmates of Saint-Lazare were permitted an hour's decorous stroll in the prison yard once per day. Nothing, to a girl of Anne's violent energies.

'Mother . . .' Anne's voice changed from anger to a kind of grieved despair. 'She blames herself, for not keeping Papa from marrying me to Daniel. Not because he chases boys – I don't think Mother even knows what a boy-chaser does when he catches one! – but because he's a Jew. Such stuff! As if anyone who married a Jew was bound to come to a bad end.' She slapped the heels of her palms together as she spoke, turned her head from side to side, the strong, auburn tendrils that framed her face catching a little in the sweat on her brow.

'I would have laughed, if she hadn't been so . . . so *eviscerated* by all this. I spent over an hour comforting *her*, promising her it was all a mistake. That I'll be all right, that of course I didn't do it . . . She was almost sick with weeping, poor dear . . . And Madame Sonnet, that frightful woman who attends her, kept shaking her head and offering her smelling salts and asking me, "How could you do this to her, Anne?"'

'We'll get you out,' said January, hearing behind the torrent of her words the fear she wouldn't acknowledge, even to herself. 'Do you know Celestin de Gourgue?'

'Philippe's brother?' Anne frowned, and gave a little shrug. 'Tin-Tin, Philippe called him . . . I've met him. A spotty little dumpling with a beard like a couple of socks hanging on a clothes line! Papa spoke of making a match between us at one point, but in the end hadn't the money to make the running, even with a younger son. I expect they'll marry him to that frightful de Taillefer girl, now that he's the heir. I can't see Louise de Taillefer letting the next Comte de Belvoire get away from her daughter, no matter who— You're not thinking *Tin-Tin* did this?'

'He was in Paris during the rioting, beautiful lady.' Old Lucien, who had accompanied January and Ayasha to the prison, spoke for the first time. 'And in the *Gazette*, his parents are claiming that he wasn't.'

'That's ridiculous. For one thing, he can't hit the side of a barn—'

'Philippe was shot at close range,' said January. 'My baby sister could have hit him at that distance.'

'For another . . .' Her words tailed off.

January waited, in her silence. After a time Ayasha asked gently, 'Do you think him capable of it? I hear he's heavily in debt from gaming.'

Another long silence as Anne thought about it. Thought about the new king's eagerness to enlist the old nobility to his side. About the 'honor' of the de Belvoire family, which would tolerate anything but a 'catamite' as the head of the family – even, possibly, a fratricide. At length she whispered, 'I honestly don't know.'

Etamps itself lay a day's journey from Paris by *diligence*. Daniel provided the ten francs that comprised the fares for January, Ayasha, and Lucien Imbolt – the only one of the party who knew the new vicomte by sight – plus the cost of lodging and food. 'A fine thing when I've been reduced to the status of a reference book,' grumbled the old violinist, but January knew he was pleased to have the excuse to retire from playing for the professional *danseuses* at Au Mandragore. In his youth the old man had been first violinist of Queen Marie Antoinette's personal orchestra, and he still (he said) had his pride.

Daniel had given January the names of as many of the de Belvoire servants as he could remember from Philippe's references to his childhood. The young man's own valet had followed his master's body back to the family hôtel and from there had presumably been re-absorbed into the Comte's household. 'Very much the old family retainer,' had sighed Daniel. 'He would have slit his own throat before allowing Philippe to stir from the house with so much as a speck of dust on his sleeve, and he looked through me as if I were Banquo's ghost. Philippe told me once the man held that his – Philippe's – bedroom preferences were his own affair, but apparently took him severely to task about being seen around town with a Jew. Extraordinary.'

Thus when the overloaded diligence had deposited them in that trim cobblestoned town, the three investigators knew to take rooms at the Porcelet Ailé in the Rue St-Martin, where Lucien presented himself as the former valet of the Vicomte de Chamarande (whose family had fled the country in 1789 and never returned), accompanied by his daughter and her husband. On any given evening, at least two of the de Belvoire servants made the two-mile walk from Noisette-le-Comte to the Porcelet, and it was a relatively easy matter to lead the conversation from enquiries about the Chamarandes to gossip concerning the de Belvoires.

'A horror, it is,' murmured Bertrille, the chambermaid who assisted Madame de Belvoire's 'dresser' in the repair and embroidery of that lady's clothing. 'Poor madame! She acts so brave, but you look at her eyes and knows she weeps the night through.'

'She won't let that little witch get away with it.' Bertrille's bosom friend from the laundry thumped angrily on the table, at which Ayasha – who had joined the two girls in the corner by the fireplace – refilled both their wine cups. 'You can bet on that.'

January, inconspicuously playing écarté with Lucien at the next table, sorted his cards and watched them over the top of his hand.

'Did she mean to murder him?' inquired Ayasha breathlessly. 'Or was it her husband—'

'Oh, she meant to murder him, all right.' Bertrille nodded grimly, a buxom Venus with a lace cap over her dark curls. 'Liane – that used to be La Ben-Gideon's maid – says as how that woman *hated* Philippe. Not that ordinarily I'd believe one word Liane says, the stuck-up bitch, but she was there after all . . .'

'Madame Ben-Gideon's maid?' Ayasha's startle and stare were perfectly genuine. 'How . . .?'

'Oh, she's working for Madame la Comtesse now.' Bertrille preened herself a little at being the custodian of such information. 'Thieving *gadoue* – helps herself to madame's purse and hints that it's *me* that's taking the money, or poor Giselle, my sister that works in the ironing room . . . Yes, madame hired Liane just as soon as the police realized it was Madame Ben-Gideon that did it. And she's right to say, that it'd go worse for any maid, if she stood up before the *juge d'instruction* and said what she knows. A girl's got to look out for herself.'

'*Yallah!*' exclaimed Ayasha. 'Yet to speak against her mistress . . .'

'Oh, she did it, right enough.' The laundress – Vig was her name – Régenérée Vigeur – nodded, and downed her wine, which Ayasha thoughtfully and immediately refilled.

'That rat dog from the Paris Sûreté – Quicherat – said there was no question she'd done the deed . . . He said he knew it was done with her pistol. Huh!' snorted Bertrille. 'As if a woman of her sort could hold onto a man, even a *pédé* like that, even if she *didn't* have competition . . .'

'Poor Philippe,' murmured Vig. 'So handsome he was, and so sweet . . .'

'A waste of good looks,' added Bertrille. 'That old *tante* Ben-Gideon was the one who led him into buggery in the first place.' This, January knew – from Daniel and Philippe both – was simply not true. 'It should have been him that woman shot, not poor Philippe. Madame says that before Philippe met him, he was as fine a man as any in the nation.'

Ayasha made a shocked noise, and offered in corroboration a completely fictitious anecdote concerning a younger brother (also imaginary) who had been similarly corrupted. 'My cousin Zuliema, who was betrothed to him, swore revenge on the old bugger who did it, but of course her parents kept a close eye on her and married her off to someone else.'

'Exactly!' agreed Bertrille. 'Though myself, I say it serves Marie de Chouvigny right – that's the girl they were trying to make Philippe marry. Nasty spoilt little wretch . . . Now they're trying to make the match with poor Tin-Tin, Philippe's brother. No wonder he disappeared on them!'

'Disappeared?'

'Yes!' The maid rocked back on her bench with delight, and Ayasha topped up her cup again. January struggled not to lean closer to listen. 'I thought I'd piss myself, laughing!'

'Now, honey,' protested Vig, 'you know poor madame is frantic—'

'Madame de Taillefer is the one who's frantic,' giggled Bertrille. 'And her ferret-faced daughter. Oh, look, here's Fleurette and Jeanne . . .' She half-rose, waving to acquaintants – also maidservants, by their dress – who entered arm-in-arm with a couple of crimson-liveried footmen, and Ayasha wasn't able to lead the conversation back to the murdered heir and his absconding brother without appearing obvious about it.

Subsequent gossip, about the town and in the inn the following evening, confirmed these facts. Celestin de Gourgue had gone off to Paris, driving himself in his own English curricle, on the twenty-sixth of July – Monday, the day before the rioting had started. He had still been absent on the evening of the twenty-seventh, when, January estimated, his brother had been killed. Philippe's body had appeared on the barricade sometime before dawn on Thursday morning, the twenty-ninth . . . the same day that young Celestin had returned to Noisette-le-Comte in the afternoon.

News had reached the family of Philippe's death late the same day, and two days later, on the thirty-first, Celestin had evidently hitched up his own horses when the grooms were occupied elsewhere, and had driven away without a word to anyone. He had not returned.

'Got a mistress?' inquired Lucien casually, and the footmen for whom he'd bought a drink laughed.

'Fat chance he'd have to find one, with old père Delabole hanging 'round his neck.'

'If you ask me,' opined the younger footman, Robert, 'his lordship wouldn't be sorry to see it if Celestin *did* have a mistress . . . not while they're tryin' to bring it off with the marquis's daughter, of course. You can't say he would, Serafine,' he added, when his older companion clucked reprovingly. 'You heard his lordship, often an' often, say as how it was a grief to him that Philippe, bein' the heir, favored beef over ewe-lamb. Last time Philippe was home – the older son,' he explained (unnecessarily) to his new acquaintances, 'that just only ten days ago was murdered by the wife of the Jew bugger he'd took up with – last time Philippe was home I thought his lordship was going to murder him himself, shoutin' so's you could hear it clear down in the hall . . .'

'My guess,' provided the older footman, shaking his head, 'is young Tin-Tin can't keep money in his pockets long enough to make it worth any tart's while to *become* his mistress. Goes through the ready like a rat through cheese. Minds what he's told out here, of course, but every time he's in town he comes back with his pockets to let and no idea how it happened, poor fish. His lordship rants about it, but pays up – to get back at madame, I'd say. Philippe was her white-headed boy, and God forbid his lordship should admit to her that his favorite lad is bait for every elbow-shaker in town.'

'My brother,' said Lucien, 'would frequently be obliged to go into hiding – once he even went the length of traveling to Italy, of all places – because the owners of some hell or other had their strongmen out after him because of gaming debts. But I can scarcely see that sort of situation befalling the son of the Comte de Belvoire.'

Young Robert shook his head. 'His lordship said, next time

little Tin-Tin ran himself "up the river Tick", as the English say, he could look out for himself, and God knows what happened in that couple of days when he was home . . .'

'Likelier that he's shamming,' opined Serafine. 'My brother used to do that all the time: "You said you'd throw me out, well, I'll take you at your word and vanish." It was usually enough to bring Papa to heel, for of course Maman would give him no rest til he'd taken Jacques back. Joined the army he did, at last,' he added sadly. 'Died at Waterloo, at Chateau Frichermont, and left his poor wife three months gone with child . . . Hullo!' He turned, as two more men entered the tavern, also in the wine-red livery of the Comtes de Belvoire. 'Old Potato-Nose let you off the chain, then?'

'Gone to Blanquefort.' The shorter of the newcomers, a sharp-faced Gascon, named the nearby country home of the Vicomtes de Beaujeau. 'Not back 'til moonset, most like.'

'And good riddance to the lot of 'em,' sighed the other. 'Lord, what a fuss-budget that lad Brancas is!' He turned toward the serving girl and January, sitting near the hearth listening to Lucien's conversation with Robert and Serafine, barely had time to duck back deeper into the shadows.

The taller, younger lackey in crimson Belvoire livery was Daniel's former footman Laurent.

TEN

During the few days spent in Etamps, the three travelers made it their business also to walk out to the chateau of Noisette-le-Comte, and linger among the coppices of the eponymous hazels long enough to catch glimpses of the household. In addition to the footmen and maids, whose notice they assiduously avoided, January got a good look at the Comte de Belvoire, a powerfully-built man whose nose did indeed resemble a potato, and whose country tweeds couldn't quite disguise the fact that he was running to fat. On the occasion of January's observation, his lordship was shouting at a groom, and when the man protested, lashed him with the riding crop he carried. A little later Lucien pointed out the whole of the holiday party, as the comte assisted the ladies into a varnished crimson landaulet. 'The tall lady in the stripes is Madame la Comtesse,' murmured the violinist. Even at a distance of twenty yards, her resemblance to Philippe was striking. 'That's Madame de Taillefer with her, a connection of hers through the Rochechouarts – dazzling in her youth, I'm told, who'd think it now? The girl in white's Taillefer's daughter—'

'I told you she looked like a ferret,' put in Ayasha, and though January tried to be generous in his judgments of others he had to admit his bride had a point.

'Butterball Senior and Butterball Junior,' the old man continued, 'are the Marquis de Taillefer and his son the Vicomte de Brancas . . . Not going driving, are we, gentlemen? Well, I shouldn't like to be trapped in a vehicle with Mesdames la Marquise et la Comtesse either, not to speak of that whining girl of Taillefer's. She has a voice that can cut glass like a diamond, you know. You could hear her above the din at every ball they attended last season.'

'That was her?' January remembered the voice, at least, but only brief glimpses of the girl's thin back.

'That was her.' Last of all a dark-haired maidservant climbed into the carriage, bobbing curtsies in every direction and with almost acrobatic adeptness, considering she was burdened with a straw basket containing silk fans (January saw her hand one to Madame la Marquise), a straw-wrapped jar (*Wine? Lemonade?*), a book, and three parasols.

'Liane Pichon,' whispered Ayasha. 'Madame Anne's maid.'

'Seems to have done well for herself,' murmured January, observing the quality of the girl's striped satin frock, and the strand of amber beads around her neck. Miss Liane took her seat facing backwards, and Mademoiselle de Taillefer evidently made such a fuss that the servant climbed down and had to be handed up (by a footman) to the seat next to the driver.

'It is true,' he added, as the carriage rolled away, 'that a servant in a position to testify against her mistress could face harassment – or even false accusations of theft – from her mistress's family . . .'

'Bet me La Comtesse offered her two hundred francs a year.'

'To say nothing of young Laurent's salary. A cheap price to pay,' speculated Lucien, 'if one suspects one's younger son of killing his brother. Nothing can bring poor M'sieu Philippe back,' he answered January's troubled look. 'And better to live with suspicion gnawing one's heart than scandal affecting the matrimonial alliances of one's younger children. The police have to guillotine *someone*, you know.'

Discreet enquiries in and around Etamps over the next few days also filled in the list that Daniel had begun, of the de Belvoire properties in Paris and its environs. The old Comte de Belvoire – the current comte's father – having retired to his estate at Gontchâtel, far away from Paris, in 1789 and renounced his title, he had managed to hang onto most of his property until the title was restored to him (for a hefty consideration) by Napoleon. The family owned four houses, two commercial properties, and an inn in Paris itself, and considerable land immediately to the north of the city where gypsum was mined. The fugitive Celestin, January guessed, might have access to any one of these, with or without the knowledge of his family – or a portion of his family.

'You can add the Convent of Notre Dame de Syon to that,' piped up Chatoine, the leader of the orphan gang in January's neighborhood, when, upon their return, a meeting of possible allies was called in Daniel's elegant turquoise-and-gold salon. 'Belvoire's grandpa got hold of their land during the revolution and then handed it back to them free when Old Fatso—' this was the local name for the restored King Louis XVIII, old King Charles's elder brother and predecessor – 'came back. They'd do just about anything for him.'

'Not hide a man on their premises,' objected Armand de la Roche-St-Ouen heatedly.

The little girl took one of Daniel's cigars from her mouth, raised her eyebrows, and stared in haughty surprise at this display of naïveté.

Armand reddened. He was clearly ill-at-ease, though January wasn't certain whether this was because of the company in which he found himself or because he had never approved of his sister's marriage to a Jewish banker's son (and had said so, often and loudly, within Daniel's hearing). 'My aunt is the Mother Superior at Syon. Completely aside from the dishonor of the thing, no patronage on earth would come before her vows. She spent the revolution in La Force prison rather than forswear the supremacy of the Pope. I know at the first hint of trouble last month she locked the convent up tight and took the girls away into the countryside.'

'We might at least have a look at the place,' temporized January. 'Find out if the caretaker there – while the sisters were away – was as faithful to his vows as the mother superior is to hers, and if any of the neighbors noticed anything.'

'What could they have noticed?' Jeannot Charbonnière shook his leonine head. 'The convent's right on Rue St-Martin. The fighting was only a few streets away.'

When January hesitated – Charbonnière was perfectly correct, and what, indeed, could anyone have seen or noticed anywhere in the confusion? – the little girl saluted, and said, 'We'll do our best, chief.'

The tavern Aux Vierges Sages – out in Montmartre near Notre Dame de Lorette – was easy enough to broach: Carnot knew the place and went with his latest sweetheart to make inquiries of the barkeep and hostlers (and the girls who worked the neighborhood). Likewise the two buildings on the Place des Victoires which housed, respectively, a fashionable silk shop and a not-quite-so-fashionable charcuterie, with a score of rental rooms behind and above these establishments. At such places it was always possible to learn about everyone housed under the roof for any length of time, and January didn't expect to learn anything that would advance his search for Celestin de Gourgue.

The houses were different. January and Ayasha went out to look at each. All were in the older parts of the city, all purchased as investments and rented to those made newly affluent by the increased stability of a Europe without war. Lucien went with them, but recognized no one who might have been Celestin in hiding, and January's inquiries among the servants at the neighboring public houses in the evenings – under pretext of searching for a naïve sister who'd been 'run off with by a toff' – in three cases elicited no protestations about any toff staying with the family.

In the fourth case, January, Ayasha, and Lucien all very quickly received the information that the house – which was on Rue Notre Dame des Victoires – had been empty for months.

'And if I'd just murdered my brother,' mused Lucien, as the three made their way back along the Rue St-Martin in the direction of Daniel's house, 'with or without our father's connivance, I should find a vacant house to which my father kept the key a great convenience, even in August.'

'We can't forget,' added Ayasha, and tucked stray curls of her strong dark hair back under her round, working-woman's bonnet, 'the places Belvoire père owns outside the city, either. A farm in Batignolles, the mines and a vineyard in Montmartre—'

'And a lot of neighbors likely to be flapping their gums about any stranger staying there,' the old violinist reminded her.

'Wherever he is,' said January thoughtfully, 'the man has to eat. If he's lying low – if he can't be seen to come and go – someone has to be providing him with food, even if he has plenty of money. He . . .' He turned sharply as they crossed the Rue St-Merci, his consciousness tugged – not for the first time, he realized – by someone or something half-recognized. A jacket or cap in a color he'd seen one too many times before? A figure whose height or bearing or shape touched his memory as familiar? In New Orleans, when he was eight or nine, one of his schoolmates – a boy named Hermes – had been kidnapped when he'd ventured down to the riverfront by himself. His distraught mother never had gotten him back.

'What is it?' asked Ayasha.

January scanned the Rue St-Martin behind them. Carts coming up from the river with hay for the thousands of horses in every mews and stableyard in Paris. Washerwomen bearing baskets of linen on their heads to customers. Water-vendors or peddlers of matches, rags, underwear or English pears; children playing with hoops, a few whores out early for a cup of brandy before starting the evening trade.

'I think we're being followed.'

He saw no more of his shadow, and when Lucien detached himself from the group, ostensibly to chat up an especially pretty shop girl but in fact to circle behind and look for potential trackers, the old man said he saw no one. Still, it was enough to make January postpone his intention of walking down the narrower street that backed the houses of Rue Notre Dame des Victoires – to see if the gate into the garden of number fifteen showed signs of recent use – until after dark. The waning moon rose late, and with most of the lamps still broken from the rioting, the streets were extremely dark. Ayasha followed him a short distance from Daniel's flat, to make sure no one was behind him.

Still he kept listening, glancing back, as he moved along the soot-black faces of the houses across the way, listening to the voices from the dim-lit windows above him. 'Don't you lie to me, I've seen the way you look at the girl . . .' 'Can't something be done? If we lose the shop . . .' 'I can't help you if you won't tell me what's wrong!' In a doorway that smelled as if the entire district used it as a public urinal (most doorways in Paris did) he stopped, and retreated into the shadow, watching. The voices quieted in the windows around him. In the garden across the way, beyond the wall, a nightingale sang its liquid notes.

The clock on St Eustache replied. Midnight.

Not long after that he heard her, the light soft susurration of petticoats – taffeta silk, he thought, remembering Ayasha's construction of such garments – and the heavier whisper of a domino cloak. The houses on his own side of the street cast shadows like ink, but the moon had just cleared their roofs. Movement on the other side of the street. January waited in silence, and she passed so close to him that he could smell the sandalwood of her perfume, and in the dusky masses of her curls could see the glint of diamonds, the moon above her brow, and the glimmer of three stars.

Why her?

His fingers paused, resting on the keys of his piano. The house had grown profoundly still – the Rue Esplanade outside as well. The candle on the corner of the piano had burned nearly to the socket, his mind noted automatically that it must be long after midnight.

I should go to bed.

The night was heavy as steamed blankets. He knew he would not sleep. It felt extraordinary to him, that after nine years he could still walk from one end of Paris to the other in his mind, could still recall the route from the rooms he and Ayasha had shared on the Rue de l'Aube to the market, to Daniel's house, to Notre Dame. As he walked them, at least once a week, sometimes oftener, in dreams.

Looking for some part of me that I left there? And does that part search, in its dreams, for me?

Why her?

The sour stink of piss, rotted cabbage, Paris muck. The glimmer of moonlight on diamonds.

She'd seemed to turn into shadow herself, in the gateway that led to number fifteen's garden. So great had been the stillness in the Rue Notre Dame des Victoires that he'd heard the metallic click of the gate-lock turning over.

He has to be getting his food from somewhere. The woman could have been concealing anything, beneath that all-enveloping cloak.

A quarter-hour passed, by the clock on St-Eustache; then a half-hour. At one end of the street a peddlar passed by, singing softly:

> *Entrez dans la danse,*
> *Voyez comme on danse,*
> *Sautez, dansez,*
> *Embrassez qui vous voudrez.*

Moving soundlessly, tensed to flee at the first whisper of noise, January crossed the street to the garden door.

She'd locked it behind her. January stepped back a few paces, but the wall was high. The garden was sufficiently long, and the house low enough, that he couldn't see whether light shone in its windows or not.

Damn it . . .

He retreated across the street, then took a running start and leaped with all his strength. His arms were long; he caught the top of the wall, pulled himself up, and looking over, got a dim impression of a narrow town garden. A small fountain in the center, dry and filled with leaves. Near the gate what looked like a miniature Chinese pagoda, its porcelain roof besmeared with bird droppings and its walls lost in a tangle of vines.

No lights in the house.

Curtains?

Or did she just go through the house – if she has a key – and out the front door?

He dropped down from the wall and realized a split-second too late that in the act of leaping up to look over the wall he had neglected to keep an eye on the ends of the street behind him. Violent movement in the darkness, men running towards him, how many he couldn't tell. He plunged toward one end of the street and tried to dodge past. A club cracked across his shins and he staggered, a second blow felled him, and a third smote him across the back of the neck when he tried to rise.

He lashed out in the darkness – only one man, he thought, and then a second one, or maybe two, came running up from the other side of the street. A brutal kick took him in the belly and he brought up his arms, protecting his head, as more blows rained on him and darkness closed in.

1839

It was partly recollection of this turn of events, as well as his customary caution about going outside the bounds of the old French Town, that prompted January to take Hannibal with him on his expedition to view Henry Brooke's New Orleans real estate on the following afternoon.

'Somewhere,' he said, as he and Hannibal guided their rented mounts from the shell road along Bayou St John and onto the track beside the smaller waterway, 'there has to be some trace of a reason for Brooke's murder. Some thread that will lead me to the real killer – or at least to evidence that someone had better reason to do away with him than poor Jacquette had.'

'*Quot homines tot sententiae: suo quoique mos,*' agreed the fiddler. 'And unfortunately, at first glance, she seems to have the best of all possible reasons.'

Of the four properties either purchased or negotiated for by Brooke in the two weeks of his residence in New Orleans, Chitimacha was the only one which had ever been actually put to use. The remains of overgrown sugar fields surrounded the house like the castle of La Belle au Bois Dormant, a massive granny knot of cane stalks, palmetto, weeds, and rat nests through which it was abundantly clear nobody had hacked his way in decades.

The overseer's house had burned down years ago, its surviving timber and furnishings looted by whatever trappers lived in the nearby swamps. Weeds and vines choked the few slave cabins – far too few, January guessed, to have housed the bondsmen needed to make the plantation a profitable concern. 'I'm guessing the former owner hauled his cane over to the widow Aury's—' he named the nearest large plantation owner – 'to have it ground and boiled. On a place this small, that's enough to burn up your profits right there, even before that flood ten years ago cut the bayou off from the main river.'

Over the seven years he'd been back, January had learned from Olympe most details about what had happened in and around New Orleans during his absence in France. He recalled clearly her mention of the flood in 1829. It happened all the time, in the high-water months of March and April. The levee would crevasse, the land along the river would be inundated six- or eight-feet deep, and when the waters retreated the big bayous like Gentilly, Metairie and St John might easily have altered their courses. New bayous could appear; old ones would find themselves isolated from the Mississippi by silting. As a child he recalled sitting on the sill of one of the high windows of the sugar mill at Bellefleur Plantation, staring out over floodwaters and watching his parents' cabin drift past.

On another occasion upon which Michie Fourchet had locked the Bellefleur slaves into the sugar house to prevent their escaping in the confusion of the flood, he'd seen a flatboat eighty-feet long – at that time steamboats were barely a rumor in the valley of the Mississippi – surge calmly past the sugar mill with all its crew struggling on the long sweep-oars and cursing fit to shock the Devil in Hell. And indeed, a few hundred feet from the ruins of the Chitimacha house, the much-decayed carcass of a steamboat lay half-aground in the shallow bayou, the faded letters – REL– half-legible under a snarl of honeysuckle and wild grapevine on its bow.

'How much did he pay for this – um – demi-paradise?' Hannibal turned in the saddle of his rented horse to survey the desolation.

'Eight thousand, according to Shaw, in three installments. And it would take three times that at least,' he added, seeing his friend's eyebrows rocket up, 'to put it into production, not even counting the cost of slaves.'

'Obviously the previous owner wanted to get rid of the place, and no wonder. Still, it's a curious thing to buy . . .'

'It's an absurd thing to buy.' January swung down from his own mount, a very large and sturdy riding-mule that Maggie Valentine at the livery – for whom he had done favors in the past – let him take for half price, given the predilection of some members of the white community to take offense at the sight of a black man on a horse. 'Particularly for a man who is already tangled up with some kind of skullduggery at the British Consulate. So let's see if we can find whatever it was that made the property worth twenty-five hundred dollars out of pocket.'

January had brought a cane knife – one of several weapons he kept cached unobtrusively around his house – and with that and two snake-sticks, he and the fiddler slashed and prodded their way gingerly up to what remained of the house. Like all plantation houses in bayou country, it stood on six-foot brick piers, the storage rooms beneath now choked with swamp-laurel, and all its floor timbers perilously rotted. As they moved from room to room, January saw little that would have made the place worth buying and nothing out of the ordinary: it had been stripped of the little furniture it had once contained, and such movables as doors, shutters, and window glass had long since been carried away. A square hole in the wall of what had been the owner's bedroom showed where a safe had once been. Even the tiles that had been laid before the fireplaces had been prised up and taken.

Systematically, he and Hannibal went through the dilapidated slave cabins, the site of the overseer's house, and even the non-flooded portions of the ruined steamboat, hung over with foliage, alive with mosquitoes and swimming with copperheads.

'Whatever he was doing,' said the fiddler, thrashing through a tangled curtain of honeysuckle and back out to the slanted planks of the deck, 'it can't have had anything to do with what's actually here. So what can a man do with land like this? Besides sell it to some other fool?'

January murmured, 'What indeed?'

I'm missing something . . .

He felt almost as if he were winding a clock whose inner gearwheels were missing teeth. A sense of things not connecting.

He climbed to the highest point of the steamboat deck, looked back toward the ruined house. Something brown – a deer? – moved in the trees beyond; Hannibal flinched, and slashed for the thousandth time as mosquitoes whined around their faces. 'Let's get out of here,' he said. '"The murmurous haunt of flies on summer eves . . ." Clearly Mr Shelley had never visited the tropics. Nothing is worth being eaten alive in this fashion.'

January slapped at the thin droning in his ear and had to agree.

But his mind went back to that . . . Had it been a deer? It hadn't moved like one.

The parcel of land that Brooke had purchased from the Labarres was even less productive of any hint as to what the Englishman – *or Irishman,* reflected January – had in mind. It lay far out along Bayou St John, halfway to the lake and several miles from the cluster of handsome houses that marked the only land along the bayou high enough not to flood repeatedly. The land here lay too low even for a sugar crop, let alone building: Shaw hadn't been exaggerating when he'd described it as being half under water. An occasional houseboat marked the dwelling of squatters or fishermen. Cypress knees jutted from stagnant pools, and clouds of mosquitoes whined in the dark-green shelter of oaks curtained with gray moss.

Before descending from the road he unpacked the veils of mosquito netting he'd brought from home, and pinned it around the brim of his shallow-crowned hat. Even Olympe's 'bug-grease' wasn't going to be much of a deterrent here.

'Is there anything there at all?' The fiddler peered nervously into the humming gloom beneath the trees, and rubbed a second application of 'bug-grease' on his face. 'Good Lord, what does your sister put into this? "Pernicious weed, whose scent the fair annoys".'

'Asafetida, cloves, catnip and wormwood.' January took the little pot from him, and handed him the other piece of gauze. 'And dead fish, from the smell of it. There isn't so much as a hog pen on the property,' he added, as he tied horse and mule to a sapling close to the narrow track of the Bayou Road. 'But I think we have to look around.'

'*Moriamur et in media arma ruamus*,' sighed Hannibal, and tucked his shirt cuffs into the cuffs of his gloves.

They skirted the standing water where they could, and once – in addition to the omnipresent snakes – January saw a five-foot alligator basking on a higher hillock of ground. But the land which Henry Brooke had purchased contained nothing visibly notable. Among the trees the heat was suffocating, and with the approach of the inevitable afternoon thunderstorm the frogs and cicadas set up their steady, persistent chorus. The long, narrow plot – some two hundred feet along the bayou and nearly a half-mile back into the woods – contained mostly oaks and cypress, and in one place an almost-impassable thicket of palmetto: 'But there isn't even enough land here to make it worth anyone's while to log it,' Hannibal protested, as they waded their way back to the road. 'I know times are hard, but land holds its value . . . any land but this, I suppose. And any land a French Creole family lets go of *has* to be worthless. Yet you tell me Brooke rode out to look at the place before he put up in his Bank of England stocks.'

'It's not the land.' January swung into the saddle again. 'It's something else. Something about *owning* land . . .'

Bags of coin, boxes of rubies . . . Our Lord with his body made of pearl . . .

'You couldn't even bury treasure on land like this,' said the fiddler, as they reined away back toward town. 'You couldn't dig a hole without it filling with water. Look at the size of the cypress knees, and the thickness of the brush – it must have been this wet for decades. You couldn't even run cows on it.'

'How many decades?' wondered January. 'And who held the land grant originally? Was Chitimacha part of the same grant? Or those other parcels Brooke was looking at?' He frowned, as thunder growled to the north, coming down fast.

'And how would he have found out about . . . whatever it was?'

January shook his head. 'There's a lot of questions,' he murmured, 'about Mr Brooke and where he went, and what he did, in the years since he stopped being Gerry O'Dwyer.'

ELEVEN

The rain caught them just short of the first houses, where the shell road from town joined the Bayou Road that led to the lake. Partly from the knowledge that his friend would not survive a bout of pneumonia, and partly from concern about being that close to a large body of water during a lightning storm, January took refuge in the stable yard of a house belonging to the banker Hubert Granville, for whom – as for the owner of Valentine's livery – he had done services in the past. Granville wasn't at home – the Bank of Louisiana had recently re-opened its doors under another name – but his coachman Marcellus knew January well, and put up the two rental steeds under the abat-vent that protected the front of the stable from the rain.

'Myself, I'd take old Voltaire here over any horse in the city,' remarked the coachman, slapping the riding-mule's neck companionably as he loosened the cinches. 'My apologies, Roux,' he added, addressing Hannibal's gelding. Marcellus was on a first-name basis with every member of the *genus equs* in Orleans Parish. 'But you know it's true. Can I fetch you some beer, Ben? I'm sure Claire—' Claire was the Granville cook – 'will draw us a couple, seein' as she got a soft spot in her heart for you.' Claire was sixty-two years old and it had never been proved she *had* a heart, but Olympe had taken a curse off her kitchen the previous year and the old cook would return any favor to Olympe's family that was asked.

'Tell her I would take it mighty kindly of her.'

'Get you some lemonade, Hannibal?'

'I will sing songs of undying love beneath the beautiful Claire's window,' responded the fiddler, 'if she, and you, would be so kind.'

Marcellus laughed, and came back not only with beer and lemonade, but with Claire herself: it was mid-afternoon, pouring down rain, and evidently Michie Granville was having dinner in town. 'Lookin' at Miz Valentine's boys there,' he added, nodding toward the two steeds as he and Claire, January and Hannibal took seats on the rough bench beneath the abat-vent opposite them, 'reminds me, Ben: that little maid over to the Marigny place, Savannah, tells me you lookin' for a blonde-headed Englishman in a green coat, supposed to got himself killed Saturday night? I think I mighta seen him out here that evenin'.'

'Calling on Michie Granville?' *A banker*, he thought. 'Six-feet tall, bukra duds, one of those new silk-plush hats—'

'Not here on Michie Granville.' The groom sipped his tin cup of weak 'small' beer. 'An' I just got a look at him as he's headin' the other way along the road.'

'When you shoulda been payin' mind to your own work,' groused Claire, who never let a remark go unchallenged. 'What you messin' round lookin' for dead white men anyways, Ben? Not your business.'

January shook his head, and spread his hands in a gesture of resignation. 'Olympe asked me to help out,' he said. 'I owe her too much not to.'

Claire said 'Hmph,' and turned her attention toward the bayou, visible, like a sheet of hammered silver, through the half-open gate of the stable yard. 'Them idiots out there gonna get hit by lightnin', sure as gun's iron,' she added, as if she personally looked forward to the spectacle. And indeed, unlike January, there were at least a dozen pirogue and keel-boat crews within sight who clearly didn't know or didn't care that bodies of water would draw bolts of electricity in a storm. A little group of riders went past the gate, unshaven Americans from the backwoods of Kentucky, by the look of them, soaking wet themselves but cherishing their rifles in long bundles of oilskin slickers.

Rose, January guessed, would have calculated the relative likelihood of each 'Kaintuck' being hit: the leading man in the brown rawhide jacket, who was the tallest, or the slouched woman riding *à l'Amazone* closest to the water itself.

He turned back to Marcellus. 'But you're pretty sure about the green coat, and the blonde hair?' He didn't ask, Could you swear to that?, because the testimony of a slave was unacceptable in court. Even that of a free black wouldn't be legal, if the culprit was white.

'Pretty sure,' agreed the coachman, nodding. 'Seein' old Voltaire reminded me, 'cause it was Tyrell Mulvaney that brought him in his cab, Tyrell drivin' mules, not horses – which to my way of thinkin' makes a lot more sense, mules bein' stronger an' a heap smarter. My apologies, Roux,' he added again, with a friendly wave at the gelding. 'But you do know that's true. Surer-footed, too. Why, a horse'll eat himself into a colic or drink water 'til he's sick, but . . .'

There followed five minutes of comparison between the equine breeds and another five of headshaking over why anyone would choose a horse for any sort of work just because they were slicker and 'prancier' and didn't have long ears – what was wrong with long ears anyways?

January inquired, did Tyrell Mulvaney get less custom by driving mules? And so gently led the conversation back to Saturday evening.

'I didn't see where he went to,' apologized Marcellus. 'I was drivin' Mr Granville out to visit one of his lady friends – Mrs Granville bein' up visitin' her kin up North – an' I waved to Tyrell as we passed, him goin' the other way. 'Bout the time we's crossin' over Bayou Gentilly Tyrell comes passin' us, goin' at a good trot back to town, so he musta dropped your Englishman – if it *was* your Englishman – someplace along between the bayou bridge and the edge of the woods there where that little Bayou Fortin runs into it, 'cause there's no houses further along than that.'

'Thank you.' January made a mental note to track down Tyrell Mulvaney, who worked out of the cab ranks at the foot of the Place d'Armes near the levee. 'You wouldn't happen to have heard anything about Juju Filoux, would you?'

'Heard anythin' other than that he's the most worthless piece of Original Sin that ever shamed his mother?' retorted Claire.

'About where he might be. Or who he might be with?'

'Since that good-for-nothing whore Lallie Gardinier threw him out, I doubt there's a soul in the town that'll believe his lies or put up with his thievin'.'

The catalog of Uncle Juju's enormities – unaccompanied by anything in the way of useful information as to his possible whereabouts – Marcellus's horse-lore and January's account of Rose's health occupied a pleasant hour of the afternoon, until the rain lightened and the thunder grumbled its way out over the lake.

With many thanks and promises to play at the festivities that would mark the end of next December's sugar harvest, January tightened up the girths on Voltaire and Roux, and he and Hannibal proceeded on their way along Bayou St John, as more and more boats appeared on the water and more passersby – foot and horse – on the shell road. January didn't want to call attention to his researches by riding back the way he'd come – the way the cab driver Tyrell Mulvaney had been heading with his fare a week ago Saturday night – but he turned in his saddle, and counted the houses that lay along the bayou in that direction.

This point – where the bayou dog-legged just beyond the half-constructed suburb of Pontchartrain – was the only place along the waterway where the ground was solid enough – and high enough – to support houses. There were about two dozen of them, counting both sides of the stream. Handsome places, some in the old Creole style and others newer and American, all surrounded by trees and by their own grounds. January had taught piano lessons to the children in three of them, though he knew the Santerre family had moved from New Orleans when the banks had collapsed and it was in the back of his mind that the Labranches had, too. He ticked off in his recollection the names of the inhabitants of the others. People he'd never met for the most part – French or Creole French or Creole Spanish, or some like the Champsverts who'd started out as Germans, several generations ago . . .

Which of them, he wondered, had land to sell?

Or information to buy?

'Whoever Brooke went calling on,' remarked Hannibal, 'you're going to have your work cut out for you, if they did in fact put quietus to the man. You know no jury in the state is going to convict a white man – or woman – when they have a perfectly good black *cocotte* to hang instead.'

January glanced back at him, brows raised in question at the second object of that sentence, and Hannibal added, 'The fact that Brooke – if he *was* this O'Dwyer scoundrel of yours – or even if he wasn't – had a *librée* mistress doesn't mean he wasn't also committing adultery with half the females in the parish as well, you know. And the fact that he was working for Her Majesty back in England may have nothing to do with some outraged husband putting a hole in him – and I speak here as a man with considerable experience of outraged husbands.'

January said, 'Hmn . . .'

In either case, most of the people who lived along the bayou had access to boats of one kind or another. Saturday night the moon had risen late, and had been on the wane. A man could have taken a flat-bottomed pirogue at dead of night and nobody would be the wiser.

A dozen yards past the Granville place the bayou jogged briefly toward town, and at the first curve the smaller Bayou Metairie joined it from the west. January turned Voltaire's head onto the track that skirted the lesser water, along a levee of barely three feet in height. As he did so he pulled from his pocket the sketched map Shaw had given him, marking the approximate location of the parcels of land whose owners Brooke had been 'talking to'. The Allard parcel lay about two miles from Bayou St John, the Aury parcel, almost five. The heat had returned, more stifling than before, and the ragged monochrome green of the swamp-forest closed in around them.

'As before,' remarked Hannibal, 'I can see why the owners would contemplate selling, but what on earth would possess anyone in their senses to buy?'

'That,' said January, nudging Voltaire to a trot, 'is what I hope to learn. Or to learn at least that there is nothing to learn.'

But if any clue could be gleaned from contemplation of the few sodden arpents of bayou land – squishy with mud and humming with mosquitoes as the sun declined – it was beyond January's ability to interpret. Now and then he smelled smoke from the dwelling of some squatter or swamp-trapper, and an occasional cow or pig could be seen foraging among the tangles of hackberry and elephant-ear. For the most part, there was no sign of human habitation at all, nor of any attempt to either farm or log this land.

'If he was buying land to bury gold on,' said Hannibal, after they had criss-crossed the portion of forest that January calculated – by the landmarks listed – to belong to the Widow Aury, 'where's the gold now? Any serious quantity of it isn't something you carry in your pockets, you know. Surely Madame Filoux would have mentioned if Brooke had had shovels or barrows on the premises? Other than the fatal handcart she's supposed to have lugged him in, but I can't really see anyone carting a corpse across Rampart Street to the basin at three in the morning unseen by *somebody*, though whether they'd notice – or care – is another matter entirely. Why else – other than the obvious reasons – take up with a woman who had a house of her own?'

January shook his head.

When the fiddler started to speak again he held up his hand for silence, listening.

For the second time in fifteen minutes – his mind had registered it the first time and he'd merely thought, fox – January heard the flurrying burst of startled birds flying out of underbrush.

And from the same direction, he thought. Between them and the road.

He remembered the flicker of brown in the woods of Chitimacha . . .

Damn it.

Shadows were gathering in the green dimness beneath the trees. It would be growing dark by the time they reached town.

Up until a few years ago, runaway slaves had had villages here in the swampy lands along the bayous beyond the back of town. But according to Olympe, the last of them had disappeared shortly after the leader of the runaways, Cut-Arm, had been captured and hanged. Single runaways still camped where they could fish in the bayous, hunt in the woods, but they'd flee from riders as the birds fled . . .

And there was no earthly reason for anyone else to be out this far from town with evening coming on.

Which means that whoever scared those birds, is here because he's following us.

He murmured, 'Let's get out of here.'

At least, reflected January as they turned their mounts' heads back toward the road, *I've got a white man with me who can claim I'm his property . . .*

1830

When he'd been ambushed in Paris – on the trail of the lady with the moon and three stars in her hair, who might or might not have known the whereabouts of Philippe de la Marche's real killer – this had not been the case. The knowledge that he was a free man and couldn't be kidnapped and sold into slavery had been very little comfort when he was being clubbed and kicked into semi-consciousness on the slimy cobblestones of Paris.

He'd thought on that occasion that they were going to kill him, and knew, through a groggy haze of pain, that they could easily do so. But they dragged him a short distance along the narrow street – there were three of them, he estimated cloudily – and shoved him into a carriage of some sort. The floorboards stank of Paris mud and tobacco smoke, and the vehicle rocked and swayed wildly as it clattered at a gallop over the cobblestones. He didn't lose consciousness, but had been sufficiently stunned to have only the dimmest notion of how long they drove; every turn and jolt slammed him into the boots of the men sitting above him, and he didn't dare let them know he was conscious by bracing to save himself. The carriage tilted wildly as it rounded a corner, one of the men yelled, 'Now!' and the door flew open. January was thrust out, trying to roll as he hit first the paving stones, then the stone corner of a gateway.

He struggled to rise but collapsed, his nose full of his own blood and his body one mass of pain. *Though not*, he thought, *as bad as being beaten by Michie Fourchet when he'd had a couple of drinks in him . . .*

Far off he heard men shouting. Iron gates squealed – *they must have flung me out in a doorway somewhere* – and strong arms got him to his feet. Steps, and then lamplight. 'Fetch some water, Jacques—'

January wiped the blood from his eyes as he was helped to a bench indoors. A gate lodge, such as a porter or concierge would sit in during the day, and an elderly man in shirtsleeves leaning over him in the greasy orange glow of an oil lamp. 'You all right, m'sieu? Can you see me? You see one finger here, or two?'

'One,' January managed to say, and a tall young man wearing a footman's crimson livery breeches came in with a tin cup of water. *At least I don't have a concussion . . .*

'Bandits!' exclaimed the elderly concierge in a scandalized voice. 'Robbers! Since the riots they think they own the night! And this "King of the French", pah! What does he do about it, eh? Why, in the days of Napoleon, a girl could have walked from Marseilles to Calais carrying a bag of money, and no one would have—'

'What is this, Etienne?' The gold light of a half-dozen candles brightened the open archway that led from the lodge to the courtyard. Looking around, January saw the Comte de Belvoire with a candelabra in his hand. 'Who is this man?'

The concierge bowed. January, conscious that the comte was his host (and it was probably his brandy that someone had considerately mixed with the water in the tin cup he'd been offered), got to his feet, staggered, and fell back onto the bench. 'He was hurled from a speeding carriage into our gateway, monsieur,' the footman Jacques explained.

Another candelabra behind de Belvoire's shoulder, and a man's cultivated voice inquired from the darkness, 'He isn't one of yours, is he, Balthasar? Or one of those others you hired to find Celestin?'

'Gran-Polisson never said he had Africans working for him . . .'

January recognized the name of a man whom Chatoine had spoken of as running one of the gangs that stole goods from the quais. In hard times like this, when even such little work as was available in the city was disrupted, of course the wharf gangs, and the crews of pickpockets and thieves that haunted the dreary alleyways of districts like St-Antoine, would hire out their services to whoever cared to pay them.

To Louis-Balthasar de Gourgue, Comte de Belvoire, certainly. *And to his son?*

But if Belvoire hired them to find Celestin . . .

'My name is Benjamin Janvier, monsieur.' January struggled to his feet again, and spoke in the excellent French he'd been taught at the Academy de St-Louis after his mother had attained her freedom. In his torn and filthy clothes, his face swollen by bruises, he was well aware that upper-class French was his quickest means of proving to Philippe de la Marche's father that he wasn't some brawling sailor who'd been beaten up on a spree.

'Thank you – thank you all . . .' He turned and executed a second bow to Etienne and Jacques, before returning his gaze to Belvoire. 'You have most certainly saved my life. I am a musician – you may ask anyone at court, from the Comte de Noailles to

Monsieur de Polignac—' he named his two most socially prominent employers – 'and they will assure you of my bona fides.'

Not that the Comte de Noailles – or any other nobleman – ever actually met face to face the musicians he hired to play at his entertainments: such things were done by a nobleman's steward. But if it came down to cases, January knew that his height and his striking appearance would guarantee that at least some of his employers could vouch for him. Besides, in the world of the court – as the Puss in Boots of legend could have attested – mention of a socially elite lord's name was usually enough. The second constellation of candle flame bobbed in the archway and January recognized the man who peeked in over de Belvoire's shoulder as Lucien Imbolt's Butterball Senior: the Marquis de Taillefer.

Whose daughter Philippe had left for the sweeter charms of Daniel's company.

That same daughter whom he now hoped to wed to Philippe's younger brother, the new-minted and now missing heir, Celestin.

A number of thoughts fell together in his mind.

'They set upon me in the Rue des Trois-Maries,' he said, 'where I had been playing for the christening party of a friend's new son. Men are desperate,' he added gloomily, shaking his head, 'if they think a man such as myself, at such a season of the year, would have more than a few sous on his person. One would think that an honest man could walk about Paris in relative safety—'

This was enough to set Etienne – and both the comte and the marquis – off on the subject of the new king's disruption of the Paris police force, and the shortcomings of the new regime in general ('Factory owners and jumped-up nobodies – what do they know of the administration of the realm?'). In the ensuing flood of indignation, the issue of why January's attackers had thrown him into the Comte de Belvoire's courtyard, with all the courtyards in Paris to choose from, disappeared without a trace.

TWELVE

'Just because Belvoire has hired men to look for Brother Tin-Tin,' said January, two hours later as Freytag – not a hair out of place – handed him a small cup of very black coffee in Daniel's impeccable Louis XV library, 'doesn't mean he didn't have a hand in Tin-Tin murdering Philippe – if it *was* in fact Celestin who murdered his brother.' The side of his mouth had begun to swell painfully but he didn't care. The coffee was like new life in his veins. 'Or that, if he didn't approve of or plan such a killing, he wouldn't nevertheless shelter an heir who'll . . .' He bit off the words, and his thought.

Daniel said nothing for a time. In the lamplight he looked as if he'd aged ten years, or walked a very long distance alone.

At last he looked up from the inky deeps of his own cup, and said, 'Who'll give him grandchildren?'

Freytag set down the tray on the library table, and January saw the worried glance the valet gave his master as he faded silently into the darkness of the silent house. 'Who won't disgrace the family with scandal?' In Daniel's quiet voice January read the fear that he had lived with for three weeks now: that it was his flamboyant *affaire* with the young nobleman which had triggered the events leading to the young man's death. His 'corruption' of his friend, which had stood in the way of the orderly succession of property and power.

'Belvoire should give himself airs about scandal,' sniffed Ayasha. She leaned from her seat in the window, which stood open to the gluey night, and held a fragment of sweet cake coaxingly out to Musette. 'His great-grandfather kept a harem of young girls in a house outside of Vincennes that would have made a Tunisian pimp blush.' Like the valet, Ayasha looked not a whit the worse for the fact that it was now close to dawn. She'd patched and stitched January's cuts when he'd made his way back to the Rue de l'Aube, and had agreed at once with his suggestion that they proceed immediately to Daniel's rather than wait until daylight: *'If you lie down now you'll be so stiff you won't be able to move. And you know Daniel will still be awake.'*

She'd been right, of course. Their friend had been reading in his library, like an enormous peacock in a dressing gown of Oriental magnificence – and even sitting still long enough to drink a cup of coffee (*did Freytag ever sleep?*) and outline the events that had befallen him since he'd taken up his vigil in the Rue Notre Dame des Victoires, January could feel every bruised muscle of his torso and limbs freezing up hard. The walk home would be agony.

'The men could have been following the girl,' he said after a time. 'They could be her relatives or friends. Or they could have been hired by Celestin—'

'Or by Celestin's creditors.' With a motion of his heavy shoulders, like a man temporarily setting a burden aside, Daniel raised his head. The desk behind him, January saw, was littered, not with the medieval and Turkish jewels that were the delight of his idle hours, but with letters in Anne's clear, rounded hand. 'From what Philippe told me about the rows between Tin-Tin and their father, the boy was forever coming back from Paris pleading for money to cover his debts. He must owe every gambling-hell in town. The local brotherhood of the galloping bones will have greeted his elevation to the status of heir with stately pavanes of delight. They wouldn't welcome his being guillotined – and they would have been in a good position to help him move the body to wherever in Paris he chose.'

'Bravos in the pay of gamblers would have killed me,' pointed out January.

'And you were being followed,' added Ayasha, 'this afternoon . . . yesterday afternoon,' she corrected herself, with a glance at the windows. 'I saw no one tonight, but that doesn't mean they didn't find you later. Or that they weren't waiting for you in the Rue Notre Dame – maybe to see if you'd find what they hadn't been able to.'

January was silent for a time. 'I saw them first – or thought I saw them,' he said slowly, 'sometime after we left the Place des Victoires. If someone heard our enquiries and got word to Celestin – or Madame la Comtesse – they had plenty of time to start watching out for us. I'm not exactly hard to miss. Whoever it was I encountered tonight,' he added, gingerly touching the back of his head where a knot the size of a quail egg was developing, 'had enough money to hire a carriage, and knew on whose doorstep to throw me.'

'Benjamin, I am . . .' Daniel stretched out a hand to January as if in supplication, then turned away. 'I call you my friend, and nearly get you killed—'

January waved the words aside. 'We didn't know,' he said, and added, 'we still don't know.'

'They could have killed you,' persisted Daniel, tears of remorse flooding his tired eyes. 'Easily. And they may next time. I couldn't stand . . .' He broke off, turned his face aside.

I couldn't stand to be responsible for another friend's death . . .

Musette whined gently at his feet, and he lifted her to his lap, staring almost sightlessly into the distance.

'If you go there again . . .'

'We may not need to.' January reached across to the desk – the muscles in his back cramping like the pincers of the Inquisition at his movement – and drew to himself a sheet of notepaper and a pencil. 'Look at this. Does this look like any work you're familiar with, my nightingale?'

Ayasha came to look over his shoulder at the sketch of the diamond moon and three stars. 'I haven't seen any jeweler's work,' January said, 'that makes the moon that thin, or the stars four-pointed like that—'

'The Vicomtesse d'Orles has a necklace with stars of that design. She wore it to a fitting.'

'*Darling!*' protested Daniel in horror. 'In the *afternoon*?'

'She wanted to make sure the dress matched the jewels.'

'Fiddlesticks! I'll wager she wanted to impress whoever it was she was with – who was she with?'

'Madame Bovinne, the wife of that fellow who makes boots for the army.'

'What did I tell you? The jeweler is Reuben Gemier,' Daniel added, leaning around her shoulder. 'His shop is in the Palais Royale – D'Orles seldom buys from anyone else. Gemier's an official in my father's synagogue, his work's been pointed out to me a hundred times. And you're quite right, he does make the moon like that.'

'Very good.' Ayasha finished off the last sweet biscuit, and the bitter dregs of her coffee. 'He'll open up shop in . . .' She regarded the gray light of the window with a calculating eye.

'He isn't going to go telling anyone the names of his customers,' Daniel warned. 'Particularly since so many of them aren't ladies of the court. He lives in terror that one of his court customers will encounter one of his demi-mondaines in the street . . .'

''amaq.' Ayasha gave him a pat on the shoulder and a brilliant grin. 'Foolish one. I'm going to ask the assistant at his shop, of course – on behalf of my mistress.' Her wave seemed to conjure this fictitious lady from the shadow and candle-gleam. 'Who will pay *anything* to learn if her husband has purchased such a moon and three stars for some trashy nymph of the pavement—'

Daniel broke into a tired smile in return, and he took her hand and kissed it. 'Beautiful nightingale,' he declared, producing a roll of banknotes from his dressing-gown pocket and tucking it into her hand, 'so will I.'

1839

'They still behind us?' January glanced around him at as much of the swampy woods as he could without visibly turning in the saddle. Hannibal, under cover of a fit of coughing, dug a hand-kerchief and what looked suspiciously like a small palm-mirror – half the size of a silver dollar, such as gamblers sometimes used to pick up signals from confederates – from the pocket of his dilapidated coat.

'Well, may crows devour him,' said the fiddler after a moment, following a second – less convincing – cough that brought the palmed mirror close to his eyes. 'I doubt I could see a fire-breathing dragon at this distance and in this light. How far are we from town?'

'Four miles back to Bayou St John. Their horses can't be any fresher than our own.'

'*Solvitur ambulando*,' agreed Hannibal, and delivered a stout kick to Roux's ribs. 'Or *cursatio*, as the case may be.'

Though no pursuing horsemen galloped up onto the road to follow them into town – and given the marshy terrain, January was fairly certain that even Voltaire and Roux could outrun the hottest-blooded thoroughbred in Kentucky under those conditions – January was careful not to return to his home. He repaired instead to Hannibal's current lodging, which was in the attic of the Broadhorn saloon at the back of town not far from the basin, a district known as the Swamp for moral as well as topographical reasons. While the proprietress, a heavily-built, bulldog-faced woman named Kentucky Williams, greeted Hannibal in a fashion that made it plain that he was expected in her chamber after closing time, January stepped diffidently to the rear door of the barroom and signed to one of the men who worked inside. He would, of course, have risked a beating every bit as bad as the one he'd gotten in Paris for venturing into territory hallowed to white men.

'Any chance I could get a couple of notes taken into town?' he asked, in the German that was the middle-aged 'bar-boy's' native language, and produced the last of his cash.

Conrad hesitated, but Mrs Williams, one beefy arm around Hannibal's shoulders, called out, 'Yeah, go ahead, we ain't that busy yet.' January scribbled a message on a notebook page to Rose, warning her to take Baby John, Zizi-Marie, and Gabriel, leave the house at once and take shelter with Olympe, and another to Lieutenant Shaw.

'If Olympe is right,' he said, as he and Hannibal climbed the rickety outside stair to the gable window – the attic's only means of ingress, 'and there's gold involved, it looks like somebody besides Brooke was interested in it.'

'*If* there's gold involved.' Like a skeleton in his frayed linen shirtsleeves, Hannibal routed around in the shabby crates that ranged along one side of the low rafters and unearthed half a dozen candle-ends, the attic being nearly dark at this hour. 'You only have Olympe's word about the gold – or the word of whatever it is that lives in that black bottle of hers.'

'Do you disbelieve her?'

'Gods, no! Any idea who that was that followed us?' He lighted the candles, adjusted the broken chunk of shaving mirror balanced on another crate, and dipped his razor in the nearest rain bucket.

'I suspect it was the men who passed us on the shell road,' said January slowly. 'Americans – Kaintucks – filibusters, they looked like.' He used the local term for American freebooters who took advantage of the current political upheavals in the Caribbean to organize raiding parties to foreign soil, secure in the knowledge that the governments of Mexico, Nicaragua, New Grenada or Spanish Cuba were too disorganized and weak to retaliate. 'I could be wrong. And anyone can hire river pirates or brawlers anywhere in town, for any purpose.'

'*Anyone* being perhaps Sir John Oldmixton himself?'

Through the unglazed opening in the wall – which served the purpose of both door and window – voices drifted up from the saloon and the yard. A man shouted perdition to all goat-fucking Irish; a woman yelled, 'You give that back, you bony-assed bitch!' Movement on the floor beside him drew January's attention and he used his notebook to swat a roach the size of a baby mouse: the attic was in a sort of annex over the Broadhorn's kitchen, and though blessed with enough heat in the winter months to keep Hannibal from freezing, it was unspeakable in the summer months.

January had slept in worse places.

'If his murder had anything to do with the papers he was carrying,' he said slowly, 'or with Chitimacha Plantation, or the gold that Olympe saw in her vision. I didn't know Gerry O'Dwyer well,' he went on. 'For all I know, he may have had a good reason not to come back to Paris when the fighting was over, in the summer of 1830. He may not even have known my friend's wife was accused of a crime of which he could have cleared her. In fact, he may have sent her a message, either then or later, that was never delivered. But someone killed him. And finding out who he knew in New Orleans will lead us somewhere – and with luck,' he finished grimly, 'it'll do so before an innocent woman is hanged because she can't prove she was innocently asleep.'

A hundred dollars. January stared out past the flicker of candle-light in the stifling attic, listening to the last of the Broadhorn's customers either staggering on their way down Perdidio Street or copulating with the four whores who had cribs on the other side of the yard. The last of the evening, to judge by the quiet in the yard itself. Hannibal had gone downstairs at about ten to play poker for the house, after helping January piece together the beginnings of a rough list of who they knew who lived out on Bayou St John – 'Although it's perfectly possible,' pointed out the fiddler, 'that Brooke was simply meeting someone out there because he'd rather not do so in town. It may be that he was being followed as well.'

A hundred dollars and 'papers'. And presumably a large sum in Bank of England stock.

Was whatever Oldmixton could tell him worth being drawn into whatever scheme the spymaster had going? For that matter, would Oldmixton tell him the truth? Had he told him the truth about anything so far?

He propped himself on his elbows on Hannibal's low pallet bed, and tried to concentrate on the fiddler's well-worn copy of *As You Like It*. But the tale of brothers seeking the lives of their brothers, of mismatched lovers pursuing one another and hanging love notes on trees, turned his mind back to Paris again. When he slept, he dreamed of the prison of Saint-Lazare, and of Anne, gray-faced and shivering with terror.

1830

'The swine!' cried Armand, as January and Daniel were ushered into the cell, the afternoon following January's adventure in the Rue Notre Dame des Victoires. 'The blackguards, to treat a lady this way! Filthy *san-culottes*! I think they revel in insulting the daughter of our house!'

'Are you all right?' Daniel dumped the food they'd bought on the way to the prison – bread, cheese, fresh peaches and figs and a bottle of pale wine – on the end of the bed, strode to the window and caught Anne's shoulders between his hands.

Her glance had gone past him to January, and she exclaimed, 'Are you all right, Ben? What . . .?'

'Just bruises.' January crossed the cell to take the young woman's other hand.

Armand took another look at him and yelped with shock. 'Did someone attack you?'

January repressed a sarcastic reply, and answered, 'I tried to get a look at one of Belvoire's houses on the Rue Notre Dame des Victoires. Someone followed me, and I was beaten up and dumped in the gateway of Belvoire's hôtel. Obviously, somebody thought I'd been sent by the comte—'

'The blackguard!' Tears of frustration and rage swam in Armand's wide, blue eyes.

That morning, while Ayasha pursued her enquiries at the shop of M'sieu Gemier, January and Daniel had returned to the Rue Notre Dame for another look over the garden gate, an expedition which had yielded them nothing beyond the information that the house – or more probably the garden – was being used as accommodation address by the lady with the moon and stars in her hair. All around the miniature pagoda beside the overgrown path, fragments of trash and birds' nests were littered, as if scraped out of the tiny structure by someone dragging something forth. As far as January could tell (standing on Daniel's back, this time, to look over the wall) the nesting material didn't look weathered or widely scattered, as it would have been had it lain there even a few days.

The house, when they'd gone around the front for a better look at it, was shuttered up tight, and the neighborhood children affirmed (for a consideration) that it had been so for many months.

('Fat lot of good any of this does us,' had groused Daniel. 'After last night they'd be fools if they used this place again.')

Still holding Anne's hand, he now guided her to the room's single chair, and January poured out a glass of wine.

'What's happened?'

Anne shook her head, unable to speak, and Armand blurted in fury, 'That swine, that . . . that *animal* Quicherat – the man from the Sûreté – has been implying that Anne set some kind of ambush for de la Marche. Followed him, or lay in wait for him . . .' He shook his head violently, trembling all over. 'It's that hag of a wife of Belvoire's! That hag wife, and her powerful friends . . . *and* that bastard Taillefer, pimping that rat-faced girl of his to whatever heir comes handy—'

'Lieutenant Quicherat is in charge of . . . of the investigation,' said Anne. She kept her voice steady, but January could see the effort it cost her. He remembered a girl on Bellefleur Plantation – Caline, her name had been: *why did I remember that? I couldn't have been more than six* . . . Caline had been twelve, bright and pretty and petted by Michie Fourchet's family for her cleverness.

He didn't remember why Michie Fourchet had taken it into his head to 'give her a lesson', but he had. *She was uppity*, January's mother had whispered to him at the time, when Fourchet had finally opened the door of the woodbarn where he and one of the foremen had 'punished' Caline. *She was spoiled. That's how they 'un-spoils' you.*

More than the pulped flesh of her back, the swollen mess of her face, January remembered Caline's eyes. The look in them, of a hurt and terrified animal, that will never suffer a human touch again.

Caline's back, and face, had healed. Her eyes had never gone back to what they'd been before.

He wondered if Anne's ever would.

Anne went on, 'He keeps trying to get me to admit that I hated Philippe. That I'd set out deliberately to murder him. That it was my gun that killed him. Daniel, I'd never—'

'Of course not!' Daniel put his hand to her cheek, a gesture of tenderness January had never seen his friend make towards his wife, pity and protectiveness breaking through the friendly bantering that had always been between them. 'Good God, Anne—'

'I was *never* jealous.' Her voice pleaded as she put her small hands on his chest. 'You know that! Not of Philippe – not of any of them. Not even that frightful bitch Apollon—'

'Anne, I never thought you were!' He caught her hands in his own. Daniel, being Daniel, had insisted on stopping home between their morning investigation and coming to the prison, to change clothes, have Freytag fix his hair, and put on a little rouge, so that he would be, as he said, 'fit to be seen'. But as he bent his head down over hers, January was aware of Armand's grimace of distaste.

'Good thing she never was,' the boy whispered furiously, 'the way he paraded them around the town.'

'I'm sorry,' whispered Anne. 'If I hurt you—'

'Hurt me?' Daniel seemed momentarily nonplussed. 'What, with those . . .' He stopped himself from one of the several joking names that, over the past eighteen months, he'd applied to her 'stable of stallions', her 'muscle-bound boys'. His voice tender, he murmured. 'Don't be a goose, Anne. And don't go talking as

if we're not going to be shaking our heads over this whole business over Freytag's coffee two months from now in our salon,'
he added. 'There's probably hundreds of those muff pistols being
sold around Paris. I saw some only the other day, at Montjoie's
in the Palais Royale. Anyone in the city could have been using
one. And Benjamin's found a perfectly brilliant way to trace little
Tin-Tin—'

'Do you really think,' murmured Anne, 'that Celestin's mother
is going to let him stand trial for murdering his brother? Even
if she knows that he did it? This . . . this Quicherat – the inves-
tigator – seems so sure, as if he had proof. But what proof could
he have? Do you really think the comte is going to lose the
second heir to his lands, and see them go to some cousin in the
Limousin? Or that the Marquis de Taillefer is going to lose the
chance to wed his daughter to Belvoire's heir?'

'It doesn't matter if Celestin is convicted,' said January grimly.
'Only that the *juge d'instruction* can be shown that there were
others who could have done the murder besides yourself. Daniel's
right, the gun means little. It's an antique type, but anyone could
have such a thing. But as it is, we're trying to prove a negative.
To show that you have no proof about where you were and what
you were doing *because* you are innocent, *because* you never
thought you'd need such a thing. Gerry O'Dwyer—'

'He's dead.' Anne turned her face aside, and gently, Daniel
tightened his arm around her shoulders, so that her cheek pressed
the dark silk of his lapel.

'If he were not dead – if he were anywhere in Paris – he'd
come forth. You knew him, Armand. He was your teacher . . .
he'd find some way.'

'Of course he would.'

She looked past her husband's shoulder to January. 'And
nothing has been heard – or found . . .?'

'He had no family in Paris, I take it?' said January, his own
eyes going from Anne to Armand. 'You'd know better than I
about that, m'sieu. You said he was your teacher?'

'No, he had no one in Paris.' The youth spoke stiffly, and
January guessed that this was how the flamboyant young Irishman
had come to know Anne. But the admission that his sister would
take a mere fencing master as her lover was clearly more than

Armand de St-Roche-Ouen wanted to admit. 'And yes, he was my teacher – in English, a little, and in fencing. The only ones he knew in Paris were the other men in his reading group – men who'd been students with him at the Faculté des Lois. Or journalists. None who'd go looking for his body, who'd dare to be seen themselves, poking about the morgue.'

His blue eyes filled again with tears. 'You have to find the one who did this, M'sieu Janvier. Anne goes before the *juge d'instruction* next week. This . . . this *monster* Quicherat comes in every day and hounds her, questions her, always, Who was your accomplice? and hints how much she hated de la Marche. Sits there digging at his hairy ears and scratching himself, stinking of pipe smoke. He was a thief himself, that one, and a murderer, before he joined the Sûreté – half of them were! Stupid as a brick and blind as a bat. To send such a one to harass a lady, a daughter of a house renowned while his own were stealing sheep! I want to kill them.' His voice broke, and he turned away, tears of anxiety running down his face.

'I want to kill them all.'

'Would the *juge d'instruction* believe such a thing?' asked Daniel, as they made their way along the Rue du Faubourg St-Denis back to town. Under his rouge and eye paint and his pomaded curls, his face was haggard with a fear he had tried to conceal at the prison. 'That Anne . . . What? *Lured* Philippe, like the villainess of an opera, to some deserted spot? *Where*, for heavens' sake? We're in the middle of the largest city in Europe!'

'And yet the house at 15 Rue Notre Dame des Victoires is deserted,' returned January quietly. 'A man could have been shot in its garden and no one the wiser, until the body started to stink. The convent of Notre Dame de Syon was deserted when its mother superior, of whom Armand bragged, took her charges out of town; the monastery of St-Honoré d'Autun in whose doorway I hid Philippe's body; the old gypsum-mine tunnels in Montparnasse, your father's town house, for that matter, for I'd bet – if I had anything to bet with – he *absquatulated*, as the riverboat men say back home, at the first whiff of hot weather . . .'

'Well, yes, but . . .'

'This is the largest city in Europe,' said January. 'And one of the most crowded.' He gestured around them at the thickening traffic: carriages, barrows of vegetables from the countryside, a hurdy-gurdy player with a trained monkey, a knife grinder and a vendor of second-hand underwear. 'Yet all throughout it there are little hollows, like the holes in Swiss cheese, where murder can happen. And does happen, every day. One only has to get one's victim alone, and stand close enough to him with a muff pistol.'

'Anne would never have done such a thing.'

'Anne's maid, and a servant who was in your house on the night Philippe went out to meet his death, are now both in the employ of La Comtesse de Belvoire. Her elder son is dead. Whether she believes or not that her younger son committed the crime, until someone is guillotined for it, that son will stand in danger of being accused.'

Daniel turned his face quickly aside at the mention of the machine that criminals jokingly called the National Razor. A small, protesting sound died in his throat.

'So let's hope,' concluded January quietly, 'that Ayasha has something to tell us.'

THIRTEEN

1839

The recollection didn't come to him whole and in order, of course.

As is the way of dreams, the images were but fragments – Armand cursing at the Sûreté, Daniel wrapping Anne gently in his arms – mingled with the pissy, moldy stink of the courtyard of Saint-Lazare and the momentary cloud of perfume as he and Daniel passed a vendor of roses in the Rue du Faubourg St-Denis. Things that had nothing to do with these events obtruded themselves with agonizing clarity: Ayasha washing her hair in a bowl and pitcher in their room, while rain trickled down the windows; morning sunlight on the towers of Notre Dame as he walked back from early Mass. Then he'd wake, and lie listening to the cicadas in the trees of the *ciprière* that stretched out behind the Broadhorn, or the yelling of the men in the saloon in the other part of the building: brags and shouts, challenges and curses, 'Fucken swine, you talkin' to me? You skunk-face French pussy, you ain't fit to eat with a dog nor drink with a nigger . . .' 'I'm cut! I'm cut! Oh, God, I'm killed . . .'

And the rest of the memories would sort themselves into logical order for a time.

Then he'd drift off, and see Anne under the arcades of the Palais Royale, with her hands on her hips and the silver muff pistol tucked into her tricolor sash: *Nobody has* ever *accused His Majesty of not being a fool*! And Gerry O'Dwyer adjusting his shabby cravat in the reflection of a shop window, before turning to her with his dimpled chin and dazzling smile.

For a moment he dreamed about Ayasha's laughter, before his visions slipped to the dank, stinking cell at the Cabildo, and a woman's voice sobbing with the horrors, 'Gimme some! Gimme some! Jesus Christ, doesn't anybody got any dope?' The smell of piss and vomit. Someone else screamed, 'Get them off me! Get them off me!' The rattle of cockroach wings and the scrabble of rats.

A slim girl in filthy white sat crammed in a corner, staring around her in the darkness.

And as one sees in dreams, even in the blackness he saw her face, and it wasn't Jacquette Filoux.

It was Anne Ben-Gideon, weeping the tears she could let no one see by day.

First light waked him.

Will they be watching the house?

Rose would get word to him, from Olympe's.

The kitchen below, the saloon and the yard, were silent, save for the barking of a far-off dog. Hannibal was still gone, presumably murmuring Classical Latin endearments into Kentucky Williams's shell-like ear. Cocks crowed in a half-hundred backyards beyond the trees. Visible through the open window – railless and looking straight out onto a twelve-foot drop to the yard – a distant hawk gyred in air like gray crystal.

Are my friends of yesterday still following me? Do I need to send Hannibal – or one of Kentucky Williams's girls – out looking for Tyrell Mulvaney?

He reviewed yesterday's visit to Chitimacha in his mind, the untouched tangle of weeds and maiden-cane that walled in the stripped-out ruin of the house, the swampy green water of the bayou like a sullen moat.

Had he seen someone in the woods? Or had that really been a deer?

Now he wasn't sure. Getting the tar beaten out of him in Paris – added to a lifetime of looking over his shoulder for kidnappers (*Something I didn't have to deal with in Paris, Secret Police notwithstanding*) – had made him wary, especially when he knew this was a matter that was worth a hundred dollars to one of Queen Victoria's agents.

Abishag Shaw boarded these days in one of the spare rooms at Valentine's livery stable. Even if the policeman hadn't gotten his message of last night, it should be easy enough to slip over there, and get him to check the neighborhood of Rue Esplanade, to see whether the house was being watched or not. If Shaw was out already, he could find Ti-Jon at the levee.

He heard the creak of the ladder below the open doorway, a single whisper of sound. His mind identified it moments before he thought, *I didn't hear anyone cross the yard . . .*

There were riders in the woods . . .

He was off the pallet bed and halfway across the attic, his boot knife in his hand, when a head appeared dark against the dawnlight and a scratchy voice whispered, 'Maestro?'

January put down his knife, and took a few more relaxed strides to reach the opening as Abishag Shaw scrambled the rest of the way into the room.

'Did you have a look at the house?'

Silently, the policeman held out a folded piece of paper. The handwriting in which the words 'B. Janvier' were written was unfamiliar and January's eyes flashed, fast, to his friend's face; his stomach sank at the bleakness in the gray gaze.

The note was in French, and unsigned.

M. Janvier

My representative will meet you where the turnpike road meets the shores of the lake, at noon today (Saturday). Your wife and children are unharmed and will remain so as long as you are unaccompanied and unfollowed. There will be no second warning, nor any other attempt to communicate with you.

'I didn't get your note til past midnight.' Hands in pockets, Shaw spit a long stream of tobacco at a turtle creeping from the ditch along one side of Perdidio Street, a few feet from a man lying half in the water, snoring. The tobacco missed the reptile by several feet.

January said nothing. Had said nothing, since they'd left the Broadhorn.

'You said in your note as how you was havin' M'am Janvier an' the youngsters go to your sister, so's I didn't think nuthin' of it, when I went by an' saw the shutters all up an' nobody there. Wasn't 'til this mornin', when I seed the shutters still up, that I went in.

'At a guess,' the guard continued, glancing sidelong at his still-silent companion, 'that note's from Jared Ganch, gambler what owns the Flesh an' Blood on Girod Street. Leastways he's the feller what employs Pasky Peever, who I seen watchin' the Filoux place yesterday. Just watchin',' he added, answering January's sharp glance. 'For Uncle Juju, most like. If anybody *is* watchin' your house, they'd'a seen me go in there already, an' won't be surprised none to see me come back with you.'

Still January made no reply. The sun was barely up. Clear and tiny above the low roofs of the shabby collection of saloons, tents, and hovels that made up the Swamp, the bells of the cathedral, and of the mortuary chapel across the street from Jacquette Filoux's house, called the faithful to early Mass. The air had begun to smell of fresh woodsmoke, as stoves were lit to boil morning coffee and to heat water for the washing of glasses in the more respectable of the district's establishments.

He felt as if electricity were coursing through his veins. *I will kill them . . .*

'Can't prove a thing on Ganch, of course.' Shaw spit again. They had reached the more respectable neighborhoods along Rue Esplanade, and the occasional Spanish plantation houses more and more mingled with the low, stuccoed cottages. The first of the traffic from the wharves began to be seen on the track that ran between the trees of the 'neutral ground' between the two lanes of the wide street. Slaves swept the brick banquettes before the steps that led up to the French doors of snug dwellings, or scrubbed them with brick dust against the night's drift of steamboat soot. 'He got friends on the First an' Second Municipal councils,' Shaw went on. 'Or anyways folks that owe him money. That ain't his handwritin' on the note – I got samples of that. He's a businessman. Cold as a witch's kiss.'

Rose would be delivered within weeks – maybe within days. Panic turned him sick. *I will kill them . . .*

'House was as you see it,' added Shaw, as January ran up the tall steps of the old Spanish house, unlocked the shutters on the French door that led into his study. Shuddered as the smell washed over him, the prosaic mustiness of plaster and paint, redolent of dreams and plans and the exquisite peace of his life with Rose.

Yesterday, only yesterday . . . 'No windows broke, nor the locks nor latches neither. No sign of a fight.'

All the other French doors looking out onto the galleries – front and back – were shuttered and latched inside.

January strode, trembling, past the huddle of tarpaulin-covered furniture in the parlor and into the dining room, where Rose would have been lighting the candles yesterday evening. And indeed, half a dozen candles in their holders stood on the table, barely burned down. The kidnapping must have taken place at about eight, as the first shadows began to fall.

He found he could barely breathe, though his mind felt curiously calm, as if he were halfway through some hideously complex symphony, everything laid out before and behind him, like a burning road.

The chairs had all been neatly placed against the walls. There was a blue glass tumbler from the kitchen on the table, with a few inches of lemonade still in it. Zizi-Marie's sewing box had been closed, but the baby dress she'd been embroidering for Secundus lay beside it.

Don't do this, he screamed at God. *Don't do this . . .*

A needle gleamed coldly where the light from his study came through the doorway. He passed through into the bedroom and saw at once that the satchel in which Rose carried Baby John's clouts and shirts was missing. Opening the dresser drawer sanctioned to his son's things, he thought a few of each were gone.

He could just hear Rose saying, Unless you're especially fond of the smell of baby urine, I suggest you let me collect a few things from the bedroom before we leave . . .

He would have wept, only a part of him – the part that had been born and raised a slave – told him that it would only waste time.

And he would not let a white man see him weep.

Crossing the yard to the kitchen, he found signs of a scuffle: fragments of a broken plate, a wooden chair set in a corner where Gabriel wouldn't have put it. Flies rose in a cloud from the pot where yesterday afternoon's dinner gumbo had been heating for supper. No kitchen candles. The doors looking into the yard had all been closed and latched, but they'd have been open yesterday evening when this happened. Gabriel had at least been allowed time enough to bank down the fire.

Your wife and children are unharmed . . .

Whoever they were, they'd taken pains. They really wanted something of him.

Or maybe they just didn't want to call attention to the kidnapping by a conflagration.

'What you need me to do, Maestro?' Shaw's voice was matter-of-fact as the clunk of a butter churn. January had the impression that if he'd replied, 'Assassinate the Queen of England and burn London', the tall Kentuckian would have shouldered his rifles and set forth to do so without a word. Knowing Shaw, he'd probably succeed . . .

'If I'm not back by evening,' he said slowly, 'go to Sir John Oldmixton at the British consulate and give him the note I'm going to write for you. And then start checking the slave pens of every dealer between Natchez and the river mouth. Even if this Ganch kills me—' he slid the note Shaw had handed him into his jacket pocket – 'he'll sell them.'

Shaw nodded, and spit tobacco out into the yard. January would have bet money his friend couldn't spit through an open French door at two paces. 'I will do that.'

'You own such a thing as a palm pistol?'

Without a word the policeman produced one from the top of his boot. The lineal descendant of Anne Ben-Gideon's muff pistol, it was small enough to lie concealed in January's enormous palm.

'Thank you.' He was well aware that Shaw had just broken Louisiana state law by handing him the weapon. 'You wouldn't happen to know,' he added, as he slipped the ramrod down the muzzle, 'whether any of those Bank of England securities – the ones Brooke used to back up his purchase of Chitimacha Plantation and the Labarre land – have turned up? Cashed in at a bank, for instance? Or put up for any other kind of purchase?' The gun was indeed loaded, not that he had for a moment thought that Shaw would carry an unloaded gun.

'Not as anybody's sayin'.' The Kentuckian followed him from the kitchen across the yard again, up the back gallery steps and into the house. 'I had a feelin' Uncle Juju wouldn't'a gone back Sunday – after Brooke's body was found – if'n he'd had luck

getting' those sustificates by breakin' into the dinin' room
Saturday night. But he's into Jared Ganch for maybe five thousand
dollars, plus whatever else he owes to every other snap-house in
town. So I'm guessin' they figure you know where they is. Or
maybe where *he* is.'

In his study, January uncapped the inkwell, sat for a moment
at his desk.

In the dining room, Rose's small French clock tinged the hour.
Eight clear notes, bringing her before him, a quicksilver smile
and a flash of spectacles. Calling forth Baby John's solemn steady
gaze, a thousand years old in his infant face; briefly conjuring
Gabriel's laughter, Zizi-Marie's sweet voice singing, from the
shadows of the paint-smelling parlor draped in old sheets. Shaw's
voice ran on in the back of his mind, and he was aware of the
policeman watching him with those cold gray eyes, asking him
what else 'they' might figure he knew.

I may never see any of them again.

*I may never see the face of my only daughter or my second
son.*

It was his childhood nightmare returned, the dread he'd lived
with for the first seven years of his life: not fear of his master's
beatings, but the sickened awfulness of not knowing, when he
came in from taking water to the men in the fields, if he'd find
his mother, his sister, his father gone.

Holy Mary, full of grace, his heart whispered, *return them here
safely. Guide me . . .*

With a steady hand he dipped his pen, wrote, 'Dear Sir John . . .'

Mounted again on Voltaire, January scanned the flat gray water,
the flat pale sand mingled here and there with low islets of gray-
green grass, as the shadows of cypress and tupelo opened out
around him. From the end of the Turnpike Road a long fishing
pier extended into the waters of the lake, and as he approached
he could see men moving about on it from the boats docked at
the far end. But it lay too far from the nearest cottages – summer
dwellings begun before the bank crash two years ago had wiped
out the credit of their builders – for there to be much activity.
His heart thudded painfully in his chest.

It was three miles from the town itself, and most of that distance through the marshy wastelands of the *ciprière*. Shaw had accompanied him through the Swamp, to make sure no one followed him: a free black man riding alone through those empty woods was asking to be kidnapped. Beneath the scrunch of Voltaire's hooves on the broken shells, January had listened every foot of the way for sounds in the trees around him. Had turned in the saddle, time and again, to scan the road behind him, the dark-green monotony of woods on either side.

White egrets picked at cow dung by the roadside ditches. A hawk circled overhead.

When he saw the break in the trees, and the lakeshore beyond, January heard the plaintive mewling of gulls.

He drew rein where the road ended, a hundred feet from the shore. Though clouds rose like advancing towers above the water, the day was grilling hot, even the storm breeze that soughed across the lake helpless before the sweltering heat.

Their names turned on themselves as they passed through his mind again and again: Rose. Zizi. Baby John. Gabriel. Rose.

Hooves ground on the shell road behind him. Two men emerged from the trees a dozen yards behind him, a third came riding fast up the road from the direction in which he'd come. Americans, he thought. The kind of Americans he hated most, 'Kaintucks' who came down the river on the flatboats, from the frontier towns of Arkansas and Missouri. Small-time land speculators, slave traders (or slave stealers), 'filibusters'. As Hannibal had surmised, mercenaries who hung around the saloons of the Swamp, waiting to be hired by smugglers or gamblers or river thieves.

One of them wore the brown Mexican jacket he remembered from the Bayou Road yesterday, coarse cowhide embroidered on the sleeves in dirty white. He wore a low-crowned Mexican hat, too, beneath which blondish-red hair straggled to his shoulders. His mouth and unshaven chin were stained with tobacco, and the paunch that sagged over his belt in no way decreased his aspect of brute strength. 'You January?' he asked, when he got close.

'That would be me, sir.' *At least this is the party I'm here to meet and not random kidnappers . . .*

'Nobody back there, Cat,' reported the third rider, and jerked his thumb back toward the road.

'Take the nigger's mule, Rocky.'

The man named Cat dismounted, caught Voltaire's bridle, and January warned, 'Watch out for him, sir; he kicks like a bastard,' even as the big animal swung his hindquarters into firing position. January reined him around, then stepped from the saddle as Rocky sprang down from his own mount and carefully took the mule's rein.

'Never met a mule that didn't,' grinned Rocky – younger than Cat, but bigger, with the same hulking frame and red-gold hair. Under the brim of a shallow-crowned beaver hat his pale blue-green eyes were both crueler and stupider.

'You stay with 'em here, Rocky,' instructed Cat, and gestured to the other member of the party – the skinny, mean-eyed, lantern-jawed woman who'd been with him on the road yesterday – who stepped up to January's other side. 'That's a fine mule,' he added, with a glance at January. 'Your'n?'

'Maggie Valentine's.'

Cat spit. 'Bet she charged you a packet. My brother'll keep an eye on him for you, give him back when Mr – uh – *Smith* – is done talkin' to you.' He took January's arm, as did the woman, and walked him toward the pier. 'I hope you ain't prey to seasickness.'

FOURTEEN

Cat blindfolded January when they got him into the boat at the end of the pier, which, he reflected, they should have done a lot earlier if they were really concerned about secrecy. It would be difficult for him to determine where they'd taken him – the newish, dark-green, twenty-foot sailing-skiff could be steered anywhere along the shore of the lake – but it would be fairly easy to trace the boat to its owner by a description, and to guess at least to within a few miles where they'd landed, given the direction of the wind.

He hoped that meant that Cat and his friends – and 'Mr Smith', presumably the gambler Jared Ganch – were careless, and not that they didn't care what he learned because they planned to kill him and drop his body over the side. They had patted his pockets, but hadn't searched him thoroughly, possibly because they knew that even with a knife or a small pistol he wouldn't be able to fight them all.

Yet looking back on the carefully banked kitchen fire, the extinguished candles, he didn't think this was the case.

They wanted him alive, and they wanted him to do something for them.

Probably, he reflected, exactly what he was already trying to do.

Find Juju Filoux.

And learn what Henry Brooke had done with his Bank of England stock certificates – and his gold.

They wouldn't have left Rocky to keep an eye on Voltaire if they hadn't been told to be polite.

His escort spoke little – a third man, addressed as Chuy, had been in the boat – and mostly about fishing in the lake, though once the woman said, 'There's the rocks – swing her around here,' in a voice devastated by tobacco and drink.

Far off, thunder rumbled across the water and Cat said, 'How fast that storm comin' in?'

'We fine,' returned Chuy. 'We put in anywhere here.'
Mexican or Caribbean Spanish.

They changed direction – January felt it in the sway of the boat, the direction of the wind on his face – two or three times in the half-hour they were on the water. January guessed they backtracked, to keep him from guessing where along the shore they'd put in. Another hopeful sign that they didn't intend to kill him, at least not yet. Still blindfolded, he was helped out of the boat when they scraped bottom, and waded some forty feet to dry rock and grass. He counted sixty more steps inland, among trees, and up rickety steps. Fishing camp, he guessed, even before he was guided to a chair (*Not pushed, they must not intend to sell me in Texas either*). The man on the other side of the table – whose edge he felt with his arm – used bay rum on his hair. A lot of it. And Parma violet to cover up the smell of clothing too long unwashed.

The blindfold was removed.

The man on the other side of the table was better dressed than his employees, but his eyes, and his clean-shaven face, had the same callous hardness. He sized January up as if pricing what he'd bring on the auction block, and folded hands that had done manual labor, though not recently. The diamonds on his stickpin and pinky ring screamed, 'I bought these because I can afford them now!' The room, as January had guessed, was plain and walled with old flatboat planks whose shrinkage let slits of daylight through, though the roof was solid. In a fishing camp you wanted a roof, but the deep galleries that shaded its floor-length windows on all four sides kept away the rain. The windows were open to the lake air.

After a first glance January kept his eyes down. He'd learned the hard way that white men didn't like to have black ones meet their gaze.

'You find anything at Chitimacha?' asked his host.
'No, sir.'
'Or at the Labarre parcel?'
'No, sir.'
'You looking for anything in particular?'
'No, sir,' replied January. 'That is, I'm looking for anything that might tell me who would have murdered Henry Brooke. I

think if Madame Filoux had done so she'd have gotten herself and her children out of town the next day – or she would have buried the body under the house, not dumped it in the basin. The bullet I found at the house wasn't nearly the same size as the one dug out of his body.'

'And that's your business why?'

Stick as close as possible to the truth. He'd learned that about telling lies as a child. *You never can tell what they already know.*

'My sister's a friend of hers. Some of the local voodoos told me Mr Brooke was supposed to be mixed up with dangerous men. The banks told the City Guards the property purchases had been backed up with Bank of England stock certificates, but I didn't find any in the house, 'cept for the one Madame Filoux had on her when she was arrested. There was some talk of gold, though that might just be ya-ya. You talk to any voodoo about someone who's been murdered and sooner or later they start saying there's pirate gold behind it.'

'Mr Smith' was silent for a time at that, studying January's face with cold dark eyes, like onyx collar studs, seeming darker still against his neatly-trimmed sandy hair. Gauging his words. Sniffing for a lie.

'So gold wasn't what you was lookin' for out in the woods along Bayou Gentilly?'

'I don't know what I was looking for, sir. But Mr Brooke bought two pieces of land, and according to what the bank told the City Guards he was getting ready to buy two more. The only thing you can do with land like that is bury something on it. The land was sure too worthless for him to re-sell. I think it was a blind, and I wanted to go out there and see what I could see.'

'And what did you see?'

'Nothing, sir. No dirt turned up fresh, and no water deep enough – barring the bayou itself – to sink a box in, that it wouldn't be found. Not that I think he'd have hidden so much as train fare on land he didn't own.'

'Smith' nodded. This was something he understood. 'You search the whore's house?'

'Yes, sir.'

'Find anything?'

'Some receipts and an old bank book. A little jewelry. The deed to the house.'

Ganch's mouth twisted thoughtfully. January put his age at forty or so, a man who'd lived all his life as a predator, robbing other men as casually as a toothed garfish swallowed smaller fish. 'A list of men's names? A strongbox? Or the key to one?'

'No, sir.' *Personal papers.* He could almost hear Sir John Oldmixton's creamy baritone pass casually over the words. *Which it is imperative that I find, and find quickly.* 'Sounds like it was Juju Filoux who let himself into the house late Saturday night, almost certainly after finding Brooke's body in the turning basin and going through his pockets. He could have searched the dining room, one of the cabinets, and the attic without his sister waking up. I don't know what he might have found, either there or in Brooke's pockets. Since he came back next day I'm guessing he didn't find anything.'

'Any idea where he is now?'

'No, sir. I've been asking around town.'

'That's what I hear tell.' The gambler placed palms together, and leaned lips and chin against them, as if praying. At length he said, 'There's no need for us to be working against each other here, January. I need another man to help me find Juju Filoux. A man who knows the colored side of town. A man who's respected among the niggers. Now, it happens that Mr Brooke and I were in the process of closing a business deal when he met his unfortunate end, before he was able to turn over to me the strongbox containing these Bank of England certificates you mention, as well as a list of his associates, and a couple hundred dollars in gold. Would you be willing to help me find that?'

January felt his neck and ears grow hot, but made himself say quietly, 'Certainly, sir.' No sense spitting in his face and yelling at him. 'Might I speak to my wife?' he added after a moment. 'She's near her time, and I would be better able to concentrate on our – *joint endeavor* – if she were where I could get her to help immediately if she needed it.'

Smith considered the matter. The man Cat spoke up, a trifle diffidently, 'I'd feel better if we wasn't worryin' about her up an' farrowin' any minute, sir. She's about ready to pop, sure as gun's iron.'

'Don't think I don't sympathize with you, January,' said Smith after a time. January closed his fists under the table so hard his nails dug into his palms.

'Don't think I don't sympathize with you' meant 'no'. Only the thought that the situation might be worked around somehow kept him from hurling table, chairs, anything he could find, at this pale-haired man, from pulling Shaw's purse gun from his boot and killing him, knowing he'd die too and not caring.

'My experience in these matters has taught me that moderate amounts of pressure tend to improve the concentration rather than disrupt it. Mrs January and your children are perfectly safe, and in no discomfort. They will be returned to you as soon as I have that strongbox, and that list of names, now presumably in the possession of Mr Filoux. Until such time, you will take orders from myself, or from Catastrophe here—' he nodded toward the ginger-haired, broken-toothed Cat – 'who can be found any day from two o'clock on at the Flesh and Blood, on Girod Street. You have—'

His dark eyes narrowed, calculating. 'You have three weeks. After the first of August it will be too late, and I will be forced to conclude our dealings, and dispose of Mrs January and your children in a manner best suited to recovering some of my financial losses in this matter. I hope you understand?'

Everything within him screaming, like a mine exploding in a holocaust of flame and shattered iron and rage, January said quietly, 'Yes, sir. I understand.'

I will kill you, he thought. He was pretty sure the words were in his eyes, and kept them properly downcast.

But he was also pretty sure that this 'Mr Smith' – this Jared Ganch – saw this, and had already made his plans accordingly.

The house on Rue Esplanade, when he returned to it, seemed still as the house of death. In the gray light of the afternoon's rain he paced from room to room, the smell of the half-repaired plaster, the mild mustiness of the packets of sizing and pigments, mingling heart-rippingly with the clean soap smells of Baby John's empty crib, the lavender and sweetgrass of Rose's pillow. He wanted to weep, to curse God, as Job had cried, and die.

A half-hour after his return, Shaw came in through the discreet passway into the backyard and mounted the back gallery stairs. 'Far's I can tell ain't nobody watchin' the place.'

'It takes effort to watch a house,' added Olympe, who followed Shaw a few moments later, by the same route. Her deep, rather rough voice was steady, but there was a look in her eyes that January had never seen there, or had seen only in a diminished or second-hand form: the cold eyes of a killer. He knew his sister understood the lore of poisons, and could make a man sicken or die, but she was generally careful to whom she sold such things. She knew the gossip of the town: knew also when to turn a prospective buyer away. But her eyes were now the eyes of one who can call up the demons of hell, and fix them like leeches to an enemy's flesh, and not care about the cost to her own soul.

'Ganch has eight men these days who draw their living from him,' she went on. 'Maybe as many as twenty others he can call on. Men who owe him money, and dare not say no, or drunkards whose loyalty can be bought for a drink. I don't see any of these hereabouts.'

January made himself say, 'Thank you' with a mouth that felt like it belonged to somebody else.

Rose. Dear God, Rose . . .

He said, 'In the boat coming back Catastrophe Watling told me that Zizi-Marie is all right.'

Olympe's eyes didn't change, but he thought her shoulders shifted a little, relaxed one-half a degree. 'You believe him?'

'I don't know,' said January. 'What he said was, "Mr Ganch says he'll break the man's arm that lays a hand on your girl or your wife". They seem to think Zizi and Gabriel are my children. How long that protection will last – or whether Ganch will in fact retaliate if one of his men harms Zizi – I don't know.'

'*Crimine ab uno disce omnis.*' Hannibal came in from the back gallery as well, followed by Olympe's husband Paul, by ashen-faced young Ti-Gall, and by Ti-Jon, whose net of informants and potential helpers was almost as wide as Olympe's. 'I have encountered Mr Watling and his brother in the Swamp on a number of occasions. Even drunk, Watling seems a man without malice, which elevates him to demi-sainthood in that milieu. Brother Rocky will cross a street to kick a dog dying in the gutter – Catastrophe won't, for what that's worth. Whether that will forestall him from . . . ah . . . other acts of malice—' he glanced at Olympe's stony face and visibly evaded the word, 'rape' – 'I know not.'

Olympe said, 'I will fry his balls with onions, and feed them to him,' in a conversational tone. She turned to Shaw. 'This man Ganch is a whoremaster, no? Might he be keeping them in one of his houses?'

'I doubt he'd hold a pregnant woman an' her child where they'd be like to disturb the payin' customers, m'am. Like as not he's got one of his madams keepin' a eye on her. Sefton?'

'I shall make it my quest to inquire. A damerel and a ladies' boy, that's me . . .'

'Just don't let 'em know you's lookin'. He'll keep a good eye on M'amzelle Zizi too, I reckon,' he added, not looking at either Olympe or Ti-Gall. 'Virgin'll bring more, on the market.'

Ti-Gall flushed darkly under his sprinkling of freckles, but January nodded, and prayed that Ganch's influence over his men was strong enough to counter their selfish contempt for a woman in their power.

'Melkie Frias runs the Flesh an' Blood for Ganch,' added Ti-Jon. 'Nobody'd tell him the time of day for free, no wonder Ganch can't find out nuthin' 'bout Juju. You stay away from where he can see you, Ben. Keep clear of the Cock as well. Frias, he a snitch with a mouth on him like a busted pipe.'

'I can go to the Flesh an' Blood,' said Ti-Gall. 'Melkie's always lookin' for boys to work there, he pays so bad.'

'Ain't a bad idea,' said Shaw.

Paul put a big hand on the boy's shoulder, and said, 'You watch yourself, son – your mama kill me if you come to harm.'

'Why the first of August?' January looked from face to face among them, the only people, he thought, who held open the door through which Rose might one day walk back to him. *Rose, and Baby John, and Zizi and Gabriel and Secundus* . . . He felt as if he were wounded and bleeding, as if it would be easier to stay lying down and simply bleed to death. *I have to get up and fight.* 'That mean anything to any of you?'

They traded a glance: two white men, three black – slave and *libré* – and a black voodooienne.

'It might to Oldmixton,' opined Hannibal, and January nodded. He'd already written another note to the diplomat, arranging a meeting as soon as the Englishman could come to the house without drawing attention to himself. Ganch might not have enough men to watch the place, but the knifepoint deadliness of the situation made all of them hesitant to run even the smallest risk. 'You need me here, *amicus meus*, until that gentleman's arrival?'

January shook his head. The rage returned in waves, turning him sick. Between them he felt simply tired and very strange. He tried to remember whether this was how he had felt in the wake of Ayasha's death, but oddly he could not remember how he had felt at all. 'I'm all right,' he said, still with that queer sense of speaking through someone else's mouth, of inhabiting a body strange to him.

'You is not,' retorted Olympe, '*all right*. Paul, you go see what's in the kitchen. I think my brother'll do better with somethin' in him. Ti-Jon, Gallie, Michie Shaw, you-all welcome to stay.'

'They be lookin' for me down the wharves, m'am,' returned the slave, 'once the rain quits. An' those lazy bastards be gettin' themselves into God knows what trouble, thank you all the same, m'am.'

Shaw also excused himself with thanks, and took his leave. A little later, as Hannibal was preparing to depart, last of the guests at that silent dinner, the fiddler rested a hand on January's shoulder. 'Find Juju, and his execrable list of names which, wherever that strongbox ended up, I'll go bail is in the hands of whoever made quietus for Brooke. That's your task. We'll find Rose.'

He stepped out onto the gallery, opened his umbrella, and departed, leaving silence in the shadowy house, and the thunderous drumming of the rain.

FIFTEEN

Find Juju, that's your task, Hannibal had said.

January had meant to make his way to the Place des Armes once the rain ended, to find Tyrell Mulvaney and ask where he'd taken Henry Brooke on Friday night. But it was still raining hard when dark fell, and he sat waiting in the plaster-smelling parlor, listening to the drumming of the storm on the gallery roof.

There is nothing further that I can do tonight, save what I am doing.

Hail Mary, full of Grace, the Lord is with thee . . .

Don't let them come to harm . . .

The faces of the men in the boat, surrounding him on the Turnpike Road by the shore of the lake, came back to his mind. Shaggy and coarse, the hard faces of those who traded slaves, who beat those who owed Mr Ganch money, who would cross the street to kick a dying dog.

Hate turned him sick. Hatred of the white race, every single man of them, every woman and child.

Shaw is white, he reminded himself. *Hannibal is white . . .*

He still hated them all.

He didn't hear a carriage in Rue Esplanade, but the footfalls that creaked on the steps up from the banquette weren't those of a man used to sneaking up on his foes. He crossed to his study, where he'd left a lamp burning and the shutters open, and unlatched the French door even before Sir John Oldmixton reached it.

The rain had ceased, and droplets glittered all along the edge of the gallery roof in the thin reflection of the study lamp. The world smelled of wet vegetation, of mould and decay.

'M'sieu Janvier.' Oldmixton held out a kid-gloved hand.

Another white bastard . . .

'I hope the secrecy of this meeting implies that you've come round to being willing to—'

'A gambler named Jared Ganch has kidnapped my wife and children,' said January quietly. He stepped aside to let him in, closed the glass door behind him against the mosquitoes. 'He says he'll sell them as slaves in the Territories, unless I get him the strongbox containing the Bank of England stock certificates that Henry Brooke had in his possession, and a list of names – presumably the "purely personal family papers" that you were so desirous of retrieving. So I think all that has earned me the right to ask you: what the hell is going on?'

'My . . . dear . . . Janvier—' By his voice the Englishman was absolutely aghast.

January picked up the lamp, and guided him through to the dining room, where all but two of the candles on the table had guttered themselves into oblivion. In their feeble light he stood, looking across into the Englishman's eyes with an anger that would have gotten him whipped – and possibly lynched – had he so regarded any American on the continent.

'I take it Brooke absconded with the Bank of England stock certificates from the consulate,' he continued in a level voice. 'Strongbox and all, apparently. What is the list? Ganch is a gambler, a slave dealer, a saloonkeeper and a whoremaster – that's only what I know about, he may be other things besides. He has friends on the municipal council. He may – or one of his hired thugs may – have killed Brooke himself, only to find that the things they wanted from Brooke weren't where they thought they were. You owe me your help.'

'This is all—' Oldmixton began with a wave, and January caught his wrist and simply looked at him.

And don't you dare *say this is all very irregular and you can't do anything . . .*

The Englishman sighed. 'Yes,' he said. 'Yes, Brooke absconded with twenty-five thousand pounds' worth of stock certificates. He left the strongbox where it was, by the way, with packets of cut-up newspaper, wrapped in such a way as to look as if the certificates were still there.'

January released his wrist, gestured to one of the chairs. 'Can I get you coffee?' The screaming hatred ebbed, leaving him tired and faintly ill.

Oldmixton, his shoulders relaxing, took a seat and nodded.

'Thank you, that would be much appreciated.' He swiped at a mosquito as January retreated to the pantry, and returned a moment later with a clean cup and the little pot refilled. 'I am sorrier than I can say,' he added, when January took a seat opposite him and slid in his direction the last plate of the pralines with which his barely-tasted dinner had been concluded.

Gabriel had made them the previous day. *Dear God, guard him safe . . .* He had to turn his face quickly aside, and Oldmixton went on, 'I pulled you into this and I would never have done so had I known—'

'In this country,' explained January quietly, 'that's something you always need to take account of, dealing with those of my race. And it wasn't you who got me into it,' he added. 'Strictly speaking, it was my sister – the mother of the two young people who were taken along with my wife. But I ask you – I beg you—'

Oldmixton raised his hand. 'Henry Brooke was a courier,' he said. 'The consul here had need to . . . ah . . . purchase a little goodwill. Brooke was sent from London with the stock certificates, which would be easily negotiable through American banks but traceable should they go astray. Brooke has worked with our department for six years, and was vetted as dependable – obviously a premature judgment on someone's part.'

'Well, the traceability of Bank of England stocks is a premature judgment on someone's part,' remarked January grimly. 'There's half a dozen men in New Orleans with the resources to purchase them and organizations large enough to hold them and then sell them quietly, in Mexico or Cuba, no questions asked. It might have been exactly the opportunity Brooke was waiting for. What do you know about him before he came to work for your "department"?'

'Personally, very little. Someone in London—'

'Was Brooke his real name?'

'Good heavens, no!' Oldmixton looked shocked at the very idea.

'Any idea what it was?' And, when the Englishman shook his head, January asked, 'Was it O'Dwyer?'

'I don't think so. But he had several, you know. And sometimes – when he was drunk, or angry – he did sound very Irish.'

January nodded. Under those circumstances the Irish lilt would return to Hannibal's voice, too.

'What about the list of names?'

'Well, that's the reason for my concern, you see. I know he gained access to my notes on a number of subjects, and I'm fairly certain he made a list of names – the marks that bled through onto the sheet of paper underneath the one he wrote on tell me that much. For one thing, I have no idea what use he planned to make of those names, or in how much danger those people will be placed. For another, if I knew who they were, it would give me some idea of where the stock certificates went – or were intended to go – and what Brooke was up to. I fear on that head I am as much in the dark as you.'

'So there's no chance of mocking up a list.'

'Not if this Ganch scoundrel knows the sort of names that should be on it, no. But I cannot at the moment call to mind anyone in the . . . ah . . . local *diplomatic* community who would consider such an expeditious solution to any problem Brooke might make for them. It's the sort of thing one would expect in South America, but I know the consuls for Peru and Argentina, and since they already *have* lists of each others' agents I can't see them killing anyone over them. Things are so confused in New Grenada these days with the revolt in Ecuador that poor Señor Melendez – the current consul – hasn't been paid in months, and I doubt he could hire anyone to murder anyone . . . And Brooke could as well have been shot by an outraged husband as by anyone else, you know. He was a good-looking devil and he had a sort of fastidiousness about his love life: he much preferred seducing the wives of the local gentry to paying for a frolic in even a high-class bordello. I had cause to speak to him on the subject.'

'Did you?' said January thoughtfully. 'Any names?'

Oldmixton frowned for a moment. 'Not off the top of my head, but I can easily find out.'

'And I assume,' continued January, 'that since you didn't mention a valet in our early conversation, Brooke didn't travel with one.'

'Good lord, no. He wasn't a gentleman.'

The casual way he said that made January smile. It reminded

him a little of traveling in Mexico, where the hire of a valet automatically promoted one to respectworthiness. The same, of course, could be said of travel on a steamboat up the Mississippi – if one happened to be white.

'If there's any way in which I can help you,' added the Englishman after an awkward moment.

January drew a deep breath. 'Some money would help,' he said. 'I don't know for what, yet, but—'

'Good heavens, my dear Benjamin, in my business one learns never to ask.' From his pocket – January never figured out how he could carry such a thing while keeping the lines of his clothing so smooth – he extracted a small sack, which clinked as he set it on the table. 'And who was this Gerry O'Dwyer?' he asked. 'It wouldn't surprise me in the least that Brooke had some secret former life – several, in fact. He was rather that type. Might someone he knew under that name have . . . I don't know, pursued him . . .?'

'I don't see how,' said January quietly. 'He seems to have covered his tracks very thoroughly. Gerry O'Dwyer was a man I knew – well, I met him only once, and that briefly – in Paris, in the summer of 1830. He disappeared immediately after the Three Glorious Days—' he could not keep sarcasm from the way he pronounced the words – 'and his disappearance was responsible for the death of the wife of a friend of mine. She was accused of murdering a man. His testimony could have saved her.'

'My dear January . . .' Oldmixton's brow creased with distress. 'I'm so sorry—'

'Nothing for you to be sorry about,' January said. 'It was a long time ago.'

It was a long time ago.

He sat in the dining room, by the light of two guttering candles, for nearly two hours after Oldmixton left. *Was it like this for Daniel?* Something about the gathering that evening took him back to his friend's gorgeous gold-and-turquoise salon, to the nights when Jeannot Charbonnière and Lucien Imbolt and Armand and Carnot and all the others would gather . . .

Their faces came back to him, street urchins and medical students, wealthy and poor, grouped around that black-and-gold table. *What can we do? How can we solve this? There has to be something . . .*

You go do this – You find this out and report back to me . . .

He felt as if he had indeed stepped back into some metaphysical river, returned to the place he'd been before.

Find Juju, that's your task. We'll find Rose.

Would they? He trusted his friends with his life, but he found he did not – could not – leave this in any hands but his own. *Only I can do it . . .* How foolish was that?

He remembered Armand de la Roche-St-Ouen pacing, unable to sit still, twisting his hands, tears sometimes running down his face. 'There has to be something else,' he kept saying. 'There has to be some way to find out.'

Daniel, with less and less to say, losing flesh, growing gray before January's eyes.

1830

When Ayasha had told them the name of the woman with the moon and three stars in her hair, January had exclaimed, 'Phaedre Hirondelle? The opera singer?' As if there were two Phaedre Hirondelles in Paris, both of whom had admirers rich enough to buy them diamond moons to put in their hair.

'It's what that poor silly *'uwz* at Gemier's said.' Ayasha shrugged, and swept into a seat at one of the little tables that cluttered the arcade outside the Chatte Blanche, in a great flounce of striped skirts. Chatoine and her little gang of snarly-haired moppets grouped around her – Ayasha took the youngest of them, a tousle-headed five-year-old named Momicharde, on her lap. The Palais Royale had returned to its customary mode of business some days ago ('And why not?' Pleyard had groused. 'His New Majesty needs the money, I'm sure.'), and music trickled down the steps from the gambling establishments on its upper floor, as if the city had not been rocked by riot and revolution only three weeks ago.

'And they were bought for her by Celestin de Gourgue,' she went on, 'because I asked – claiming, you understand, to be the confidential maid of Celestin's other mistress. And you owe me twenty francs,' she added, turning to Daniel. 'Or else there is no bread and no oil in our house tonight, and no charcoal for the stove. And a cup of coffee would not be out of order either. And some frites for my bodyguard.' She waved grandly at the children.

'O jasmine that twines upon the wall of Paradise . . .' Daniel rose from his chair and bowed deeply over her hand, to the evident amusement of a group of students and their girlfriends at the next table. 'I would pay double that amount if it meant going without bread and oil myself.' He dug in the pocket of his cream-colored silk jacket and produced a packet of Banque de France notes, then went in quest of a waiter, several of these gentlemen having made themselves scarce in the days since the end of the riots. Watching him, January reflected that in the weeks since the uprising his friend had gradually abandoned the extravagant coats of brocade and antique silk. This didn't make Daniel any less recognizable in a crowd – the banker's son would have stood out anywhere with his height and the velvet glory of his voice. But the quiet grays and silvers of his jackets, and the subdued conservatism of their cut, were like a species of mourning – or a desperate apology for leaving that gorgeous regalia where Philippe could snatch it up, slip it on, before hastening out into the deadly night.

As for Phaedre Hirondelle, there was no question where she might be found. January had seen her only a few weeks previously, when an illness in the orchestra of the Opera Française had given him several days and nights of extra work. He'd watched that tall, too-thin, plain-looking young woman transform herself through Boieldieu's music, filling the theater with a golden magic until it was irrelevant whether she was pretty or not.

Everyone in the beau monde in Paris – even in the heat of August in a year marked by rioting and the fall of kings – knew where the *chanteuse première* of the French Opera lived. Still nursing the bruises acquired in the Rue Notre Dame des Victoires, January hesitated to ask for volunteers among the little group of Daniel's friends.

But when he mentioned this to Daniel as he returned with Ayasha's coffee, Chatoine – taking from him the newspaper cone of fried potatoes – piped up, 'Don't be a *canarie*, they'll see you coming a mile away.' She licked the grease (and printer's ink) from her fingers. 'You stick out like a whore in a church, Ben, and for a second offense they'll give you more than a warning.'

January was aware of this, too.

'And what'll they do to you?' he asked grimly.

'Chase us 'til they're knackered,' retorted the little girl with a cheeky grin. 'And then cuss.'

'I can't let you,' said Daniel.

'You can't stop us, *copain*. Me and the *marmousins*—' Chatoine gestured around her at Momicharde, Grivot, and Poli – 'can back Ben up when he goes and watches La Hirondelle, so while he's getting whalloped by her *lascars* we can follow her . . . Or we can save Ben a thumping and he stays back here and we follow her and then come back and tell him where she went.'

'You could be killed.' January's eyes rested for a moment on the little girl, tiny and thin in the cut-down, faded third-hand mourning she still wore for her brother Poucet. The men who'd beaten him, January knew, would swat these infants aside with barely a thought to the force they used, enough to break those tiny bones.

'They got to catch us first,' pointed out Poli, the older of the boys.

So January, with deep misgivings, agreed, and within two days Chatoine caught up with him on his way back from Mass one morning with the news that Phaedre Hirondelle wasn't staying in her stylish apartment on the Rue de Plessy. 'The porter of the building don't know where she is,' reported the little girl. 'Grec the courtyard sweeper says the porter don't know – and that wife of the porter's knows *everything*. Grec says, La Hirondelle turns up every afternoon to ask whether she's got mail or not. She's got her own closed coach and two horses and a driver named Roquille, but they're not at the local mews. The horses are match bays with white stars. The coach is dark red with cream panels.'

January sighed. 'At least it'll be easy to follow.'

Like many young men of wealth, Daniel 'kept his carriage', as they said: the rather expensive mark of a gentleman, in that it entailed not only the vehicle itself (Daniel's barouche was an English model, varnished a deep turquoise-blue and gold) but a pair of horses to draw it, a coachman, a groom, feed bills, and stabling in the nearest mews. Furthermore, Anne – who would never sit in a carriage if she could ride, preferably astride (to the horror of her parents) – owned her own assortment of horseflesh, two beautiful Arabian mares and a long-legged Irish thoroughbred which could outdistance anything in the hunting field.

'Too light for you,' said Freytag judiciously, when he took January and Daniel on a tour of the stables the afternoon of Chatoine's news, and had the groom bring out one of the carriage horses. 'Madame always speaks well of this lad's performance under saddle, and if I may say so, sir, his nature is calmer than any of madame's.'

The handsome black Frisian had a white blaze down his face, but the valet showed himself to be surprisingly adept at horse-coper tricks, and before nightfall, when January returned to the mews, the blaze – and the animal's white near-fore stocking – had disappeared.

'Good luck,' said Daniel, as January swung himself into the saddle. By the stable lanterns his friend looked haggard; it was the twenty-third of August, and the following Monday Anne Ben-Gideon would appear before the *juge d'instruction*. 'Whatever you can learn, anything . . .' He handed up to January a fat leather wallet which contained – when January glanced inside – a startling quantity of bank notes. 'Father,' explained Daniel shortly. 'He's always been as horrified of her behavior as her parents are, but one must, as he says, keep these things out of the police courts.'

A shadow of pain crossed the big man's painted eyes. 'All this is bad enough,' he added quietly, 'without Father – and Mother as well – wailing and beating their breasts over how they knew I would bring them down in sorrow to their graves. Completely ignoring the fact that it was they who wanted me to marry, and to marry Anne . . .'

'Why?' Ayasha swung into the saddle of a gentle black mare lent them by Armand. Her hair tied back, her figure startling in a pair of slop-shop breeches and one of Lucien Imbolt's old coats, she had taken it on herself – against January's violent objections – to follow him at a distance. It was a measure of the growing desperation of the situation, January reflected, that

Anne's brother had finally consented to the adventure. The effort to track Celestin de la Marche could not afford to fail.

'I assume your parents asked about the girl before they started negotiations with the family . . .?'

Daniel sighed. In the distance, the church clock of St-Roche sounded eight; January estimated that *La Dame Blanche* would be well into its second act, in a gaudy blaze of gaslight and harp arpeggios. Would Celestin de la Marche be in the audience?

'Mostly,' said Daniel quietly, 'they enquired into the social connections of the Vicomtes de la Roche-St-Ouen and their willingness to admit to society at large that they were connected to bankers and Jews. It was, I'm sorry to say, a point on which Father insisted. One can go only so far in the financial world – or at least one could under King Charles, God knows what things will be like under the Citizen King – without introduction to the more select salons of those who sit on the Chamber of Deputies and have the ear of the king.'

His brow puckered, as if he recalled some pain or distress. 'Anne's parents had little enough desire to so admit. But their case was desperate, and Father was not only lenient in matters of dowry but offered an extremely handsome settlement to the family as well. And finances aside – though of course with both Father and the vicomte finances are *never* aside – to whom else would they marry Anne? Even were she not . . . not *Anne* . . . with a marriage portion of fifteen thousand francs, nobody would look at her. They'd been trying for months to arrange a match between Armand and one of the Comte de Noirchamp's girls. I am sorry to say . . .'

He took a deep breath, all the blithe confidence of wealth – which January now realized suddenly was a shield against the scornful Christian world – drained from him, by grief, by fatigue, by anxiety for a woman he had come to love as a sister. 'I am sorry to say that Father simply didn't care. And neither did hers.' He seemed to come to himself a little, and pushed the wallet into January's hand. 'But that doesn't stop him from moaning that all of this is my fault.' He managed a wry smile. 'And, he says, if he has to buy his way out of disgrace, he's perfectly willing to do it. Better, he says, that one should be prepared. I have *no* idea who he thinks you may have to bribe before the night is out, my dear, but he did tell me to count whatever funds you bring back.'

Sitting above him on the black horse, January wanted to dismount and embrace him, an outsider even among outsiders, incomprehensible to his family and to his family's society alike. It came to him for the first time that he himself – even in slavery – had always known he was part of a community. Part of a family that would take him in if his mother, his sisters, his father were torn away from him.

No wonder Daniel sought the bohemian world, and the love of a young man who, like himself, was a stranger to his own kin. No wonder he and Anne, despite their forced marriage, found a kinship in one another.

He made himself beam, and replied, 'I shall turn in accounts to the penny.'

Daniel returned the extravagant smile. 'It will make my life *so* much easier if you do, darling. Good luck! And to you, my orchid of the desert.' He took Ayasha's foot from the stirrup, and kissed her ankle. 'I would have let you use my back for a mounting block, but this jacket is velvet and it smudges so easily—'

Dark-clothed on a black horse, the small weak gleam of a bullseye lantern bobbing against the pommel of his saddle, January rode into the blackness of the mews.

It was early enough that some light fell from upper windows, in the Rue de l'Université and Rue des Juives, but January still felt as if he were navigating underwater in a river of ink. Sometimes when he turned down a quiet street he thought he could hear the click of hooves on the cobbles behind him, where Ayasha followed in the dark. But when he glanced back, there was nothing. She'd wrapped her face in a dark scarf, like a highwayman – and he prayed that the soldiers who still patrolled the streets wouldn't take her for one.

The Rue le Peletier was crowded with carriages and fiacres – the evening's performance was drawing to a close. Even as he rode along it, watching for the red-and-cream coach, the bay horses with white stars on their foreheads, he saw gentlemen emerging from the Salle le Peletier's massive doors, sometimes alone, or in little black-clothed groups, sometimes with ladies on their arms dressed far too fashionably to be respectable wives.

Lucien Imbolt had spoken of seeing Celestin de la Marche – as he must be called now – in a cabaret only a few streets away, the night before the rioting began. Had he come into town, like so many of these young gentlemen, to see his mistress? Would he risk capture in order to continue to do so?

He found Phaedre Hirondelle's carriage without trouble. *If Celestin de Gourgue bought that for his beloved*, January reflected, *no wonder his parents believed he was losing tens of thousands of francs gambling.* The vehicle stood far up the street, almost to the Rue Chateaudun, and he rode past it, taking note of the little knot of coachmen at the corner, gruff quiet voices amid a blue whiff of tobacco smoke. From the corner of the Rue Chateaudun he could keep an eye on the vehicle – he had not the slightest idea of where Ayasha was, but guessed she was still behind him somewhere – and as the clock on St-Nicholas des Champs struck ten a boy came running along the street, lantern in hand. A big man in a coachman's many-caped greatcoat sepa-rated himself from the group, with the usual handshakes and mock-punches and jests, and carefully removed the light rugs from the star-browed bays of La Hirondelle's coach. Following them to the Opera itself was easy – the street was choked with carriages by this time and January hadn't the slightest fear of being noticed – and he was within a few yards of the coach in the crowded little canyon behind the Rue le Peletier where the stage door opened, among a scrim of noisy admirers. He saw La Hirondelle herself when the coachman led his team to the door. She emerged alone, and was as January recalled her from the rehearsals back in June. Her strong jaw and beak nose prominent until she smiled, when all was eclipsed by the dark, sparkling beauty of her eyes.

Tonight, as she had three nights ago in the Rue Notre Dame des Victoires, she wore the moon and three stars in her dark hair. Men handed her flowers, pressed for a word with her. An employee of the theater guided her through the crowd to where the carriage waited, and for a time January saw the pale glimmer of her glove as she leaned through the window, letting her hand be clasped and kissed, and laughing with her too-big mouth, the moon and stars flashing in her hair.

He suspected she'd head for one of the customs gates of the

city, where the roads ran out to Montmartre or Courtille and on into the countryside, but she didn't. Instead, the driver guided the coach along the Rue St-Antoine toward the Marais, the old district of crumbling hôtels which had once been fashionable, and convents where the daughters of the old king's pious friends were educated in the old way, behind high gray walls. January had to fall farther and farther behind, guiding himself by roof-lines and church towers as he had in his childhood guided himself through the Louisiana swamps by the shapes of bent trees and the clumps of palmetto and swamp-laurel; if you lost your bearings there, you were lost indeed.

At least there's no alligators in the Marais.

Just the coachman to watch out for . . .

The lane they halted in was somewhere near the Rue St-Denis, a narrow side street with a gray wall at one side, and a small tradesman's gate. He saw against the pale wall the cloaked woman step from the coach, hurry to the gate. A small light burned above it, and he saw beyond the wall the stumpy tower of a small church, and heard the soft stroke of a bell summoning worshippers to Mass. *A convent . . .*

Phaedre Hirondelle unlocked the garden gate, slipped in (*And what do I do* now?) but he saw the coachman waiting, and knew she'd be out soon, and she was. At the end of the lane, cloaked in the darkness, he saw her come to where the coachman sat in the soft glow of the carriage lamps, and unfold a piece of paper she carried.

Another drop box. What had Chatoine said, in Daniel's peacock salon? *You can add the Convent of Notre Dame de Syon to that . . .*

She climbed in the carriage.

He leaves her word of where he'll be.

He's in hiding. If it was simply gambling debts he'd speak to his father, and have his creditors turned away, as he has for years.

This is a man hiding for his life. Hiding until someone else is convicted, and executed, for his crime.

These thoughts were in his mind as the carriage began moving again, and January gently nudged his borrowed black horse after it, trusting in the clatter of eight hooves, the jangling of trace-chains and cobblestones, to cover his own mount's iron tread. The dim glow of the carriage lamps bobbed before him, moving east. *Damn it, they're heading for the Barrier du Trône.*

Already they were moving through the grim tenements, the smelly wet streets and low warehouses of the Faubourg St-Antoine. *That's all I'll need*, reflected January. *To be ambushed by the local toughs. The men at the customs house will let through a coach and pair but if I'm anywhere near enough to them to follow them on the Vincennes road they'll stop me for a highwayman, and little wonder . . .*

He reined into the darkness of the houses as the carriage rattled into the faint starlight of the Place de la Bastille, the huge absurdity of Napoleon's plaster elephant looming against the night.

'*Malik . . .*' Ayasha's sharp whisper came at the same moment that he heard hooves clack the cobbles behind him. January swung around in the saddle. 'You go around to the Barrier de Bercy. I'll keep behind them here, tell the gate guards a tale.'

January veered off at once, following the tangle of dirt streets towards the canal, then swung east again along the river to where the palings of the city customs 'wall' stood like a finicking reminder of the government's unpitying demands, and revolutions be damned. In the daytimes the barriers – or more accurately, the areas just beyond the barriers – were lively places, taverns and cafés thriving just beyond the city tax-collection line. Now in the deep of night a few lamps were still lit, and young gentlemen laughed and toasted the girls who'd walked out with them in the clammy warmth of the summer evening. Someone played a guitar in a little *estaminet*, and a girl sang some raucous ballad about sausages.

January put his horse's head to the north, and spurred back through the fields and lanes toward the Vincennes road where it ran through the little village of Picpus, farmhouse dogs barking at him as he passed.

In the drumming rain, the flickering candlelight of his plaster-smelling parlor – in this other world, this other life – he looked back on that distant, sweltering night. That former self, riding at a hand-gallop and trusting to the night eyes and good sense of his borrowed horse, with the moon barely more than a fingernail hanging above the dark trees. *We can't lose her*, he remembered thinking. *We have to keep her in sight. Follow her to the young man who killed his brother, the young man who put Anne in danger of her life.*

He remembered how it had felt, to know that he had his quarry in sight at last. To know that this one final knot would be unraveled, and then Anne would be safe, and all would be well.

Ayasha was there, in the main street of Picpus, a dark shape against the pale daub of the cottages, a hundred feet or so from where he emerged from a back lane. She signaled him with her lantern and then trotted to him. 'Down here.' Another lane snaked away, and January could see the dim orange spot of lamp-flame in a window, and the whisper of moonlight on the coach's pale panels. 'The driver's on the box, but he's rugged the horses.' Her voice was barely a murmur in his ear. 'They'll be there for a while.'

January slid from the saddle. Ayasha tied their own mounts outside a shut-up inn – as he'd ridden cross-country January had heard one o'clock strike from the village church – and the two of them slipped through back lanes and across somebody's garden, until the lights of the house, the largest on this side of the village and the only one still illuminated, shone before them. He signed Ayasha to stay outside, in the little orchard behind the house, pistol in her hand, then slipped through one of the wide kitchen windows. They were not yet shuttered, and like the American houses back in New Orleans, French dwellings had their kitchens as part of the main building, separated from the front rooms only by a wide, sanded passage.

He heard no sound as he moved quietly along toward what had to be the door of the room at the front. Doors to his left and his right – *servants' rooms? Does he dare have servants? And if so, how many?* He rubbed gingerly at the bruises, still swollen and painful, on his shoulder and ribs.

Without a sound, he pushed gently at the door.

Two candles burned on the small, plain table in the center of the room. Their light picked triangles of flame in the jewels that lay beside them, the moon and three stars, and the gems of a necklace, coiled like a glittering little snake around a dueling pistol. The woman kneeling before the pale bulk of a chair near the window had let her hair down, and the man seated in the chair, his face against her shoulder, had both hands buried in that river of dark silk. For a moment January only looked at them, clinging together, as he and Ayasha would cling on those endless sweet evenings by the open window of their rooms . . .

Then the man raised his head sharply, and the woman turned, and her hand went for the gun.

January saw the resemblance to Philippe de la Marche at once. Celestin's face reminded January rather of an unbaked loaf, round and soft-looking, decorated with a sparse Van Dyke beard of the sort which was just beginning to be popular again. His eyes, in the gloom, seemed weary and his mouth twisted a little, in exasperation rather than fear.

He wore, January saw, mourning black.

Phaedre Hirondelle stepped back from her lover, pistol leveled on January, her body stiff with anger and pride. 'It's your father's Negro—'

Celestin touched her wrist, shook his head.

January, his own pistol in hand, had been about to snap, 'Don't call out—' but didn't. Neither of them seemed about to do so.

'Oh, put that away,' said Celestin. 'I'm sure Father didn't order you to haul me back to Noisette at gunpoint. You, too, beloved. And it's no good anyway.'

He stood, and the opera singer – not releasing her weapon, but lowering it to her side – took his arm defensively. He drew her close, his left hand moving to cover hers.

'Tell my father – with my compliments – that whatever he does, I will not marry Mademoiselle de Taillefer. If he annuls my marriage to Mademoiselle Hirondelle – to Madame—' he tightened his arm, pressing the woman's hands against his ribs – 'I will only re-marry her in two weeks, and there will be nothing he can do about that.'

SIXTEEN

January lowered his weapon. '*Marry* her?'

In that first moment all he felt was a sense of let down, of exasperation – and of enlightenment. He knew of, and had often heard Ayasha expiate upon, the French law which permitted the heads of noble houses to annul the marriages which their sons might make, up until the age of twenty-four. *A law doubtless enacted precisely to keep fresh-faced boys like Tin-Tin from marrying opera singers.*

He even remembered someone saying recently that Philippe's younger brother was twenty-three . . .

'Before the priest at the church of St-Christophe, in Creteil.' La Hirondelle raised her chin, and January saw, despite her defiance, the glimmer of tears in her eyes.

And in the next moment the meaning of the whole chain of events crashed down on him, like an avalanche, like the roof of a collapsing building.

Only it was not he, he understood, who was in danger of perishing in the ruins.

'And your twenty-fourth birthday is . . .?'

'The thirtieth of August.' The new Vicomte de la Marche frowned at the question. It was something any of his father's servants might be expected to know.

The day Anne will go before the juge d'instruction.

'Were you with madame—' he inclined his head just slightly to the singer – 'on the night of July twenty-seventh? You were seen at Au Mandragore on the twenty-sixth,' he added. 'Though your parents claimed in the *Gazette* that you were at Noisette. The twenty-seventh was the night that we believe your brother was actually killed.'

Celestin's mouth fell open in shock, in the moment before outrage flared in his eyes. It was Hirondelle's turn now to silence him, which she did with a quick squeeze of his arm.

'He was with me,' she said. 'Both on the twenty-seventh and

on the night before. And no,' she added, as if she read January's next thought, 'I'm not playing the opera heroine here, M'sieu . . .?'

'Janvier.'

'M'sieu Janvier. Any of the girls in the ballet, or any of the stagehands, can tell you that M'sieu de Gourgue – M'sieu le Vicomte,' she corrected herself, with a sudden grimace of distress, 'waited backstage for me on the Monday night, and was with me on the Tuesday, dressed very much not in his best, at the house of Claud Boulanger – the assistant director of the Opera ballet – in Vincennes. The man who owns this house, in fact.'

'Does my father honestly think,' De la Marche broke into her words, nearly breathless with indignation and disbelief, 'that I would . . . Would what? *Murder* my brother? I was angry at him of course: who wouldn't be? It was only a matter of time before he would have dragged our name through the police courts! And knowing what he did with . . . with those boys he took up, and with that degenerate wretch of a Jew banker's son, I prayed nightly for his soul.'

'The murder of a brother,' replied January softly, 'is quite literally the oldest crime in the world, monsieur. Forgive me for coming to the wrong conclusion when the other obvious suspects were proved to have been elsewhere.'

'Even Ben-Gideon's wife?'

'Do you know Anne Ben-Gideon?'

The young vicomte shook his head.

'I do. And believe me, she would not have—'

'But she sent him a note,' said Celestin. 'A note to lure him to a meeting with her. Or to lure her husband, I . . . I don't know really which of them she intended to kill . . .'

January could only shake his head. 'She never sent such a thing.'

'She did,' insisted the young man. 'Her maid saw her write a note that morning. And Laurent – one of the Ben-Gideon footmen – took it in and laid it on the hall table. She must have known my brother would be there. It had "Urgent" written on the outside, Laurent says.'

'You've seen this note?' January fumbled through his memories: Anne, Tuesday morning, at the Palais Royale, an English hunting-rifle on her back and the little silver muff pistol stuck in her tricolor sash. Gerry O'Dwyer hovering respectfully at her elbow.

Daniel ducking into the house behind the St-Denis barricade later that afternoon: *The dear boy is as beautiful as an angel but has* no *sense whatsoever* . . .

'Anne was on the barricades,' he said slowly. 'I don't know what time she set forth that morning. Was the note written in pen or in pencil?'

The young vicomte shook his head. 'I didn't see it. But Laurent swears such a note was delivered, and that it wasn't there after my brother left Ben-Gideon's house.'

'Laurent was hired by your father,' protested January. 'As was Madame Ben-Gideon's maid—'

'To protect them,' returned Celestin. 'Naturally. Can you imagine going to the law with such knowledge, if you were still at the mercy of that family? By what I have heard, if Moses Ben-Gideon knows what a scruple is, he hides the knowledge well. And that poor fool Armand, madame's brother . . . I think he would say anything to destroy testimony against his sister. I have spoken to Laurent,' he added quietly. 'And to Liane Pichon. You say you know Madame Ben-Gideon, but how well do you know her? Liane says she hated Philippe like poison. Hated her husband as well, for disgracing her before the whole of society. How could she fail to do so? He's the one who drove her to take lovers—'

'That's ridiculous,' January snapped, and bit back a comment – which would have helped nothing – about the upcoming disgrace in the de Gourgue family when it was revealed that they now numbered an opera singer in their ranks.

'It *is* ridiculous, Tin-Tin.' Phaedre Hirondelle put a hand on her husband's wrist. 'No man *drives* a woman to misbehave herself . . . certainly not a woman of so strong a character as madame. And that note Laurent saw – and you will admit, m'sieu,' she added, turning to January, 'that Madame Ben-Gideon's hand is a distinctive one – could have been anything. She might have written any number of notes that morning. Myself, I would not believe the word of a woman's maidservant, particularly when she has been hired by that woman's enemies. Or the girl could have been unsure as to the date. It is easy for a new mistress to push one's recollections one way or the other, if one is afraid for one's own livelihood.'

The velvet swags of her hair shifted across her shoulders as she shook her head, and her eyes were dark with the recollection of, perhaps, her own days of fear.

'But unfortunately I am not the *juge d'instruction*. And unfortunately, the note no longer exists. It was undoubtedly in Madame Ben-Gideon's hand, Laurent says—' she glanced for confirmation to her young husband, who nodded – 'which Laurent knows quite well, of course. It was sealed hastily with a wafer, he says, and the word, "Urgent" was written across the face of it . . .'

'Urgent?'

The young man nodded. 'My mother would have it,' he said, 'that Ben-Gideon destroyed it, rather than have his wife accused—'

'Not an action,' put in La Hirondelle, 'one would look to see, if his wife had murdered his lover.'

Celestin shook his head, his face suddenly tight with grief. 'I don't know what to think,' he admitted. 'Everyone at Noisette was talking about it, and accusing madame . . . My father shut himself up in his room for hours, weeping, I think . . . He *never* weeps. And then that horrible old Taillefer and his wife started asking, What about the marriage? Father . . .' He hesitated, twisting the fingers of his right hand with his left, then raising his hands to stroke and straighten his moustaches, as if he feared they would come loose.

'Father loved Philippe very much,' he went on after a time. 'But he has all his life thought first of his land, of the heritage of our family. He has recently entered into business partnership with the marquis, on the strength of an understanding that my brother would marry Mademoiselle Marie. Here,' he said suddenly. 'I speak of the honor of my family and I don't even offer you refreshment . . . Please, sit down.'

He looked a little helplessly at his bride. 'I have no idea what sort of amenities Boulanger left for us here—'

'I'll look.' La Hirondelle picked up one of the candles. To January, she said, 'Of course Milord the Comte has had his grooms out looking for M'sieu le Vicomte – and I do beg your pardon, for I know Roquille – my coachman – and the two stagehands who've been helping him guard me treated you roughly. But they'd seen you asking questions around the Place des Victoires, and de Belvoire can be *unscrupulous*. Particularly with a woman whom he considers a danger to his family.'

She shook her head. From playing for her at Opera rehearsal, January knew her to be exacting where her art was concerned, and more knowledgeable about music than many of his fellow musicians. Looking now at the strong lines of her face, he suspected that she was several years older than her bridegroom – whether Tin-Tin knew it or not – and that she'd be the brains of the marriage.

'For nearly a month we have had to be completely invisible,' she said. 'I have sung, and rehearsed, and behaved precisely as I always have, but from time to time I know I've been followed, and not only by yourself, m'sieu. Though for two years now my husband has been tucking money away in different banks to take us through this time, because of poor M'sieu Philippe's death, Celestin hasn't been able to show his face anywhere in Paris where he could be recognized. He has keys to all his father's properties, and in them I'll leave information as to where and how he can find the packets I leave, of money, and instructions as to where I have found for him to stay. Food, too, sometimes, if the house or the apartment or wherever it is, is vacant. Sometimes our friends are good enough to leave food and wine, but it is always something of a surprise, like a bean in a twelfth-night cake.'

She disappeared into the dark of the kitchen passage. January saw how her young husband followed her with adoring eyes. Turning back to January, he said, 'I apologize for my anger earlier. I thought – we all thought – that Philippe . . .' His voice cracked a little on his brother's name, and he pulled himself together with an effort. 'We thought he had left Paris. He said he was going to, when the trouble started. It was Friday before our parents heard he was . . . heard what had happened – and by Saturday, they were planning my wedding.'

He shook his head, not in amazement, but in a sort of pain, like a horse tormented by biting flies. Then he managed a wry little smile. 'It's ungallant of me to say so of any woman, but it was always quite clear – to me, at least – that Mademoiselle Marie had no affection for my brother. She didn't really care whether he was a sodomite or an assassin or a drunkard. Her only concern was that he would one day be the Comte de Belvoire, and she would have a wealthy establishment of her own.'

'And for all the girl's tantrums and spite,' added La Hirondelle quietly, returning with a tray containing bread, cheese, some wine glasses and a chunk of paté wrapped in paper, 'from what I have heard of her mother I can scarcely blame the girl for wanting to escape.' When she passed close to him, her hair smelled of sandalwood. 'Did you bring other bravos with you, M'sieu Janvier? I have water boiling for coffee.'

Ayasha was beckoned in, with the signal January had long established meaning: 'All is really well', and she listened with somber eyes to the true story of Celestin's flight and concealment. In her stillness, January could tell that she knew what it meant.

'The thing is,' said the vicomte diffidently, 'my father is not a man to take "No" for an answer. He put tremendous pressure on Philippe – not about his way of life, but earlier, when he had friends of whom Father didn't approve. One friend – not the louche degenerates he later came to favor, but a quite honest young officer – Father bought up his debts, and forced the man out of the Guards and out of Paris entirely, only because he was a socialist. Father thought him a bad influence. He's had several of Philippe's friends arrested – I'm sure they deserved some sort of punishment for their sins, but not . . . not quite so savage. One man, Father used his influence with the colonial office to have sent to Guiana, where the poor fellow died. Sometimes I thought it was his way of punishing Philippe.

'Please understand, m'sieu.' Again he shook his head, struggling with thoughts he had pushed aside. 'I know my brother was a sinner, but . . . There was much in him that was good. In any case between Father and Monsieur le Marquis and his awful daughter, I panicked. I fled Noisette. I married Phaedre as quickly as I could, under my family name . . .'

His hand sought hers, and she returned its pressure. On the table, the candles guttered, the gold light flicking over the diamond moon, the diamond stars, and calling echoes in the black coffee dregs.

'And I have been in hiding ever since. But because of Philippe's death I haven't dared to simply leave Paris. In case of some emergency, some sudden event – whose nature I can't even begin to imagine! – I wanted to be on hand. As Phaedre says, she would leave me keys, and instructions, of where to find money, and food, and shelter. One night I slept in the crypt of Notre Dame de Lorette, whose sacristan is the brother-in-law of one of the stagehands and the most venal being God in his wisdom created. On another, Phaedre's arrangements fell through and we slept in her dressing room at the Opera, with Roquille keeping guard in the street. But you see,' he finished, 'on the night my poor brother was killed, whether it was by Madame Ben-Gideon or by someone else, Phaedre and I were together, at our friend Boulanger's apartment. And Boulanger, and the tenor Valette, and five members of the ballet, were with us. I am sorry.'

1839

And so they left them, together in that comfortable little house in Picpus: the soft-faced young gentleman who later did indeed, January recalled, become the Comte de Belvoire, and his wife, the beautiful Hirondelle.

The candles were burned down. It was almost dawn.

The new comtesse, he remembered, had been roundly snubbed by the whole of French society – at least during the two years between that stifling night and the terrible cholera summer that had ended with Ayasha's death and January's departure from his adopted homeland. He had read not long ago of her death, at the age of thirty-six.

Childless, the newspaper had said. Almost certainly, January guessed, because of earlier abortions undergone for the sake of her career. He had not read anywhere that the comte had married again, but such things often didn't make the American papers.

In any case, six mornings after that meeting in Picpus, Anne Ben-Gideon had gone before a *juge d'instruction* and had her case remanded for trial before the red-robed judge of the assizes, on the testimonies of Laurent the footman, Liane Pichon ('*hated all her husband's men-friends like poison, she did . . .*'), and Apollon Michaud ('*A more spiteful woman I never encountered in my life . . . in spite of all the men who paraded through* her *bed!*').

Two months later, on the seventh of November, she had gone to the guillotine.

*   *   *

In Rue Esplanade, the charcoal-seller's wailing cry rose: 'My donkey white, my coal be black, buy yo' charcoal, ten-cents sack, *chaaaaar-cooooal . . .*'

January blinked, but beyond the last guttering flare of the candles, he could see no whisper of light past the jalousies. A mosquito lighted on his wrist: he swatted it to a blot of gore. In an hour the bells would ring for morning Mass. Somewhere – he was virtually certain – Rose, and Gabriel, and Zizi-Marie would be hearing that bell. Like the bells of Paris, he thought, as Ayasha and he rode their black horses through iron darkness that smelled of cut hay and wood smoke, not speaking. Wondering what to do next. What they *could* do.

He rose, and the smoking candles bent and flickered, the gold light dancing momentarily on the black coffee dregs in the cups on the table.

Honeysuckle, he thought. For a moment he almost smelled it.

What had Olympe said? *The gold smells of honeysuckle*; the way the diamond moon, the diamond stars had smelled of the sandalwood in Hirondelle's hair.

What can a man do with land like this? Hannibal had asked, thrashing through a tangled curtain of honeysuckle that hung over the doors of the ruined steamboat that was slowly rotting on Henry Brooke's new-bought land.

And January knew the answer. La Hirondelle had told him, with the memory of the diamond stars in her hair, and the scent of sandalwood in the night.

Use it as a drop box.

Like the birdhouse pagoda in an overgrown garden on the Rue Notre Dame des Victoires.

I'll leave information as to where and how he can find the packets I leave, the singer had said, the lamp in her hand and her dark hair tumbled over her shoulders.

You have three weeks, Ganch had said.

The other pieces of land – cheap and worthless – were only blinds. Diversions.

And the question is now, reflected January, *how to retrieve whatever is in that 'drop box' without having Ganch follow me to the place and rob me of even the leverage of making a trade.*

SEVENTEEN

With gray light growing in the sky and the last balmi-
ness of the night yielding to morning's thick heat,
January fetched rough brown soap, and tepid water
from the cistern, and washed himself in the yard. The 'spit bath'
(as his mother called them) made him feel better. So would the
last of yesterday's rice, he reflected. But instead he bolted every
shutter and window of the house, and walked the ten streets –
over and down – to the cathedral, where he knelt among the
marchandes and laborers, to hear Mass and receive the Body of
Christ.

Instead of praying that Jared Ganch and all his men would
roast screaming in Hell, he made himself pray: 'Thank you for
giving me this chance. Thank you for guidance. Thy will be
done.'

He couldn't imagine what life would be like without Rose.
Without his son. Sometimes it felt to him that when Ayasha had
died, his heart – and a huge amount of the surrounding flesh –
had been carved, bleeding, from his chest. When he had met
Rose, loved Rose, he had acquired a new heart, of a different
color, a different consistency, a different composition than the
heart that was gone.

If that, too, were taken from him he suspected that this time
he would simply bleed to death.

*If the gods really want to do this to me, I won't fight them
anymore.*

In any case he knew that if something went wrong and Ganch
made good on his threat to sell his family, the gambler would
almost certainly have him killed; *Just to be on the safe side*, as
he would undoubtedly explain, without any personal animosity.
It's only business.

Then as he rose from his knees to walk back to the outer
world, he saw the cab driver Tyrell Mulvaney kneeling just within
the doors.

Mulvaney's cab, with its two beautiful bronze-bay mules, was tied near the cathedral steps. January stood by the team's heads, genuinely admiring the animals, until their owner emerged, a square-built, craggy-featured man in his forties wearing a cinnamon-colored coat and a top hat with a rose stuck in its brim. January said, 'Mr Mulvaney,' and held out his hand. 'Benjamin January. Could you spare me a few minutes for a word, sir?'

Mulvaney's eyes narrowed, placing him. 'You're the feller what plays for the opera,' he said after a moment, and returned his grip.

'I am that, sir. Granville's Marcellus told me where I might find you.' Which wasn't entirely the truth, since anyone in New Orleans who was paying attention to what went on around him would know where Mulvaney had his stand, but the driver's shoulders relaxed and he smiled.

'Ah, now, there's a man what understands horseflesh!'

'And from what I can see of those beauties of yours,' returned January, 'he didn't lie about your eye for a good mule.'

Respectable artisans and their wives, both white and colored, were arriving for the later Mass – the very few wealthy who remained in town wouldn't put in an appearance until the ten o'clock Mass – but the driver took no notice of them. After a good ten minutes' discussion of the intelligence, willingness, saint-like forbearance and esteemed parentage of mules in general and Tulip and Hotspur in particular, January brought up the English gentleman in the bottle-green coat whom Mulvaney had conveyed to Bayou St John on the last day of June. 'For I won't deny to you, sir, the man was found shot the next day, and the woman he's been staying with is accused of it. A friend of my sister's, who was asleep in her bed at the time – and of course, being asleep in her bed by herself, can come up with no witness . . .'

'Lord, the damn' guards'd have you be robbin' a bank where everybody can see you, rather than waterin' your flowers in your own backyard!' Mulvaney flung up his hands. 'Pigs are all the same, they are, the whole world over!'

'Certainly every part of the world that I've seen, sir,' agreed January ruefully.

'Cheap bastard he was, too, your Englishman,' added the driver.

'Give me an argument about the fare, an' then tried to get me to come back in an hour, an' *then* wait about til he came out to me . . . pah! All the same, bloody Sassenach . . .'

'Where did you drop him?'

'Bloody should have dropped him in the bloody bayou, is what I should have done. Got himself shot, did he? Good job on somebody.'

'Bad job on the poor girl he's been living with,' returned January, 'if we can't find where he really was that evening before he ended up floating in the basin.'

'How'd he end up in the basin, then?' Mulvaney leaned one elbow on Tulip's back and frowned, working out the geography in his mind. 'There's not current enough in that bayou to float a paper boat, not ten feet in a year. And I left the man just on the town side of that big bayou, what's it called? The one that divides the Widow Fortin's land from Howe's . . .'

'I know the place,' said January. 'Which side of the bayou?'

'Upstream,' replied the Irishman, using the standard Orleanean topography rather than the North-South-East-West directions favored by the rest of the world.

'You turned around and left him there?' Bayou Fortin was a good hundred yards beyond the last of the houses; Brooke must have either turned around and walked back, or have walked on to a meeting place further up the shell road. A place which would, he reflected, have had every trace of a meeting, fatal or otherwise, wiped out by the daily aspersion of summer rains. 'Could you swear to that in court?'

'That I can, sir,' promised the driver, 'that I can. Anythin' to help a little lady that's shot an Englishman.'

Nevertheless, reflected January, crossing the Place des Armes toward La Violette's coffee stand beneath the market arcade, he would have to go out – with Hannibal along for protection – and search along the verge of the shell road and back into the woods.

After we finish at Chitimacha, he thought. *And maybe whatever we find there will tell us what we need to know to free Jacquette Filoux – without having to track down the execrable Uncle Juju . . .*

'Uncle Ben?' He turned sharply, and yes, it was Ti-Gall, tall and solemn and awkward in a much-stained calico shirt.

He must have just come off-duty at the Flesh and Blood . . .
'I think I found where they got Zizi and M'am Rose.'

The bordello operated by Cassie Lovelace on Harter Street stood
at the very edge of the Second Municipality, a few blocks beyond
the last of the built-up area. It was early enough that none of the
whores would yet be awake, particularly on a Sunday: the inhabitants of the Second Municipality, though they might own
whorehouses, didn't like to see the Sabbath violated. Nevertheless, January kept to the trees on the next lot. The kitchen windows
at the back of the house were open and he could see a servant
woman come and go to the woodpile and the outhouse, and it
wouldn't do to have even the chance of word getting back to
Jared Ganch – the house's owner – that a black man six foot
three and built like Hercules had been loitering around looking
at the place. It wouldn't take him long to guess who *that* was.

Ti-Gall had said to him that Mrs Lovelace – a trim blonde not
much over thirty – had visited Ganch at the Flesh and Blood,
dressed with a severe respectability one didn't often encounter
on Girod Street. This wasn't something a madame would often
do – she wasn't trolling for customers in the gambling parlor
– and the coincidence of timing was marked. After five minutes
in Ganch's office the pair of them had entered the saloon and
sought out a fat, balding, rather bleary young man whose air of
crushed defeat seemed to stem less from the alcohol he'd imbibed
– 'He been there all evenin',' Ti-Gall had said – than from the
fact that he'd run through all his money at the craps table and
the house wouldn't front him any more. They'd talked to this
individual for some minutes and he'd nodded, but had finished
his drink with no air of hurry before accompanying Mrs Lovelace
out the door. Later inquiry of the barkeep had told Ti-Gall that
the young man was Dr Sparger, one of the dimmer lights of the
American medical community.

'It didn't seem like there's any emergency,' Ti-Gall had
concluded, as he and January had walked towards Canal Street.
'But I thought you'd want to know.'

January had sent the young man home when they'd reached
the wide strip of 'neutral ground'. He himself, if recognized,
might face a reprimand or, at worst, a beating from Catastrophe

Watling and his boys, but Jared Ganch needed him for the moment. There was a real possibility that Ti-Gall would be killed for snooping, and the New Orleans City Guards probably wouldn't even investigate the random murder of a black saloon-boy. Watching the house now, January guessed that Rose, Gabriel, and Zizi-Marie weren't being held on the premises itself. Deserted as the place seemed at this hour of a Sunday, in the evenings there would simply be too many people around who might see or hear something. It wasn't fancy, but it was no dockside dive, either. Even Jared Ganch's influence with the municipal council might not serve to keep him out of trouble.

Particularly, reflected January, if the trouble involved information acquired from foreign consulates.

But two hundred yards further on, beyond even the last of the staked-out promises of streets and lots, he found what looked like an old indigo mill, a ruinous brick building recently repaired with the usual back-of-town resource of old flatboat-planks, and flanked by a similarly reconstructed overseer's house, and what had undoubtedly been a slave jail.

The outhouse was newly dug, within the last few weeks, January guessed. The earth thrown beside where its pit had been delved hadn't completely settled. By the midden of broken cigar boxes, eggshells, breadcrusts and chicken bones outside the back door, the house had been in occupation for roughly that long. A makeshift corral near the old mill housed a dozen horses, among whom he recognized a stripe-backed dun like the one Catastrophe Watling had been riding yesterday (*was it only yesterday?*).

Do not *be caught* anywhere *near this house*.

The place was silent – it was still only eight in the morning – but January knew a hideout when he saw one, and the fact that the place was this close to town told him roughly what was going on. He backed, very quietly, into the woods, and though his whole skin prickled with danger at being alone in the *riprière* outside of town, he made his way back to Rue Esplanade by the most circuitous route he knew, looking over his shoulder all the way.

Now was *not* the time to be seen taking even the slightest interest in Jared Ganch's plans.

*   *   *

Upon reaching home, he made himself a cup of coffee. A yellow-ware bowl that he recognized as Olympe's sat, covered with towels, on the table outside the kitchen; it contained some of his sister's excellent 'hoppin' john'. Evidently La Hirondelle wasn't the only woman who left secret offerings of food for her menfolks. He reflected wryly that for a woman who had a sometime reputation as a poisoner, his sister was a marvelous cook.

He couldn't bear to return to the stillness and shadow of that unnaturally empty house, filled with the smell of drying plaster and fresh paint. *Rose's dream*, he thought. *Rose's school*. When the first of the girls arrived in October, would Rose even be alive? *Will I?*

He settled at the worktable that stood in front of the kitchen's open shutters, gazed across the crooked yard at the barred and shuttered house. *I'd better write something*, he thought, *leaving the house to Olympe*. Otherwise, he knew, their mother would lay claim to a portion of it, and force a sale. *If I leave it in a will, I can stipulate that Olympe give shelter to Hannibal, so he won't have to go on towsing Kentucky Williams to keep a roof over his head.*

There had been summers, he recalled, when his friend had fallen afoul of the saloon owner (or when Williams had a new boyfriend) and Hannibal had taken refuge in the attics of disused houses here and there around the French Town, whose owners had gone to the lake. He'd spent two and a half months once, in the loft of Lorette's livery stable, his presence unsuspected by anyone. January shook his head, smiling a little. *Like Tin-Tin in his father's various houses to which he had the keys . . .*

With an almost audible click, a dozen things fell together in his mind at once.

The moon and three stars.

Phaedre La Hirondelle bending to unlock the gate at fifteen, Rue Notre Dame des Victoires.

He set his coffee cup down and said, 'Oh . . .' as the streetgate of the crooked little yard opened and Hannibal Sefton slipped through.

'*Ave, amicus meus.*'

Still feeling a little dazed at his revelation, January said, '*Ave*. You're just the man I wanted to see.'

'Every time anyone says that to me,' said Hannibal plaintively, 'I find myself in danger of my life or facing an accusation of paternity.'

It was so early in the day that he, like Ti-Gall, must have been just coming from his night's activities rather than just arising from his bed. January had never known his friend to waken of his own free will earlier than noon, even after he'd quit drinking. The fiddler carried a long loaf of bread – fresh, by the scent of it, God knew where he'd acquired it – a newspaper, and two peaches. 'Are you all right? All things considered,' he added, with an air of apology, and set his chimneypot hat on the table beside Olympe's dish.

'I am,' said January. 'All things considered. I think I've found where they're holding Rose. And I think I know what's going on.' And as he fetched the coffee beans from the kitchen shelf and the roaster from its place on the wall, he delivered a brief but thorough outline of his interview with Oldmixton, and his morning's expedition. 'Taken together, it seems clear to me that Jared Ganch is gathering men for some illegal purpose that is being winked at by the local authorities, as long as they keep quiet about it.'

Hannibal paused in cutting and buttering the bread. 'Sounds like mercenaries for some kind of filibustering excursion.'

'Hand me the newspaper, would you? There's two places I can think of,' he went on, as he paged slowly through the *True American*, 'that filibusters could make money right now – Chile, and New Grenada. Ten years ago filibusters could just raid Mexico, but since Santa Ana took over he's strong enough to retaliate. Ganch might be putting together mercenaries to take to the fighting between Chile and Peru. He could hire out to one side or the other, or simply raid convents and town houses in Lima or Santiago. They must hold hundreds of thousands in gold, but that's a long way to go. But a big raid in New Grenada, where anything can be blamed on the fighting . . . Cartagena and Carracas are just across the gulf . Even when you've paid for a ship and paid off your men, you'll still net a fortune.'

Bags of coin, boxes of rubies, Our Lord with his body all made of pearl . . .

Convents. Churches. The government of New Grenada in

the throes of civil war, its armies occupied in fighting one another . . .

'But they need a bankroll,' concluded Hannibal.

'That they do.'

It's the gold they're after. Gold that M'am L'Araignée had whispered about, the dark spirit that lived in a black bottle on an altar in Olympe's parlor. Gold that smelled of honeysuckle.

'And an enterprising gentleman like Henry Brooke can be easily pardoned for thinking that a fifty percent share of the take might well be a better use for the Bank of England stock certificates that he's carrying, than whatever use the British Foreign Office intended for them.'

'He might indeed,' Hannibal agreed.

January went on, 'I'm pretty sure Rose and the others are being held in the old slave jail behind the indigo mill, out on the Pontchartrain Road. It actually takes a good deal of trouble to keep someone prisoner, you know, if you want them in good condition. It has to be someplace where there are your own men always around. Cassie Lovelace has been told to keep an eye on Rose—'

'Then I—' Hannibal rose from beside the fire, dumped the roasted coffee beans into the grinder and saluted with the empty pan as with a dueling saber – 'shall take it upon myself to keep an eye – and perhaps more – on the beautiful Cassie. I don't think we dare get closer to Rose than that at the moment . . . That's what you were going to ask me, wasn't it?'

January shook his head. 'You're right,' he agreed quietly, 'about not being able to get close to the indigo mill without risking one or more of them being killed – or mutilated – in retaliation if we're seen. But it's not something I would ask you or anyone to do.'

'Then I'll do it in spite of you,' retorted Hannibal. He settled at the table with the coffee grinder before him. 'I'll do it because for eight years now I have nourished an unrequited passion for Rose in my secret heart, *Da mi basia mille, Rosa, deinde centum* . . grinding my love in the mills of our friendship as I now grind these coffee beans—'

January gave his friend's shoulder a sharp shove, and his friend an unwilling grin. 'That's not what I was going to ask.'

'Well, I won't pull resurrection-fern out of your roof—'

'Not that, either. I want you to come back out with me to Chitimacha – now, this morning. Right now,' he added, 'while it's early – we can make coffee when we get back.'

'*Festina lente* . . . I thought we ascertained on Friday there was nothing out there.' He emptied the contents of the coffeemill into the pot – regretfully – for later boiling.

'That,' said January, 'is because we didn't know where to concentrate our search. *Assiduus usus uni rei dedities ingenium et artem saepe vincit*,' he added. 'And bring your picklocks.'

EIGHTEEN

J anuary dug two dollars from the small horde that Sir John Oldmixton had given him the previous night, and sent Hannibal off to Maggie Valentine's livery for Roux and Voltaire. It was an expense, and mounted men would be more conspicuous, but Hannibal didn't look in shape for a four-mile walk out to Bayou des Avocats. While the fiddler was about this errand, January himself walked over to Rue Toulouse. For the past five days, since Jacquette Filoux's arrest, in addition to taking the young woman food, clean linen and ginger water – for the food in the prison was worse than execrable – and her children to visit her, Olympe and her husband Paul had paid daily visits to the shabby cottage, to see that all was secure. Now January did the same, walking around the yard in a perfunctory fashion, checking the shutters, briefly rattling the handles of those that covered the French doors into the dining room and bedroom, checking likewise the locks on the kitchen door and the latches that were the only defense on the doors of the outhouse, and of the children's rooms above the kitchen.

He returned to his house in a thoughtful mood, and by the time the shops were open, and the wastrels of the town were stirring, he and Hannibal had reached the stretch of the shell road where Tyrell Mulvaney had set Henry Brooke down on the late afternoon of the twenty-ninth of June.

'There are thirteen houses on that side of the bayou, along this stretch of Bayou St John,' he said. 'Three more lie further back in the trees. There's the Eagletons and the Almonasters, Pandely and Arrowsmith . . . maybe Arrowsmith is this side, I don't recall. I've sent a note to Shaw, asking for a list.'

They were passing the Bayou Bridge as he spoke, and across the water January could glimpse the houses, set back in the trees. One or two of them were old, raised on stilts against the periodic floods. Even the newer, more American-looking dwellings stood high on foundations, their 'main' floors – like the *piano nobile* of European town houses – standing above storerooms or waste-space that functioned as above-ground basements. Even so, he reflected, the mosquitoes must still drive the householders crazy.

Servants of course had been about their business for hours. But now the owners themselves were visible, those of them that hadn't abandoned the state entirely until cooler weather came. A young lady in pink paused on a gallery to have a word with the slaves who swept the steps. A black groom held the heads of a beautiful chestnut team while their owner – and his – climbed into a buggy. A young gentleman in a blue coat helped his crippled wife to walk among her roses, leaning on his arm and a stick.

Was Henry Brooke really Gerry O'Dwyer?
Who had he gone to Bayou St John to meet?

Not someone connected with Jared Ganch, January was willing to bet. Did one of Ganch's wealthier competitors have a place out here? Or the spymaster for some other country?

Or did one of those houses shelter a discontented wife who'd taken the Irishman's roving eye one day while he was on his way out to Chitimacha?

Fastidious, Oldmixton had described him.

Beyond Bayou Fortin – a desultory stream that would probably lose its identity in the next flood – the land grew marshier. Instead of houses along the banks January saw only the occasional flat houseboats, and half-naked children, white or brown, digging vegetable gardens or herding cows in the woods. He glanced behind him a dozen times, but saw no sign of pursuit or surveillance. Catastrophe Watling and his 'boys' had evidently taken the same cursory look around Chitimacha that he and Hannibal had performed, seeking for obvious signs that something had been hidden there.

'Maybe they just assume that we'd have found whatever there was to be found.' Hannibal adjusted the veils of mosquito-bar that he'd pinned around the brim of his hat, so that they covered his face as they turned off along the edge of Bayou des Avocats, and fanned nevertheless at the mosquitoes that swarmed around them. 'And maybe they just didn't want to come back and look very hard. Are you sure it'll be there?'

'Not in the slightest.' January lowered his voice, the heavy stillness of the deeper *ciprière* pressing around them. On the other side of the bayou, an alligator hauled herself up onto the remains of what looked like a stranded pirogue, decaying where it had long ago been beached. Waterstriders made tiny movement on the green-brown sheet of the stream, where the sun-dapple glinted like stolen gold. 'But I trust that thing that lives in Olympe's bottle. And it's worth a look.'

January left Hannibal holding horse and mule some distance from the plantation itself, and went ahead to cautiously circle the house and grounds, to make sure that they were in fact deserted. He saw no sign of anyone (*Not that* that *means anything*, he told himself with a sigh, *after it's rained every afternoon for weeks*). Nor was there evidence that anyone had been there since his former visit. Tying Voltaire and Roux in the canebrakes out of sight of the road, the two men stripped to their drawers, shirts, and veil-draped hats, and, armed with January's cane knife and the stoutest snake-sticks January could cut, they returned to the vine-choked hulk of the steamboat.

The wreck lay heeled slightly to port. She had, January guessed, torn out her belly on a submerged snag trying to get back down Bayou des Avocats to the larger Bayou St John after a flood. 'I wonder whether the owners cleared her out,' he murmured, as they half-climbed, half-pulled themselves up the tilted stairway to the upper deck, 'or whether the locals beat them to it?'

'I keep expecting to see tigers.' Hannibal surveyed the clumps and clusters of resurrection-fern which had taken root on every windowsill and bunk of the men's cabin. Spanish moss hung from holes where the ceiling had decayed. A snake whipped down from a bunk and away into a hole in the floor.

'Don't worry about that one,' January advised, as Hannibal drew back in alarm. 'Black and yellow longways stripes are garter snakes, not poison. The ones you want to watch out for are the copper-colored ones with diamond markings, or the dark gray with bits of yellow—'

'I shall watch out for *all* of them, thank you. I presume they're . . . er . . . friends of your sister?'

'In fact,' said January with a smile, 'they are. She – and I – learned from the time we were Baby John's age to tell the poison snakes from the safe ones, but Mambo Jeanne, back on

Bellefleur, would tan our hides for us if we disturbed any snake.
Damballah Wedo – Li Grand Zombi – created the world, Mambo
Jeanne would tell us, and his descendants share his wisdom.'

Hannibal made a noise usually written as *Eeugh*, and
shivered.

'And they do eat mice and cockroaches,' added January, leading
the way out onto the upper deck and around to the ladies' cabin
– much smaller, and with only a few bunks remaining. There
was little to be seen there, nor in any of the other rooms of the
upper deck, as January had seen during their first inspection of
the steamboat. It was one of the older types, a stern-wheeler with
a very shallow draft, as any boat would be that anyone would
even consider taking, no matter how high the water, up Bayou
St John. From the crazy ruin of the stairway to the top deck he
could see into the pilot house, perched high above the river to
give the pilot the best view of those small ripples and eddies that
gave clues to sub-surface dangers. The state of the ceilings of
both men's cabin and women's told him that trying to cross the
upper deck would result in the rotting boards giving way.

'All right,' grumbled Hannibal. 'I'll give them that. *Ave atque
vale, amice*, all is well . . . I don't see where a strongbox full of
stock certificates *could* be hidden up here. For one thing, I don't
think the floors would stand it.'

'Just making sure,' returned January. 'Let's have a look below.'

'I was afraid you were going to say that.'

The forepart of the hold stuck up out of water, but was an
even worse tangle of vines, resurrection-fern, elephant-ear and
swamp-laurel, the broken hatches surrounded with clouds of
mosquitoes as with plumes of brown smoke. Hannibal whispered,
'*Di nos protegat*,' as they edged past that sinister pit – *God knows
what else is down there*, January thought – and they made their
way to the engine room, submerged knee-deep at its forward end
and shoulder-deep at the far end – the end which they had formerly
explored by poking their snake-sticks into the murky green water
before retreating in the face of the local serpent life.

The boat's engine was of the older type, and much of it had
been salvaged – or looted – years before. The great pivoting
crossbeam had been taken down, and lay rusting under a mantle
of waterplants and slime. The valves and gears were likewise

gone, but the furnace remained, and the two boilers – probably, guessed January, because they were old and may have been too cheaply made to be worth salvage.

Nothing in the furnace. 'Of course not,' sighed Hannibal, 'it's in the dry end of the room.'

The small iron strongbox – roughly four inches square by a foot long – had been wedged into the flue of the first boiler, and when, wet and slimy and hot, January extracted it from its hiding place and got it out onto the deck, Hannibal made short work of its lock. The neat roll of Bank of England stock certificates had been wrapped for safekeeping in several layers of oiled silk, sealed with wax. Separately wrapped were ninety-six gold eagle five-dollar coins.

There was nothing else in the box.

Without a word, January returned to the boiler room and searched the second boiler, the furnace, and every cranny and nook he could probe beneath the water. Hannibal stood by with a snake-stick and they were both, in spite of liberal coatings of mud and Olympe's bug-grease, bitten repeatedly by mosquitoes above the water and crawfish beneath it. They found nothing.

'It has to be here somewhere,' said January stubbornly, when they emerged at last, exhausted, filthy, and almost dizzy with thirst.

'Does it?' Hannibal retrieved the little strongbox from where they'd cached it under the stair during their second search, and followed January out through the curtain of honeysuckle to the deck. 'If Brooke was going partners with Ganch, I can see him handing off the money and the stocks as seed money for the expedition. But he'd want to keep the more valuable commodity – the list of names – to himself. I presume he compiled the list from Oldmixton's notes about people in New Grenada who'd assist filibusters in their little looting expedition, if that's what they were planning . . .'

'That's what I figure,' said January. From the little bundle of their clothes he fetched a corked jug of ginger water that he'd had the wits to bring from home – the taste of it brought Gabriel, its brewer, back to his mind, with painful and furious clarity. 'People who know where the convents and churches around Cartagena, or wherever they're planning to visit in the war zone, are hiding their gold. And I'm afraid,' he went on wearily, 'that you're probably right.'

'Were I dealing with Jared Ganch,' said Hannibal, 'I'd be sure to keep *something* that he needed up my sleeve – and make sure I knew where all the exits of the room were during any conversation. I suspect Brooke had it on him when he was shot, and *that*,' he concluded, 'unfortunately, brings us back to Uncle Juju.'

'I fear – again – that you're right.' January passed the ginger water to his friend and tucked a corner of his bandana handkerchief under the lock of the strongbox as he shut it, to keep the lock from catching again. 'Let's do what we can to conceal the fact that we were here,' he went on, 'in case one of Ganch's myrmidons is clever enough to figure out why a man with something to hide would buy land with a wrecked steamboat on it—'

'Could happen,' agreed Hannibal, with a certain amount of regret but no evident belief in such an eventuality.

'And then I think I'll just conceal this in my cellar for the time being. Until I have *everything* Ganch is asking for. Or at least until I've talked to Juju, and seen what he has to say.'

Hannibal raised his eyebrows almost to his hairline in question.

'I found Juju this morning. While you were getting the horses.'

The eyebrows went higher. For a moment January thought his friend would actually be at a loss for words, but Hannibal said, '*Aurora Musis amica*. Where was he?'

'Exactly where L'Araignée told Olympe he'd be.'

Hannibal offered to go into the Flesh and Blood that evening to fetch forth Jared Ganch, if he was there, or Catastrophe Watling, who would almost certainly be among those present. January shook his head. 'I don't want them to know you,' he said. They were in the yard of the crooked house on Rue Esplanade again, sponging off in a tub of tepid water after hiding the strongbox in one of the small, secret chambers beneath the house, where January often concealed the runaway slaves who would make their way in from the countryside, seeking passage to New York or Canada. 'If things go wrong tonight – if we don't manage to net Uncle Juju, or if he doesn't have this list of names – I'm going to need you to fall in love with Cassie Lovelace, so that you'll at least be hanging around her house if something happens with Rose. I don't want them knowing that you're likely to be spying for me.'

'*So the boy love is perjur'd everywhere* . . . Your sister wouldn't happen to have given you any remedy for mosquito bites, would she? I feel like I'm coming down with the smallpox . . .'

January – whose skin was dotted with growing bumps where neither the bayou-water nor his shirt-tail had succeeded in protecting him – went into the tiny garden patch that Rose culti-vated at one side of the yard, and cut a fleshy leaf from one of the aloes that grew there. From the kitchen he fetched the little pot of beeswax Olympe had given him, the astringent smell of witch hazel blending with the softer odors of lavender and cloves. Beyond the shelter of the kitchen's abat-vent, the afternoon's rain had begun to fall, soft and steady, making the whole town smell of mold. 'It's probably not going to kill the itch completely,' he warned, slitting the leaf and squeezing the drops onto the fiddler's reddening skin. 'But it should help. Rose tells me mosquitoes are fonder of men who drink.'

'Hmph. That must be what my tutor back home meant, when he said I would regret my fondness for brandy for the rest of my life. Nasty little vampires. I wonder if they get drunk themselves? How would one tell?' And in another tone he asked, 'Will you be all right?'

January anointed his own bites, first with the juice of the aloe, then with the itch-paste. 'I don't know.' He returned to the kitchen, for the remainder of the hoppin' john and for another jug of ginger water. 'It depends on what time I get there, and how drunk the clientele is, that I might meet in the yard.' In truth, faced with the prospect of venturing after dark across Canal Street and down to the waterfront upriver of the French Town, he hoped he would reach the saloon at all.

The rain was barely a whisper today, and scarcely touched the heat. January stirred up the kitchen fire to fry sausages, and reflected that he'd have to cook tomorrow, if he lived til tomorrow . . .

Sleeping, in the exhaustion of last night's wakefulness, he could still smell Rose's hair on the pillow: chemicals, lavender, and soap. He feared – as he had feared in the early hours of this morning, in the wake of Oldmixton's visit and the rush of blood to his heart when he'd realized where to find the treasure that Jared Ganch sought – that he'd dream of Rose. Dream of her in the dark of the old slave barrack behind the indigo mill, listening to the men in the house nearby shouting drunkenly at one another.

Dream of her fears – fears she had only with difficulty confessed to him – of this second childbirth . . .

Dream of Zizi-Marie, and the way such men as Cat Watling would look at her . . .

But when he slept, dragged into the dark realm by chains of exhaustion his body could not break, he dreamed of the chill rain of autumn in Paris, and of Anne Ben-Gideon in the prison of Saint-Lazare. Anne thin now, in the wake of her trial, and terrified, clinging to Daniel's hands. 'I sent no note,' she kept saying. 'How can they say they saw one when I didn't write such a thing?'

And January, who had spent the weeks between the preliminary hearing before the *juge d'instruction*, and the assizes, in tracing down the movements and whereabouts of the Comte de Belvoire himself (at Noisette, irritably deploring the absence and habits of both his sons), of the comtesse (ditto), of the Marquis de Taillefer, and even – without letting Daniel know – of Daniel's father (he'd been in and out of meetings with representatives of Jacques Lafitte and Rothschild Frères), could only say, 'There has to be something we're missing.'

But what that might be, he never knew.

NINETEEN

January waked to the stifling heat, and the sound of quiet voices briefly in the parlor, then the shutting of a door and the soft retreat of booted feet across the gallery and down the steps. The rain had ceased. By the gray quality of the light he knew it was near sunset, and thought, *Ganch should be at the Flesh and Blood soon.* But for a time he didn't move. Only lay staring at the cradle that stood in a corner of the bedroom, ready for tiny Secundus who might never lie there. He could turn his head and look through the door to the chamber that he'd been painting and fitting up as a nursery for Baby John.

Please, dear God . . .

He wanted to grab the hem of God's mantle and scream. Promise anything . . .

Don't do it! Don't do it! Please don't do it!

Like Armand de la Roche-St-Ouen, all those days in his sister's prison.

In time he got up, and passed through the parlor to the dining room and thence out to the back gallery, where Hannibal sat reading over a list of names. For a moment – though he knew it had to be Shaw's list of the inhabitants of the up-river bank of Bayou St John – his heart gave an illogical jolt: *Brooke's list . . .*

'Shaw left this for you.' The fiddler looked up. '*Miles Kentuckiensis.*' As he came to the rough table January could see the Kaintuck's familiar, painstaking blockprinting, dotted with spots and smears. 'Five of American extraction, seven of French. Four took up residence there within the past two years. All seem to be respectable owners of property and slaves: two cottonbrokers, a banker, two *rentiers*, the owner of the steamboats *Red Dog* and *Memphis*, a wine merchant, a widow who seems to live on the income of various securities, two importers, two planters, and an officer of the Bordeaux and Havana steamship line. Ages, names, and the names of slaves, wives and children appended.

I'm not sure how we'd determine why any of these would wish to murder Henry Brooke, though that widow looks promising.'

'With luck,' said January, 'Uncle Juju will have whatever Brooke – or O'Dwyer – had in his coat pockets, and we can deal with the issue of who actually murdered Brooke, and why, next week, and still be in good time for Jacquette Filoux's trial. Without luck . . .'

He stood for a time, turning the folded pages of Shaw's list over in his fingers.

'Without luck—' The fiddler took them back from him – 'we would neither of us have waked up this morning. Well, yesterday morning, in my case. *Damnéd spirits all . . . They willfully exile themselves from light/ and must for aye consort with black-browed night.* With your permission, *amicus meus*, I am heating water in the kitchen wherewith to shave and otherwise adonize myself in preparation for sweeping Madame Lovelace off her feet with passion. Might I borrow a clean shirt? Your nephew's should fit me – I fear if I return to the Broadhorn I might find myself pressed into service at the gambling tables again: Stuss-Finger Scrump having fallen afoul of a large gentleman from Missouri Friday night, the Pearl of Lexington is temporarily short of a dealer.'

An hour and a half later, January slipped across Canal Street, and worked his cautious way past the handsome houses of Lafayette Square and down into the less salubrious precincts closer to the waterfront. The yellow glow of cheap oil lamps made gaudy rectangles in the blackness, but threw little light onto the wet brick streets, and the noise of rattling pianos or small orchestras of fiddle and coronet – to say nothing of men's voices arguing politics with drunken fervor – effectively prevented him from listening behind him to see if he was being followed. In addition to the knife he usually carried in his boot – wholly illegal for a black man to use – and Shaw's equally illegal little pistol, January had armed himself with a slung shot, several ounces of birdshot tied in the toe-end of an old sock, a weapon which could be thrown away without regret and without possibility of identification. Not that a member of the Second Municipality's City Guards would have the slightest hesitation in identifying him as the owner of an illegal weapon, should he offend them in any way.

Around his neck he wore, on a string, a tin 'slave badge', identifying him as some other man's property – in this case, the property of Hannibal Sefton, from whom he carried a letter author- izing his slave 'Ben' to be out after curfew. A free black man might be abducted with virtual impunity: a slave was worth fifteen hundred dollars to somebody, and kidnappers knew a man's owner would come after them. In addition to this he carried an extra copy of his freedom papers – Hannibal's forgeries were nearly indistinguishable from the official documents – in case someone happened to tear up the copy he carried in his jacket pocket.

When a free black man ventured into the American section of the city – or anywhere near the waterfront at night – virtually anything was likely to happen.

Close to the wharves, Girod Street boasted half a dozen saloons within a few blocks. Some of them were larger and more solidly built than the collection of shanties and canvas-roofed makeshifts around the basin or in the Swamp, but as many were as squalid as anything to be found at the back of town. The Flesh and Blood fell into the former category, in that it was built of bricks, had a sort of plank sidewalk in front of it, and was three stories tall, combining the amenities of barroom, gambling parlor, whore- house and bathhouse under one roof: panel house and opium den as well, January suspected. In the alley behind it was what was locally termed a 'grocery', meaning a shop which sold liquor to blacks, both slave and free, as well as an assortment of cribs housing the bottommost dregs of the waterfront prostitutes, most of them black, all of them too old, too diseased, too damaged by abuse, alcohol and opium to command more than a dime from the drunkest of sailors, or the most penniless of slaves.

One of them was cursing a customer – or possibly a rival – as January made his way down the alley, a spew of abuse screamed at the top of her lungs. In the door of another crib he saw two children sitting, a boy and a girl, listening indifferently. The girl looked up as he passed and said, 'Twen'y cents for a blow-job, mister?' It was to avoid this, he understood, that Jacquette Filoux had put up with Henry Brooke's abuse.

Ti-Gall was sitting on the back step of the Flesh and Blood, smoking a cigar with a look of tired misery on his face. His eyes widened when he saw January and he leaped to his feet.

'Mr Ganch in?'

The boy shook his head.

'Cat Watling?' January removed his slave badge and pocketed it.

'Cat's here, yes, sir. Did you . . .?'

January touched his finger to his lips. 'I think so. Not where you think. But I need to speak to Cat. He sober?'

'Pretty much, sir. He don't drink as heavy as his boys.' And with this rather surprising piece of information, Ti-Gall ducked back into the lamplit gloom of the barroom.

From this gloom Cat Watling emerged a few minutes later, smiling genially around a cigar himself. 'Mr January.' He stuck out his hand. 'I was hopin' that'd be you.'

'I think I've found Juju Filoux,' said January quietly, shaking the man's hand. 'But the place needs to be surrounded, and we'd need to go in fast, or he'll be away and disappear again like a cockroach.'

The American whistled softly, and said, 'That's damn fast work, my friend. You got a hella better organization than Mr Ganch an' that's a fact – not that some of the sorry-assed tosspots Ganch keeps around him give you much competition in that department, mind you.'

'I wouldn't know about that, sir,' returned January respectfully. 'But if you've got any choice in the matter, you might want to bring in your better men on this, not just whoever's handy. The place is in the middle of town, and the man's slippery.'

'You're a man after my own heart, Mr J. You want to wait for me here? Corrine,' he yelled back into the kitchen, 'get this man a drink. You hungry? No? He holed up? Or just sort of roostin' in a tree?'

'Holed up,' said January. 'I think – but I can't be sure – one of his girlfriends has been dropping off food for him in the middle of the night.'

'Wimmen.' Cat shook his head. 'You give me half an hour, an' I'll have my best dogs ready for the hunt. Where's he at?'

January gave the man a thin but genuine smile. 'Where I should have seen him all along,' he said. 'Right under our noses.'

*   *   *

Catastrophe Watling stationed one of his 'best dogs' – a stocky Tennessean named Joe – in Rue Burgundy, just on the Swamp-side (as they said in New Orleans) of Jacquette Filoux's house. The boatman Chuy loitered in Rue St Louis, one street upstream; the lantern-jawed woman, whose name was Esmeralda, in Rue Dauphin in case Juju headed for the river itself. It was early in the night – just after nine o'clock – and the streets still clamored and rattled with the business of summer nights – the Sabbath notwithstanding – at the back of town. Whores sat in the windows of Sally Boudreaux's house next door, or lingered by the door of Shinna Gordon's two houses down towards the river. *Marchandes* called their wares with lungs of brass: rags and horseradish, pralines and melons. 'Sand yo' kitchen, sand yo' floors, sand yo' doorstep, sand yo' doors . . .' A few ragged children played in the open gutter.

'I'd say, wait til later,' said January softly, as he, Cat, and Cat's brother Rocky walked up the street, 'but if Juju's going to go out, I'd guess it'll be later in the night, when the crowds are less. And if we wait til he's gone and hide there to wait for him, he could be carrying what Mr Ganch wants on his person, and someone in the neighborhood might warn him.'

'Not to speak of Chuy an' Joe at least bein' in the habit of gettin' shit-hammered drunk by ten o'clock, come what may.' The big Kentuckian scratched his bristly chin. 'No, Mr J., this's the best way to come callin'.' He paused, and studied the rundown little house, shuttered up and dark.

'Sure as gun's iron looks deserted to me,' opined Rocky, who had been about to close a bargain with one of the whores at the Flesh and Blood and hadn't liked being called out to work. 'Why'd anybody want to stay in town when Mr Ganch's lookin' for 'em?'

'Yeah, if Mr Ganch was lookin' for *you*,' retorted his brother, 'you'd keep a light on just so the boogie-man didn't scare you in the dark, wouldn't you? Lord God, if I was as stupid as you I'd hang myself.'

'And I think once we get inside, sir,' added January, in his most placating voice, 'you'll see Juju's spent the past four days searching that house with a nit comb, trying to find those stock certificates of Brooke's. The place has a kitchen in the back, across the yard, sir,' he added, to Cat. 'The kids' rooms were above that, and Juju may be living in one of those, instead of in the main house.'

'Well,' said Cat, 'if that's the case he got to come through the yard. Rocky, you hit the rooms above the kitchen, same time Mr J. an' me goes in the main house. Just the one stair goin' up to 'em?'

January nodded. 'My money's on the main house, though.'

'Why's that?'

'The lock plate on the dining-room door. It's scratched up – scratched far worse than it was when I had a look at it first, on the fourth of July. Somebody's been unlocking that door, and unlocking it in the dark. Madame Boudreax, and some of her girls, have been keeping an eye on the house; they've said no one's been in or out. That means somebody's been sneaking in and out at dead of night.'

'Well,' said Cat admiringly, 'ain't you the clever nigger.'

January thought it wiser to shake his head, and reply deprecatingly, 'I just have way too many friends who're burglars, sir,' which got a laugh. He'd learned a long time ago that despite an occasional flash of admiration, on the whole, white ruffians preferred their niggers dumb. 'The real tip-off was the outhouse,' he added. 'In a hot summer it doesn't take brains to tell that somebody's still using the place.'

That got another laugh. *These men would haul Rose out to Texas and sell her for a cottonhand*, he thought, *and rape her on the way. Sell my son for a couple dollars and kill the baby rather than take the trouble to keep a child that young alive. Dear God, don't let her have gone into labor yet! Sell Zizi to a whorehouse and Gabriel to some planter in Florida . . . So they'd* better *not think I'm smart enough to realize all this, and resent them.*

And they apparently didn't, any more than that rufous-bearded American businessman at the Verandah Hotel had realized that it did not behoove him to insult and make trouble for people who handled his food.

'You stand in the yard,' breathed Cat, as they drew near Jacquette Filoux's dark and silent little house. 'I'll go in the front. You got a gun?'

January shook his head, another complete lie. 'I'll get a stick off the woodpile. Like as not I'd shoot myself in the foot if I had one.'

Cat was still chuckling over this as January and Rocky moved out of the main stream of foot traffic on Rue Toulouse, and opened the latch on the passway between Jacquette's house and that of Madame Boudreaux. Only the dimmest reflections from the whorehouse windows filtered into the yard's pitchy darkness. January and his hulking companion stood for a moment at the inner end of the passway, blinking as their eyes adjusted to the deeper dark. The wooden upper story of the kitchen seemed to loom above the shadows in the yard like an island over a lake of ink, and January pointed silently to the stair that led up to the garçonnière. He did go to the woodpile, collected the stoutest stick of firewood that remained.

Evidently Uncle Juju, despite his treatment of women in general, retained his charm, because the next moment a hand and arm thrust out of the little gable window of Madame Boudreaux's, a metal handbell gripped in a delicate fist. The bell rang wildly, then was dropped as the girl – whoever she was – bolted into hiding. (*As well she better, if she doesn't want her nose broken . . .*)

January heard the crash of a body against the shutters in the front of the house, and in the same instant one of the dormer windows that overlooked the yard was flung open, and a man's form slipped through. January yelled, 'Cat! In the back!' and Rocky, his bear-like clumsiness vanishing as if by magic, bolted half-down the garçonnière steps and then leaped over the rail into the yard. Uncle Juju dashed across the roof and sprang the four feet to the roof of the house next door – he was lucky he didn't break his neck, thought January – and dashed across that . . .

This was all he saw, for even as Juju was making that portion of his escape, January dashed from the yard, nearly colliding with Cat and Rocky when he reached the passway. 'That way!' he gasped, pointing downriver; all three ran in that direction, knowing Juju had to drop into a yard somewhere soon and then would try to disappear into the street. They spread out, watching the gates of the dark little passways between the cottages – the yards behind were high-walled, for precisely that reason: so that slaves couldn't dodge from one yard to the next. January had tried escaping across roofs once or twice in the French Town and knew one couldn't get far that way.

Cat meanwhile scanned the roofline against the dark of the sky. 'He's got to came down there.' He pointed to a passway between a two-story house and the taller brick block of a town house. Three floors, nobody could jump up that distance.

The Watling boys charged into the passway and January headed for the front door of the house, recognizing it as one which had been converted into rooms to let.

Sure enough, Juju Filoux, slim and graceful as his sister even in the gloom of the ill-lit street, slammed out the door as if shot from a gun moments before January got close enough to intercept him. Faced with the same circumstances, January guessed that Hannibal would have strolled out calmly, betting on the fact that the single street-lamp on this block was fifty feet away and one of the old whale-oil type – and probably would have got clean away while Cat was searching the house. Juju, panicked, ran, and January pounded after him, yelling 'There he goes!' *If he has that list on him I will run him to earth if it kills me . . .*

Hannibal would have sprung into the nearest cab or carriage with a desperate tale of 'Those villains are trying to murder me' and again, might possibly have gotten away with it. But, January reflected grimly as the passers-by dove out of Juju's way, Hannibal was white and this was the back of town, where beatings outside the whorehouses and barrooms were becoming more and more common.

Juju streaked like a terrified squirrel up Rue Toulouse, heading for the maze of saloons, bordellos, and thick stretches of utter darkness around the basin, where the canal would lead into the open dark of the true swamps, the impenetrable *ciprière*. He was a much smaller man than January, and lighter on his feet, but Chuy and the woman Esmeralda headed him off when they reached Rampart Street. The darkness there was thicker – the width of the street made it impossible for chains to be stretched across with lanterns – and only Juju's wild flight made him visible as movement in the darkness. The young man dodged among the mud, trees, and weeds of the neutral ground – *if he'd just go to ground we'd lose him* – and January realized that was exactly what he was going to do.

Go to ground in the darkness.

He wanted to yell to the rest of the pack, 'He's heading for the cemetery', but it was obvious by that time that was where he was going.

Juju reached the cemetery's wrought-iron gate twenty feet ahead of the closest of his pursuers, scrambled up it like a monkey. A gunshot crashed behind January and he ducked aside; Juju's jacket caught on one of the spear-pointed tines of the gate, ripped audibly without seeming to slow the young man down in the least. The gun cracked again – looking back January saw it was Esmeralda, with a cavalry pistol that could have downed an ox – and he knew better than to yell 'Stop shooting, you idiot!' at a white woman, albeit a tobacco-chewing hell-cat like that one. But Esmeralda stopped to reload both her pistols, and in that moment of respite – Juju having vanished into the darkness of the cemetery – January pelted across the remainder of the neutral ground and scrambled up over the gate.

Even in daylight, visibility in the cemetery was less than a yard. All around him, tombs crouched in the starlight, eerie blocks of pale stucco, patterned with blackness where resurrection-fern had taken hold in the cracks. Now that his eyes were adjusted to darkness he found the starlight easier to hunt by than moon-light, frail and shadowless. Mosquitoes whined in his ears and he heard, behind one of those stubby rectangles of plastered brick, the scrabbling rustle as his quarry swatted at one – or a dozen . . .

He hoped Cat had the good sense to send for reinforcements, once Esmeralda told him Juju had taken refuge in the cemetery. On both sides, and at the back, the eight-foot walls fronted the shabby, dirty neighborhoods at the 'back of town', and there were sufficient vacant lots and saloons to swallow up a fugitive, if he could temporarily lose his pursuit in the maze of sepulchers. Moving silently, January slipped across to an old bench tomb, crumbling under the onslaught of summer rains and semi-tropical vegetation, and helped himself to a handful of broken bricks. The soft New Orleans clay decayed easily and the cemetery was dotted with these dilapidated relics, wherever the families of the dead neglected to renew the stucco and clean away the fern on the Feast of All Saints. He moved by guess and when he gathered the fragments he felt something living – a cockroach or a crayfish – dart away from beneath his fingers, and made himself freeze.

Make him tell you where he is. Don't you tell him where you are.

He'd encountered plenty of cockroaches in the sugar mill on Bellefleur in his childhood and though they disgusted him, they didn't impress him. Freeborn, Juju probably hadn't been inured to the things.

He pitched a fragment of brick in the direction in which he'd heard Juju's flailing, watched the starlit aisle between two tombs . . .

There he went.

Good.

When he tries to go over the wall, he'll be vulnerable.

January slipped across an aisle, stood in the blackness between two tombs listening, to see if Juju had seen him and fled. Nothing, save the drone of mosquitoes, the faint pitter of crumbling stucco-crumbs as something – cat? rat? – moved along the top of a nearby monument. He trod in a puddle, felt crayfish wriggle away from his foot – the starlight showed him two or three of the things, moving around the cracks in a fresh-sealed tomb. The whole night smelled of mortality.

Movement there – January saw Juju's thin shape and flung another chunk of brick, startling the hell out of him and driving him toward the wall on the canal side. A moment later he himself dodged a little closer to where he guessed the younger man was, slipped around the side of a huge family tomb. This part of the cemetery, the front part, he didn't know as well as he knew the rear where the free colored had their tombs. For seven years now he'd gone with his mother and his youngest sister Dominique, ostensibly to clean and tend the graves of family friends but mostly so his mother could picnic with her fellow *plaçeés* and learn the latest gossip, both white and black.

His education, both in New Orleans as a child and later in Paris, had sponged away most of the tales his aunties had whispered, in the muggy dark of plantation nights: the Platt-Eye Devil that waited in the blackness to devour children, the half-human

Stiff-Leg that could nevertheless pounce with a tiger's speed, the demon Onzoncaire. The witches that would seize and ride those who wandered in the night, and the ghosts that seeped from their graves to drink the souls of those so foolish as to walk past them when the sun was gone.

The stink of decay in the tombs, the recollection of three cholera summers, put such childish efforts at frightfulness to shame. But in the darkness, the memory of old Mambo Jeanne's tales returned, and he guessed that for Juju, the effect was probably worse. He could hear the distant clamor of the saloons near the basin from over the wall on the St Louis side. He flung a tiny pebble behind the darkness where Juju would be, to get him to turn (*Is that danger? Is that just a cat?*) so that January could slip a little further toward the wall.

A moment later he heard the young man's footsteps, running, splashing, tripping in the mud; *that's it, he's breaking for the wall . . .*

January saw him flick across the aisles, dashed from shadow to shadow, until the cemetery wall loomed ahead of them, a black bar of shadow rimed with starlight at its top. Juju flung himself at the wall, scrambled in its cracks and furrows of broken brick, and January plunged from the concealing blackness of the tombs and seized him around the waist. The young man twisted, kicked, but couldn't get purchase for a telling blow. He fell backwards, January wrapping his arms around him, knowing he probably had a knife and pinning him to keep him from drawing it. For a moment they writhed on the ground together, Juju struggling to get a hand free and into his pocket.

If he can get to a knife I'm a dead man . . .

Juju began to yell as figures crowded around them, hands grabbed his shoulders and torso. January loosed his hold and broke free, guessing that these were Cat and his minions – a guess confirmed when Cat yelled an obscenity as Juju bit him. Juju's hand dove for his coat front and January grabbed his wrist as Juju dragged forth a gun, wrenched the weapon away from him. The next moment someone sapped the young man with a slung-shot, and someone yelled from the direction of the wall, 'Pigs!'

The City Guard was belatedly on its way.

'Get him to the house,' said Cat, and the men scooped Juju up and hustled him into the blackness of the cemetery.

January said, 'This way,' and led them – half by guess in the dim starlight, half by recollection of years of visits on the Feast of All Saints – back toward the Rampart Street gate.

TWENTY

C at whispered, 'Well, dip me in shit,' as he entered the dining room of Jacquette Filoux's house and January lit a lucifer-match. One of the dozen men with them (Cat had indeed fetched reinforcements) whistled and said, 'Fuck me, what's he been doin' here?'

'Searching the place,' replied January softly. A single candle stood on the table in the center of the room, where all the other furniture had been huddled. January lit it, the sulfur smell of the lucifer-match hanging in the room's stuffy air. Someone else closed the shutter and the glassed French door behind them, though January knew the feeble light would show through the jalousies. Turning, he saw, rather to his surprise, that one of Cat's ruffians was Abishag Shaw.

Shaw disappeared immediately into the dark bedroom and among the milling men, in the low and uncertain light, his absence wasn't any more remarked than his presence had been. If Ganch was hiring men for a raid on some South American town, January guessed, it stood to reason his freebooters wouldn't all know one another. In the back of town, the absence of street lighting of any sort would make it child's play for one more unshaven thug to join a group of unshaven thugs . . .

Still, January had to admire the Kentuckian's nerve.

He raised the candle, and – like Cat and his men – gazed around him at the ruined dining room. As he'd surmised, Juju had clearly spent the days of his hiding there – Cat had taken the key to the dining-room's shutters from his pocket – going over the house with a nit comb. The rugs were rolled up and tossed onto the table, three boards had been pulled up from the floor, reminding January a bit of the looted house at Chitimacha. The chairs were on the table as well, and the daybed on which Olympe and Manon had sat five days ago had had its upholstery ripped open and the lining of its bottom pulled loose. The sideboard in which glasses and dishes had been stored had likewise

been dragged away from the wall and the dishes removed – they
were stacked on the table – and all around the room the base-
boards had been pried free.

Rocky looked around for another candle, found none, and took
the single light from January's hand to peer briefly through the
bedroom door. 'Same in here,' he said, which told January that
Shaw had retreated to the cabinet – the creaking of the floor had
undoubtedly given him ample warning – and returned to the
dining room, where Cat was in the process of stripping the
reviving Juju of jacket, vest and shirt.

'Can I have his gun?' asked January, and looked around for
a napkin with which to scrape the cemetery mud from his arms
and face. 'You got this from your sister, didn't you?' he asked
Juju, who nodded in terror, his eyes darting from face to face of
the men gathered around him in the semi-darkness. 'His sister's
charged with murdering Brooke,' he added, to Cat. 'Between this
– the bullet that killed him was from a bigger gun – and the
testimony of a cab driver who took Brooke out to Bayou St John
that evening, they'll probably be able to get her off. She's a good
girl,' he added. 'I've talked to her, she had no idea what he was
up to.'

'Oh, hell, yeah.' Cat handed him the weapon. 'I wouldn't let
a dog hang on account of killin' that slick snake—'

'You need me to come into court,' piped up Esmeralda, almost
the first non-scatological comment January had heard from her
lips, 'tell 'em this sorry bastard says he stole it from her, you
just let me know.'

January turned in surprise, bowed, and said, 'Thank you, m'am.
That's most kind of you.'

Esmeralda spit, and relapsed into her usual silence.

'Nuthin' here, Cat.' Rocky finished going through the pockets
of Juju's jacket and waistcoat.

'Look, I . . . I don't got nuthin',' stammered Juju. 'I didn't
take nuthin'. Nuthin' 'cept that gun,' he added, with a quick,
enquiring glance from January to the woman. 'I . . . I don't know
what you're talkin' about. I'll have the money for Mr Ganch next
week, I swear I will, I know where I can get it—'

'An' where's that?' Cat drew a skinning knife like a young
sword from his boot.

Juju's eyes bulged. He was, January judged, younger than his sister – going by the sparse fluff of his undeveloped mustache – and prettier. Like Jacquette's his complexion was little darker than a Spaniard's, but his features, though delicate, were unmistakably African. The waistcoat and jacket lying on the table – mud-slobbered from the struggle in the cemetery and now slit in a dozen places by Rocky's knife – were silk, and costly. January wondered who'd paid for them, if anyone had.

'I'm . . . uh . . . I know this man, owes me money—'

'Always a man,' murmured Cat, 'what owes you money.' He rested the tip of his knife in the pit of Juju's throat and drew it delicately down his bare chest and over his abdomen, leaving a trail of blood like a paper cut behind.

Juju began to scream. 'I didn't find nuthin'! I didn't find nuthin'! Only that key that was in his pocket . . . Oh, God, please—'

'Where is it?'

'In the desk!'

Rocky took the candle and went to look. He came back with a small double-sided Chubb key, of a size to fit the lock of the strongbox.

'What about the list?' asked Cat, and began to cut the buttons off Juju's trousers.

'There wasn't no list! There wasn't no list!' the young man screamed, his face blanched in the candlelight; January thought he was about to be sick, and little wonder.

'May I, sir?' he asked Cat, and the Kaintuck looked at him in surprise. 'He's gonna faint in a minute,' pointed out January, 'or have hysterics—'

Cat smiled, with perfectly genuine friendliness. 'Be my guest, Mr J.'

January wondered what he'd do if nothing came of his own questions. Let Juju be tortured to reveal the location of the strongbox? Let him die, rather than give up his own possible leverage in getting Rose back?

His own immediate reaction was '*yes*' and he winced at the promptness with which he'd answered his own question. He felt contempt for Jacquette's brother, and distaste at all he'd heard about him, but he certainly didn't deserve this.

At the motion of his hand, Cat stepped back a pace, though the cut-throats who held the weeping Juju's arms didn't slacken their grip.

'Tell me about Saturday night.'

'I saw him floatin' in the basin, when I come out of the Cock.'

'What time was that?'

'Twelve thirty. I'd run outta money, see. The moon was full, I seen him . . .' Juju sniffled, threads of snot stringing from his nose.

'You know who he was?' January hoped Shaw was close enough to the bedroom door to listen.

'Not when I seen him first. I got a boathook off one of the boats, dragged him ashore. There wasn't hardly nobody around. When I turned him over I saw it was Michie Brooke. I went through his pockets, but anyone woulda! You know anyone woulda! You woulda yourself—'

January slapped him. Not hard, but hard enough to break his terrified stammering. 'What'd you find?'

Juju gulped. 'Don't let 'em hurt me,' he whispered. 'I swear I—'

'What'd you find?'

'Keys,' sniffled the young man. 'The key to Jacquette's house, that key that man found in the desk, couple others – they's right there—'

'Hotel room, looks like,' reported Cat, bringing it over to the candle. 'You got any more lights in this place, boy?'

'Place'd be bright enough to search,' pointed out Chuy, 'if we set his hair on fire.'

'What else?'

'Note from some girl, askin' to see him. Hundred dollars from the National Bank of New Orleans, three five-dollar gold pieces, 'bout ten dollars in silver. But that got stolen from me,' he added, gabbling in panic, 'stolen that same night. I was gonna bring it along to Mr Ganch but this man . . . these men . . . they . . .'

January slapped him again. 'You take that up with Cat,' he said. 'Was that all?'

'Couple receipts. His watch, an' his stickpin, an' a ring, but those men, that stole the money, they stole that, too, I swear it. Nuthin' else, I swear it, I swear it on my mother . . . I pushed him back in the basin. Then I . . . I thought I'd go over here, to my sister's house, tell her Michie Brooke was dead. But when I let myself in she was asleep, an' I . . . I couldn't stand to waken her up. I knew she'd be grieved. I figured I'd come back and tell her in the morning . . .'

'And did you?' asked January, knowing that he hadn't, and Juju began to cry again.

'Don't let 'em hurt me,' he begged. 'I swear I searched this whole house top to bottom – I . . . I knew she'd need his money, see. He always had gold, an' he had what Jacquette said was certificates of some kind, stock certificates . . .'

January was silent for a time. It was as if he could feel the heavy beating of his own heart. *Oh, no, I found those myself . . .*

Looking at the grinning faces around him, he knew these men would cut off Juju's balls just for the pleasure of hearing him beg them not to, and without the list, the certificates themselves had only a limited value. Enough, maybe, to buy Rose free, to buy Zizi and Gabriel and Baby John free . . .

But I can't just walk away and let them.

Not even if I think Juju is a completely contemptible human being.

He doesn't deserve that.

He frowned, as if he had heard what Juju had said for the first time. 'How was that hundred dollars carried? In a wallet?'

'No, sir. Just in his pocket.'

'Rolled up, or folded?'

'Rolled up. Inner money wasn't hardly damp.'

'So he hadn't been in the water but a few minutes. This note from a girl – could you read it?'

'Oh, yeah, it was in this wax-leather wallet, inside his waistcoat. It wasn't hardly damp neither . . .'

A body dead when put into the water would be slower to sink.

'Nothing else in with it? No papers, no letters of introduction, no British passport, no documents about the land he'd purchased?'

'No, sir. Nuthin' like that.'

January turned to Cat, said, 'He's done everything but take this house apart brick by brick. If he'd found that strongbox here, he wouldn't be here now.' Taking the candle, he crossed to the desk, and added, 'No wallet. No passport. Whoever killed him, searched him before dumping him in the drink. And didn't take the money or the watch.'

The filibuster pondered that, as if trying to sort out its implications – or perhaps merely struggling with the concept of someone who wouldn't have taken the money. He said, 'Whoever the fuck that was . . .'

Whoever the fuck.

January glanced briefly at the keys – one of them indeed looked very much like a hotel-room key and the other, by its size and age, he guessed to be the key to the house at Chitimacha – then took up the folded note beneath them.

Whoever it was who wrote to Brooke – *making that assignation on the bayou road*? – the moment he identified her – pointed to a name on Shaw's list – he'd bring her to the notice of Jared Ganch and the men who stood grinning around the terrified Juju, their eyes gleaming in the near-darkness. He could smell them from where he stood.

And if she – whoever she is – was only making a rendezvous for a few kisses in the twilight, knowing nothing of who and what Brooke was . . . Will she convince Ganch that she doesn't have this filthy list?

What will the result be, if I learn her name and give it to them? What will the result be, if I don't?

Virgin Mary, Mother of God, guide me, because I don't know what the hell is right.

He unfolded the note. It was written in French.

'Gerry,' it said. 'I must see you. Come to the spot where the little bayou comes out of the Fortin place, into Bayou St John, at sunset. A.'

January took a deep breath. His hands shook as he folded the note again, and slipped it into his pocket. He felt as if he'd been slammed over the heart with a bargepole. To Cat, he said, 'Give me three days. I should be able to lay hands on both the list, and the strongbox, by then.'

His voice must have sounded as strange to Cat Watling as it did in his own ears, because Cat glanced at him sidelong. 'You ain't thinkin' of doin' somethin' funny on me, now are you, Mr J?'

January shook his head. For a moment the only thing he could say was, 'No.' In his ears sounded the voice of a priest reading the *De Profundis*, with the cold steel of the guillotine's blade gleaming against a gray autumn sky.

De profundis clamavi ad te, Domine:
Domine, exaudi vocem meam

'I'm sure there's no need for me to remind you, what'll happen to Mrs J. an' them kids of yours—'

He shook his head again, still too stunned even to feel anger. He repeated softly, 'No, sir. I remember. Would you do something for me?' He turned to face the man. 'Will you throw Juju in with the bargain, sir? He doesn't know anything. Don't kill him. Turn him loose with the others, when I bring the strongbox and the list?'

Cat looked over his shoulder at Juju for a moment, then shrugged. 'I can do that, sure. Boys'll pout some, but I'll do that.' He cocked his head for a moment, green eyes narrowing, and he spit tobacco on the floor. 'You're playin' this pretty close to the chest, my friend.'

January raised his eyebrows, and glanced – as Cat had glanced – back at the 'boys': dirty, bearded, vicious, and – by the smell of them, at least – one or two of them more than a little drunk. 'I have to, sir. This is life and death to me.' He made his voice as apologetic as he could. 'And this is . . . delicate. If your child,' he went on, lowering his voice as he fished for an analogy that would mean something without coming out and insulting a white man, 'had her hand caught in a bear trap, and you had to replace the spring in it, for her to get her hand out safely . . . Which of those men would you trust to do it?'

To his enormous relief Cat's unshaven face split in a laugh. 'Well, you just said a mouthful, Mr J!' He clapped January on the arm. 'So we'll play it your way. An' we'll throw in this worthless pimp into the bargain. Three days.'

January said, 'Thank you, sir, from the bottom of my heart.' And he meant it.

When Cat and his 'boys' had departed, dragging the stumbling Juju with them, Shaw emerged from the dark of the bedroom, chewing ruminatively. 'That was smart talkin', Maestro. If'n I'd had all the men on night duty with me, I'm still not sure we'd a' been able to take Ganch's gang, always supposin' the men'd risk their lives for the likes of Juju Filoux.' He picked up the candle, the light making tiny pinpricks of gold in his gray eyes.

'You're probably right, that havin' that little purse gun, an' a cab driver to testify to takin' Brooke out to Bayou St John that night, will go a long way to turnin' M'am Filoux free—'

'If those don't,' said January quietly, 'this will.' He held out the note.

Shaw glanced over it, nodded, and spat. Between the torn-up condition of the floor and the presence in the room of Cat's 'boys' for half an hour, there was no point in looking politely around for a cuspidor. 'Should do it,' he agreed. 'An' you think this "A" gonna know where them papers is, an' that strongbox of securities?'

'The papers, anyway,' said January.

Sustinuit anima mea in verbo eius:
speravit anima mea in Domino

Shaw was watching him as Cat had watched him, and, January thought, probably for the same reason. He knew he must still look shaken to his bones.

'You figure she's one of them on that list I give you?'

A distant figure in a green dress, her chestnut hair cut short. The flash of a descending blade . . .

'I think so.' He knew he didn't sound any too sure of that.

'You need help?'

'I will, yes.'

Shaw led the way out onto the banquette – every neighbor on the street must have been watching from behind their curtains. Before following him, January turned the note over in his fingers beside the candle flame. His hand no longer shook, but he felt very strange inside, as if, in the cemetery, he had heard someone call out to him from one of the tombs. Had seen someone he knew emerge from one of those shut stone doors.

Then he blew out the light, and followed Shaw out into the darkness.

The handwriting on the note was that of Anne Ben-Gideon.

TWENTY-ONE

'She was executed.' January laid the note on the table, went into the kitchen for the coffeepot that sat on the hearth. He had slept, after a fashion, but in his dreams he'd found himself, again and again, in the Place de la Nation, with the smell of the open fields blowing over him, and the guillotine rising against the dawn sky. Autumn, on the threshold of winter, and bone-cold. Daniel had stayed home, swamped in an opium stupor which had lasted for nearly a month.

'I saw her die.'

1830

The crowd hadn't been much. Executions took place at dawn, and the rebellion in Belgium and fighting in the Netherlands the previous month had completely eclipsed the few newspaper accounts of the trial. As the tallest person in almost any gathering, January saw easily over the heads of those closer to 'The Machine' than he, and in any case he and Ayasha had stood within twenty feet of the platform. There had been no mistaking Anne for anyone else as she stepped down from the carriage in which she'd been brought, climbed the steps. There were police with her, as well as a priest, and her hands hadn't been bound. He hadn't been quite close enough to see if she wept, or to tell if she scanned the crowd, looking for a face she knew.

He, Ayasha and Daniel had visited her in the prison the previous night. Neither her parents nor Armand, she had told them, had done so.

The nuns had already been in, last night, to cut off her beautiful reddish-brown hair. She'd clung to Daniel, not weeping, only taking comfort in the warmth of his solid shoulders, the strength of his arms.

On the platform she had looked very small in the green foulard dress Armand had brought her. Her head was high, as if telling

herself, 'I can do this. I can do this'. She was two months short
of her nineteenth birthday.

'Do they drug them?' Ayasha had whispered, when Anne had
stood against the bascule, to be strapped, and that swiveling table
had been tipped to horizontal, so that Anne's neck could be
fastened in place beneath the blade.

The priest had spoken the *De Profundis*: 'Remember not, Lord,
our iniquities, nor the iniquities our forefathers; neither take thou
vengeance of our sins . . . be not angry with us for ever.'

January had shaken his head. Ayasha – tough as she was –
turned her face against his shoulder in the moment before the
blade dropped.

Remember not our iniquities . . .

1839

At the table, Hannibal said, 'Wait – *what?*' His startled voice
brought January back from Paris, from dawn, from the flash of
steel, to see the fiddler turning the note over in his fingers. 'Anne
Ben-Gideon?'

'That's her hand.' January poured him some coffee, set the
pot down next to Shaw's list of the inhabitants of the up-river
side of Bayou St John, and the dish of cold pork and grits that
Olympe had left here sometime before dawn. 'I've seen it a
hundred times in Daniel's house.'

'Anne Ben-Gideon was *Anne de la Roche-St-Ouen?*'

*He was in and out of Paris for the preceding year, or two
years . . . He went to every fashionable party, every opera and
gambling-hell. Why did I never think they might have met?*

'You knew her.'

Hannibal shook his head. 'But Armand was one of our Merry
Band. We'd been drinking together the whole of that spring. And
this is *exactly* the way he used to forge his sister's handwriting
when he was sending their parents reports corroborating whatever
he'd told them he was doing with his time and their money.'

January drew up a chair and sat down, almost without being
aware of it. The little yard behind the house on Rue Esplanade
was still filled with morning shadow – it was nearly nine o'clock,
an unthinkable hour for Hannibal to be abroad; he must not have

been to bed yet. From the street beyond the wall drifted the rumble of dray wheels, the shrill sweet voices of women walking toward the markets.

'Armand could forge her handwriting?'

His hand lay on Shaw's report. There were only two house-holders on that stretch of Bayou St John young enough to be Armand de la Roche-St-Ouen – *he'd only be twenty-six or -seven now* – and one of them, a cottonbroker, was American.

'Good Lord, yes. Armand worshipped his sister – she had all the spirit he lacked, did all the things he wished he had the nerve to do – but that didn't mean he wouldn't use her name to stay on the good side of their parents. Apparently she always agreed with his story, if they asked her. He often told us, that winter, how he used to take her to taverns and race meetings, when she'd dress up as a boy in his clothing. Before she married and got her own establishment he'd buy things for her like cigars and brandy and guns.'

'Guns,' said January softly. 'Did he ever buy her a muff pistol?'

'The silver one with the designs on the barrel? It was a pair of them,' said Hannibal. 'I was with him – about six of us were – when he bought them, at Montjoie's in the Palais Royale. He said one was for his sister; he bought them with her money. He himself could never save a sou.'

'There were two of them.' January had the sense of seeing a distant building slowly emerge from fog. 'Was he one of the group that went out to Rambouillet with you that summer? Did he ever say anything about her husband? Or her husband's lovers?'

Hannibal shook his head. 'He seldom spoke of him. Never named him – just called him "that Jew pig". Or, to give him his complete title, "that Jew pig my parents sold my sister to". And this while buying champagne with the money his sister had sent him – which presumably originated in her husband's counting house. I never knew,' he added, all his customary blitheness leaving his voice, 'that this was your friend that he spoke of. Or what Armand's sister's married name was. And yes,' he added, 'he was with us in Rambouillet, until the Monday, the night before the rioting started. He went back to Paris then. We heard his sister had died, but the family hushed it up – I can understand why, now – and he never returned to our . . . revels. Knowing how he felt about his sister, I wasn't surprised.'

'There were two pistols,' repeated January, at first feeling only a kind of shaken shock, akin to what had gone through him last night in that little cottage on Rue Toulouse when he'd seen the handwriting on that note, and known it for Anne's.

As if he'd heard her voice.

As if he stood again in the crowd on the Place de la Nation, watching that small green figure mount the steps . . .

Rage swept him, almost stopping his breath.

Quietly, Hannibal continued, 'That was the last I saw of him. He didn't roister with us after that, and I left Paris myself the following year. Armand told me once – we were both pretty drunk, and I'd raised the subject of an old cent-per-center back in London I'd gone to, when things were at ebb tide with me, Armand went off onto a poisonous denunciation of the Chosen People: men, women, and children unborn. He seemed to think the possession of an Israelite brother-in-law was what had scuppered the proposed match between himself and the daughter of the Comte de Noirchamp, not the fact that his own family hadn't a pot to piss in and was in debt up to their collective hairlines. He wrote sonnets to her for months that spring, presumably under the impression that being addressed as "Nymph, who puts the gold of dawn to shame" would somehow induce her to fly in the face of her parents' expressed wishes and elope with him . . .'

'Philippe was wearing Daniel's coat,' said January softly, 'when he was shot. Daniel's footman testified that a note had come from Anne to his house – urgent was written on the outside. Philippe must have read it . . .'

'How would Armand have found O'Dwyer, after all this time?' Hannibal touched the note that lay between them, on the scribbled page just above the scrawled legend: Francheville – Bertrand, 26, clerk Bordeaux & Havana Shipping – wife Belle, 3 children. 'And why? If Armand was the man who killed de la Marche – and then kept his mouth shut and watched his sister go to the guillotine for it . . . Unless O'Dwyer did it, and fled from Paris.' His sparse brows pulled together. 'But if that were the case, how did Armand know O'Dwyer would be coming here? It says—'

He turned the list around – 'this *M'sieu Francheville* came to New Orleans in 1835.'

He looked up, and met January's eyes. 'Would you like me to ask him, *amicus meus*?'

The house belonging to Bertrand Francheville stood at the very end of the short stretch of higher ground that lay along the crook of Bayou St John, where the little suburbs of Pontchartrain and St-John came to an end. It was an American-style house, like a large version of a cottage in the French Town but with a deep gallery across the front and a kitchen built into the main house. The whole affair was set back a good thirty feet from the shell road, and prudently raised on a six-foot foundation, the gallery supported by brick piers. Several of the original oaks of the *siprière* still stood around it, but at least half of the lot was in its original condition – too low to do anything with, riotous with swamp growth, and undoubtedly flooded in the spring.

This fact permitted January – accompanied by Abishag Shaw – to get within twenty feet of the house, standing unseen in the untidy thickets of palmetto and swamp-laurel which bordered a small garden on the swamp side of the house. Someone had taken great pains to prune the tidy box hedge which divided this wilderness from the neat beds of roses, tulips, and (in the soggier end of the plot) iris. As January and Shaw edged as close as they could, January could see a youngish, fair-haired man in a blue coat walking slowly among the plantings under the hot, noon sun, supporting his crippled wife on his arm.

At this distance he recognized Armand de la Roche-St-Ouen at once, though the boy he had known in Paris had put on forty pounds and grown a skimpy Van Dyke, reminiscent of Tin-Tin de la Marche's, nine years previously. *You can't step twice into the same river*, he thought. *And the Mississippi was a long way from the Seine.*

The woman who clung to his arm had clearly once been beautiful and was still pretty, though her skin was of an unhealthy pastiness, and her illness had aged her.

Her eyes, when she looked at her husband, were a young girl's still.

'. . . if he didn't insist on being the center of attention,' she was saying, with a schoolgirl's animation, 'he wouldn't make such a ghastly dinner guest!' She spoke English, with a light inflection of southern German; it was only with difficulty that she kept herself from letting go of her cane to emphasize her words with gestures. 'Mama used to say of people like that, "He has to be the bride at every wedding and the corpse at every funeral".'

And her husband, Bertrand Francheville – Armand de la Roche-St-Ouen – flung back his head and laughed. 'I knew a man like that in Paris . . .'

His words stopped and he froze, as Hannibal came walking down the broken shells of the garden path in the dappled green shade. 'The girl in the house told me you'd be back here,' said the fiddler in French, 'Armand.'

Armand stood as if turned to stone, and his wife looked from Hannibal to her husband, inquiring; *she speaks no French*, thought January. Her brow clouded, as she saw her husband's shocked face. She murmured, '*Liebchen* . . .?'

Armand appeared not to have heard her. Stiffly, he said, 'Alec.'

'It's not a name I go by these days,' said Hannibal apologetically. 'As I understand, neither is Armand de la Roche-St-Ouen. Madame . . .' He removed his hat, bowed to Madame Francheville, and kissed her hand.

For a moment, it seemed to January that Armand would have made a run for the *ciprière*, or the road, or the house. But he looked at his wife, and tightened his fingers reassuringly over the hand that held to his arm. 'Would you wait for me here, *liebling*? This is Mr . . .?'

'Sefton.' Hannibal bowed again, and addressed the lady in German. 'An old friend of your husband's, though we have long fallen out of touch.'

Her smile was radiant, and she replied, also in German, 'Of course.'

Armand steered her gently to a garden seat beneath an oak, where some fragments of the morning cool might have lingered. Taking Hannibal by the arm, he led him to the bottom of the garden, so close to the hedge that January feared for a moment that they'd pass on through into the thickets and give the game away entirely.

But they stopped, where the shadows of the trees grew thick.

Quietly, in French, Hannibal said, 'I know what you did.'

Armand turned his face away. For a long moment there was no sound but the rattle of the cicadas in the swamp, and the voices of children somewhere beyond the trees in the next yard. January understood that he himself wasn't the only one who looked back over the chasm of years to a different world, a different planet. Paris in the last days of the Bourbons. And a different man who had worn his flesh.

'I could have wept,' whispered Armand at last, 'I could have thrown myself in the river, when I turned his body over and saw that it was de la Marche that I'd shot, not that sodomite Jew.'

He doesn't even think of Brooke, realized January. *It's as if he has forgotten that murder completely. He's still in Paris, in his heart.*

Maybe he has been so for the past nine years.

Armand was trembling as he looked back at Hannibal, desperation in his eyes. 'A man of good family, a grandson of the Noailles . . . A connection of my mother! And then when they arrested Anne, and that poisonous Madame de Belvoire got it into her head that unless and until someone were executed for the crime, her precious Tin-Tin would live under a cloud . . . Did you know he married some slut of an opera singer? God, I could have laughed—'

But he was sobbing instead as he clutched at Hannibal's sleeve with frantic hands. 'I kept telling myself . . . Kept hoping they'd find someone else, anyone else . . . Kept praying they wouldn't really send a daughter of a good family, of an ancient house, to the guillotine! A girl with the blood of the Valois kings in her veins! If King Charles had still been on his throne it would never have happened!'

His voice fell to barely more than a frantic whisper. 'Do you remember, Alec, that day whenever it was, in '28 or was it '29? When the whole pack of us went to watch that execution after spending the night at the Yellow Palace, drunk as David's sow, to see that fellow, what was his name? Chirac? Thierry? The fellow who'd killed his wife or her mother or whoever the hell it was . . . Do you remember how he fought them?' Words tumbled faster and faster from his lips, and even at that distance, January could see the glint of white all around the pupils of his staring eyes.

'Remember how he kicked and struggled as they dragged him up the steps of the platform? How he cried and pissed himself and fell on his knees, and they had to pick him up and shove him against that horrible little table, to strap him down? Remember how he wept and begged? And when the blade dropped . . .

'It's never left me,' he whispered. 'While Anne was in prison I kept dreaming of that morning. Dreaming it was me up there, screaming for mercy and slipping in my own piss on the platform and I couldn't . . . I couldn't . . .'

So you let Anne go through it instead. January saw again that small slender form in the green dress, that shorn proud head held high.

'Alec, you were there! You saw it! You saw how his mouth went on forming words after his head was off. You saw how his eyes moved, looking from one to another in the crowd, *aware. Alive.* His eyes looked into mine, Alec, and the head lived yet . . .'

'I was there,' said Hannibal gently. 'And yes, I saw his eyes. I dream about it, too. But I wasn't talking about that, Armand. I know you killed Gerry O'Dwyer.'

Armand began to weep, burying his face in his hands. At the other end of the garden, his wife struggled to rise from the bench where she sat, levering at her cane with all her strength, and called out in English, 'Bertie? Bertie, is everything all right?'

He swallowed hard, raised his head and put all the cheer he could into his voice: 'It's all well, *leibling.* Just – news of a friend. It's all well.'

He turned back to Hannibal, as the woman sank again to the bench. 'He knew what I'd done, you see,' he whispered. 'I needed his help to get rid of de la Marche's body. They're . . . heavy. Bodies. When I saw it was de la Marche I'd shot, I needed someone to help me get the body away. I'd sent for the Jew pig to the garden of the convent of Notre Dame de Syon, where my aunt was Mother Superior: I had the key to the garden gate, I knew all the nuns had gone, when the rioting began. I'd been in and out of the place since I was a child, I knew the drains under the balneary opened into the sewers. And Anne had told me about how the rebels would move about through them. Anne had told me they'd be building barricades on the Rue St-Martin and the Rue St-Denis, if trouble started. So I sent him a note, in her hand, to come that night . . .'

He shook his head, trembling again, as if, thought January, he were still in that convent garden, waiting. Listening for a footfall approaching the gate, hearing the gunshots and the shouting, nursing his grievance. Not that his sister had been given in marriage to a man who might easily have made her unhappy – his sister whom he loved. But that the man was a Jew and compromised his own social chances.

'I stood waiting for him just inside the gate. I shot him as he stepped through it, there were so many shots being fired all over Paris that night, nobody would even hear. But when I tried to lift him I realized I'd need help. I didn't . . . I'd never tried to lift another man before.'

'It's not something one thinks of,' said Hannibal quietly. '*Tamdiu discendum est, quamdiu vivas . . .*'

'And he was tall, as tall as Ben-Gideon. I couldn't get him through the sewers alone. I dragged his body down to the chapel crypt, and sent word to Gerry at his rooms. For a wonder he was there. He didn't reach me until well after daylight. I gave him two hundred francs – it was all I had. Then when the fighting died down the following night we moved him, when everyone in the city was asleep. He was stiff by that time, Gerry had to break his shoulders . . . Gerry must have fled Paris that same night. The man always was a coward . . .'

You should talk, January bit his tongue not to say.

'I didn't think anything of it, until Anne was arrested. How was I to know musket bullets are that different? By then I had no idea where Gerry had gone. He would have said Anne was with him! That's all the police needed to have known!'

Hannibal said nothing, only looked at him with a kind of wondering pity.

'I couldn't . . . every time I thought about telling the police what I knew, I remembered . . .' His voice caught on a sob. 'I was Father's only son. The only heir to the title. I couldn't do that to our house. To our name.'

'But you could do it to her.' Hannibal's voice was so soft, January wasn't certain Armand even heard him. He certainly gave no sign that he had.

'But then he came back.' Armand's voice, which had risen, sank again. 'Two years, three years . . . sometime after the cholera. O'Dwyer came back to Paris. He came to our hôtel and asked for money. He was calling himself Preston then. He threatened to tell what he knew. Mother had died the year before, and Father not long after her. I knew Father was in debt, but . . . even with what King Charles had given us for the lands the revolution had confiscated, there was almost nothing left. I don't know what Father was thinking, or what he'd spent the money on . . .'

January saw his friend's eyebrows lift and guessed he was remembering some extravaganza of carriage horses and waist-coats, gaming debts and good quality champagne. *Whatever he'd told them he was doing with his time and their money . . .*

'I gave O'Dwyer what he asked. It crippled the estate, but I couldn't let the name of our house be sullied. Then two months later he came back, and asked for more. I fled from France, changed my name, came here. I found work – what Father, or Mother, would think of it I can't imagine, but better that than our name disgraced. I met Belle . . .'

His face softened as he looked back along the garden walk, to the thin, tired-looking woman on the bench. 'Who would have thought that I'd find such joy, such peace, with a penniless, dowerless girl of no family? My parents would never have looked twice at her. But she – and our children – have changed my life, Alec. She is so . . . good. That's the only word for her. Good. Even in her pain – and she has been in pain, ever since little Nicko's birth last winter – she is cheerful and thinks of no one but our children. When O'Dwyer showed up again, three weeks ago, I knew I couldn't flee again. I couldn't leave Belle. I knew I had to make sure of him.'

'So you sent him a note in Anne's hand,' said Hannibal softly, 'knowing he'd come.'

Armand nodded. 'I bought concert tickets for a musicale in Mandeville that night,' he said, 'and made arrangements to rent a cottage for a few days. I try to do that every summer, because Belle feels so much better in the cool by the lake. At the last minute I pretended to be sick, and told them I'd join them later. She took the servants with them – we have only the two – and the house was empty when O'Dwyer arrived. It was just before sunset, when you often hear shots from hunters in the woods. I doubt anyone in this neighborhood thought twice about them.'

'I take it you shot him in the house?'

'Just inside the hall door,' the young man replied. 'I'd laid down an oilcloth, and layers of old carpet, so the blood wouldn't stain the floor. It . . . it took rather more than I'd thought it would. In the end I had to pour linseed oil on the floorboards, and come up with a tale about having had some delivered . . . there are rugs over the place now. I managed to drag him down under the house – we store wine down there, and there's a flight of stairs from inside the kitchen. Then a little after midnight I slipped out, and borrowed a pirogue which my neighbor Sansome keeps tied near his house. I thought if I dumped O'Dwyer's body in the turning basin, amid all those saloons and bawdy houses, everyone would assume he'd been shot in some brawl.'

Hannibal cocked his head like a skeletal bird. 'As you assumed de la Marche's death would be attributed to the rioting. *Was* anyone arrested for it?'

Armand waved dismissively. 'I think they pounced one of the local whores. I took all his papers from his pockets – bodies become unrecognizable very quickly when they drown in the bayous, don't they? Because of the . . . er . . . crayfish. With luck he'd sink very quickly and wouldn't be recognized at all. It isn't as if he didn't deserve his end,' he added. 'Had he not fled Paris the way he did, Anne would still be alive. I would have stayed in Paris . . .'

He looked back down the garden again blinking in the dense sunlight, in the direction of his wife, and his face changed.

Had you not fled Paris, thought January, *you would not have met Belle.*

As I would not have known Rose, had I remained with Ayasha. Had Ayasha not died . . .

But the thought of not knowing Rose, of not holding her in his arms, of not feeling the tiny grip of his son – her son, *their* son – on his fingers was too terrible to consider.

And what would I, and Rose, and Ayasha, be then? He felt strange, and for an instant just a little frightened, as if coming down a hall in darkness he'd missed a doorway that he should have gone through. A doorway beyond which Ayasha waited for him. Had been waiting for him for nine years now.

But one cannot step twice into the same river.

'It's about those papers,' said Hannibal in his light voice, 'that I wanted to see you. It so happens that I'm in need of another identity just now, and particularly of someone with a British diplomatic passport . . .'

Armand seemed to wake himself, and nodded. 'Of course,' he said, with unquestioning alacrity. 'I have them in the wine cellar, where I kept O'Dwyer's body. I'll show them to you.'

He took Hannibal's arm, led him up the crushed shells of the path and toward the gallery steps, pausing for a moment to speak to his wife. January touched Shaw on the arm, and the two men skirted through the underbrush and around the opposite side of the house; Shaw breathed, 'They's only two servants an' one of 'em's bound to be a cook.'

'That means they'll both be in the kitchen.'

'I'm guessin' he keeps his gun in his study, when he ain't layin' in wait for somebody behind a door . . .'

The door that led into the low ground-floor rooms beneath the main house – the enclosed wastespace among the tall brick piers of the foundation – was at the front of the house, beneath the wide gallery. Presumably, guessed January, it was through this door that Armand had dragged Gerry O'Dwyer's body at midnight, a week ago, to the little skiff on the bayou's brink.

The door was locked, but Shaw had not come unprepared. From the satchel he had brought he took a thin crowbar and a hammer, fitted the metal to the lock and dealt it a blow that Hephaestus in the forges of the gods would have been proud of. The two men ducked inside, both stooping under the low rafters. January closed the door after them, lit a lucifer-match to orient themselves – it was indeed a wine cellar, though most of the racks were empty – and listened to the footfalls of the men in the house above.

Brick piers and cobwebs. The stuffy smell of mud and mould. Boxes and barrels near the ladder-steep wooden stair at the far end of the big chamber, clearly where the household stored apples and yams. Three or four large clay jars which had once held oil – one of them, by its stopper, still did.

January lit another match and Shaw slipped behind the nearest pier, which supported the front of the house. The ground-floor cellar itself, with its brick floor and supporting line of piers, was a single immense chamber and its front doorway was a good fifty feet from the stair from the kitchen. January, stooping, crossed the room in less than a dozen long strides, guessing that a clever man would steer his victim to the front of the house – to lessen the sound of a shot, though Armand would probably send the servants outside on some pretext. Whether Armand – who clearly didn't keep his head in an emergency – would think of this, he didn't know. And he didn't want to risk Hannibal's life on a wrong guess.

Footsteps in the kitchen above.

He blew out the match.

'I wasn't entirely sure what to do with them,' Armand was saying, as he opened the door above. 'Watch the steps,' he added. 'They're a bit steep.' Lamplight staggered and veered across the barrels and oil jars. Like Americans, Armand preferred the illumination of oil lamps, rather than the candles which the French – and their *libré* cousins – invariably used.

Armand descended first, carrying the lamp. It was one of the Argand type, six or eight times brighter than a candle but barely able to illuminate even one end of the dark ground-floor chamber. Certainly Shaw would have been completely invisible at the far end of the room, even had he not been concealed behind a pier.

'I didn't dare leave them in the study upstairs, with the servants, you know,' Armand was saying. 'Darkies are horribly inquisitive. And . . . well, I also worried that Belle might perhaps stumble on them, and ask questions. But because he was in the diplomatic, I thought perhaps a reward might eventually be offered, and it would be easy enough to come up with some plausible story about finding them.' His voice echoed from the low rafters as he and Hannibal walked down the length of the big chamber. January slipped after them – a childhood in slavery had taught him, even at his huge size, to move as silently as a cat when he had to.

The circle of light halted by the wine racks. Armand set the lamp on an empty barrel, turned so that his back was to Hannibal and it looked as if he were taking something from behind one of the racks. From where January stood he could see the young man withdraw a slim sheaf of papers from his pocket.

'I'd be careful about using the passport if I were you, though.' Armand passed them to Hannibal. 'I'm sure the consulate here can trace such things.'

'Good Heavens, I wasn't going to leave O'Dwyer's name on it.' The fiddler checked them over. 'What are the deeds for? A *plantation*?' He sounded convincingly surprised, for a man still covered with mosquito bites from searching a house and a steamboat on the property in question. 'Good Lord. I'd better not try to sell that one, either, or at least not in the United States. Still, it might be worth—'

He broke off, as Armand turned around to face him with a gun in his hand.

A silver muff pistol. Lamplight glinted on the stubby barrel.

'I'm sorry,' said Armand. 'I truly am, Alec. But you can see that I can't take chances. I'm the only support Belle has, the only support for our children. She has no family, no one to turn to. It isn't that I don't trust you—'

Hannibal dove, as if trying to duck behind a wine rack, then dropped flat as Armand pulled the trigger.

The boom of the shot echoed like thunder in the huge darkness, and the next instant – as Armand fumbled in his coat pocket – Shaw stepped out from around a pier with a pistol in his hand.

Armand wheeled to flee toward the kitchen steps and jolted to a halt to see January step from the darkness directly behind him. He gasped, 'Benjamin!' and Shaw's hand fastened like a rat trap on his elbow, jerking his hand away from his pocket.

Hannibal got to his feet, brushing dust from his threadbare trousers. 'You hear all that?' he asked. Then he knelt, to gather up the papers that had scattered from his hands.

'Every word.' Shaw spat, the tobacco making a dark splat on the side of the nearest barrel. 'Them the papers Ganch is askin' you for, Maestro?'

He kept his grip on his prisoner's arm – and his gun pointed at the young man's side – so didn't see when Hannibal flashed January a brief glimpse of a list of names before slipping it into his own pocket. January took the rest of the papers from the fiddler, pretended to look through them, and said, 'Seems to be.'

He didn't see any reason that Shaw would confiscate them, or feel that he had to return them to the British consul. But like Armand, January wasn't about to take chances.

TWENTY-TWO

T he meeting was set for Chitimacha Plantation at noon on the following day, the tenth of July. Accompanied by Hannibal, January returned the strongbox to the ruin of the steamboat just before midnight Monday night, concealing it behind a wall of honeysuckle creepers on the upper deck. Although he was fairly certain that the Bank of England stock certificates didn't legally exist, he wasn't at all sure that Abishag Shaw wouldn't feel obliged to return them to the British consulate anyway. He got Shaw to follow him at a cautious distance to the rendezvous the next day, and rode up to the decaying shamble of the old house, ostensibly alone, to find Ganch, Chuy, and Rocky Watling waiting for him on the front step.

'Cat tells me you're pretty good at finding things,' said the gambler. 'Looks like I was right about a moderate degree of pressure.'

January said, in his meekest voice, 'That you were, sir.'

The gambler held up the key they'd taken from the little pile of Juju's effects. 'I don't see a strongbox, though.'

January shook his head, and tried to appear as if he weren't thinking about what this man would look like with a red-hot crowbar shoved up his rectum. 'You will, sir. It's right here on the premises.'

Ganch tilted his head: *Oh, yeah?*

'But we did have a deal, sir, begging your pardon. And I was hoping to see my wife.'

Without turning his head, Ganch called out, 'Cat?'

Rose emerged from the house first, Gabriel walking at her side, as if ready to grab her elbow to steady her should she show signs of giving birth. Zizi-Marie followed them – cautious and scared, but one look at her face told January she hadn't been harmed – and behind her, the woman Esmeralda, armed with pistol and rifle. Cat came behind them, carrying a rifle in one hand and Baby John on his hip. The only one whose hands were bound was Uncle Juju, who brought up the rear, not exactly cringing but keeping as close to Rose as he possibly could.

Baby John was minutely examining a fancy Mexican tobacco pouch and seemed the most at-ease of the entire party.

'Are you all right?'

'We're fine,' Rose called out immediately, and January felt as if he could fall on his knees and kiss the Virgin Mary's feet.

Rose looked fine. Just very, very pregnant.

He turned to Ganch, said, 'Thank you, sir. It's not every white man who keeps his word to a man of my race, and I am grateful, beyond words.' *And I will tear your heart out and eat it, if you go back on me now . . .*

For the first time in his life he was grateful that he was ebony-black, African-black, because he knew by the heat beneath his skin that his neck and ears would have been crimson with telltale rage.

From his pocket he drew the list of names that Hannibal had given him that morning – meticulously copied in an excellent forgery of the original handwriting, presumably Brooke's – and handed it to the gambler. Ganch glanced over it, nodded in satisfaction, and tucked it into his own pocket. January wondered whether he had already met some of the men whose names were on it, the men who were his contacts in whatever scheme they would undertake of raiding and looting in South America. The names had been mostly Spanish, with one or two Frenchmen, and the list had included as well the names of half a dozen convents near Cartagena.

Bags of gold, boxes of rubies, Our Lord with his body made of pearl . . .

'The strongbox has been under our noses, all this time, sir,' said January, keeping his voice steady. 'It's over in that old steamboat, up on the boiler deck. Where you come off the stair, go forward to a big mass of honeysuckle. It's just sitting right behind it.'

Still, his heart hammered – audible to everyone who stood before the old house, it felt like – as Cat and Rocky made their way down the path they'd cut in the snarls of cane around the house, and across to the vine-covered hulk. He was well aware that Rose, Gabriel, and Zizi-Marie would bring several thousand dollars altogether, if sold in Arkansas or Texas. Was well aware also that with his raid on New Granada imminent, Jared Ganch might well have had enough men at his command to make him willing to risk this kind of wholesale kidnapping.

Was three thousand dollars enough to offset the trouble there'd be with the US government if the raid in preparation came to light? January didn't know.

As if he read his mind, Ganch said quietly, 'Now, you wouldn't have gone and told anyone about our dealings, Mr Janvier, would you?'

'Only to ask my friends to watch the slave pens, sir, should something happen to me.'

The sandy man smiled. 'Cat told me, you're a clever nigger.'

The five minutes or so before Cat appeared on the boiler deck of the steamboat seemed to last an hour. But the Kaintuck was grinning broadly, and waved his hand to Ganch.

The gambler turned back to January and stood for a time, studying him with those dark eyes like onyx beads. Evaluating. Then his glance went back to the little group on the porch: Gabriel looking grim and very young; Zizi only tired, as if she had lain awake for most of four nights, listening to drunk white men cursing thirty feet away . . .

When Ganch looked at January again he wore a wide, gracious smile.

And January thought, *He's going to kill me later.*

'Looks like you came through in all respects, Mr January. Of course there's no need for me to remind you, that nothing of this – not names, not places, not events – gets said to anyone, and that includes Mrs January and your children.'

'I understand that, sir.'

'I've already had a little talk with Mr Filoux,' Ganch went on, 'about what might happen to him – and to you – if any of this gets out.'

'Yes, sir.' No leverage there, January knew. Any revelation he could make would not be believed, and certainly no protection would be extended to him.

Ganch clapped him familiarly on the arm. 'Mrs January will tell you – won't you, m'am? – that no harm came to any of them while they were my guests.'

'It's quite true,' said Rose, coming down the steps – exquisitely, absolutely matter-of-fact, completely herself. 'And in fact on the one occasion that I felt ill a doctor was sent for. Whatever they wanted from you—' She glanced in the direction of the steamboat with raised eyebrows – 'they must have wanted it pretty badly. Truly,' she added, her voice lowered to his ears alone, 'we are well.'

'Then let's get out of here,' he said softly.

'And it will all be, I trust,' smiled Ganch, 'as if it had never been.'

Esmeralda produced a skinning knife from her belt and cut the ropes on Juju's wrists, and without waiting for the others he fled like a shot from a gun. Ganch and his men roared with laughter, and that laughter followed January and his family, as he lifted Rose to Voltaire's saddle, and they walked back along the trace towards Bayou St John.

'It doesn't seem fair,' Rose said quietly, that night when the attorney Vachel Corcet left the house.

The little lawyer had brought the news that charges against Jacquette Filoux were being dropped, on the strength of the testimonies of Abishag Shaw and the cab driver Tyrell Mulvaney. 'Francheville – de la Roche-St-Ouen – is swearing he never said a word about Henry Brooke or about any of the events of the night of June twenty-ninth,' he had said. 'Between Shaw, Sefton and Mulvaney – not to mention the passport and documents being in his possession, and the bloodstain on his hall floor – I can't imagine any judge in the parish is going to believe him. His wife's down with him at the Cabildo.'

'*Has* she family?' January had asked, and Corcet's plump face clouded with sadness as he shook his head.

'She's a German from Frankfort, who came to this country as a lady's maid with a Frenchwoman who was visiting the Almonasters. Francheville – de la Roche-St-Ouen – was reasonably well-off when they married, but lost pretty much all of his savings in the bank crash two years ago, and the house is mortgaged to the eaves. If her husband is hanged, God knows what the poor lady is going to do.'

'You've spoken of how you can't step twice into the same

river.' Rose's words now echoed January's earlier thoughts, as he came into their bedroom now, with the house growing quiet around them. The voices of Gabriel and Zizi floated from the gallery, where they were bidding Ti-Gall good night.

'Brooke – O'Dwyer – was after all trying to blackmail Armand, over events that happened nine years ago. Things done by another person, in another lifetime. This poor woman – and her children—' her hand rested instinctively on her own swollen belly – 'can have known nothing of them, or of the person who did them. Only that she and her children will be turned out of their home.'

Baby John's staggering steps followed Gabriel's back across the parlor to the dining room, punctuated by the occasional soft thump as the toddler lost his balance. From Shaw's list, January knew that Armand's youngest son – whose birth had cost his mother her health – was the same age.

'He was just as ready to let someone else die for his crime on this occasion, though,' he replied after a time. 'He evidently felt perfectly justified in letting "one of the local whores", as he put it, hang. And he apparently thought nothing of murdering Hannibal to cover his tracks. All with good reasons, of course. Maybe you can't step twice into the same river . . . but sometimes you choose a river that's awfully similar to the first.'

Rose acknowledged his point with a nod. She'd taken off her spectacles – she had, of course, remained in her room and in bed during January's talk in the parlor with Corcet. Without them her hazel-gray eyes seemed softer, the eyes of the girl who hid behind her air of matter-of-fact briskness. The eyes of the girl who'd sometimes smile a quicksilver smile. 'What you say is true. But his wife is the one who'll suffer. Probably for the rest of her life.'

As Anne suffered, thought January, later, lying awake in the darkness at Rose's side. Midnight, moonlight through the jalousies, stifling heat and the thin whine of a lone mosquito outside the tent of netting that swathed the bed.

As Daniel had suffered, in the days before and after Anne's trial, and in the long nights following her death. Two years after the incidents of the Three Glorious Days – when January had left Paris – in many ways his friend had still not recovered that double loss.

He slipped from beneath the mosquito bar, his body striped with needles of moonlight as he padded from the room. In the parlor the furniture was still huddled together under canvas, and the air was fusty with the smell of plaster and paint. His heartbeat hard as he unlatched the French door that led out onto the gallery, unlocked the shutters.

Beyond the absolute blackness of the gallery he could make out the dim shapes of the neutral ground up the center of Rue Esplanade, the shabby trees and the glimmer of water, where once the town rampart had stood. Cicadas droned, a heavy, metallic rattle; a thousand frogs peeped in the ditch. Among the trees, just for an instant, he saw the minuscule red coal of a cigar, and a moment later, smelled the whispered echo of smoke.

One of Jared Ganch's men.

Watching the house.

Behind his shoulder, Rose's voice breathed, 'So what do we do?'

'Jared Ganch has friends on the municipal council. I can't imagine that a complaint against him, even from a white man, would get him more than a night in jail and a slap on the wrist.' He put his arm around her waist, subconsciously raised his other hand to stroke the jamb of the French door beside him.

His house. Her house.

The school they'd worked and waited and struggled to put together for four years now.

Do we run away? As Armand had fled Paris, left his title and what remained of his family estates? Close it down? Leave it?

Do we have a choice?

'We watch our backs,' he said at last. 'Oldmixton may be able to help us. Right now Ganch's focus will be getting a ship and getting his men down to New Granada before the hurricane months begin in September. He doesn't want trouble just now. That gives us time to plan. That gives *you* time,' he added, tightening his arm around her slim shoulders, resting his hand on her belly, 'to unburden yourself.'

She gave him a little shove, like a schoolboy, and a breath of laughter.

When they looked back out into the darkness, the red coal of the cigar was gone.

'I should write to Daniel,' said January, as they closed and locked the doors, padded across the dark parlor to the bedroom. 'Tell him what happened. Every letter I've had from him – and I haven't had many – has been . . . superficial. Purple-trimmed persiflage about the opera or his latest boyfriends, but saying very little. Freytag answered my last letter, after half a year's delay, explaining that his master "wasn't well". I'm not even certain, at this distance, that Daniel will care.'

'Do you care?'

Do I care?

He didn't reply at once. They opened the door of Baby John's room, the tiny light of the china veilleuse just enough to show them his round little face, serious even in sleep, against the white of his pillow. According to Rose the boy had slept well and peacefully every night of their imprisonment, and had, in fact, seemed to treat the entire experience with his usual grave curiosity rather than fear.

When he held the mosquito bar aside, to let Rose climb into their bed, he said, 'I do care. Do I think saving Jacquette Filoux from hanging is worth us losing our house, our school? The life we've worked for? Worth having to flee from New Orleans? I wish it were otherwise, but I can't say that I don't. Anne Ben-Gideon . . .'

'And in exchange—' Rose removed her spectacles, reached under the gauzy tent to lay them on the bedside table – 'Armand de la Roche-St-Ouen is hanged, and his wife is the one who loses her house, her support. How is it that one man can spread such carnage – such grief – in all directions, down through the years? Except,' she added, 'that that's what handsome scoundrels do.'

January saw nothing of a watcher the following day, though he found the fresh stubs of three cigars on the ground where the man had stood. According to Hannibal, who was still dealing faro and romancing Cassie Lovelace out in Faubourg Pontchartrain, there was a great deal of coming and going around the indigo mill. After checking the vicinity of his own house carefully, January risked a visit to the British consulate, to give Sir John Oldmixton the original copy of the list.

'That's New Grenada, all right,' said the diplomat, glancing over the names. 'I know only one of the men personally, and he's always impressed me as the sort of blackguard who'd conspire to rob a convent while the government troops are busy elsewhere. Dear, dear! The others are men we've used now and again. Was Brooke this Mr O'Dwyer you spoke of?'

'He was,' said January. 'And he was killed for reasons that had nothing to do with the list.'

'I trust – I hope – that you passed a copy of this list along to this fellow Ganch you spoke of? And that your family is . . . is in good health.'

January smiled grimly at the euphemism. 'They are,' he said. 'Though someone was watching our house last night. When we arrested Brooke's murderer, I got this list, and what looked like a strongbox key, from his desk, and Ganch accepted them. He may have had the strongbox itself already. Nothing more was said of it.'

'Dear me.' Oldmixton shook his head. 'I've repeatedly told Lord Melbourne that more care needs to be taken in appointing couriers. There's more fuss being made about ladies of the new queen's bedchamber, evidently, than men who come from God knows where carrying thousands of pounds' worth of negotiable paper. And on the subject of negotiable paper . . .'

He went to his desk, and brought out a small sack that clinked heavily when he put it in January's hand.

A new start. A place to hide. Money for a hasty journey . . .

The money he'd turned down, knowing what entanglement with Oldmixton might mean.

January closed his eyes. *Virgin Mary, guide me . . .*

'Would you give this instead,' he said, 'to a woman named Belle Francheville, whose husband murdered Henry Brooke? It was . . . a long story. I never wanted anything to do with the job – and she needs it more desperately than we.'

Returning home, he was met by Olympe on the gallery with the news that Rose had gone into labor an hour previously.

January had been away at the birth of his first son, returning from six months in the western mountains[3] on the day Baby John

---

[3] See *The Shirt on his Back*

had been born. When Rose was delivered of the child she asked
to call Alexander – ('Alec,' she murmured, with a sleepy glance
at Hannibal, later) – January helped in the birth, and afterwards
brought in Baby John, and held his wife and his two sons in his
arms, feeling deeply at peace and almost as if he could have
slept. For all the fear and uncertainty of the summer, for all
the darkness that lay ahead – for all his rage at the power of the
whites that he knew would give him and his no protection from
a man like Ganch – he had the curious sense that the core of the
world was whole.

He emerged from the bedroom leading Baby John by the hand,
to find Olympe with their younger sister, the beautiful Dominique,
and a little group of the other ladies of their circle: Rose's friend
Cora, the Metoyer sisters from across Rue Esplanade, his own
dear friend Catherine Clisson (with whom he'd been desperately
in love at the age of fourteen), Jacquette Filoux and her daughter
Manon, looking shy but determined, like the others, to bring gifts
of jambalaya and spoon bread, 'dirty rice' and sausage, to tide
the family over days in which cooking was likely to be disrupted
(*As if Rose ever went into the kitchen in her life*, reflected January).
Gabriel made coffee and batches of fresh pralines, and Zizi-Marie
did the honors as hostess, greeting all the ladies with kisses while
Ti-Gall – shy also in the presence of the strong January women
– went about the room lighting candles.

Rain had fallen. The banquettes had smoked. The sun had set.
A little later January's mother arrived, complaining like an
affronted queen about the heat and dressed, clearly, for a leisured
afternoon at the lake.

'A little scrap of a thing, isn't he?' she commented about baby
Xander and inspected the rim of the candy plate for chips.

The only male present who wasn't a member of the family
was, not at all to January's surprise, Hannibal. The fiddler was
stunned at the news that the child would be named Alexander
('After someone I knew long ago,' he explained to Dominique),
and was left uncharacteristically speechless. The only thing he
said on the subject was, tentatively, 'Are you sure?'

'I can think of no one better.' January put a hand on his
shoulder.

Later, when the ladies started helping Gabriel carry what

remained of the food out to the kitchen, or to be put in the cool jars buried in the garden, the fiddler took January aside and told him, 'I was out at Lovelace's this afternoon. Jared Ganch has been arrested.'

Uncle Juju.

January felt for a moment as if he could have wept. Or driven his fist through the smooth new plaster of the parlor wall.

He blabbed to someone. And Ganch will blame me. Stupid, stupid bastard . . .

He had hoped that, by staying quiet, he would have time to make plans, that Rose would have time to recover if they needed to flee. The fragile joy he'd felt an hour before seemed to splinter in his hands, cutting the flesh to the bone.

'He'll be out by morning.' *And on my doorstep.* 'Half the municipal council is in his pocket.'

'I don't think so,' said Hannibal. 'The charge is treason.'

According to Abishag Shaw, whom January visited at the Cabildo the following noon, the charge had nothing to do with the missing Bank of England stock. 'Don't rightly know what it's got to do with,' confessed the policeman, scratching his greasy hair. 'All I know is, yesterday afternoon Captain Tremouille calls me in, says I'm to take three of my boys down to the Flesh an' Blood, an' wait for Ganch to come back from seein' off that brig he bought – the *Hecate* – on her way to Cartagena. When we got him back here that slick lawyer of his was here, with Prado an' Wiltz from the municipal council, goin' on about how he's an upstandin' citizen an' a property owner, an' that's when Tremouille breaks it to 'em that actin' on information from confidential sources, they had grounds for arrestin' the man for treason against the United States of America.'

He nodded toward the stair which led to the more sanctified offices on the Cabildo's upper floor. 'They's up there now,' he said. 'Arguin' it. But I don't look for any results soon. Nor does Ganch, I gather. He's paid off the parish prison to have his own cell, private-like, an' made arrangements for food to be brought in to him. Better'n what most of the councilmen gets at their homes, I gather. There he goes,' he added, and gestured to a tall deliveryman in a scarlet coat who crossed before the wide outer doors of the watch room, presumably on his way to the parish prison a block away, bearing two cardboard boxes and a bottle of wine.

January said, 'If anything changes – if there's any word of his getting out on bail – would you let me know of it?'

'That I will, Maestro. Is M'am Janvier all right? Sefton brought me word this mornin' you's a daddy again – I hope an' trust they's both well?'

They spoke a little, of Rose, and of Baby John ('He still fixin' to be a professor of philosophy, soon as he learns to talk?'), and of the students who would be coming to Rose's school as soon as the weather began to cool. Spoke also of Armand de la Roche-St-Ouen, in the common cell of the parish prison. 'Though he's in the infirmary last night. Seems he got into it with another prisoner 'bout bein' really a nobleman back in France, an' that's not a good idea in a cell full of half-drunk flatboat men. That poor wife of his comes in two, three times a day, an' speaks of hirin' a lawyer for him – seems she got some money from some-place – but I told her, it won't be no use.'

As January left, Shaw walked him to the doors, open onto the Place des Armes and the tepid breeze off the river. Thunder grumbled over the gulf, where hurricanes would be brewing in a few weeks; clouds gathered for the afternoon rain.

Shaw put a hand on January's shoulder. 'I don't know what's to come of Ganch, nor where he'll be tried nor by who, seein' as it's a federal charge. If'n he's let out I'll give you warnin'. An' if'n he's let out, I'll keep a eye on him, an' on you.'

January said, 'Thank you,' and turned away.

As he did so, he nearly collided with the red-coated food deliveryman, returning from the parish prison, whistling a little tune.

It was the slave Ti-Jon.

The following day January received a note from Shaw, informing him that Jared Ganch had been taken sick in the night with what appeared to be cholera – to the frightened panic of the staff and the other prisoners, though no one else had as yet come down with the disease and as it turned out, no one did. Ganch himself had died, in great agony, in the early hours of the morning.

The next time January went to confession – which was the following Wednesday – he confessed to rejoicing in another's death, and gladly did the penance Père Eugenius prescribed for him. But as he walked back in the sweltering evening from the novena, his mind kept straying to M'sieu Naquet, the maitre d'hote at the Verandah Hotel, and that fat, red-bearded American who insulted the waiters. And he could not keep from remembering the way the cooks had grinned and slapped each other on the backs and whispered, 'Well, he ate it.'

And of what Naquet had said, about white men who 'ain't yet figured it out, that you don't cause trouble for them that handles your food'.

Or, evidently, them who were friends with them that handled your food.

At Mass on Sunday he thought, when his sister Olympe traded smiling greetings with Ti-Jon, that a glance might have passed between them, but he couldn't be sure. No more sure than he'd been that Ganch had intended to have him killed. If he asked Olympe about it he knew she'd only protest that no such thought had even crossed her mind.

Certainly the City Guards were no more interested in investigating the death of a gambler and whoremaster than they'd been in taking trouble to prove the innocence of a young woman of color.

Later that same week, a small paragraph in the *New Orleans Bee* mentioned briefly that an attempt by American filibusters to take advantage of the disordered state of things in war-torn New Grenada had come to grief. The men – and one woman – who came ashore from the brig *Hecate*, had evidently been under the impression that the government troops would be elsewhere than the convent of St Helen of the Blessed Shroud, which it was their intent to rob. To their surprise and dismay, government troops had been waiting for them.

They had been captured and shot.

'I'm not sure I want to be beholden to Sir John Oldmixton to that extent,' said January, folding up the newspaper and dropping it to the floor of the gallery. Baby John – or Professor John, as they were beginning to call him now there was another baby in the household – picked it up and began trying to fold and re-fold it in patterns known only to himself. 'And I suspect it will lead to trouble later. But I can't say I'm not grateful for so many . . . fortunate coincidences.'

'You did say,' pointed out Rose, 'that he owed you.' And she adjusted the linen cap over tiny Xander's wispy brown curls.

Something in the tone of her voice made January wonder for a moment whether his wife knew anything about whatever Olympe might or might not have put into the food that Ti-Jon took to Jared Ganch in prison. Then he let the thought go.

The sun was setting behind their roof line, dyeing all the tops of the raggedy trees on Rue Esplanade with gold. Up and down the wide street, every window and door was open to the breath of breeze from the river. From behind the house, from the streets that had once been the quiet and proper domain of the *plaçeés*, voices drifted: raggedy children, two women arguing, a man shouting them both down. A whispered reminder that towns changed even as lives did. Here, facing the Rue Esplanade, there was quiet, and peace and the thrum of frogs and cicadas. He had finished the last of the painting in the parlor that afternoon, and his muscles were just starting to stiffen – a reminder that lives changed, bodies changed, even as towns did.

The first of their students would arrive in October. Rose would have her school again; January, a little coterie of piano students to teach.

Somewhere close by, one of the little cottages on the other side of the neutral ground, someone was playing on a piano – badly – a Chopin sonata that had been popular in Paris, the summer of the Three Glorious Days.

Another world and another life. Another self, who would have recoiled in disbelief at the suggestion that he would ever live in New Orleans again.

Across a chasm of time he looked back at himself, sitting in the window of the rooms on the Rue de l'Aube with Ayasha and the cats. Like the gallery, their room had faced roughly east, and at this time of the afternoon, as here, the city visible across the river had been blue with shadow, gold-crowned from the setting of the sun. Memory filled him – the Rue de l'Aube, the Palais Royale, moss on ancient cobblestones and the yelling of mobs. Daniel in his gorgeous coats, frail old Lucien Imbolt and the Société Brutus, Ayasha – the structure of his life . . .

As Bellefleur Plantation had been, he supposed, in the days of his childhood: the dark-green bayous, the platt-eye devil that lurked in the night, his aunties and uncles and the burnt-sugar smell of the fog during the grinding season. The fear and the wonder of childhood.

But it was true that you couldn't step twice into the same river, and the Mississippi was a long way from the Seine. These things had once existed – they would exist forever in his heart – but they were things which were no more.

Armand de la Roche-St-Ouen had lived within a few miles of him for the past four years, without his knowledge – and arguably had not been the same pampered youth he'd known in Paris. Nor was the wastrel fiddler who'd spent the early part of the summer of 1830 with Armand entirely the same man who'd been January's friend for these past seven years.

Nine years later, January was here. And this was what truly mattered, within the circle of his arms: now, this evening, this moment. Rose, Professor John, Xander . . .

The smell of paint, the voices of Gabriel and Zizi-Marie, the cursing of draymen on the road to the bayou that ran before his door. The plaintive (and badly-played) echoes of the world he'd left came to him like the ghostly ringing of church bells that fishermen were said to hear, from cities drowned in the sea.

New Orleans. Not a misstep, or someplace he'd accidentally wandered when he should have stayed in Paris, in whatever world it was in which the cholera hadn't come and Ayasha hadn't died.

Cras amet qui nunquam amavit; quique amavit, cras amet, Daniel had written to the man he had loved.

May he love tomorrow who has never loved before; may he who has loved, love tomorrow as well.

This was where he needed to be.

This was home.